08-BUt-581

THE FIFTH HORSEMAN

THE FIFTH HORSEMAN

A NOVEL OF
BIOLOGICAL DISASTER

Richard Sherbaniuk

A Tom Doherty Associates Book
New York

THE FIFTH HORSEMAN

This book is printed on acid-free paper.

Book design by Jane Adele Regina

Map by Michael Fisher, cartographer

A Forge Book
Published by Tom Doherty Associates, LLC
175 Fifth Avenue
New York, NY 10010

www.tor.com

Forge® is a registered trademark of Tom Doherty Associates, LLC.

Library of Congress Cataloging-in-Publication Data

Sherbaniuk, Richard.
  The fifth horseman / Richard Sherbaniuk.—1st ed.
    p. cm.
  "A Tom Doherty Associates book."
  ISBN 0-312-87435-9 (alk. paper)
  1. Environmentalists—Fiction. 2. Weapons of mass destruction—
  Fiction. 3. Biological warfare—Fiction. 4. Conspiracies—Fiction.
  5. Middle East—Fiction. I. Title.

  PS3569.H3987 F54 2001
  813'.6—dc21   00-048448

First Edition: March 2001

Printed in the United States of America

0 9 8 7 6 5 4 3 2 1

To my wife, Bonnie Dorish, without whose endless love, help, and encouragement neither this work, nor its author, would exist.

To my parents, who instilled in me a love of reading and learning.

Acknowledgments

I am grateful to the following people for sharing their time and knowledge. Any errors in this book are mine and mine alone.

Clive Cussler, whose immense success has not prevented him from being a generous and considerate man, and for giving me the biggest break of my literary life.

My wife, Bonnie Dorish, for her editorial and psychological advice.

Dr. R. W. Sherbaniuk, my father, Professor Emeritus of Medicine, for providing me with wise advice.

Environmental scientists, detectives, and enforcers: Dr. Bruce Taylor, Wayne Inkpen, Jim McKinley, Ken Simpson, and others.

Dr. Alan Bean, professor of theology, for his eagle-eye and vast knowledge of religion.

Ruth Anderson, MegaSearch, for her diligent research into biological warfare.

Ken Yackimec, editor, polymath, and forest ranger, for his keen wit and inherent sense of drama and psychology.

Janet Bliss, Janice Laurie, Tim Perrin, and Christopher Taylor for their editorial skills and suggestions.

Olga Dorish, for her meticulous reading of the story.

David Hunter, Joint Chairman/Managing Director, HR Aviation Group Limited, United Kingdom, for his patient and comprehensive help on Soviet-era aircraft.

Jaron Summers and Robert McKee for their sage advice on how to tell a story.

Dr. Will Orram for his elegant and detailed explanations of *monoamine oxidase* and medivac surgery, supplied during a busy time in his life.

Wayne Logus, physicist, for his meticulous and enormously detailed technical information on subjects ranging from nuclear warfare to environmental detection to medicine.

Dr. Jonathan Tyler, Tyler Research, for reading the manuscript and offering insightful advice, and for his thermal reactors and Eppendorf tubes.

Father Don Stine for his advice on religion.

Dr. Sean Graham for his herbarium and greenhouse and demonstration of PCR.

Mark Tilden, Dr. Max Meng, and James Smith, robotics experts.

Susan Crawford, my agent, the best, most dedicated, most supportive, and hardest working agent in the world.

Natalia Aponte, my editor, for her perceptive, unerringly accurate suggestions about how to make a manuscript better.

Author's Note

It may seem incredible, but the history, politics, and science depicted here are true, and the events in this story are either happening now or could happen tomorrow. I have taken some literary and technological license to keep the narrative flowing. A fuller explanation of how much of this story is true can be found in the Afterword at the end of the book.

Turkish is rendered in a variation of the Latin alphabet, and there is a confusion of spelling and usage. I have tried to choose the simplest route, which is why, for example, I call the town of Sanli Urfa (or Sanliurfa, or Sanlurfa) just Urfa, and Catal Hüyük is Catalhoyok.

In the last book of the Bible, Revelation, Chapter 6, verses 2–8, the four major disasters that befall mankind are personified as the Four Horsemen of the Apocalypse: death, war, famine, and pestilence.

Now, there is a Fifth Horseman.

Myths are the things that never were, but always are.
                    —STEPHEN OF BYZANTIUM, 6TH CENTURY A.D.

Happy nations have no history.
                              —CESARE BONESANA BECCARIA

Water, like truth, is precious.
                              —MIDDLE EASTERN PROVERB

THE FIFTH HORSEMAN

 Mike Zammit stood at the lip of the pit, wreathed in poisonous yellow fumes.

He tried to estimate the extent of the damage, aware that he could easily slip to his death down the steep greasy slope. The iridescent green lake a hundred feet below at the bottom of the pit was almost pure acid, and his protective suit would dissolve in seconds. Flakes of white ash from the toxic waste burning in the garbage dumps danced in the air around him, their edges glowing red, like Satan's version of a winter storm.

He had heard Dzerzhinsk called the City of Death because it was the most polluted place on earth. Now he knew it was true.

Gazing through the plastic visor of his helmet, with the hiss of oxygen in his ears, feeling its sting in his nostrils, he was grateful his suit was completely sealed. If you smelled anything but oxygen, you were in trouble—you'd sprung a leak. Breathing the yellow fumes would sear your lungs in seconds. He stared at the cascade of rusted drums that spread far below like an avalanche of corrosion. Many had burst and were leaking. He knew some contained industrial acid, but the others? Cyanide, fluorine, PCBs, spent reactor rods—the worst stuff on earth.

He looked at the slimy green river that trickled from the factory complex, belching foul black smoke. The few dying trees were the color of charcoal from their coating of soot. They seemed to be lifting beseeching arms toward the diarrhea-brown sky.

The mosquito-like whine was unnerving. Zammit turned to his two partners, also encased in the orange bulk of protective suits. "I haven't heard a Geiger counter scream since Chornobyl. Frankie, what's going on?"

Frances Fitzgerald Richards held up the black box in her hand as Zammit leaned over to look. The red needle quivered at the far end of the dial. The pit zone was as hot as the aftermath of a nuclear explosion.

Constantine Palaeov's muscular body-builder frame tensed as he also leaned to look. At twenty-four, he was new to the emergency field team and the most likely to panic. "Boss, I think we should get out of here."

"Connie, we're still OK," replied Zammit. "I've been through this a thousand times. There's a reason we get hired as environmental detectives. We're thorough, and we take risks no one else will take. Frankie?"

Frankie Richards pointed to a pile of ruptured drums, then looked again at the Geiger counter. "Some of those could cause cancer in a block of concrete. We have time, but not much."

Zammit nodded and turned away from the pit. "Over here."

Their boots squelched as they slogged to a crater filled with pink liquid, like melted candy. In this black contaminated landscape, the bright pool was as incongruous as a party hat on a skeleton. Glancing back at the smoke from the factory, Zammit noted the direction of the slight breeze. Gesturing for the others to follow, he walked away from the crater and around the rim, moving upwind and farther away.

Facing the pool again from a distance of twenty feet, he ripped open the Velcro flap on one of the pockets of his protective suit and removed what looked like a black golf ball. He pressed a sequence of buttons on the bomblet and a red light glowed. Silently Zammit counted to five, then stepped forward and tossed it underhand into the pool. The instant the tiny incendiary device disappeared into the pink liquid there was an explosive *whomp*. Electric blue and acid green flames licked toward the sky and black smoke roiled.

Zammit glanced at his chronometer and waited. Twenty seconds. Thirty seconds. Sixty seconds. The pool was still burning.

"You want me to collect some samples of whatever that crap is, when it finally burns out?" asked Connie Palaeov unhappily.

"There's no point," replied Zammit. "I'm not a miracle worker, and that's what it would take to clean up this mess."

"Besides, with all this radiation we better get out of here," added Richards.

Zammit took a final look at the crackling flames and tried to lessen his sense of defeat with some black humor. "Hey, Connie. Got any more of those sausages we had for breakfast? It's not often you can have a weenie roast in hell."

Palaeov suddenly pointed. Zammit turned. Yury Bogov, their official translator and fixer, ran toward them, stumbling in his bulky protective gear as he gestured back the way they'd come. A former member of the disbanded KGB, Bogov was now a freelance spy, a definite asset in a country as corrupt as Russia. Zammit wiped greasy brown film off his visor so he could see better.

A couple of hundred yards away, by his mobile lab, two Mercedes limousines disgorged half a dozen large men. The athleticism suggested by their brightly colored track suits was belied by heavy, slope-shouldered gaits as they shambled toward the troops guarding the lab. They all walked from the shoulders, like bears. Big Russian bears. Zammit's escort of young soldiers was backing away. Mafia thugs. Bad news.

Bogov reached them, panting. "I told you there would be trouble. We shouldn't have argued, we should have just paid what they asked."

"Maybe," said Zammit. It wouldn't be the first time he'd been threatened by people who didn't want an environmental detective investigating their affairs.

They trudged through the barren, devastated landscape toward the mobile lab, black muck sucking at their boots.

It was now another fifty yards to the vehicle. Flakes of ash still swirled through the air, but the Geiger counter finally fell silent. Zammit stripped off the helmet and gloves of his protective suit. He wiped his streaming brow and coughed as the air bit his lungs with the acrid smell of sulfur and smoke. How to deal with the six men?

"Frankie, what do you think?"

Frances Richards pulled off her helmet and gloves, as did the others. She plucked a piece of grit from her long blond hair. "The mafia chief didn't seem unhappy with the deal we made. Maybe his boys are bored, out for a Sunday drive."

As Zammit assessed the situation, the natural warmth in his sea-blue eyes vanished and hard lines appeared around his eyes and mouth. Three of the track suits stared down the troops, arms folded on top of their huge bellies. The five pale young soldiers supplied by Moscow to protect Zammit's team were slouched in a tense but hangdog posture of submission that said they were already beaten but still feared attack. Two other track suits poked their heads into the open doorway of the mobile lab. One watched them approach. As they drew near he used his fingers to clear first one nostril, then the other, spraying wads of snot onto the ground.

"I thought Neanderthal man was extinct, and here he is having a convention," said Zammit.

"Chechnya war vets," said Bogov. "We might as well be protected by Boy Scouts."

One of the track suits was urinating against the side of the mobile van. "There can't be many forms of life lower than these guys," remarked Zammit.

Bogov shrugged. "They exist to eat, drink, fuck, and kill. Mainly drink and kill."

"Any suggestions on how we deal with them?" asked Richards.

"More bribes are good. Unless they have orders to murder us. More money would've . . ."

"Yury, for the last time," said Zammit, "our agency isn't a bank with limitless funds, and we can't spend that kind of money just to pay off a gangster. We negotiated a fair price."

"Besides," added Richards, "we're here on behalf of the government in Moscow."

Bogov coughed. "Here they wipe their asses with the government in Moscow. And our troop bodyguards are conscripts who only shave once a week and never get paid."

As they got closer to the lab, one of the track suits pulled the dead two-headed calf from the interior of the vehicle. Zammit had collected the badly deformed animal from a nearby farm. Holding it by the legs, the gangster spun around as if throwing the hammer, finally sending the carcass soaring through the air toward them as his friends roared with hoarse laughter.

"Good distance," said Richards. "This guy's a definite for the mutation Olympics."

They passed the dead calf, its two tongues lolling from its two slack mouths. Zammit made a decision. "Frankie, where did you plant the gun?"

"It's clipped behind the third structural rib on your left as you reach through the door."

They walked through the group of six track suits to the lab, ignoring them. The men had the bloated, overfed look of people who ate nothing but fatty, salty food, and too much of it. There was a strong smell of alcohol. Zammit caught the eye of one man and held it briefly. He saw dull curiosity, nothing more. One of the track suits removed his sunglasses to fix Frankie Richards with a predatory stare. As he nudged the man next to him and whispered something, she coolly returned his gaze.

Zammit leaned into the vehicle, tossed his gloves and helmet on the seat, and picked up the satellite phone that would connect him with headquarters in Seattle. Pressing the speed-dial with his left thumb, he braced against the door frame, ready for trouble. He faced a hulking crew-cut blond in a magenta-striped navy track suit. The slit Mongol eyes betrayed the genetic legacy of a 13th-century rape that had mingled the genes of Genghis Khan with those of some flaxen-haired Slavic peasant. The thug stared with flat hostility.

With his right hand Zammit reached inside the door for the Heckler and Koch .33 caliber automatic. Had they found it? A surge of relief as he grasped the butt. "Me good guy," he said to the blond. "You bad guy."

Suddenly the connection came through. "Get me Cairo Jackson." Without taking his eyes from the thug, he delivered a terse report. "Cairo, this is the most poisoned environment I've ever seen. Dzerzhinsk's been a chemical production center for fifty years—mustard gas, DDT, Agent Orange, you name it. They weren't too careful about how they disposed of their waste. Also, lots of illegal incineration and dumping of radioactives. You can cut the air with a machete and the soil is soaked with dioxin. Flammable pools of chemical cocktail on the surface, drinking water's cloudy and stinks of kerosene, everybody's gray-faced and coughing. The only thing higher than the mutation rate is the incidence of alcoholism. There's nothing we can do. Only Mother Nature can clean this place, and it's going to take her a long, long time. Anything at your end?"

He frowned as his eyes met Frankie's. "Thousands of people dying in a remote region of Turkey after drinking water from the Euphrates River. That's all you've got?" He listened intently. "The source appears to be the reservoir of the Ataturk Dam." He raised an inquiring eyebrow at Frankie. She shrugged and shook her head. "If the White House is supervising data gathering, it must be important. You'll have to brief me later."

Zammit glanced at the track suits surrounding him. Two of them took experimental steps forward as the soldiers shuffled and averted their gaze. It was the thugs' job to be intimidating, and they must be armed, but there were no weapons in sight. Maybe they just needed a deterrent.

"The local primate population is hostile. Hang on." He pressed the hold button as he swung the gun around the door frame and pointed it at the torso of the blond in the navy track suit, moving the barrel in a slight circle to keep his aim limber. Without taking his eyes from the man, he tilted his head toward Connie and said, "Beads."

The muscular young Russian disappeared into the van and returned immediately with four bottles, two of Martell cognac, two of Johnny Walker whiskey. Smiles split the faces of the track suits, gold bridgework gleaming among teeth the color of tree stumps. Tension disappeared as the bottles were opened and upended. The blond backed away and grinned. He hawked and spat before drinking, then handed the bottle to one of his friends. Frankie was right—the lads were just out for a drive, looking for some fun.

"Yury. Remember we got drunk one night and you taught me some Russian insults? I forget how you call someone a walrus's penis."

"Please, Dr. Zammit, that's not funny. You don't have a wife and kids. I do."

A grinning turquoise-blue track suit with lank black hair wiped lips wet with liquor and said something to the translator. Bogov listened, eyes flicking back and forth. "Do you want a missile, very cheap? An SS-25. Forty grand. There's no launcher, and the guidance system doesn't work anymore. But the warhead is still live, and it checked out OK a month ago. If you pay cash in American dollars he'll throw in an armored car and a couple of girls."

Zammit spoke into the phone. "I thought it was impossible, but this place has suddenly gotten filthier. Cairo, I'm coming home."

In the gathering dusk, the huge maintenance vehicle reversed and ground to a halt.

Ruslan Glinka looked up into the evening sky twinkling with faint stars and filled with the heavy *whump-whump* of ceaselessly circling helicopters. He nervously adjusted his mask, making sure his oxygen supply was secure. He hated this task almost more than he hated the Turks, but it had to be done. He tried not to think about his fate if they caught him.

He jumped from the cab and walked to the rear of the vehicle, which now faced the reservoir. After checking the huge tanks in the back one last time, he walked to the edge of the concrete and surveyed the area. Half a mile away, 600 feet high, loomed the dam's gigantic concrete wall, its mile-long crest curving into the descending darkness. No one was close enough to see that he was doing anything more than his job. To be sure of concealment, he always did it at twilight. Back at the truck, he pushed a button to activate the winch that would unspool the heavy giant hoses, then walked again to the water's edge.

Or what should have been the water's edge. Instead of water, and extending as far as he could see, there was a thick, gelatinous mat gleaming iridescently in the setting sun. He knew it stank like millions of tons of putrid flesh, and men vomited, fainted, and sometimes died when they smelled it. Heart pounding, he again checked his oxygen unit.

Most of the mat was bright green, but in places there were fleshy, greenish-black lumps growing like slowly inflating basketballs. He knew from previous tests that the gluey mat was far deeper than it looked. It now extended almost fifteen feet deep, and it was getting deeper and denser all the time.

Returning to the truck, he adjusted the nozzle on one hose, clipped a shell-shaped weight to the end, fitted the weight into the gas cannon mounted next to the tank, aimed, and fired. A heavy thud, and the truck bucked with the recoil. Carried by the weight, the hose made a lazy parabola far out into the reservoir, then sank without a sound into the viscous muck. He punched a bright blue button on the tank's console as the motor whirred into action, heard the sloshing sound coming through the hose and into the tank. He waited until he heard the beep that said the tank was full and punched the button again.

So far so good. He looked around once more. Seeing no one, he quickly adjusted the feed hose on the second tank so that it connected to the base of the first hose, its head still sunk beneath the surface of the reservoir. When it was secure, he took a deep breath, hearing the rasp and hiss of his oxygen unit in his ears. While making a show of adjusting his tool belt, he touched the yellow button of the small remote control nestled in one pouch. He didn't want to take his eyes from the glowing red dial of the device, but he had his instructions. In an elaborate pantomime he folded his arms and waited as the second tank, instead of sucking up samples, started spewing its contents into the reservoir.

It was feeding time.

Elated, Abdul Jamal waved the remote control at the big-screen TV like a conductor orchestrating a symphony of disaster.

The TV set was incongruous in this fake 18th-century suite. He gazed around the cavernous room. One of hundreds in the palace—the personal residence of the brutal dictator of Tuvanistan and his vicious wife—it was the size of a ballroom. It reeked of bad taste, with its gilt French antiques, pink velvet upholstery, and purple watered-silk wallpaper.

His eyes returned to the screen, again absorbed in the tape of the CNN newscast. I could watch this forever, he thought. A perfect plot, unfolding perfectly.

He sipped from his snifter of cognac, savoring the amber liquid as it burned like liquid smoke. On the screen, a huge crowd of people. About a hundred thousand. A podium, a woman making a speech. The camera veered wildly as mobs of angry men rushed the stage. They were beaten off by club-wielding police in visored black helmets. He listened carefully, relishing every word.

". . . as the riots continue in Istanbul. In the midst of the most important election campaign in this republic's history, the prime minister of Turkey, Thamar Amurkhan, seems powerless to deal with a situation that is deteriorating by the moment. With no end in sight to the worst drought in history, and facing the Kurdish insurrection, it may take a miracle to save the world's only successful Muslim democracy. The winner is expected to be the fundamentalist party known as Strength. . . ."

Jamal heard a heavy tread behind him, the footsteps deadened by the expanse of silk Bokhara carpet. A toneless voice said, "Sir, a call from your Black Sea friend."

His assistant and bodyguard Wurban Ice, the only other person with a key to the suite. "Have him hold for a few moments. You've scanned the room for listening devices?"

"Yes, sir. Nothing. Also, President Popov and his wife inquire whether you wish to join them again for dinner?"

Jamal sighed and paused the videotape. He turned to Ice, thinking again how appropriate the man's name was to his personality. Built like a 300-pound fireplug, the Hungarian had white-blond hair, a flat face, and cold blue eyes.

"I suppose it's necessary, although their taste in food is as bad as their taste in interior design." He took a sip of cognac. "Tell them yes, and make it sound both graceful and grateful. We can't afford to antagonize them at this stage."

Ice nodded and left the room. Jamal pressed the remote control and continued watching the tape.

"As Syria and Iraq demand that the Turks supply them with more water, it seems—incredibly—that the opposite is happening. The president is said to be seeking assurances that the Turkish government will honor its commitment to maintain the flow to the parched lands of what was once the Fertile Crescent. Meanwhile, the threat of war looms larger every day in one of the world's most volatile regions. And no one knows why the Turks refuse to release more water. According to the State Department . . ."

Jamal smiled as he turned off the TV. *I know why.* He walked to the window and twitched the heavy purple curtain aside. The setting sun filled the flaming orange horizon, studded with the spires and domes of minarets and mosques.

He remembered the waiting phone call and reflected on the inconvenience of partners. So much explaining and persuading, invariably to people of inferior intelligence. Then, if they proved incompetent or became a liability, you had to get rid of them. And blood was a big expense.

He set down his drink and lifted the receiver. *"Da?"* Eyes closed, he listened for several moments before interrupting, again in Russian. He tried to keep the irritation out of his voice. "Everything is on schedule. No one is going to be able to stop us."

He listened again. "Don't worry about Zammit. I know every move he makes."

His jaw muscles clenched. For a man supposed to be so tough, the Russian worried about the stupidest things. It was insulting. Perhaps he'd been drinking again, out of control. A feral snarl appeared on Jamal's lips, transforming his handsome face into something frightening, as if a mask had been ripped off. But he kept his voice steady—at least he could control that. "Of course they'll talk. I expect Turkish Intelligence to conduct the interrogation with their boots, if not worse. They'll babble about the Koran. If you're going to worry about anything, worry about your task."

Jamal hung up, then stretched, bones cracking. He thought about his partners, especially the Russian he had just spoken with and his drinking. But he didn't want to think about that right now, so he didn't. Instead he gazed at his image reflected in the mirror on the opposite wall. He liked what he saw. He ran his hand over his ebony hair, silvering at the temples, and considered what a handsome devil he was.

Forty-five years old, six foot three, and built like a Greco-Roman wrestler, there was not a line on his coffee-and-cream complexion. His eyes were always watchful beneath the inch-long eyelashes that melted female hearts, until more intimate knowledge froze them with fear. A cleft chin was accompanied by dimples when he smiled. Jamal smiled now at his favorite sight, himself. He turned and walked to the window, humming his favorite operatic melody, "Au fond du temple saint," from Bizet's *The Pearl Fishers*. His family had for centuries been pearl fishers and merchants in Oman. Now, just as Saint Peter had been a fisher of men, so was he.

Finally he would achieve everything he ever wanted in life, and reel in Dr. Michael Zammit as well.

Mike Zammit contemplated the woman asking about the slaughter of baby seals.

He still felt the sting of Dzerzhinsk air in his eyes as he squinted into the hot TV lights. It felt as if his TV makeup was melting. He had returned from Russia longing for sleep and a decent meal, only to find that his communications and public relations director, Earl Stone, had booked him onto a national talk show hosted by bottle-blond celebrity Molly Katz. Jet-lagged and irritable, he soon discovered that the *Chats with Katz* audience was crammed with environmental activists and New Agers. Something was being shown on the monitor to his left. From the sound track and the audience's horrified gasps, he figured it was an old video of seal pups being clubbed to death.

I've been set up, Zammit thought. He'd have a few words with Earl. "You do great work as an environmental investigator. People should know about it," Stone had said. "Communications, Mike, that's what it's all about in the Information Age."

But for now, in front of a hostile audience, he had to tough it out. "Yes, seals have historically been a source of fur," he continued. "But hunting has been banned for years. And now they're breeding by the millions, destroying the fishery—"

Molly Katz interrupted, "But isn't there a *moral* issue here?"

Zammit fought a sudden surge of irritation and lost. He wished he weren't so tired. "Yes, there is. Whether people who have lived on fish and seals for centuries are being driven to welfare and despair by people like you, who've never even seen one of the damn things."

There was a roar of outrage from the audience.

"But don't all creatures have a right to life?" insisted Katz.

"You're talking about the Disneyfication of the animal kingdom, where every creature that looks cute like Bambi should be saved." He knew he was making a mistake but couldn't stop himself. A rising murmur from the audience threatened to drown him out. "If baby seals looked like cockroaches, nobody'd give a damn how they die."

As boos erupted, Molly Katz shouted, "We have to go to commercial break! We have with us environmental detective Dr. Michael Zammit, Director of the International Environmental Response Team, based right here in Seattle. Now we will be joined by the Reverend Edward Pompo, head of the Spiritual Brotherhood of the She-Manitou. You've read his books by the millions. Don't go away!"

Zammit leaned back and tried to ignore the catcalls from the audience. He watched Edward G. Pompo wave to the audience as he walked onto the stage to loud applause. The gray hairpiece had been carefully chosen to match the color of his Old Testament prophet's beard, and his mock Native American outfit looked expensive enough to have been designed in Italy. As he sat in the chair next to Zammit, beads glinting, fringes swaying, Pompo offered a politician's hearty handshake and looked the scientist straight in the eye with a faint smirk Zammit couldn't read but didn't like. *Probably thinks it's hilarious that I've been set up in front of a hostile crowd,* Zammit thought. He noticed that as soon as Pompo sat down, the hot lights made the false hair at the back of his head start to curl upward.

Molly Katz moved to the stage and took Pompo's hand. She smelled as if she'd recently dived into a vat of cheap perfume. "I love your books." She flashed a smile at Zammit. "Tough audience for you, huh?"

As if you didn't know, he thought sourly. Before he could say something rude—"I hope your ratings tank"—she turned away.

Zammit glanced into the wings and saw Cairo Jackson waving a cell phone. He rose and walked over.

"What?" He'd known Jackson since shortly after his parents had died in a boating accident, when the tough black kid had befriended him.

"An update on the situation in Turkey. The death toll is spiking incredibly fast. The Turks have now completely cut off the water supply for both Iraq and Syria. That could mean war. The White House can't get coherent answers about what's going on in the Ataturk reservoir."

"Sounds bizarre. It's in the middle of nowhere, miles from any pollution source."

A sound technician was beckoning urgently.

"I'll get off this show as fast as I can." Jackson nodded. Zammit headed back to his chair and sat down.

Thunderous applause. "We're back!" shouted Molly. "With us today we have Dr. Michael Zammit and Dr. Edward Pompo. We've been talking about planet Earth and how to protect it."

Zammit tried to recall what Pompo had done for a living before figuring out he could make millions peddling pseudo-religion. Used cars?

"Today Dr. Zammit has been telling us that the human race, as a superior species, can exploit animals at will," explained Katz.

That's not what I was saying, thought Zammit wearily, but hey, it's TV. Molly Katz looked down at some notes in her hand and read, haltingly: "But in his best-selling books, Dr. Pompo has taken a different approach to the reality of our world, an approach based on love and caring for the soul of Earth, the mother of us all." A beaming smile at Pompo, his cue.

Pompo's brow crinkled earnestly. "To survive, the human race must re-ensoul itself. Move back to the land, live in cooperation, not exploitation, with the animals. This will be possible in the coming global postindustrial society."

"Wait a minute," interrupted Zammit. "In a few years there will be nine or ten billion people on this planet. They'll all want cars, refrigerators, computers, and everything else that must be manufactured or processed industrially. There will never be a postindustrial society unless there's a global disaster. What are you babbling about?"

Pompo's eyes darted. "We were talking about an animal's right to life." He turned to the audience, searching for a laugh. "I must say you're not demonstrating much political correctness."

"I don't care about being politically correct," said Zammit. "I'm content merely to be correct."

The guru suddenly stood and faced the audience. "Let's save the life of an animal *right now*. Think as hard as you can of a beautiful little panda or a baby seal. Let us meditate together." He began to chant, and to Zammit's surprise, a lot of the audience seemed to know the monotonous dirge and joined in immediately.

He hated this smarmy exploitation of people's search for meaning. The religion business was booming. It was the same pattern over and over. Take a group of intellectually or emotionally needy people, and mix with an American culture whose primary religion was that peculiarly unsatisfying cult called Consumerism. Stir in a manipulative leader who cobbled together a new cult made out of bits of Buddhism, Native American beliefs, and popular delusions about UFOs and angels. Although Zammit considered most such cults harmless, he knew that others were not. With the wrong cult, the wrong type of leader, you ended up with brainwashed zombies. And if you washed your brain too often, it fell apart like an old rag.

Zammit realized the chant had stopped and Pompo was again seated and speaking. He picked up his coffee cup and sipped. Cold.

"Everything in the universe is connected at the subatomic level. Just looking at a single atom can influence the spin of another atom hundreds or thousands of miles away. This has been proved by science, as I am sure Dr. Zammit can attest." Zammit said nothing—he had heard of this phenomenon, but he wasn't a quantum physicist.

"From this it stands to reason that your being, your soul, even an individual thought, can affect events here in the real world. If you allow yourself to have negative thoughts, it affects events in the real world."

Molly Katz frowned. "You mean not just, like, with atoms?"

"From the microworld of the atom to the macroworld of forests and cities, all is connected," said Pompo. "I teach people how not to have bad thoughts so as not to provoke retaliation by the universe. For less than a thousand dollars, one of my seminars can teach you—"

Pompo's sales pitch for his cult was too much. A surge of anger snapped Zammit's patience. "You charlatan."

The audience was shocked silent. Pompo gazed at Zammit, his mouth an O. "Most people think science is a can filled with facts, and every once in a while a scientist finds a new fact and tosses it into the can. But science isn't a can full of facts, it's a way of thinking."

Katz was fidgeting already.

"That's what we're talking about, right, Molly? The influence of thought. And science enables you to spot sloppy thinking."

He turned to Pompo. "You're a sloppy thinker whose only interest is peddling spiritual trash."

A rustling in the audience, the sound of leaves before a great storm. Pompo swelled with outraged dignity. "My research has proved it to be a fact. Nothing bad can happen to you unless you *want* it to happen. You may disagree as a point of philosophy, but you cannot disprove it."

Mike Zammit glanced at the coffee cup he held in his lap, then threw its contents directly in Pompo's face. He leaned forward into the great silence that followed. "Hey, swami. Something bad just happened to you. Why did you *want* it to happen?"

Sputtering, Pompo struggled from his chair. Coffee dripped from his beard, and his swollen neck was dark. As he stepped forward, Zammit swung his left leg in an arc that swept Pompo off his feet. Fringes flying, the guru landed on the hollow floor with a bang.

"Two bad things in a row," said Zammit.

Pompo tried to struggle to his feet, hairpiece askew, got tangled in his beadwork, and fell to his knees. Zammit stood and faced the audience. "What you've just seen is science. An observable, repeatable experiment that proves the truth, or in this case the falsity, of a particular proposition. Beware of false prophets, especially when they make a profit." He stalked off.

Cairo Jackson stood with his back to the stage facing two men, one stocky and ruddy with curly black hair, the other lean and blond with a triangular face and bloodshot blue eyes. Obviously barring their way. Zammit could see the tension in the big man's broad back and knew that right now he was as alert as a pit bull and twice as dangerous. Zammit wondered what was going on. When they saw him approaching, the two tried to move forward but Jackson held them back. "This is America, fellas. Knock it off."

Zammit stood beside Jackson, his anger ebbing but still not gone. "Well, Dr. Zammit," sneered the blond one in an Irish accent. He mispronounced it deliberately—Zam*meet*.

Zammit stepped forward and thrust his face close to the other man's. They were the same height. The reek of whiskey enveloped him like an aura. He hoped his breath still smelled of all the garlic he'd eaten in Russia the past week. He leaned even closer, gazing deep into the man's bloodshot eyes.

"It's Zammit. Rhymes with dammit."

The blond tried to stare him down. Zammit knew the man could see the aggression in his eyes. The blond poked Zammit in the chest, hard. He stopped when he saw the scientist raise his right fist. "Come on," said Zammit. "Do it again. I'll hit you so hard they'll find your head in Cleveland."

The blond hesitated until Jackson stepped forward, his looming 250-pound presence as menacing as a black death star. The blond blinked, then backed away. Zammit let Cairo tug at his arm and pull him away. The dark one called out, "We'll meet again, Zam-*meet*!"

As they walked out of the building, Zammit turned to Jackson. "Have I suddenly become a thug magnet, or what?"

"Sir, would you like a woman today?"

Abdul Jamal turned away from the window. He glanced at Wurban Ice, then at his Rolex. "Yes. But let's avoid a repetition of last time. You know how I hate it when they kill themselves."

As Ice plodded away, Jamal again twitched the curtain aside. From his suite of rooms he had a panoramic view of the soldiers patrolling the electrified fence that surrounded the palace of President Ivan Popov and his First Lady, Anastasia.

He could also see the edge of a vast plain filled with oil wells, their pump heads moving rhythmically up and down like a vast herd of disoriented elephants. Oil fueled the wealth of this renegade state carved from an ex-Soviet republic.

The death of an empire is a messy business, he reflected. But chaos created opportunity for the clever and ruthless. The demise of the Soviet Union multiplied his business opportunities like so many cancerous cells. But money wasn't enough. For all his wealth, he had no home. He was just a guest in this vulgar palace, in this pitiful excuse of a country. His refuge had been purchased by a cash payment to Ivan and Anastasia. His favorite haunts were denied him—the Plaza Athenée in Paris, the Excelsior in Rome. No nation of laws would welcome him. His lips tightened as he recalled the past few years, slipping from banana republic to tinpot dictatorship to gangster haven, all around the world.

But soon he would have a country. His own.

He heard sounds of struggle behind him. A new acquisition. He did not turn around, savoring the anticipation of seeing her for the first time. He stared at the swarming streets of Blavatsk, Tuvanistan's chaotic capital, as ugly as its name. It was a wonderful source of supply. He enjoyed cruising the streets in his armored car, appraising, selecting, abducting. Or he would send Ice to do it. He had a good eye for the fiery ones. Soon the whole world would submit the way his women did. It wouldn't be easy, but submit it would. And he would have a country.

Jamal turned away from the window. Two presidential bodyguards leered in the center of the room. They were thugs who would run at the least sign of trouble. He also knew that Anastasia

Popov took an unhealthy interest in his sexual appetites and that the guards would ensure news of his latest acquisition soon reached her avid ears.

The guards held the new victim, a manacled young girl with sherry-colored hair and crocus-blue eyes, a Kurd, perhaps, or a Circassian. A bruise purpling under one eye, her mouth taped shut. She was very pale and clearly terrified. A refugee, probably no family. She would never be missed. But she was beautiful and frightened. Jamal found other people's fear a marvelous aphrodisiac. He couldn't wait to sample the nectar from this particular bud.

"Get her prepared, with a minimum of bruising," he said to Ice. "Make sure the harness is secure, administer the new sedative, and remove all sharps from the vicinity. Then call me." He waved dismissively. "I want to read my bible."

As Ice turned away, Jamal remembered. "You've arranged for the donations to the Imam Hatip?"

"Yes, sir. The response has been grateful, as usual."

"Good."

As Ice and the guards dragged the girl away, Jamal poured himself more cognac. Now he could cross his annual *zakat* from his list of tasks. It was advantageous to fulfill the injunctions of the Koran, especially when they coincided so perfectly with his business interests. *Zakat*, one of the Five Pillars of Islam, required rich Muslims to give money to poor ones. As a wealthy man, even though an international fugitive, Jamal chose to pay his *zakat* to the Turkish schools called Imam Hatip—Parson-Preacher schools. The Turkish separation of church and state was almost as rigid as it was in the United States, but these schools were allowed to provide a religious education to those who wanted it. As a powerful patron, he kept an eye on the best pupils, the boys whose intelligence and personality suited his needs. Upon their graduation he financed their university education, hired them to work for him personally, or got them jobs in organizations where their loyalty might prove useful in the future.

As for the thousands of children he did not choose as star pupils, they received a free education at his expense. He improved the lives of others and at the same time paid his *zakat* to Allah. What was wrong with combining religious obligations with business? The generosity of the one more than made up for the rest of it.

He sipped his cognac. *Zakat*. The Prophet Mohammed had a good idea with that one. A clever man. He looked at the amber liquid in the snifter. He chose to ignore some of the other teachings of Islam. He listened to the sounds of struggle coming from the bedroom. Ice had chosen a fiery one.

Jamal walked over to a gilt and ivory rococo table. A silver tray held fluted glasses and a pitcher filled with mineral water. He poured a glass and drank. It was imported especially for his use. Blavatsk's water supply system was a tangle of broken pipes beneath its teeming streets. With the influx of so many refugees, it had been overwhelmed with raw sewage. There were constant outbreaks of cholera, dysentery, and typhoid.

Which was how he had gotten his brilliant idea.

Beside the table lay a lumpy metal object the size of a large footstool—a fused block of ancient coins. Jamal stooped to peer at a face staring out of the lump. He could discern worn Greek lettering on the button-sized coin. He winked at the unseeing eye of the dead god Apollo that stared back at him. Probably Sicilian, he thought. Others also stared at him—Alexander the Great from Thrace, Silenos from Naxos, Poseidon from Salamis. "So many gods, and they're all dead," he said aloud. He wagged his finger at Alexander. "And the empires that created them, too."

Three hundred pounds of didrachmas, decadrachmas, and tetradrachmas, worth millions. His men had recently looted it from an ancient city, eventually to be inundated by the waters of a reservoir. There were some 200 such lost cities in southeastern Turkey, untouched by archaeologists. Once drowned, they never would be. He wanted to loot them all, but there wasn't time.

He straightened and lifted a leather-bound book from the table, the book he regarded as his bible. He settled in the Louis XIV chair and opened the volume at random. His eyes fell on a sentence: "The character of peoples varies, and it is easy to persuade them of a thing, but difficult to keep them in that persuasion. And so it is necessary to arrange things so that when they no longer believe, they can be made to believe by force."

Jamal smiled. He closed both the book and his eyes, then let the volume fall open. As he read again he laughed silently: "When you acquire those states which have been accustomed to live at liberty under their own laws, there are three ways of holding them.

The first is to plunder them; the second is to go and live there in person; and the third is to create within the country a government composed of a few who will keep it friendly to you." He had read this before. He intended to do all three.

He reviewed his list of tasks. Call in the debts of loyalty owed to him by the recipients of two decades' worth of *zakat*. Karl Marx said religion was the opium of the people. So it was, and a most useful drug too. He thought of his Russian partners. Lenin described those the Bolsheviks exploited and then ruthlessly discarded as "useful idiots." His Russian partners were merely useful idiots.

He looked up as Wurban Ice approached. "She's asleep."

Jamal laid the book on the table. As he walked toward the bedroom, the setting sun shone on the gilt letters of the well-thumbed volume—*The Prince*, by Niccolo Machiavelli.

Onstage, Jesus Christ writhed on his cross as the music boomed. Rivulets of blood running down his forehead from the crown of thorns looked black in the acid-yellow neon light. His tossing head lashed sweat-soaked ropes of hair against the wood. The fingers of his nailed hands fluttered in agony and his chest heaved as he struggled to breathe, slowly suffocating as his weight dragged him down the wooden shaft.

A blue fog of tobacco smoke hung from the nightclub ceiling like a storm cloud. A tall man in a coarse brown monk's habit suddenly appeared on stage, his pale face framed by shoulder-length greasy black hair and a black beard, a red Christian cross painted on his forehead. His bulging eyes were as big as eggs and the gray color of badly rinsed glassware. The audience screamed the Russian name for a peasant holy man, "*Starets! Starets!*" Ignoring the crowd, the monk glided up to the man on the cross and observed him closely, then walked off stage.

Strobe lights flashed as the music pounded. The audience of a thousand people tossed their heads in unison, a bloody cross painted on each forehead. Most were soldiers and sailors, young men with the shaved heads and emaciated faces of abused recruits. They sang and swayed to the music, the pupils of their eyes as big as dimes from the drugs they had taken.

At a table near the rear of the club, a huge man in a green uniform with red tabs paid no attention to this modern staging of Christ's Passion. He tossed back a brimming shot glass of vodka. "*Democrazia!*" He pronounced the word with spit and loathing. He wagged a finger at his even drunker companion. "Lieutenant, what Russia needs is a strong leader. A *tsar!*" he shouted, slamming his fist on the table.

Two young soldiers turned to stare. He glared at them. A look of panic crossed their faces. They hurriedly rose and darted to another table. He did not notice the slim young private who remained alone at the next table, apparently stoned beyond the ability to move.

"In the 19th century the Russian Empire conquered an area larger than the entire continental United States. And we didn't do it with democracy. We did it with a *tsar*! Not with a drunken pig like President Bugarin."

The lieutenant slurred, "General, do you hate him because he's a drunk or because he's a democrat?"

The huge man threw back his enormous shaved head and roared, "All Russians are drunks! A Russian without a drink is like a man without a soul." He gripped the lieutenant's arm. "It is against our traditions. Russians are used to venerating one leader. A strong leader. A *religious* leader."

He belched. "The communists failed because they tried to replace the one true religion with a theory of economics. Dreamed up by that idiot Karl Marx in the British Library, where he hid from his creditors because he couldn't figure out even the economics of his own household. Who the hell can worship a theory of economics?"

The general stared around blearily. "Those politicians in Moscow, they should be selling vacuum cleaners. We don't need politics, we need a *tsar*!" He shouted the word like an anthem. "Someone who will act against those destroying Holy Mother Russia." His eyes narrowed viciously. "Jews. Muslims. I say we march into those Islamic republics and pave them with bones."

He pounded his chest with a massive fist. "Between 1941 and 1945 *our* armies ground the Nazis into sausage meat. *Our* sacrifice bled Hitler to death. Our so-called allies didn't even launch the D-Day invasion until 1944. You know how many Americans died in that war? Three hundred thousand. You know how many Russians? *Twenty-seven million.* And the Americans strut around saying, 'Look how *we* won the war.' And then tell us we can't have Eastern Europe!"

He raised his face to the ceiling and laughed, a terrifying series of crazy barks. "In the Cold War the Americans had nuclear missiles right at our borders. We were *surrounded,* wrapped in nuclear barbed wire. When we gave them a taste of their own medicine by putting missiles in Cuba, America wrung its hands like a virgin about to be raped." He gripped the table with both hands as if to tear it in half. "Krushchev should never have backed down. We would have won a nuclear war. That rich boy Kennedy, he looked like a dance instructor."

He swelled with drunken self-pity. "We've paid for everything in blood, and now what? Do you know, sometimes I can't even pay my troops? It's like the Roman Empire, with the barbarians surrounding you, and you need soldiers but you can't pay them, and suddenly everyone's running away through the sewers and it's over. Our Russian civilization, the greatest ever known, over."

He swept his arm to encompass the sailors and soldiers in the room. "I have to deal with the mafia and worse, just to get food and vodka for my men." He leaned forward conspiratorially. "We need a strong leader, a holy leader, allied with God, to overwhelm our enemies. All the enemies, everywhere."

At last he noticed the music had stopped. The nails had been removed from the wrists and feet of the dead Christ as he was taken from the sweat-soaked, bloody cross and laid on the stage. The tall monk in the coarse brown habit knelt over the acolyte of his cult, one of the few who was permitted to undergo this agonizing initiation ritual and achieve, in their own minds at least, a Christlike sanctity. The audience rose, hands clutched to their mouths as they awaited the miracle.

The holy man prayed, arms to heaven. He leaned forward, made the sign of the cross, and pressed the voluminous robes of his left arm to the dead man's chest. The corpse twitched. Suddenly the whole body convulsed. Gasps and screams from the crowd, as hysterical prayers rose to heaven.

Lurching from his table, the general staggered toward the arisen Christ, now sitting up on stage with his blood-streaked arms wrapped around his legs. At the sight of the uniform the crowd parted. Falling to his knees with a crash that shook the building, the general tenderly removed the crown of thorns. As people gasped in ecstasy, he pursed his lips and smeared them back and forth along the bloody forehead. The monk raised his grotesque staring eyes to heaven at this display of devotion, but as the devotee somehow regained his feet and staggered back to his table, they followed him with a sidelong reptilian interest.

Lips beslobbered with blood, the general leaned toward his nearly unconscious companion. The monk half emerged from the shadows and listened as the general looked around in a drunken caricature of conspiracy, his voice louder than he realized. "No longer hidden, the Holy Chosen One awaits. Soon our new tsar will be crowned in the rose-red church, Hagia Sophia. He will reign where he *should* reign, in the holy city, no longer called Istanbul, but its rightful name, Constantinople. And then—"

He looked up, startled, as the monk leaned over and whispered in his ear. For the next two hours, as he pressed shot after shot of vodka to his blood-caked lips and poured them down his throat, he didn't utter another sound.

He didn't notice the slim lone figure at the nearby table, dressed in a private's uniform, rise and slip through the still chanting, still swaying crowds.

 As Cairo Jackson drove the car away from the television studio, Mike Zammit could tell the big man was watching him from the corner of his eye. He gazed at the skyscrapers of Seattle's downtown, their tops hidden in a swirl of gray fog. Wipers slashed at the sheets of water cascading down the windshield, and colored lights gleamed blearily through the rain.

Finally Jackson said, "You think Pompo's going to charge you with assault?"

Zammit shrugged. "I don't care if he does or not."

"What about his goons?"

"You heard those accents. Couple of Belfast hard boys. Ex-IRA, Provo Army. Strange company for a New Age scam artist."

Zammit gazed at the scudding clouds as they exited Stewart Street and entered the stream of traffic on the I-5. "Let's look into it."

Five minutes later they took Exit 170 off the I-5. After a three-minute drive along Lake Union, its deep blue surface covered with whitecaps, Jackson dropped Zammit at the front door of a nondescript building on the shores of the lake and went to park the car. Several of the world's most innovative biotechnology firms were located beside the big lake in the heart of Seattle, including the three-story warehouse that housed the headquarters of the International Environmental Response Team. A discrete yellow sign said INERT. Zammit's people loathed their organization's acronym, chosen years ago by some faceless bureaucrat, and never lost an opportunity for wordplay with it.

As Zammit walked through the automatic doors into his agency's headquarters, he felt his fatigue slowly infused with something close to happiness. Home.

He'd designed the building himself. From the cavernous lobby a white metal staircase spiraled up to connect all three floors. The artificial waterfall had been turned on, its plume filling the air with energy-inducing negative ions as it cascaded from the third floor to the first, splashing into a rock-filled pool near the entrance to the gymnasium, kitchen, boardrooms, and studios. The constantly refreshed air kept the staff alert, happy, and productive. There was a dock at the back, facing the lake, where DeHaviland TurboBeaver pontoon planes rolled up to deposit the bright yellow biohazard containers with samples taken from the sites of environmental crises all over the world, samples that needed urgent analysis, the core of INERT's business. The third floor was his apartment, while the second contained the forensic laboratories, a machine shop, and other facilities INERT needed for its operations and Zammit needed for his inventions.

Zammit had come to the agency in 1994 after running his own business, ZAM Research Instruments Corp., inventing customized tools for DNA analysis, biomedical research, and environmental cleanup. After registering a series of patents, he found his products in use all over the world and came to the attention of the federal government. With budget cutbacks, the environmental protection agency INERT was dying from lack of money just as ecological crises around the world became more frequent and severe. Asked to take over, Zammit drove a hard bargain. He offered to roll most of the income from his patent royalties back into INERT in exchange for a virtually free hand in operating the agency. To his surprise, the government agreed, although the noninterference clause hadn't worked as well as he would have liked.

As Zammit walked past the workstation area, Dikka Spargo waved him over. He'd hired her, now nineteen, after hearing about an experiment she had done in high school two years previously. An inventor himself, Zammit recognized ingenuity when he saw it.

For a school science project, Spargo had made a couple of insect robots, one the size of a thumb, the other the size of a hand, using cast-off electronics that cost less than fifty dollars. She had taken silicon chips from old computers, wiring cannibalized from microwave ovens, twenty-five-cent hardware store hinges, old three-pronged plugs, obsolete sensors, and other debris, soldered them together to make artificial creatures, and then given them life through some highly creative programming. Citing the pioneering research of robotics expert Mark Tilden, Dikka had said, in the brief but cogent four-page paper explaining her robot life forms, that all artificial intelligence projects had failed miserably over the

previous twenty years because they concentrated on building robotic intelligence from the top down, which she maintained was
impossible. Her inspiration was to follow Tilden's ideas and mimic
evolution by building intelligence from the bottom up. There were
now about thirty of the insectoids roaming through the building.
Spargo's creatures had three basic commands built into their software, the first and most important of which was *Always be on the
lookout for food.* More than one pompous congressman, on a tour of
INERT headquarters, had jumped three feet off the ground as a
metal and plastic tarantula scuttled down a hallway, found a wall
socket, inserted its plug for a quick fix, then darted away, all the
while evolving bizarre behaviors that were impossible to forecast.

The insectoid Zammit found most intriguing was the biggest so
far, from metal tentacle tip to tentacle tip slightly larger than a
dinner plate. In addition to being the biggest, it was also the most
complex and intelligent, its brain consisting of an entire mother-
board taken from an old Aptiva. Zammit had named it Catula
because it had somehow taken an aversion to the resident feline,
named Cat, and stalked it constantly. Zammit figured that Cat had
probably batted the insectoid around when it first started to roam,
and in some unfathomable robot way Catula remembered and re-
sented it. He'd finally asked Spargo to reprogram the metal cat-
hater to spare the organic creature any further torment. He
couldn't wait to see if the behavior reestablished itself.

Dikka Spargo looked up with a faint smile. She had sparkling
hazel eyes, freckles, an astonishing variety of body piercings and
tattoos on her slender frame, and long brown hair, at the moment
tied up into a haphazard chignon that was rapidly coming apart.
She had stuck a variety of pens and pencils in her hair. Her powers
of concentration were amazing. Zammit had once found her on
the floor in a dead faint and discovered she had been so intent on
a project that she'd forgotten to eat or sleep for three days.

A slowly rotating three-dimensional neon red, blue, and yellow
simulation of a molecule floated on her computer screen. "Hey,
boss. Not exactly an *inert* performance."

Chats with Katz was broadcast live, so he should have known
they'd all see it or hear about it. "Dikka, with all that metal in your
body, stay away from magnets." As she grinned, he leaned over
to look at the screen. "What's this?"

"Tissue analysis of those marine corpses floating in the Gulf of
California."

Zammit nodded. There had been mysterious kills of sea birds, pilot whales, dolphins, and sea lions in a sparsely populated area. "Identify anything?"

Spargo turned the monitor and pointed at the image of the molecule. "The killer. Cyanide."

"From what? There aren't any *maquiladora* factories in that part of Mexico."

"There's a theory we came up with while you were gone. Actually, us and the Feds." Dikka's chignon finally came apart, and a tousled curtain of brown hair suddenly veiled her face like that of some unlikely teenage oracle, as pens and pencils hit the floor. She pushed at her hair impatiently. "Apparently the Gulf is used as a transfer point on a drug route from Colombia through Mexico. Shipments are dropped by plane into the water. To mark the drop-off spot, the smugglers have started using a photosensitive dye called NK19. It shows as a red stain during the day and a blue phosphorescent glow at night. When NK19 decomposes, it releases cyanide. Bingo, bouillabaisse."

She pulled the screen back toward her. "Sure tells you how active drug traffic is in that area." She piled up her mane and reached into her white lab coat for a couple of barrettes, clipping them into her hair in an ineffective effort to bring it under control.

"Good work," said Zammit. "Any news about Turkey?"

"Not that I know of."

After checking with the technicians working on other projects, Zammit walked across the soundproofed flooring to the reception area, where Frances Fitzgerald Richards was going through a sheaf of files. She had returned from Russia two days before, as Zammit flew to Moscow to deliver his report on Dzerzhinsk. Her title was Deputy Director, Technical Operations, her training in botany and molecular biology, particularly DNA sequencing. Thirty-four years old, she was tall for a woman at five eleven, just two inches shorter than Zammit. She had a heart-shaped face, hair the color and texture of corn silk, tied back in a ponytail, and green eyes the color of new leaves. They were always alert. She often appeared sardonically amused at something or other, her fair skin crinkling naturally into laugh lines at the corners. She looked like a friendly Viking. Her looks were marred—endearingly, Zammit thought— by a slight overbite and a crooked nose, the result of a childhood fight with her brother.

It was supposed to be her day off, but since the disappearance of her husband, Adam, eighteen months before, she had never taken a day off. A paleobotanist, Adam Richards had been on a field expedition collecting medicinal specimens in the primary jungles of Sumatra when he simply vanished. Frankie had taken it very hard. As hard as Zammit had taken the death of his wife, Claudia, from cancer three years before.

"Frankie, it's supposed to be your day off. Why are you here, and if you're here, why aren't you in the lab or your studio?" He always tried a half-hearted I'm-the-boss routine with her, and it never worked. He suspected she was smarter than he was, but it didn't bother him.

"I'm here because I wanted to look at some test results. I'm not in the studio because I'm stalled on a portrait. Also, I had to meet a potential client today."

"And the result?"

"It appears he'll get his ego rubbed and I will get lots of money."

"So, Renaissance Woman. Is this new commission in your career as a famous portrait painter going to interfere with your scientific duties here?"

"Not at all."

"May I ask who the client is?"

"I don't want to say the name. I'm sure you can guess anyway. A wealthy man with a huge ego who owns a lot of real estate in New York. Wants me to paint two portraits of him. One with his family, all smiley and decent. The other of him stark naked, posing as a Greek god. In a winged helmet, throwing a javelin."

Zammit raised an eyebrow. "You're kidding."

Frankie Richards shook her head. "Obviously leads a rich fantasy life."

Richards was much in demand for her portraits. Trained in Italy and France in traditional techniques, she had an uncanny instinct for color, proportion, and perspective. Despite lavish enticements, she refused to license the reproduction of her work, so the rich and famous pursued her relentlessly, eager to be immortalized by a talented original artist, someone whose work would be forever one of a kind.

Even though he knew she could handle herself, Zammit always felt protective of Richards. She wasn't as tough as she pretended to be. Hell, he thought, I'm not as tough as I pretend to be.

Zammit said, "Just make sure you're in a situation where you can protect yourself, in case this naked fan of Greek mythology decides he wants to play Mars to your Venus. And if you're not sure, call me."

Her eyes flickered, and he changed the subject. "Speaking of protecting yourself, is Cat still having problems with Catula?"

"I would never have believed it, and Dikka swears she erased the memory of that nasty little thing. Stalking my cat indeed. It's doing it again."

Zammit blinked, intrigued. "Well, both creatures live in the same environment, and that hasn't changed. The pattern of behavior has again become the same. An interesting insight into convergent evolution."

"Not really," disagreed Richards. "They don't compete with each other for anything. It's not as if Cat and Catula fight over who gets first dibs to stick themselves into a wall socket."

"True," admitted Zammit. "But its memory of cat-hating was erased, yet it still reverts to cat-hating. Must be some sort of evolutionary pressure. Maybe space."

"You're telling me that glorified toaster on legs is territorial?"

Zammit shrugged and gave in to the impulse to tease. "Apart from shedding some light on evolution, you know what this means."

"What?" challenged Frankie, warily.

"Any creature with minimal intelligence, natural or artificial, is smart enough to figure out it hates cats."

Richards threw a playful punch at his arm. Zammit said, "OK, enough fooling around. Anything important happen?"

Frankie examined her nails. "You mean apart from a possible dry-cleaning bill from the pompous Dr. Pompo? I'm sure he won't demonstrate much *inertia* in demanding restitution."

Zammit groaned. "Why can't I have a straight man around here instead of all you comedians? Well?"

Richards reached for her coffee cup. "Lab results, some promotional stuff, and tons of general agency e-mail, most of it the usual waste of bandwidth."

"Anything more about Turkey?"

"Rumors, bits and pieces, dribs and drabs. Nothing useful. Terse phone calls from important people who should know what's going on but obviously don't because their voices contain too much brown and gray with shrill little yellow highlights. That always means ignorance with flashes of panic."

"What does it tell you, Frankie?"

Her face was impassive. "We're in the eye of the hurricane, the calm before the storm. This is going to be a nasty one."

As Zammit absorbed this assessment, her sardonic green eyes appraised him. "You look awful. If you promise not to throw it at me, I'll get you a coffee."

"Thanks." He rubbed his face and thought for a moment. "I want a briefing on the results and anything else that came up while I was in Russia. Have somebody run the protocol and retrieve anything interesting from my private e-mail address. I'll be down in fifteen minutes."

Richards waved Dikka over, then headed back to her office. The teen sat down in front of the monitor and keyed the sequence that would automatically scan the electronic mail that had built up in Zammit's personal file during his absence.

A controversial and aggressive agency despite its name, INERT was constantly dealing with politicians, animal rightists, and environmental extremists, including the occasional eco-terrorist. They liked sending e-mail. Most of it was electronic junk. To cope with the volume, INERT used a software program that recognized key words and addresses. Any mail containing them was pulled and the rest trashed. But the addresses of the world's known remailers were also pulled automatically. Offering anonymity to people who wanted to send e-mail but didn't want the recipient to know where it came from, remailers stripped off the sender's electronic address as easily as slitting open an envelope, then substituted their own address—in effect, putting the message in a new envelope—before sending it on. Zammit figured that anyone who didn't want him to know who or where they were was someone whose threat might be very real.

As he headed upstairs to his apartment, Zammit felt eyes watching him. He turned. Glowering down from the wall was a life-size portrait of Vladimir Ilyich Lenin. He'd been given it a few months earlier by a grateful Moscow official after breaking a crime ring that had been smuggling thousands of tons of illegal ozone-eating chlorofluorocarbons from former Soviet factories under the brand names of legal refrigerants.

The bureaucrat had shrugged and gestured at the portrait, taken from storage, saying vaguely, "We have so many of them. . . ." Like the insect robots, it was a surefire conversation starter with visitors.

Dressed once again in civilian clothes, Jack Morgan, his face flushed, stood before his boss and argued.

His all-American good looks seemed out of place in the shabby 19th-century room. Modern steel desks and computers contrasted strangely with the rest of the headquarters of the CIA shell corporation called the AmeriSlav Import-Export Company. Dusty French-looking furniture with worn velvet upholstery stood against pale green wallpaper that rose two-thirds of the way up the walls, faded and peeling away at the corners. Above the wallpaper rose cream-colored plaster covered with a crazed network of thin cracks.

Morgan's lanky limbs gestured in frustration. "Sir, my Russian is fine. And it wasn't just him babbling about a Holy Chosen One being the new tsar and reigning in Constantinople. It was his uniform. He was a *general*. This area houses two of the world's most important military and naval bases. We're the CIA, for Christ's sake. I think we should investigate."

"How old are you, and how long have you been here in the Crimea?"

"Twenty-eight. I've been here six months." As you damn well know, he thought.

Yarham's chair creaked as he clasped his hands behind his head and leaned back, making a pretense of thinking deeply. He always did this, and Morgan detested it. Lance's head was round and his skin yellowish from hepatitus B contracted in Guatemala early in his career. He had dyed his thinning hair an improbable shade of red, but half an inch of gray root was showing. The combination of yellow skin and reddish hair looked so peculiar that Morgan assumed the man's eyes must be going. Yarham had already gone to fat, and the act of leaning back in his chair thrust his bulging belly, like a half-full sack of wet sand, farther over his straining belt. He was close to retirement and had given up even the pretense of staying in shape. And, as far as Morgan could see, even the pretense of doing his job.

"Six months," Lance Yarham said complacently. "Harvard,

Langley, then six months at this station. And already you know something huge, something nobody else has ever heard of."

Before Morgan could reply, Yarham slowly lowered his chair and leaned on his elbows. "I'm what you'd call an old Russia hand. I've studied the former USSR for twenty-five years, since you were barely out of diapers. . . ."

Inwardly Morgan seethed at this patronizing lecture.

". . . and I can tell you this for sure. In the old days, under the tsars if you tried to do anything against the system, the Okhrana—the secret police—beat the shit out of you and sent you to Siberia for a couple of years.

"Under Lenin, if you tried to do anything, the Cheka—the Bolshevik secret police—tortured you before beating the shit out of you. Then they sent you to Siberia for twenty years.

"Under Stalin, if you so much as *thought* of doing anything against the system, the NKVD came along, tortured you, beat the shit out of you, and wrecked your brain with drugs. Then they either shot you or sent you to Siberia for life."

Lance Yarham gave a weary shrug. "And now the whole country is run by gangsters, and their pathetic currency doesn't even make good toilet paper. So they drink vodka to blot out their horrible lives. Sing sad songs, weep about their country's awful history, and talk big before they slide off their chairs in a drunken stupor."

He wagged a finger at Jack Morgan. "My point is, despite all the big talk, they never actually *do* anything. A thousand years of serfdom and secret police have kicked all initiative out of them. The only thing that would get these people aroused to do something would be the reincarnation of Christ himself."

"But sir, he was a *general*."

"You've had a chance to review the security files by now. Did you recognize him from the photos?"

"No, but—"

"Did you see him arrive or leave in a staff car?"

"No, but—"

"And he was at one of those rituals staged by that creepy monk Smegyev? In the old days you moved up the ranks in the Soviet army by being a good Communist, which meant being an atheist. The person you're describing would never have gone into the army in the first place."

Yarham looked up sharply, his first crisp movement since the young agent had been at the station. "You were there. Does he really raise the dead?"

"I assume they're not dead. But they have doctors there, with monitors and stuff. You can check the equipment. No life signs before they're revived. How they fake it I don't know. But the general, sir. And what he said."

Yarham waved his hand dismissively. "Just some drunk talking big at this country's equivalent of a backwoods revival meeting. Forget it."

Morgan tried one last time. "But the uniform . . ."

Yarham sighed. "You've seen the street demonstrations. Members of the Monarchist Party wearing old tsarist uniforms? Doesn't mean they're military men, does it? I could walk out of this office and be back in fifteen minutes with a genuine Russian general's uniform I bought from a street vendor for a five-dollar bill. Everything is for sale in this country. This is a place where young women *aspire* to be hard-currency prostitutes because they make real money and meet men who don't stink of vodka and despair."

He turned away and reached for a pen. Morgan knew he never used his computer if he could avoid it. "I know we have to keep tabs on all these weird cults, and I appreciate the fact that you volunteered for that duty, but where this general is concerned, forget it, kid. File a report, but forget it."

"Yes, sir," said Morgan as he turned and walked out the door. He had no intention of obeying Yarham's order.

Boris Kazov stared at the cuticles of his fingernails, brimming with bright red blood.

He leaned back into his big leather armchair, put his hands to his face, and tried to rise. A sudden wave of nausea pitched him forward over his cluttered desk as he gagged. Through eyes teared with pain, he finally found a steady visual reference in his battered leather briefcase propped against the wall. Breathing shallowly, back aching, he tottered like an old man over to the mirror that hung on the wall across the room and straightened with an effort. A gray face he barely recognized as his own stared back, slick with the sheen of sweat. His eyes were bloodshot and his hair was falling out in clumps. He tried to take a deep breath and a stabbing pain made him snort, sending two rivulets of bright red spurting from his nostrils. He wiped with the back of his hand, grimacing at the rusty taste of his own blood, and shook his head.

Think. The mysterious illness had now plagued him for two weeks. At fifty-five he knew he had a weak liver and bad lungs from the hard-drinking, chain-smoking life of an investigative journalist, but why would that make him bleed from practically every pore? He held up a shaking hand and touched his throat. It was hot, swollen, and sore. He tried to stick out his tongue and choked from the pain.

For the first time he realized he was dying.

Like an animal at the end of the hunt, sick and exhausted, his bleary eyes roamed the familiar confines of his office as if searching for a way out. There was none. It was time to save what he could.

Slowly he dropped to his knees and crawled over to his briefcase, taken from a storage locker that morning. Panting, he inserted the key in the lock and lifted the flap. It was all there. Luckily he had taken the material home with him the night his office had been broken into and every filing cabinet ransacked. He pulled out the sheaf of folders and papers, bound with elastic bands. Clutching the documents to his chest, he slowly rose to his feet and groped for the desk. Dizzy, he reached for the edge to steady himself, his arm brushing a stack and sending a cascade of paper crashing to the floor. He sat down again in his chair, gasping with the effort.

The office door opened. "I heard a noise. My God, Boris." Irina Markova, his best young journalist, stood in the doorway.

After decades of reading the lies in *Pravda* and grinding his teeth, Boris Kazov had made the best of it after the collapse of Communism. He founded his newspaper, the *Glory of Sevastopol*, and built a reputation searching out corruption in the new capitalist countries carved from the carcass of the USSR. He never had to search far, and he made enemies by the hundreds among the rich, the powerful, the brutal, and the bought. But even he couldn't uncover every filthy secret alone. He hired Irina Markova after a story he ran about a slave prostitution ring enraged a mafia kingpin and he was attacked on a lonely night street and beaten almost to death. Irina, fresh from school, had visited him in the hospital, bringing vodka and cigarettes. "You need some help, I think," she had said. They argued for hours, and she had finally talked him into hiring her. It was the best decision he had ever made.

She knelt before him and took his hand. Her violet eyes were filled with concern. "You are much worse. I'll get the doctors."

Boris Kazov shook his head. "They didn't know what was wrong a week ago, and now it's too late," he whispered. With trembling hands he thrust the package at her. "You know what to do."

She kissed his hand and then his face, now streaked with tears mixed with blood as he sobbed with pain. "I'm getting the doctor anyway. You stay here."

"You know what to do," Kazov rasped. "Do that first."

Her eyes searched his face, then she caressed his cheek with the back of her hand and strode from the office. For almost a minute he was able to continue sitting slumped in his chair. Then he started to pitch forward, face first, and with slow surprise found he couldn't even lift his arms to break his fall.

 Zammit rubbed his face as he walked through his loft home on the third floor of the INERT warehouse.

On marble pedestals stood busts of Roman emperors, frowning with imperial disdain at small squat figures carved five thousand years ago from golden yellow stone on the Maltese islands. The tiny figures from the dawn of history looked so modern they could have been sculpted by Picasso. Persian carpets covered the floor. The loft's vast expanse was separated into sections by folding screens, silk carpets hanging from bronze rings set in the ceiling, and arrangements of rich leather furniture.

In a far corner, half-hidden in shadow, stood a suit of armor. The mailed right hand grasped the pommel of a huge sword. It was tarnished, leaned a bit, and was badly dented. Mike Zammit smiled at his most prized possession. He patted it fondly on the shoulder as he headed for the shower.

He undressed quickly. In the bathroom he turned the water on as hot as he could stand it and adjusted the shower nozzle to spit out stinging needles. Just as he felt the heat making him drowsy, he turned the water to cold. Breathing hard, he forced himself to stand completely still under the icy torrent for sixty seconds.

Toweling his numb body, now thoroughly awake, he walked back into the bedroom and reached for the remote control, aiming it at the TV in the big entertainment unit against the wall. He watched the screen as he pulled a pair of chinos and a black turtleneck out of his closet. Some male action star was being shot three times by one of those improbably huge and menacing weapons he'd seen only in action movies. The fallen actor, spouting fake blood from containers concealed under his clothing, writhed briefly and unconvincingly on the pavement, then sprang to his feet, pulled his own phallically large gun, and sprinted down the street after the bad guys. Zammit shook his head. Only in the movies. In real life when you got shot like that, all you wanted to do was curl up in a little ball and start whimpering for your mama, before you went into shock. He clicked the remote to CNN.

As he dressed, images of angry crowds, deserts, and soldiers told him that the big news was still the ongoing drought in the

Middle East and the unrest in Istanbul. No mention of the deaths downstream of the Ataturk reservoir. Zammit remembered the first time he'd met the Turkish prime minister, Thamar Amurkhan, at the beginning of her political career, when she was the junior cabinet minister in charge of environment. There'd been a problem with Russian oil tankers dumping contaminated bilgewater into the Bosphorus. He had found it hard dealing with her, not because she was difficult—on the contrary, she was intelligent and charming—but because she bore a disconcerting resemblance to Sophia Loren, and he always found himself tongue-tied in her presence. I must be a romantic, thought Zammit.

He bent to pick up his favorite pair of battered brown loafers and started violently. Two little red eyes stared at him from under the bed. As he leapt back, the metal insectoid scuttled rapidly out of the room. Zammit took a deep breath. Of course. Spargo's second programming command: *Hide.* He made a mental note to talk to Dikka. Although he encouraged innovation and creativity among his staff, the situation was getting out of control when he was as twitchy as Cat. At the age of forty, he didn't fancy being given a heart attack by one of Spargo's little experiments.

Zammit looked at the screen as he sat down to put on his shoes. Suddenly a repellent image appeared there—pale face framed by long greasy black hair and a scraggly black beard. On the forehead was painted a red Christian cross. The gray eyes bulged, as big as eggs.

"... *Lazar Smegyev. The mysterious monk heads a cult that preaches the need for a religious revival and the fulfillment of Russia's historic destiny. Hysterical riots preceded his arrival here as word spread of his alleged ability to raise the dead. Sources in Moscow say the monk has gained an influence unprecedented since the days of Rasputin. Like that infamous monk, who held the last Russian tsar under his spell, he appears to be protected by powerful elements in government. As stories circulate about bizarre initiation rituals, it is rumored ...*"

Zammit turned off the broadcast. Another cult. He thought of Pompo and his cult, his exploitation of people's search for meaning. At least he didn't claim to raise the dead.

The dead. He glanced at the stack of videocassettes hidden in shadow at the back of the entertainment unit. He selected one and looked at the label. After a moment's hesitation, he pushed the cassette into the VCR and turned on the TV.

Four years ago. A summer picnic. His wife, Claudia, mixing

potato salad. Sleek and dark and interesting looking, a wide smile on a face like a Renaissance portrait. Not like the end, wasted and wan in the palliative care unit. Adam Richards at the barbecue, wearing a white Tilley hat and a big grin, cooking steaks. Balding, his short beard peppered with gray, he appeared every inch the academic, even in an apron. Looking at him, you'd never suspect he spent months on end in the most dangerous and inaccessible jungles on earth hunting for rare medicinal plants. For the hundredth time, Zammit wondered where and how he had died in Sumatra. Frankie Richards, in slacks and a sleeveless blouse, eating chocolate ice cream. A messy kiss for Adam, his cheek now smeared with chocolate. Frankie blew a kiss at the camera as Claudia held two fingers up behind her head. Foolish fun. The frolicking dead.

He thought of Frankie, never taking days off since Adam disappeared, not knowing how he had died, not wanting to be alone with her grief. His own loneliness, now Claudia was gone.

He watched for a few minutes, then turned off the VCR and walked back into the bathroom. He splashed cold water on his face and stared in the mirror. Short black hair, sea-blue eyes, hard lines around the eyes and mouth. He waited until he looked normal before heading downstairs.

 As Zammit walked toward his office over-looking Lake Union, Frankie handed him a steaming cup of coffee and a pile of folders. Her appraising gaze told him she knew he felt badly about losing it on the Molly Katz show. She also, somehow, picked up on his recent distress from watching the video. "Thanks. I promise I won't throw it at anyone."

"I appreciate that," smiled Richards. "By the way, it's been on the news. Everyone comments on your terrific aim. Also, I intend to avoid the board meeting. I want to complete a polymerase chain reaction."

"I know you hate meetings. We'll be discussing routine stuff. No need to waste your time, and PCR is fascinating. You still investigating the Abominable Mystery?"

"Yes."

"Great. Let me know what you find—I see a Nobel Prize in your future. Unless some news comes in from Turkey, we're on our own."

"OK." Frankie walked away toward her lab.

Cairo Jackson's massive frame was wedged into a chair in front of his workstation. His office was a few feet from Zammit's. The big man was forty-one, and his face shone like a basalt star. He always wore a white shirt and tie to the office, usually with an expensive Italian suit. Through sheer intelligence, hard work, and a couple of big paydays during his brief career as a heavyweight, he had scrabbled out of the projects, obtained both a law degree and an MBA, and was now Deputy Director, General Operations at INERT. Zammit had once asked him why he hadn't continued as a boxer. Cairo had growled, "I like my eggs scrambled, not my brains." Zammit stuck his head into Jackson's office. Cairo swung around, brown eyes alert. His eyes never looked anywhere long, and never without a purpose.

"In addition to checking on our Irish elves, could you put together a briefing on Pompo? You ever read any of his stuff?"

Cairo shrugged. "The usual New Age crap. Crystals, channeling, UFOs, after-death experiences. Lights at the end of the tunnel and choirs of angels, my ass."

"So why read it?"

"Because my kids are getting into it through their friends at school. It's a form of hysteria, I think, since the beginning of the new millennium." He crossed his arms across his chest. "By the way, since we met at the TV studio and not the airport, I didn't have a chance to ask how things worked out with Connie. Did he go nuts not being able to spend hours in the gym?"

Zammit knew Cairo had doubts about Constantine Constanti-novich Palaeov, the twenty-four-year-old Russian student who had joined INERT several months before to learn environmental science.

Part of the agency's mandate, insisted upon by Zammit, was the training of young people from other countries. Palaeov had written to Zammit personally from St. Petersburg, begging for a job. Taken with the kid's eagerness, and knowing that Russia was one of the world's most polluted countries, Zammit had pulled some strings to get the kid sponsored. It was Frankie Richards who nicknamed him Connie, explaining, "Constantine is *way* too formal, and I'm not going to call anyone Con. Besides, he's cute, and Connie is a nice warm burnt sienna kind of name."

At first they had struggled with Palaeov's lack of idiomatic English. During his first week with INERT, he had come to Zammit holding a newspaper and a dictionary, black eyes burning, bony face flushed with frustration, straw-blond hair askew, his raw-boned limbs quivering with frustration. "I know what is food. I know what is junk. But what is junk food?" Apart from language difficulties, now resolved, the intense, hard-working Russian was devoid of a sense of humor, something Zammit would ordinarily have found intolerable. But, he reflected, remembering the little he knew of Connie's personal history, if I were an orphan who'd been raised in a monastery in Siberia during the collapse of the Soviet Union, I don't think I'd be inclined to see the funny side of life, either. Besides, Zammit had a soft spot for underdogs, and he intended to give the young man every opportunity.

Connie spent many of his off hours in INERT's gymnasium using the weight machines and free weights. He got big so fast that Zammit became alarmed. Cairo Jackson had said, "I've been watching too. He's not using steroids. He's just an insecure kid from a screwed-up country trying to build himself a living suit of armor so he can hide behind all those muscles."

Zammit had pondered this insightful observation. One day in

the gym, as he worked his circuit, from skipping rope to calis-thenics to speed bag to heavy bag, he tried to talk to Palaeov as the Russian strained at the weights.

"You know, I used to do that. Got bored with it. Maybe you'd like to try swimming or boxing or karate. You could spar with Cairo. Speed up your reflexes and build some endurance instead of just show muscle." He went to the kitchen next door and took two big crisp apples from the fridge. He gave one to Connie. "Watch. This is a trick the Roman Emperor Tiberius used to do." Placing his second finger and his thumb on either side of the hard fruit, he squeezed his muscular hand, effortlessly penetrating the apple until finger and thumb met at the core. "You try."

The kid had tried, muscles bulging, and only made a couple of small dents. Zammit shook his head. "Connie, show muscles are no good." But the kid ignored his advice, lifting weights with re-newed vigor, and he hadn't pushed it.

Zammit shrugged at Cairo. "Connie worked out well. Kept his head when we confronted the local thugs. I left him in Dzerzhinsk for a few days to do some more analysis, but he'll stay away from those red-hot nuclear garbage pits in case it provokes another visit by the knuckle-draggers." He looked at his watch. "Boardroom."

 Frankie Richards entered her lab.

The room was a long rectangle. To her left, lab benches, the centrifuge, and the old-fashioned hand-controlled microtome for sectioning specimens. There were computerized ones on the market, but she preferred to do it by hand. She even sharpened the steel blade herself, using her own special combination of mineral oil and volcanic pumice, which led to jokes about Crusaders whetting their swords before going into battle. But the jokes always stopped when they saw the results. Zammit often remarked on her "touch" and the fact that she could, by hand, section a specimen so fine it was only two microns, so thin it was almost invisible, like gossamer. It was an art, just like painting, and it was the elegance of the controlling hand that determined the result, a result no computer could match.

There was a fume hood to waft away the poisonous solvents she used in fixing specimens. Under the fume hood, the storage containers for the acetone, toluene, xylene, and other solvents and chemicals. And a 1200-degree Celsius autoclave for incinerating contaminated equipment and rotting specimens.

To her right, windowed cases were filled with equipment. Glass jars, slender glass tubes called pipettes, racks of glass slides and covers, bottles of hematoxylin and eosin dyes, and plastic baskets containing thousands of Eppendorf tubes, from 0.2 to 1.5 milliliters—the small ones the diameter of a thin pencil and the length of a thumbnail, the big ones as thick and long as a little finger.

For the experiment she was about to perform, she'd use the little Eppendorfs. Their walls were incredibly thin to conduct heat, and they had flexible, hinged contamination lids that expanded so the tiny tubes wouldn't pop open during the extreme temperature changes involved in the polymerase chain reaction and ruin the results.

Richards walked to the far end of the lab, which contained her vasular plants herbarium of dried specimens and her greenhouse of live ones—her passion, apart from painting. It had originally been both hers and her husband's passion, but with Adam's disappearance in Sumatra she was determined to continue the work.

Her favorite photograph of him was pasted to the glass wall of the greenhouse: in a jungle somewhere, balding, short beard peppered with gray, big smile, holding a rare white orchid—and hard as iron, despite his professorial appearance. She stopped in front of it, a ritual she was determined to keep—never, ever would this image become so familiar that it was just another object the eye glided over unseeing. The same thoughts always ran through her mind: We were such a great team. You always called me an introverted extrovert—content to be completely alone, doing my research for weeks on end, and then hitting the social circuit in a cocktail dress, being charming, in my role as a society painter. How could you die? You were so strong.

The loss of Adam had been an agonizing sharpness that slashed her soul, but now, thanks to time's grace, the memory of him was being coated with nostalgia, just as the grit inside an oyster is transformed into a pearl.

By the greenhouse entry, Cat was grooming herself in her basket; sleek, snow white, shorthaired, with pale blue eyes. Frankie picked her up and gave her a kiss and a snuggle. "Poor baby, being hunted by that awful spider thing."

She put Cat back in her basket, entered the greenhouse, and quickly shut the door as the heat, humidity, and scent enveloped her. She closed her eyes and inhaled. As a child she'd spent a couple of months a year on her grandparents' estate in Hawaii, and scent and heat always made lush, exotic images dance in her head. Even then, she'd been fascinated by flowers.

After a few moments, Frankie opened her eyes. Time for business. She suspected that somewhere in this protected environment lurked the secret of what Charles Darwin had called the Abominable Mystery—the origin of flowers. I love this place, she thought as she inspected the humidifier nozzles and squinted into the lights. "Hello, babies," she said to the strange array of plants. "Which one of you is it? Who can unlock the mystery?"

It was a struggle to keep them alive in the same space. Ginkgo, a primitive, weird, spindly tree, here about four feet high, with a bilobed, fan-shaped leaf unlike any other. Familiar to the dinosaurs, it used to cover the planet but was destroyed in the last Ice Age, apart from remote pockets in Northern China. Now extinct in the wild, it survived only because Buddhist monks had recognized the medicinal value of its cherry-sized nuts and the tea that could be brewed from its leaves, a tea that miraculously restored memory, and so had planted it in their monastery gardens and worshipped it. Frankie drank gingko tea every day.

Magnolia. The scent was intoxicating. Another very primitive flowering plant. The only one on earth whose floral parts were arranged spirally instead of in whorls. Why?

An aquarium filled with African water lilies. Her recent experiments had shown they were far more primitive than anyone realized, throwbacks that predated even the narrow-leaved monocot grasses.

The newest addition, perhaps—just perhaps—the oldest living fossil among the flowering plants, just recently discovered. A tiny flower called *Amborella trichopoda* that grew only on the remote Pacific island of New Caledonia, near Australia.

And the ugliest plant in the world, now surviving only in the deserts of southwestern Namibia. Belonging to an ancient group of gymnosperms, the hideous *Welwitschia mirabilis* could live for a thousand years or more. Lying partially buried in the ground, the barrel-sized plant produced only two straplike leaves, which grew continuously until they reached lengths of thirty feet or more. It also grew a tap root almost thirty feet long. There was a huge box filled with sand beside its case to accommodate both leaves and root, so the thing could grow in comfort. It looked as if it belonged on Mars, not Earth.

Which one was it? thought Richards. Or none of them? Which held the key to the Abominable Mystery? The question had driven Darwin half-crazy. According to his theory of evolution, there was no reason at all for flowers. A hundred and thirty million years ago they had appeared in the blink of an eye, in evolutionary terms, competing with seed plants and grasses. Petals, stamens, anthers, pollen, all together. Why? And flowers had to coincide with pollinating insects. How had *that* happened?

Darwin's theory had holes, and Frankie was determined to plug them all, once she had solved the current puzzle. Which of these primitive plants was genetically closest to the first flowering plants? There was only one way to find out, and that was to do a series of polymerase chain reactions and analyze their DNA.

Frankie left the greenhouse and walked to a lab bench. She paused in front of the Tyler Research T-96 Thermal Reactor. A foot and a half high, a foot wide, with a laptop computer on top, it had a CD-style rack hidden in the middle. It didn't look like much until you saw the results. Other thermal reactors on the market used boiling water baths and robotic arms, with the attendant difficulties of scalding, mechanical breakdown, and inability to regulate temperature precisely. She had tested them all, and this was her favorite. The Tyler machine was completely self-enclosed, used hot air, and could ramp from temperature to temperature, from 5 to over 100 degrees Celsius and back down again, in a few seconds.

Frankie pulled out the rack, preloaded with eighty-eight tiny Eppendorf tubes. Each tube contained several substances. First, a miniscule fragment of DNA (she had clipped tiny pieces of leaf with a pair of scissors, although dried, long-dead specimens worked just as well—she called it the Jurassic Park effect). Second, ultrapurified water. Third, DNA primers, called primase, to start the whole process. Then a big dose of the four DNA nucleotide bases (adenine, cytosine, guanine, and thymine) known as A, C, G, and T. A and T always joined with each other, as did C and G, to form the DNA double helix, the root of all life, its twisted strands held together by hydrogen bonds.

Finally, the polymerase itself, called Taq. Taq was to biology what the atomic bomb was to physics—it revolutionized everything. It allowed researchers to Xerox millions of copies of DNA in a matter of hours from the tiniest samples. Taq was derived from *Thermus aquaticus*, a bacterium accidentally discovered in the hot springs of Yellowstone National Park. To analyze DNA sequences, you had to first "denature" the DNA—unzip it—making the double helix fall apart by dissolving the hydrogen bonds. The only way to do it was through heat. The problem was, most enzymes capable of scissoring unzipped DNA into usable lengths were heat sensitive. Not *Thermus aquaticus*. Its DNA copying mechanism remained stable at high temperatures.

All three parts of PCR took place in the same tiny Eppendorf vials. Frankie typed commmands into the computer that rested on top of the reactor, and stared at the readout display that would precisely determine the timing, sequence, and results. First, denature the DNA by heating it to 90–95 degrees Celsius (165 degrees Fahrenheit) for thirty seconds. But the primase couldn't bind to the DNA at such high temperatures, so the vials had to be cooled within seconds to 55 degrees Celsius (100 degrees Fahrenheit). At this temperature, the primase would bind, or anneal, to the ends of the DNA strands. This took twenty seconds. The timing was crucial because otherwise the two strands of the double helix would rezip.

The final step of PCR was to make complete copies of the denatured DNA template—biological Xeroxing. Since Taq worked best at about 75 degrees Celsius (the temperature of the hot springs in which it was discovered), the reactor would ramp the heat accordingly, again within seconds. Taq would then begin adding loose nucleotides to the primase, which would then bind at the appropriate A, C, T, and G points of the unzipped strands. The end result would be a precise copy of the target DNA.

The three steps of PCR took less than two minutes. But Taq was durable enough that the sequence could be repeated thirty times or more. Each time, whatever DNA was in the vials would be duplicated exponentially. At the end of a few hours you had millions upon millions of copies, which you could then analyze at your leisure.

Today Richards intended to examine the genetic differences between magnolia and *Welwitschia mirabilis*. She pushed the tray back into the reactor, noted the Tray Interlock light, and typed commands. Thirty cycles. The screen glowed. The Reactor Power and Primary Turbine lights blinked as the chain reaction began.

Now, the agarose gel and the horizontal electrophoresis system.

Agarose came from a family of polysaccharides called agars, obtained from seaweed. They had amazing antidessication properties—one gram (one twenty-eighth of an ounce) of agarose could bind up to twelve liters of water. The food industry used thin agarose as an ingredient stablizer to make jelly, ice cream, whipped desserts, and other products. Frankie used a thicker agarose for her biochemical experiments.

Once the PCR cycles were completed, the contents of the Eppendorf vials were transferred to the gel and then into the horizontal Tyler Electrophoresis System, just sixteen inches long, nine inches wide, and less than four inches high. Trays of agarose were slipped into the unit, which had positive and negative electrodes at either end. Depending on the charge of the DNA sequences, they migrated through the gel to one electrode or the other with the gel acting as a sieve, the smaller fragments moving faster than the larger ones. A stain was then used to make the DNA stand out for easy visualization. Of the three stains available—all blue—she

didn't much care for Carolina Blue or methylene blue. She preferred the faster and more stable ethidium bromide, even though
you needed an ultraviolet transilluminator to make it fluoresce.

Richards looked at the reactor's blinking lights as it flashed
through the series of chain reactions. She'd had some fun with PCR
and INERT's staff. Bringing them into her lab, she had them use
small plastic spatulas to scrape cells from the inside of their cheeks
(such cells contained the gene sequence of their entire bodies).
Then she'd done PCR to determine their genetic heritage. Because
the human genome was so large, about 3 billion DNA base pairs,
and she wasn't targeting anything specific, it was like sticking your
hand into a bowl containing lottery tickets—you never knew if
you'd pull out something valuable. But she'd had some interesting
results. Dikka Spargo, despite her protestations that her family was
pure Irish, had some odd genetic sequences which indicated une-
quivocally that she had ancestors who were Basque, from northern
Spain, the aboriginal people of Europe, long predating the Indo-
European invasion of 40,000 years ago. Zammit's chief computer
wizard, Kitson Kang, was Japanese, but some sequences showed
he had ancestors who were bear-worshipping Ainu, the ancient
Caucasian population of Japan, now surviving only on a couple of
remote islands. Zammit had declined to participate ("I know who
I am"), and so had Cairo Jackson ("My ancestors were slaves, for
God's sake. Where they came from, I don't know and I don't
care"). It was also intriguing that after these initial experiments,
which she had thought were fun, no one was interested in going
any further.

She checked the reactor, then punched a button on the CD
player beside it. The cool rhythmic tones of the Blue Note Jazz
Quintet provided the sort of kinetic mind space that allowed her
thoughts to free-associate. It worked best this way. No interrup-
tions. Her time, her space. That was the wonderful thing about
INERT's environment—they all respected each other's space.

Except Mike Zammit. He'd barge unannounced into her lab or
studio whenever he felt like it, without phoning first or knocking.
He was always intense and preoccupied, always full of questions.
Often the questions were about a crisis somewhere in the world,

but sometimes they were trivial—the biochemical composition of chocolate, why the print on newspapers rubbed off on your fingers but the print from magazines didn't.

Often he'd slam through the door to announce a theory or conclusion, seeking her endorsement. Any flaws she pointed out were usually dismissed on the spot, but it always came to her attention that they were surreptitiously looked into anyway. God, he could be irritating.

Zammit often reminded her of an overgrown boy sitting in a patch of dirt with a forgotten half-eaten candy bar beside him, fiddling intently with some kind of mechanical device. She'd seen him like that many times, in his lab and machine shop or conferring with the technicians. No wonder he and Dikka Spargo got along so well—the same self-absorption, endless curiosity, physical and intellectual stamina, and twisted sense of humor. At least he didn't insert metal into his body.

And then there were the other times.

The times when his cold, handsome face would get that look, and he would deduce something no one else could deduce. He and Cairo Jackson pounding each other in the boxing ring in the gym, two big guys trying to destroy each other but not really, because they were friends. His muscled frame, gleaming with sweat, chest heaving. Lying on a couch, sea-blue eyes fixed on the ceiling as he figured something out, something he—maddeningly—wouldn't talk about. His tenderness when his wife was dying. The time when they were about to be shot to death outside an illegal insecticide factory in a Colombian jungle, and Zammit had faced down eight heavily armed thugs through sheer cool and bravado, using a Spanish dialect she didn't even know he knew. It was his apparent lack of fear that was scary, and the thugs felt it. She suspected that in a very real way he truly did not care if he lived or died, and that was the scariest thing of all.

The polymerase chain reaction was finished. What would it show?

As Frankie removed the tray of Eppendorf tubes, she felt something rubbing against her leg. Cat. Demanding. She wanted attention and wanted it now. Tray in her left hand, she picked up Cat in her right hand, gave her a kiss, put her on the counter, and moved toward the electrophoresis equipment to analyze the PCR results.

Suddenly she heard an unearthly scream and started violently.

The tray hit the floor, little Eppendorfs scattering everywhere. She saw Cat launch herself from the counter, flying five feet through the air onto an adjacent bench, back arched, teeth bared, like some Halloween cartoon. She turned to look.

Catula.

The insectoid was at the counter's edge, red eyes glowing, as if contemplating making the jump itself. "Go away, you evil thing! And leave my cat alone!" Catula scuttled away, dropped to the floor, and disappeared somewhere.

How had it gotten into the lab, much less onto the counter? She searched for Catula and Cat and couldn't find them. Poor Cat—probably cowering someplace. A thought struck her. Natural creation versus artificial creation. Was God's work being overtaken by man's?

She knelt and began collecting the scattered tubes. A lot were broken, and razor-sharp shards were everywhere. She paused, knowing she'd end up cutting herself. Why does Zammit allow Dikka to make so many of those damn things and let them roam around at will? Two days' work ruined, thanks to that bloody robot.

 Dikka Spargo was in the boardroom, along with Kitson Kang. At twenty-five, clad in a tight black muscle shirt and camouflage cargo pants, the wiry Japanese-born computer expert was a younger version of martial arts movie star Jackie Chan. He grinned as he tugged at the gold earring that made him look like a samurai turned pirate. "Boss, I understand today you made your TV fight debut. Hey, Cairo—how are things in the Valley of the Kings?"

Cairo grinned good-naturedly. "I've said it before, I'll say it again. One more Egyptian joke, and you're a dead man."

Kang turned to Spargo. "Is that a new one? It's hard to tell, there's so many of them. How do you breathe with all those rings through your nose?"

She grinned and fingered the new silver hoop inserted through her left eyebrow. "Like it?"

"I guess. But Dikka, if you put any more metal through your face you won't be able to lift your head off the pillow."

Zammit smiled as he sat at the head of the table and sipped his coffee. A glowing panel of neon-bright colors occupied the entire north wall, showing the location of some two dozen actual or potential environmental hot spots around the world. He studied the wall closely. The new Turkish crisis was on the screen as Code Red.

Zammit briefed them on the Dzerzhinsk situation, then Spargo expanded on the NK19 dye problem.

"Anything else?" asked Zammit.

"Yeah," said Cairo. "Recall that guy who invented the super-sorbent for mopping up chemical spills in any kind of weather? He asked for our assessment of the stuff."

Zammit nodded, remembering the product. "You spray the sorbent foam onto the spill, on land or water, and whether it's heavy crude oil at forty below or pulp mill effluent in the tropics, it soaks up every last bit. Sounded good to me."

Cairo Jackson's chair creaked as he leaned back. "Every silver lining has a cloud, as my sainted grandmother used to say. Stuff works like a dream. Only one problem. Let's say you use several tons of this sorbent to mop up a big nasty spill. The ground or the water is pretty clean, but now you have tons of contaminated sorbent. You can't landfill it because it's hazardous. So you have to burn it. Dikka, I believe you are our current expert on this particular substance."

She grinned, pulled another barrette from her lab coat, and clipped it in her hair. "Whereupon it emits such enormous quantities of hydrogen cyanide gas that no smokestack scrubbers currently on the market can get rid of it."

Zammit shrugged. "Back to the drawing board."

They discussed how to avoid paying so much for the huge amounts of chemical reagents, glass pipettes, Kleenex-style Kimwipes, and other material they used when doing lab analyses.

"I've checked out some suppliers and prices," said Kang. He reached under the boardroom table for his briefcase, then let out a yell. There was a fingernail-tapping-on-a-table sound, fading as something ran away.

"Sorry." Kang took a deep breath, blew his lips out, and stared across the table. "Jesus, Dikka, do those things have to be so ugly? Can't you make them so they have wheels and look cute, like R2D2? I've got a thing about spiders, girl."

Dikka Spargo tried to look sorry and failed. "No can do, Kit. Things with wheels are unstable. If wheels were sound evolutionary strategy, we'd all be rolling along like shopping carts. Too easy to knock over. I employ Mark Tilden's BEAM principles—biology, electronics, aesthetics, and mechanics. I make them like spiders because the thorax is flat and oval, which makes for easy engineering. With the body mounted on the eight articulated legs, the guts of the thing are like a weighted trampoline on springs. Very low center of gravity. Can't be easily knocked over, and if it is, it can right itself. A thing with wheels can't do that. The little retractable hooks on the ends of the tentacles mean it can climb, it can—"

Zammit knew what Spargo was like when she got going. "Dikka, I feel pretty much like Kit does. I'm glad we now lock them up at night in the storeroom, but I think something more is needed." He had insisted on this after waking one night to find a particularly beady-eyed specimen sitting on his chest. Dikka had sulked for a week because the robot had smashed to pieces when he hurled it against the wall. They decided that putting the robots in the storerooms was preferable to switching them all off every night and then having to turn them on again. It was Spargo's responsibility to round the creatures up every evening, which would ordinarily have taken hours since they were often in hiding, obeying the second programming command. To resolve the problem, she installed a switch in each creature that responded to a particular sequence of tones on her cell phone. It still struck Zammit as odd to see the long-haired Spargo dancing down the hall, waving her phone like a high-tech Pied Piper of Hamelin, leading a trail of scuttling insectoids.

Dikka's face fell in disappointment. To cushion the remark, Zammit said, "Can't you have them make a noise or something? Anything so we don't get taken by surprise all the time?"

The teenage inventor's face was instantly thoughtful. She fingered her new eyebrow hoop. "I could modify the sensors and the video card and install little speakers." She brightened. "When they get within five feet of someone, I could have them make a noise like the roadrunner in the Bugs Bunny cartoons. You know, 'meep meep.'"

Zammit struggled to keep a straight face. "Whatever. I'm sure Cat would appreciate it as well."

Spargo was suddenly distraught. "But being programmed to make a noise like that is not evolutionarily sound, because it draws attention to you. It—"

"Dikka, think about it. Flashing lights, a siren, 'meep meep,' right now I don't care. Just come up with something." Zammit yawned uncontrollably. "I'm beat. I'm going upstairs for some shut-eye. Don't wake me unless we hear more about Turkey."

As he stood, Frankie Richards stuck her head in the door. "Earl Stone is on the videophone. I don't think he wants to give you an Oscar for best actor."

"Not now," said Zammit.

"There's something else. He didn't say, but it must be Turkey."

He rubbed his eyes. "OK. All you guys, stay here. Frankie?"

Richards nodded. "I'll be in right away. Had a little accident, have to clean it up." As she closed the door she punched the button to activate the videoscreen and the room's cameras.

Zammit jabbed at the speaker console as Stone's furious face appeared on the flat five-foot by-seven-foot display panel at the far end of the room. "Hello, Earl."

Stone noticed the other men in the room. His news anchor baritone was accusatory. "Make yourself at home, Mike. Hit somebody."

"Come on, Earl—"

"All this effort to get you on that show. The theme is animals, protecting the environment—a natural. Fits perfectly with the work you're doing identifying whatever's killing those creatures in the Gulf—"

"Cyanide," said Zammit, stifling a yawn as he realized he was going to have to let Earl vent.

"But do *you* play to the crowd, being warm and huggy to get some first-class exposure? No. You spend your time figuring out how to use coffee as a weapon."

"Sorry, Earl. Won't happen again. Not this week anyway. Incidentally, where are you?"

Stone took a deep breath and finally regained his composure. "Washington, D.C."

"What's up?"

"Thamar Amurkhan contacted the White House a few hours ago and asked to use your services immediately. She thinks you can walk on water after what you did for her last time. Apparently they've got a really ugly situation."

"We've heard," said Zammit. "But we don't know any details."

Stone ran his hand over his hair. "Randy Berkowitz is on the president's staff. I told him a few days ago you were in that ghastly place in Russia whose name I can never remember. He called me a few minutes ago and wants to talk to you urgently."

"What kind of situation?"

"According to Randy, they're still trying to figure it out. Thousands of people are dying of something. But he also used the word Armageddon."

13

"I don't know if I'd call it Armageddon," said Colonel Walter Graves. "Description's a bit biblical for my taste. But based on what we've learned so far, it could lead to an all-out war in the Middle East and the deaths of millions of people."

Speaking from Washington, the colonel's rugged face filled the videoscreen as he briefed them on the situation in Turkey. He peered over the top of his half-moon glasses, eyes red with fatigue beneath bushy gray eyebrows. Sixty years old, a former Marine, he was now with the CIA and an adviser to the president. They had worked together on a dozen crises over the years, and his attention to detail and meticulous planning were legendary. Constant worry had carved deep lines in his face, and he looked very worried now.

"The Turkish government has ordered nonstop emergency airlifts of fresh water," continued the colonel. "Trucking it in too. They've evacuated some of the local population, which is a problem because of the Kurdish insurrection in the area. They've also shut off the dam and cut all nonmilitary access to the region. Place is closed up tighter than a tick."

Zammit interrupted. "How many casualties so far?"

"About 100,000 people have drunk enough water to become violently ill. I understand about 20,000 have died in the last few days."

Zammit scribbled notes. Twenty percent kill rate, so soon.

"Thousands of animal deaths have also been reported. It's a good thing this part of the country is a virtual zone of occupation, so military resources are on the spot and the media is kept away. And that it's sparsely populated. Unfortunately, that particular demographic changes once you move downstream."

The picture on the videoscreen suddenly kaleidoscoped. Now Colonel Graves was a tiny figure walking through a virtual reality landscape. "I'm afraid our enhancements aren't based on optimal data. All we've got so far is what the Turks gave us, and they're confused as hell."

He stopped by the banks of a river. "As you can see from our simulation of the death plume, the number of fatalities decreases proportionately the farther away you get. This suggests that what- ever is in the water is diluted as it moves downstream. The prob- lem is that we don't know what it is or where it came from, much less how to get rid of it. And based on what we've heard, the concentration is likely to get higher and higher. That's where we're counting on you, Doc."

"OK. But I'll need a lot more background on this dam and res- ervoir. And eventually I'll have to talk to the Turks directly."

Graves nodded. "I realize that. I didn't think the Turks would like hearing some of what I have to say, which is why I'm giving you this preliminary briefing. The geopolitical implications of this are crucial. Mishandled at any level, we could have a catastrophe on our hands."

Graves continued walking across the virtual landscape. "To summarize: The Middle East has always been short of water, even in antiquity. The region is currently suffering the worst drought ever recorded. The only country with a decent supply of fresh water is Turkey."

Suddenly the colonel was standing in the midst of a desolate landscape of low rolling brown hills. "The two countries with the worst water problems lie to Turkey's southeast: Syria and Iraq, side by side. Until the end of the First World War and the defeat of the Turks and their German allies, both countries were part of the Ottoman Empire. They still hate and fear their former over- lords."

Graves pointed to a thin blue-green ribbon snaking its way through the chocolate-colored desolation. "Syria's main water source is the Euphrates River. After flowing all the way through Syria, on a diagonal of about thirty degrees, the Euphrates carries on into Iraq, where it eventually joins up with the Tigris River and they flow to the sea. The Tigris is Iraq's only other source of water, but with the drought, the flow is nonexistent. Which means the Euphrates is vital."

Another dizzying kaleidoscope of colors, and the colonel was standing in front of a glowing multicolored political map of the area. The number of countries, both large and small, made it look like a patchwork quilt sewn by a blind man. "The headwaters of both rivers rise in the barren highlands of southeastern Turkey and flow through that area before entering Syria and Iraq. Three de- cades ago the Turks looked at all that water dribbling away in the desert and figured they could make better use of it. They started building one of the world's largest irrigation and hydroelectric complexes. It's called the Southeastern Anatolia Development Project—the Turkish abbreviation is GAP."

Zammit interjected. "I'm no expert on the subject, but these huge dams are almost by definition environmental disasters. They alter the ecology of entire regions."

Graves nodded. "So I understand. That may be the cause of the present problem. GAP has been under construction for over two decades now—twenty-two dams and nineteen power stations. The project services an area larger than Austria."

"Holy cow," said Dikka Spargo.

"The Turks use the water for two purposes. The first is generation of hydroelectric power. They sell it to their electricity-starved neighbors, including Russia and those crummy little gangster countries like Chechnya and Tuvanistan. The second purpose is irrigation."

Suddenly the colonel was standing in front of a gigantic concrete wall. "The centerpiece of the whole project is this monster, the Ataturk Dam. It's the last one and the closest to the Syrian border. It's four times larger than the Aswan Dam. The fill material used in this thing is sufficient to build a three-by-three-foot wall circling the equator twice, with three thousand miles to spare. Has a reservoir ten times larger than the Sea of Galilee."

"Wow," breathed Kitson Kang.

Now the colonel was dwarfed by the vast pipe in which he stood. "The water irrigates the Plain of Harran. The Turks figure they can get three crops annually off that land and improve agricultural productivity twentyfold. And in the process turn an impoverished desert back into the Garden of Eden and make the Kurds happy. The Turkish government has stated that GAP will make Turkey the breadbasket of the whole Middle East. Thanks to the Ataturk, that arid wasteland recently had endless fields of high protein crops and cotton. That is, until this drought. With the water shut off, under the blazing sun, all those crops are already dead."

Zammit stood and paced. "What's the bottom line?"

"The Ataturk Dam gives Turkey absolute control of water resources in the region. They can literally turn off the lifeblood waters of both the Tigris and the Euphrates whenever they want. It makes them the most powerful nation in the whole Middle East, nukes or not. Turkey has the biggest land area and the second biggest population of any NATO country east of the Atlantic. Already their neighbors complain about a new Ottoman Empire. As a result of all this, the Syrians and Iraqis are scared shitless."

Graves now stood in the midst of a rumbling herd of Iraqi tanks. "Both states appealed to international tribunals, trying to either stop the project or get the Turks to bring them in as partners. But the Turks are proud and stubborn. They've said all along that no one is going to tell them what to do with a resource that originates within their own borders. That pretty much summarizes international legal opinion too."

The tanks clanked on in a computerized never-never land. "In 1975 and 1986, the Iraqis rolled their tanks right up to the border. They had to back down because Turkey has a standing army of half a million men, the biggest of any NATO country, including us, and they are fearsome soldiers. An attack would be suicidal. Unless, of course, they have nukes. We don't believe they do."

Once again, Colonel Graves's craggy face filled the screen. "That's it. Syria and Iraq are drying up and blowing away. They tell the Turks to release more water, and the Turks won't do it because there's something in the dam's reservoir that's killing their own citizens downstream, and they don't know what it is. Earlier I mentioned demographics. The Turkish part of the Euphrates basin is thinly populated. But just one hundred miles downstream from the Ataturk is the first big city, Aleppo, in Syria. Population over two million. Their sole source of water is the Euphrates."

Zammit leaned forward. "Something lethal is in the reservoir's water. The Turks can't release more water because they'll kill their own citizens and eventually millions of Syrians and Iraqis downstream. But if they *don't* release more water, millions will die anyway, of thirst and famine. It's a no-win situation. But in either scenario, the two nations can't stand idly by."

"Exactly," said Graves. "Remember how relieved we were when Saddam Hussein was assassinated? It never occurred to us that his son Anwar would be even worse than the old man. In a fit of paranoia, Anwar may conclude that the Turks have hatched some sort of plot. And do something stupid."

The colonel took off his glasses and rubbed his eyes. "I can't emphasize how important this is. Turkey stands now where West Germany did during the Cold War. Right on the front line, face to face with our biggest geopolitical problem—that rancid mix of oil, fanatical Islamism, and decrepit dictatorships called the Middle East and Central Asia. We need Turkey as a powerful buffer between us and the Syrians, Iraqis, and Iranians. It's not only a deterrent to aggressive nations in the area, it's the world's only successful Muslim democracy. It's a shining example to every other Islamic country on the planet that you can be prosperous and respected without fundamentalism. If it weren't for Turkey we'd be seeing a lot more crazy mullahs returning their countries to the Middle Ages. And even Turkey has fundamentalist factions." He sighed heavily. "I know the president is worried. Turkey is a faithful ally and a member of NATO. If anything happens to Turkey, we get dragged in too."

Frankie Richards interrupted. "Colonel, could I have another look at the geographic map of the area side by side with the political one?"

"Of course."

"There's another problem. See where the Tigris and Euphrates join? Right at the bottom of Iraq? And then the two flow to the sea?"

Cairo Jackson nodded. "Into the Shatt al Arab delta. So?"

Zammit said, "And from the Shatt al Arab into the Persian Gulf."

"From whence," said Richards, "using the world's largest desalinization plants, all of the bone-dry Arab oil states get their sole supply of water."

Graves had gone pale.

"Oh, swell," said Cairo Jackson. "Not a regional crisis, a global one. My fave."

"Colonel," said Zammit, "I need the names and numbers of the appropriate Turkish officials. I want White House authorization to contact federal departments and agencies if I need more people. And I want the last three weeks' worth of scans from the Terra earth-observing satellite system."

"Of course," said Colonel Graves.

Mike Zammit turned to his staff. "Showtime."

On the bright auditorium stage, a choir of brown-robed monks chanted the hypnotic liturgical music of Old Russia. The rows of seats, which stretched into the darkness, were filled with hundreds of young men in uniform. On the wall of the auditorium, a huge square of red cloth.

General Vladimir Bled strode to the microphone, boots creaking, red-tabbed green uniform immaculately pressed. A thin sheen of sweat gleamed from his bullet-shaped skull, evoked by the hot lights and a thudding hangover.

At the podium and microphone, he pulled himself to his full height, gazing imperiously at the rapturous faces in the audience. As the music swelled, he pointed at the drape of red cloth. The chanting suddenly stopped.

With a hiss the drape drew aside, revealing a huge icon. It was an ancient portrait in the traditional Russian and Byzantine perspectiveless style. A melancholy dark-haired man of about forty-five, in armor, loomed out of the picture. There was a cross behind him but not the traditional gold ring of a halo to indicate a saint. The striking impression was of a strong man shouldering an unendurable burden.

"Constantine XI!" boomed Bled. "The last of the Roman Emperors. The Ottoman Turks had reduced the Byzantine Empire to a single city. Constantinople. The birthplace of our religion. The great walls endured twenty-one sieges in 1100 years. They would not endure the last."

Bled gripped the podium as if to tear it in half. "Tuesday, May 29, 1453. The day the city fell to the infidel. The emperor had fourteen miles of walls to defend and only 7,000 men. Led by Sultan Mehmet II, the Turks had a 100,000 soldiers. The emperor fought courageously, but a swarm of Turks overwhelmed him and he disappeared."

His voice dropped to a sepulchral whisper. "But his body was never found." A ringing, expectant silence. "There was a Russian monk in the city that day. Nestor, a visiting novice, from the remote monastery of St. Sava, near Keremovo, on the far side of the Ural Mountains. Knowing the battle was lost, the emperor entrusted his greatest treasures to Nestor, to spirit them to Russia where the Turks could not pursue. The holy icon of the Virgin Eleousa, painted by Saint Jerome himself; the gold crown of Constantine IX Monomachos, encrusted with emeralds and rubies; the diamond-rimmed chalice of the Emperor Romanos, carved from a single sapphire; and the emperor's gold signet ring.

"Nestor escaped. So did the emperor. Near death, he was taken first to the Despotate of Morea. When the sultan conquered Morea, he was taken in secret to the St. Sava monastery, where Nestor waited with the treasures. He took years to recover and lost the ability to speak. In old age he married and fathered a child, so the dynastic line was continued. To ensure their safety, all was concealed and the monks took a vow of silence, which they have kept to this day. Nestor lived to be almost a hundred and wrote an account of the city's fall, *The Secret Chronicle*."

Bled held up a leather-bound, gem-encrusted book. "In it, Nestor prophesies that one day Constantinople will be retaken. The Holy Chosen One, a descendant of the last emperor, will reign as tsar and sit again upon his golden throne in the rose-red church called Hagia Sophia."

Bled touched the book to his lips. "In the 17th century, a copy was discovered, but its contents were dismissed as myth and legend."

He wiped his brow and took a sip of water. "So fell the last tiny fragment of the Roman Empire, just thirty-nine years before Columbus discovered America. Without Constantinople to block them, the Ottoman Turks poured into Europe, brimming to the gates of Vienna, subjugating Greece, the Balkans, and Hungary and raiding Italy and France. All Christendom was aghast. But none was more horrified than Ivan III, Grand Duke of Moscow. He brooded on the fate of the lost city. He married Sophia, a niece of the last emperor. She brought with her to Moscow the ancient imperial rituals of Constantinople. Ivan took the title tsar—Caesar—and added the two-headed eagle of Byzantium to his coat of arms. Enslaved eastern Christians lifted their eyes in hope during the long centuries of bondage, knowing that in Russia the true faith still lived. The memory of Constantinople did not fade. Down all the dark centuries, they told their wide-eyed children, late at night by the fireside, how the city was defended, of the heroic emperor, abandoned by his allies, who refused to abandon his people. How he fought courageously to the end until his enemies overwhelmed him—and he disappeared, to bide his time in the darkness, in a secret place, until the dawn should come and the empire, like a phoenix, be reborn."

Bled pointed at the icon, his voice hoarse with emotion. "The dawn has come."

There was a sigh from the audience, as from some huge, suddenly aroused beast. "Four times in the past four hundred years we were within a few hours' march of the city. Each time our enemies prevented us from seizing the prize."

Another sigh, louder than before. Bled leaned forward. Time to really let them have it. "Holy Mother Russia is being raped." Enraged screams from the audience. Bled raised his hand to stop the outburst. "Raped by foreigners. Americans and their Jew overlords. German businessmen, Nazis without uniforms. We beat the Nazis. Now veterans stand on streetcorners and sell their medals for kopecks, as Germans speed past in their limousines. We are mocked by gangsters from Chechnya and Georgia, little countries we once ruled with a fist of iron. They loot our gold and uranium, our forests and oil. They buy our women and use them as prostitutes. And all the while they laugh at us."

There were hoarse shouts from the audience, the sound of stamping feet, the sweaty smell of rage. Bled blinked furiously and held up both arms. "They laugh and mock where once they feared. They will fear again. Marx and Lenin said history is driven by class struggle. They were wrong. History is a titanic spiritual battle between Russian, Western, and Muslim civilizations. Always, satanic forces have conspired against us. We have become spiritually empty. We are materialistic, rootless, weak. And so the parasites gather to feed on the carcass."

He pointed again at the icon. "We will fulfill Nestor's prophesy. We will establish dominion over the inferior peoples who wash over a borderless world like garbage in a tainted sea. Faith will be our shield and our sword. We must recover our lost territories and lost greatness."

His voice rose to a hoarse shout. "We will have dominion! We will rule again, from the place where we should rule, the birthplace of our religion. We will have a tsar. The Holy Chosen One will reign as emperor in the once and future imperial city, Constantinople. A strong Russia! A spiritual Russia!"

He paused as cries of *"Derzhava!"* and *"Sobonost"*! rang out. Sweat trickled down his face and neck, staining the tight collar of his uniform.

"But I am just a simple military man." He spread his arms wide. "You all know me. How many of your fellow men at arms do not get paid, so their families are forced to sell everything they own to the Jews and the Nazis?"

There was a roar. "Do I not pay you? Do I not feed you?" Shrieks of affirmation echoed through the cavernous room.

"Our cause has many enemies. But with God's help we will crush them, we will kill them all!"

To deafening cheers he backed away from the microphone. As the choir again began to chant, a figure in a coarse brown monk's robe emerged from the shadows on sandal-clad feet. Bulging eyes stared straight ahead as the hot lights shone on his long greasy hair. The audience roared the name for peasant holy man, "*Starets! Starets!*"

At the podium he lifted his arms and his great staring eyes to heaven. "Russia is God's instrument." Wild cheers.

"Church and state, working together, the union of the tsar with the people, is the best bulwark against Satan. Always we must guard against the enemies of righteousness. It is in the New Testament itself, Saint Paul's letter to the Corinthians. There can be no intercourse between righteousness and lawlessness, as there is nothing in common between light and darkness, the true God and false idols . . ."

As the *starets* spoke in his hypnotic monotone, an odorless, tasteless mist so fine as to be invisible wafted down from the pipes and nozzles concealed in the distant gloom of the ceiling. As they inhaled the atomized drug, the audience began to scream. By the time the choir's voice soared majestically and General Bled and Lazar Smegyev left the stage, the soldiers and sailors in the audience would have invaded hell itself.

Bled threw himself onto a laboratory bench and wiped his gleaming head with a handkerchief. Smegyev followed him through the foot-thick stainless steel security door that separated the research laboratories and manufacturing facilities from the auditorium.

"Good speech." The monk rubbed the eye he had pressed against the sensor so that it could read the pattern of his iris and make an indisputable identification.

Bled grunted and gestured irritably. An aide hurried over with a dispatch box. He opened it and withdrew a glass and a bottle of Stolichnaya. "It's thirsty work."

Smegyev's distended eyes bulged with disapproval. Bled shrugged and took out another glass. He filled both and offered one to the monk. Bled raised his glass to make the toast that always accompanies drinking in Russia: "To success." Both men downed the vodka in a single gulp, the only acceptable way of drinking. Bled tilted the bottle to fill his glass again, but the monk laid a hand on his arm.

"Enough. When you drink too much, you talk too much. You must keep a clear head."

"Very well, *starets*." Bled replaced the bottle and glasses in the case.

"Besides," said the monk, "we have work to do." The two men walked into the adjacent cavernous room, with its laboratory benches, computer monitors, and storage facilities. They stopped at a surgical table with a uniformed body strapped to it. The young soldier stared vacantly, his face deathly white beneath his shaved head, saliva trickling from the corner of his mouth.

"As you can see, the dosage is very important," said the technical director, Dr. Bratko Cabrinovic. His nervous fingers plucked at the lapel of his white lab coat. To stop himself, he shifted his pen-based computer tablet from one hand to the other. He cleared his throat and continued in a thin piping voice. "With something this powerful, there is a fine line between suggestibility and senescence."

Bled leaned over and stared into the young man's unseeing eyes. He grunted. "Nobody home." He fixed his gunmetal gaze on Cabrinovic and noticed with satisfaction how the physician flinched. He reminded Bled of an emu, and the general always tried to play the lion, to keep this birdlike man twitching and alert. "Is the damage permanent?"

The doctor tried to meet Bled's gaze and failed. "Yes. We're still adjusting the mix of the two drugs. With the first, they must be suggestible but not to the point of complete docility and still capable of understanding and carrying out orders. With the second, they must be physically unimpaired, able to make quick decisions, and incredibly strong and aggressive."

Cabrinovic bounded over to a bed where another soldier was lying on his back. A metal helmet covered his head and face, and electrodes and wires trailed across the pillow to the glowing monitor next to a stack of graph paper and digital scan images. As the technical director leaned over the bed, he turned his head and stared at the helmet with one eye, like an emu contemplating a defective egg. "The problem is that everyone's physiology is a little different, so we must find the optimal range of effectiveness."

With spindly fingers he fanned the sheaf of scan images. "Positron emission tomography, or PET scan. Investigation of brain physiology and neural activity. Look here." He pointed to a series of scan images. "The blue area, before the drug is administered. It is the hypothalamus, the conductor of the body's hormonal orchestra. Along with the pituitary gland, it coordinates, among other things, body temperature, hunger, and manifestations of rage. Blue indicates areas of low uptake." Another series of images. "After the drug is administered." Now the hypothalamus was bright red. "Red indicates areas of increased uptake. It's now lit up like a Christmas tree. Tremendous activity."

Bled grunted again. "Is it reliable? How, precisely, does it work?"

Cabrinovic straightened and gazed into the middle distance, as if taking an exam. "The drug suppresses the production in the brain of the enzyme *monoamine oxidase*, or MAO, which is one of the key inhibitors of aggressive behavior in humans. Based on the information provided by our supplier, natural MAO production can be impaired in early childhood by physical, sexual, or even extreme verbal abuse. This is why so many serial killers and other psychopaths, all with very low levels of MAO, have been found to be victims of such abuse."

"But will it work?" insisted Bled.

"The technology is still too new for me, or anyone else, to have built up a reliable database. Our supplier doesn't have much data either. But mix this with methamphetamine, beta-endorphin, the other hormones, and drugs, and there's no question it will work. Any soldier who takes the mixture will be incredibly aggressive, absolutely fearless, and capable of fighting for days on end without food or rest."

"How long before you refine the final mix?"

"A few days."

Smegyev fingered his greasy beard. "Excellent. Keep going. If you need more subjects, just ask." He smiled at Bled. "The general has a plentiful supply."

As they walked away the monk asked, "Has anyone resisted?"
"They do what they're told," growled Bled.

As with many cults, they had discovered that bad food, lack of sleep, and unremitting bullying were perfect conditions for brainwashing. Using a variant of the carrot and the stick, Bled maintained iron discipline but made sure brutal hazing rituals didn't get out of hand, while ensuring that his men got paid. As a result, the general was both feared and revered by his men and obeyed unquestioningly, even when it came to medical experimentation. The situation was also helped by the drugs supplied by their partner, which ensured that Bled's men were extremely suggestible.

As they walked through the cavernous room, warehouse shelving units rose forty feet high, towering over the laboratory benches, beds, isolation chambers, and other equipment far below. The shelves were stacked with crates and drums made of wood, white plastic, or black metal. Every one had on its side a sign or symbol indicating its contents. Some held weapons, from antitank guns and machine pistols to surface-to-air missiles. Others had the international symbol for radiation or the black and yellow emblem of a circle intersected by three horned crescents that indicated a biohazard.

"How is our arsenal coming along?" asked the monk.

"We'll have the best-equipped fighting force in the world," said Bled. "And the most motivated. No one will dare attack us. How is the Holy Chosen One?"

"He is here. No one suspects a thing."

"It is stupid to risk the future tsar like this. He should be in seclusion, praying and preparing."

"He insisted. A God emperor must be a warrior emperor, and he must prove himself. And how are our silent partners?"

Bled smiled grimly. "Which one? The green one or the brown ones?"

"All three."

"The green one is succeeding even beyond our expectations. Our first brown partner doesn't care much for his present residence or his hosts. But I understand he is amusing himself in his usual way. I know he is impatient. As for Anwar, he is impatient as well."

"Have you acquired the smallpox yet?"

"I don't understand why you want it. Our scientists have supplied us with sarin, ricin, anthrax, tularemia, botulinum, bubonic and pneumonic plague, plus we have enough polio virus to wipe out a galaxy—"

"I want smallpox," insisted Smegyev. "It is the most destructive disease in history. There is no cure, ninety percent of the world's people have no immunity, and no one in the industrialized nations has been vaccinated against it in decades."

Bled knew that since the eradication of the dread disease in the wild in 1977, only two samples of smallpox virus officially existed in the world. One was under impenetrable security at the Centers for Disease Control and Prevention in Atlanta, the other at the Russian virology institute called Vector, outside the city of Novosibirsk in Siberia.

The general shrugged irritably. "All right, I'll arrange to have it stolen. An old *babushka* with a crowbar could get into that institute, but it's still risky. Even those idiots in the Kremlin are going to figure it out sooner or later. And that business with the cobalt-60 was stupid. If I'd known, I would have stopped it."

"Soon it won't matter," said the monk. They approached the research laboratories and isolation chambers near the manufacturing facilities. In a clear plastic tank, a naked young man was soundlessly screaming as he convulsed, his back arching at an impossible angle. Even though the clear walls were so thick as to be virtually soundproof, they could still hear thumping sounds as his thrashing limbs shattered on the thick, unyielding plastic. His eyes stared at them beseechingly as his jaws clamped again and again on his thick protruding tongue. Finally it severed and lay on the floor as he gave a final twitch before he died.

Smegyev fingered his beard. "We are all God's children, and we all serve His purposes." He made the sign of the cross. "A martyr to the faith. May he dwell in Heaven forever, with the Holy Father."

Rain pounded on the roof like jungle drums.

Holding yet another cup of coffee, Mike Zammit stared at his reflection in the board-room window as water cascaded down the glass. It was three in the morning. He'd always hated this long dark night of the soul, when the rich colors of day turned into stark black and white, like one of Goya's prints about the horrors of the Peninsular War. He'd been through this more times than he cared to remember, that time of night when a man sits exhausted and stares at the carpet, and his whole life sits on the carpet and stares balefully back. Through the night's darkness and the fog, against the lights of Seattle's skyline, smeared like a doused watercolor, he could dimly see whitecaps on the storm-tossed surface of Lake Union.

So much water.

Throughout the night they had tried to find out what was happening in the parched deserts of southeastern Turkey, in the reservoir of the Ataturk Dam. They had examined the images from the earth-observing satellite system known as Terra.

The brilliantly colored photos, taken hundreds of miles above the earth, had revealed a startling picture. The filters and lenses used by the special cameras picked up changes in light emissions, and when the photos were artificially enhanced by computers and false color images produced, whatever contamination was in the dam could be made to stand out visibly from the water in which it was found. The latest images showed a huge purple stain hard against the Ataturk Dam.

"That was taken today," said Kitson Kang. He looked wearily at his watch. "Or rather, yesterday." He punched a few keys. "This was a week ago." The violet smear was smaller and fainter. "This is two weeks ago." A barely detectable smudge. "This is three weeks ago." Nothing at all.

"Well, it tells us something's there," said Zammit, forcing himself to concentrate on something other than the buzzing board-room lights and the smell of stale coffee. "A lot of something that got there fast. But it doesn't tell us what it is." He knew he had to force his people to concentrate too. "Let's review the theories so far."

The INERT team was sprawled around the table. No one looked fresh or alert. Frankie Richards was wearing jeans and a heavy black turtle-necked sweater. She was rocking back and forth and had her sleeves pulled down over her hands like a little girl, the way she always did when she was cold. Zammit knew she got cold when she was very tired. He gazed around the table. It wasn't the first time they'd brainstormed most of the night, nor would it be the last. It wasn't the nature of crises to be booked months in advance.

Cairo Jackson rubbed his face with both hands. "OK. Theories so far. Industrial pollution. Chemical spill."

"Logical first choice," Zammit agreed. "Only there's no industry of any kind in the area, and with the drought, and all the crops dead, there's just brown rolling hills with the river running through them, then the reservoir, then the dam."

Spargo spoke. "They're using something at the dam that's leaking. The stain is right up against the dam, so it's logical it comes from there."

"I don't think so. We know they've got eight huge turbines for generation of hydroelectric power, some 90 billion kilowatts since the thing fired up. But as far as we can tell, there's nothing they use to run the turbines, or anything else at the dam itself, that is poisonous."

Richards said, "It could be something that got into the river *before* it flows into the reservoir. The Euphrates is over a thousand miles long. Contamination could get into it anywhere along the way, and it would inevitably end up in the Ataturk reservoir."

Zammit couldn't stop himself from yawning. "But that reservoir covers over six hundred square miles. If the contamination had been introduced that way, then we should see it where the Euphrates initially empties into the reservoir, in the north. But that's not where it is—it's at the far end, hundreds of miles to the south, right against the dam itself. Besides, there are other dams on the river. Stuff would have to get into the Euphrates between the second last dam in the GAP complex." His mind suddenly went blank from fatigue. "What's it called again?"

Kitson Kang's gold earring gleamed under the bright halogen lights as he shone the beam of the laser pencil on the huge geographical computer map of southeastern Turkey glowing on the far wall. The beam stopped and automatically magnified the name on the map so it was readable. "The Karakaya," he said.

"Right. Between the Karakaya and the biggest and last, the Ataturk. Once again, nothing there but shepherds and their flocks."

There was a beep, and INERT's communications director, Earl Stone, appeared on the videoscreen. "Got him."

Colonel Walter Grave's right-hand man in Turkey was Lloyd Lavender. Stone had been trying for hours to reach him. "Finally," said Zammit. "Cross-reference the imaging, and put him on."

Lloyd Lavender's face was jowly, his hair strawberry blond. His blue eyes were as opaque as marbles under sandy lashes. Parchment skin webbed with fine lines now sagged with exhaustion and worry.

"Hello, Dr. Zammit. I've got some information for you."

"Go ahead."

Lavender started to read from a sheaf of papers in his hand, as Zammit scribbled notes. "Twenty thousand downstream civilian casualties confirmed. People die horribly, literally vomiting their guts out. Their skins turn yellow as their bodies swell with fluid like balloons. In the final stages, they either drown in their own vomit, suffocate from the fluid filling their lungs, or suffer cardiac arrest. The whole process takes two to three days."

Zammit frowned. "All the symptoms of poisoning, liver disease, and congestive heart failure combined."

"No theories at all as to the type of toxin in the water," continued Lavender. "And one military casualty as well, at the dam itself."

Zammit's head snapped up. "What?"

"A corporal. Died while taking a sample from the reservoir."

"Died how?"

"Vomited to death."

"Did he drink any water?"

"No."

"Did he *fall* into the water?"

"No. The Turks say he was heading to the water to collect a sample when he suddenly fell, started vomiting, and couldn't stop. Then he died."

Jackson stared at the screen in disbelief. "It's lethal by *inhalation* as well?"

"I wouldn't be surprised," said Lloyd Lavender. "The stuff in the reservoir stinks like you wouldn't believe. Since the corporal's death, no one goes near the water without wearing an oxygen unit."

"Don't assume anything," said Zammit. "Ask the Turks to do an autopsy on this soldier. And what is this 'stuff in the reservoir' you just mentioned?"

"Masses of slimy green organic material, nature and origin unknown. Tons of it. That's why they've had to shut off the turbines. This stuff is thick and gluey, and it's clogging the dam's intakes, penstocks, and the machinery. It smells like rotting meat."

There was dead silence. Zammit had never heard of anything like this before. "Enough. We're guessing. I hate guessing. I want evidence. I gather they have succeeded in obtaining samples?"

Lavender nodded. "They're in Urfa, the regional capital. About a half hour from the Ataturk."

"We need somebody on the ground to analyze those samples. The only member of the team in the general area is Connie." He turned to Frankie Richards. "Contact him, brief him, tell him to drop the other stuff and get to Urfa pronto."

Cairo Jackson objected, "Mike, do you think he has enough experience? I don't know what sort of lab facilities they have over there, and he might have problems."

"It should be easy enough. He just patches through a satellite feed to our computers here." He turned back to the screen. "Thanks, Lloyd. I'll be in touch. Anything else we should know?"

The pale face lifted briefly in a baggy, humorless smile. "You know everything I do. Sayonara." The screen went blank.

"Masses of slimy green material," echoed Zammit. He turned to Frankie. "Some sort of organism. You're the botanist. What could it be?"

"I have no idea," Richards replied. "It would be different if the Euphrates were like the Nile, laden with silt and nutrients. In the reservoir of the Aswan Dam, as the water sits stagnant under the blazing sun, an amazing variety of pests breed out of control. But according to my information, the Euphrates is nutrient-poor. And that still doesn't explain how the contamination got there in the first place or why it's growing so fast."

"Then we'll have to study the samples. Where's Stavros Costopoulos?"

"Somewhere in Thessalonica, last I heard. Maybe Athens by now. He was supposed to deliver a paper at some academic conference."

"I want him to meet me in Malta." Frankie nodded distractedly, her face suddenly blank.

"What's the matter?" asked Zammit, concerned that she was exhausted. It wasn't often she looked stunned.

"Wait a minute." Richards strode from the boardroom and returned moments later with a piece of paper. "When Dikka finished the scan on your private e-mail yesterday, the only thing that stood out was this. It got automatically pulled by the program because it's from that remailer in Sweden—we've had significant stuff from him before. It read like nonsense, and I was going to throw it out. But now I'm not so sure."

Zammit read the brief message aloud. "Greetings, gallant knight, help of the helpless. Your sword is of no use against the primordial soup, and by the rivers of Babylon you will lie down and weep."

"I don't get it," said Kitson Kang.

"Me neither," said Dikka Spargo.

Zammit gazed intently out the window, like a man trying and failing to remember something. Richards watched him for a few moments, as if trying to read his mind. Finally she said, "There are other names for those two rivers."

"I know that," said Kang. "We been encountering them all evening. In Turkish the Euphrates is called the *Firat* and the Tigris is the *Dicle.*"

Zammit spoke. "Before they had those names, before there was a Turkish language or a Turkish people, about 4,000, 5,000 years ago, they were the heartland of Mesopotamia, the Fertile Crescent." Again he looked at the message. "The rivers of Babylon."

Once more he seemed lost in reverie as he stared at the strange message. "What is it, Mike?" asked Cairo Jackson.

"The remailer has stripped off the date the message was sent as well as the address of the sender. Did anyone scan my e-mail between my leaving for Russia and yesterday?"

"No," said Dikka. "We never check your personal mail unless you ask us."

"So yesterday was the first time in a week. Kit, how long does it take a remailer to pass on a message?"

"Depends how busy he is. It's not like he's the post office and has to make daily deliveries. Might be two minutes, might be two days. Maybe more. Why?"

"So this thing could have been sent eight or ten days ago."

Cairo Jackson grasped the situation before the others could speak. He turned to Zammit. "I have three questions. One, how did this person know about the contamination at the Ataturk Dam before the Turks did?"

"And," said Richards, "why does he want you to know that he knew it?"

Jackson nodded in agreement. "Second, how can you threaten somebody with soup?"

Faced with silence, he turned and pointed at the sole decoration on the east wall, a big white Maltese cross embroidered on a red background, lovingly hand-stitched by Zammit's Aunt Julia, far away on the sun-baked island of Gozo. "Finally, how does this person know you're a knight?"

 When Mike Zammit came downstairs after a few hours of restless sleep, it was still raining. Kitson Kang still sat in front of his computer looking haggard and frustrated. Empty cans of Pepsi littered the floor around him.

"Anything?"

Without taking his eyes from the screen, Kang said, "In the merchant marine they have a saying. When you're sailing around but not getting anywhere, you're steaming to Bamboola." He flicked at his gold earring. "I'm steaming to Bamboola."

He turned away from the screen. "I've been running hundreds of scenarios since our meeting broke up. The program keeps spitting out the same one it did before." He handed his boss several sheets of paper. "*Exactly* the same one. So the program is telling us the only possible scenario is the one we all agree is physically impossible."

"Take a break and get some sleep. I'll be in touch when I'm in Malta. Did Frankie find Stavros Costopoulos?"

Kang nodded. "He's going to meet you on the island. Frankie's painting in the studio if you want to talk to her."

"Okay. You and Dikka work in shifts. Grab any other staff you need to help you."

Zammit headed for Frankie's studio. She always said she thought better when she was painting.

A riot of color greeted him as he opened the door. Richards was a brilliant artist but not a neat one, and the walls and floor looked like the aftermath of a multihued paint bomb explosion. He inhaled the thick scent of oils and the sharp sting of turpentine as he walked over to where she was frowning at a canvas, in a paint-smeared smock, her hair tied back in a ponytail. She sighed. "Don't you ever knock?"

"Sorry. I always forget." She wasn't wearing makeup and her face looked pale and drawn. "How did you sleep?" asked Zammit, concerned.

"Badly. I had that nightmare again about Adam, the one where he's lost in the jungle and so weak he can't stand anymore and he falls and the fire ants swarm into his eyes and he calls for me—"

"Please, Frankie," said Zammit. "Don't do this to yourself." It wasn't like her to be so wound up. To get her off the subject, he asked, "What are you working on?"

"A disaster." She began scraping wet pigment off the canvas with her palette knife. "I just can't concentrate. Has Kit found anything more?"

"No. We have the same scenario we did last night—it's impossible for any kind of organic contamination to be in the reservoir. We won't be able to figure out anything until we get some samples. In case Connie's analysis doesn't tell us anything, I'll pick up the prototype microlab I've been testing in Malta."

"I got hold of Stavros in Athens. I didn't tell him much in case the lines weren't secure, so you'll have to give him a complete briefing. When do you leave?"

"Three hours. Lots to do before then."

Richards seized a sable brush, dabbed it in a gleaming, copper-tinted pool of chocolate color on the palette she held in her left hand, and smeared a wide arc of burnt sienna on the canvas. "I've been thinking about last night and how peculiar this is. How can there be anything in the Ataturk reservoir, especially something that lethal? The Euphrates is nutrient-poor, and with the drought everything's dead, so there's nothing for miles in any direction except dust."

"I've racked my brains. I'm sure I've never heard of anything like this before," admitted Zammit. "And I can't get that damn message out of my head."

She faced him. "There's something fishy about the whole thing. You know my instincts are good. I think you're being set up, for God knows what reason. You be careful."

Zammit forced himself to grin. Her instincts weren't good, they were superb.

There was a beep from the paint-encrusted intercom. She put down her brush and reached for it.

"I'm amazed that thing still works," said Zammit. "Why don't you try boiling it in glue to see if you can finally manage to destroy it?"

"The creative mind is not necessarily a neat one. If I wanted things tidy I'd be a maid."

She listened to the handset for a moment. "It's Cairo. Wants to know if you want him in Malta too." She smiled and spoke into the mouthpiece. "You can't fool me, Mr. Jackson. You just want to go fishing in that gorgeous clear sea."

Zammit took the handset. "Cairo, I think it's best if you stay here and act as liaison with Colonel Graves and the White House. Depending on what the analysis of the samples reveals, we might need help from other agencies. Frankie will start working on a solution as soon as I can send data. Besides, Connie will be there to help me."

As he hung up, Richards said, "Optimist. If there *is* a solution."

She suddenly leaned forward and kissed him on the cheek. He was so startled he was speechless. "You be careful, mister. If you don't come back alive, I . . ." But she didn't finish the sentence. They gazed awkwardly at each other. Zammit couldn't read her expression. To lighten the suddenly heavy mood, he said, "I'll come back alive. All you have to do is hold down this fort while I'm at the other one."

"Fair enough," said Frankie, picking up her brush, as well as on his attempt to cover their discomfort. "Say hello to Aunt Julia and Rocco for me."

 As the plane made a lazy descending circle in the scorching azure sky, Mike Zammit stared out the tiny window at the Mediterranean far below. The brown hills of his ancestral home rose from the aquamarine sea like five tanned knees. He returned to them often, although he had been born in the United States to parents who had emigrated from the islands.

The flight from Seattle to Heathrow and the final leg from London on Air Malta had been uneventful. He had discussed with Colonel Graves using an air force plane, but they had agreed it would be too obvious. The United States had no bases on Malta, and someone would be bound to ask unwelcome questions. Zammit used the time to catch up on his sleep and ponder the scenario the computer program had identified, its machine certainty not acknowledging that it was impossible. He thought about Frankie, how much she enjoyed the islands, and wished she were with him.

"*Bongu*," he said in the Malti language to the smiling immigration official who greeted him and stamped his passport. Although most Maltese spoke good English, Zammit liked to practice the language of his ancestors, which was unlike any other. Originally derived from ancient Phoenician, a Semitic, tongue, it had also been influenced by Arabic, Old French, Spanish, and Italian. It was the only Semitic language that used the Latin alphabet. Rendering Semitic consonants was a problem, leading to some weird-looking words, with lots of *xl* and *xx* combinations. Many times Zammit had given directions to head-scratching tourists who were unable to pronounce the names of their intended destinations: Mgarr (Imgar), Xhagra (Shagra), Xlendi (Shlendi), and the one that always baffled them, Marsaxxlock (*Marsa* meant "harbor", *xxlock*—pronounced schlock—meant "of the southeast wind"). Another one that threw them was that Pope John Paul II was Papa Gwanni Pawlu.

He collected his bags and walked out of Luqa International Airport. After the rain and fog of Seattle, the hundred-degree heat made him gasp. He squinted in the harsh sunlight that glowed on the yellow limestone buildings. Located ninety-five miles southeast of Sicily and just over 200 from the coast of North Africa, most of the Maltese archipelago was as hot and brown as a freshly baked loaf of bread.

At the heliport office he bought a ticket for the chopper flight to Xewkija, on the neighboring island of Gozo. The twenty-seat helicopter had only a handful of passengers. There really was no better way to see the islands, reflected Zammit as they circled Luqa airfield. Off in the distance he could see the capital city, Valletta, and the squat menace of the massive fortifications of the Grand Harbor, the medieval equivalent of a nuclear deterrent, turning golden orange in the late afternoon sun.

It took only minutes to traverse Malta, the main island, just nineteen miles long. Sweeping over Mgarr Harbor, he could see bobbing in the waves the gaily painted traditional fishing boats used by Maltese sailors. They might bear the names of saints, but each had open, ever-watchful eyes painted on either side of the prow to ward off evil, just as they had since Phoenician times. Although a deeply religious people, converted to Christianity by Saint Paul after he was shipwrecked on the main island in 60 A.D., the Maltese, like all people who live by the sea, knew it was wise to hedge their bets.

As they landed at the Xewkija helicopter pad and disembarked on the eight-by four-mile island of Gozo, Zammit heard his name shouted and looked around.

"Hey, Mike! Over here!" Waving at him from the parking lot was his eighteen-year-old cousin Rocco Pullicino. He was sitting behind the wheel of the small white Mercedes convertible Zammit used to get around in whenever he visited. Zammit fetched his bags and walked over. The blinding sun reflecting on the white paintwork made him wince even behind his sunglasses.

"Hello, Rocco. Been taking good care of my car, I see."

"Of course." The handsome teen's teeth looked even whiter than usual in his mahogany complexion as he pushed his jet black hair out of his eyes. "It's strange to see you here in the summer."

Zammit smiled as he tossed his luggage into the backseat. "At this time of year the climate is only fit for nudists, Germans, and Brits. Man, it's hot."

As they drove leisurely down the narrow winding roads, they passed a few other cars and the occasional wooden cart pulled by a sleepy mule. Malta was crammed with tourists, discos, and fast-food joints, while Gozo, less than four miles away, half the size and much greener, had never lost its pastoral simplicity. The misty green terraces wrinkled their way up the low hills of the island's interior like the face of some friendly, mossy ancient.

Fifteen minutes later they arrived. The square golden tower of Lascaris by the edge of the sparkling sea had been built by the Knights of Malta, known also as the Knights of the Order of Saint John of Jerusalem, Hospitallers, in the 17th century. A member of the U.S. chapter of the Order since the age of twenty-seven, Zammit was one of several thousand modern Knights of Malta in the world. He found it odd to be both a scientist and a member of an eight-hundred-year-old Order of crusaders whose military role in fighting evil had ended so long ago. Now the knights delivered humanitarian services in Third World nations. Personally, he would rather concentrate on his scientific endeavors, but he'd joined when asked because of his family's historic connection with the Order.

Perched on a sheer cliff near Ramla Bay, the old fort was Zammit's home away from home. After the success of ZAM Instruments, he'd spent a lot of money renovating the place. When his Aunt Julia's husband died, she and Rocco had moved from their small villa and now lived there year-round. Zammit liked to visit during the spring and late fall. It was close to Europe and Asia and a quiet place to think and reflect.

A steep path led down to a tiny sandy beach, almost entirely hidden by craggy pillars of sea-worn limestone. It was a great place to go fishing or diving. The sapphire and cobalt blue waters, the cleanest in the Mediterranean, had a visibility underwater of more than 100 feet.

Rocco helped him lift the bags from the car and carry them up the four broad, shallow steps. "Michael!" It was his Aunt Julia, Rocco's mother, waving from the immense stone doorway. Like many Maltese women, she had ivory skin, huge hazel eyes, jet hair, and a full figure, a legacy of Greek, Roman, Arab, Norman, and Sicilian genes. She looked remarkably like her older sister, Zammit's mother, Adriana, who had disappeared with his father, lost at sea in their yacht during one of the terrible winter storms that could spring up so suddenly. Now, twenty-eight years later, he found it curiously comforting to know that there was a living reminder of what Adriana might have looked like.

"Hello, gorgeous." At fifty-six she looked ten years younger. He kissed her on the cheek and put his arm around her shoulders as they turned and walked into the cavernous coolness of the great entryway. "I'm parched."

Julia led the way to the back of the old fortress as Rocco took the luggage upstairs. Their footsteps banged hollowly on the flag-stones in the dim passageway that led into the kitchen. Despite its rusticated appearance, modern wiring and plumbing serviced the gleaming appliances. Zammit opened the fridge and pulled out a bottle of Hopleaf ale. "Is Costopoulos here yet?"

Julia shook her head. "He phoned. All he said was, he'd be arriving tonight in time for dinner."

Zammit nodded. "Ordinarily I'd take you all to the Sea View and we could eat and listen to Lino's guitar and watch the boats come in. But Stav and I have some business to discuss and I'm afraid it's private. Rocco, could you drive back to the heliport and pick him up? You won't have to wait long, and besides, in that Mercedes you should be able to attract a girl or three."

As the teen clattered down the stone hallway Julia said with mock severity, "I always forget what a bad influence you are on that boy."

"It never hurts a guy to become a man of the world," smiled Zammit.

He finished his beer and went outside as Julia started getting the meal ready. He strolled slowly around the old fort, along brick-red paths whitened with fine dust blown all the way from the Sahara. Under an enamel blue sky, he passed fields of sharp stones and even sharper gray thorns and cactus. Only heat-stunned lizards watched him, and the hot air stood on the ground in shimmery waves.

He walked back to the kitchen through the dark, cool stone hallways and sniffed experimentally. He peered over Julia's shoulder, knowing what the answer would be. "I'm setting a bad example for a modern sensitive male. Can I help?"

She shooed him away. "Take a bottle of wine and wrestle with this problem you hinted at on the phone." Her hazel eyes were shrewd. "You've been doing a lot of work in Russia. Another Chornobyl?"

"No. Hard to believe, but it might be worse than Chornobyl. In Turkey." He looked at her closely. "Heard anything on the news?"

"Just about the riots and the election campaign." Her nostrils flared in distaste. "Turkey. What, are they massacring people again?"

Zammit had to smile in spite of himself. Like most ancient peoples, the Maltese had the memory of a collective elephant, and what they remembered best was how they had saved Christian Europe from a Turkish invasion in 1565.

Through treachery, the Knights of Saint John, after two hundred and fifty years on the island of Rhodes, were forced out by Suleyman the Magnificent in 1522. They finally relocated to Malta, given to them as a gift by Emperor Charles V. The Order, formed in the early 12th century as a crusading Order of nurses, had been forced into militancy as the early crusading successes came under attack. The knights were the most fabulous heroes in Christendom, deploring violence but more than capable, as a last resort against unspeakable evil, of climbing into suits of armor and proving their worth. Out of gratitude for Charles's donation, the knights sent him every year the gift of a Maltese falcon.

The Turkish Ottoman Empire expanded rapidly from 1300 to 1680. In 1564, at the age of seventy, Suleyman decided he wanted to conquer Sicily, then Italy, then recapture Spain. The only thing blocking him was Malta. He sent 200 warships and 40,000 soldiers to besiege the tiny islands, which were defended by 8 galleys, 450 knights, 400 Spanish auxiliaries, and some 9,000 native Maltese. If they had lost, the whole history of Europe would have been different.

But they didn't lose.

Suleyman thought the whole thing would be over in three or four days. He was wrong.

Almost the entire four-month conflict took place in about half a square mile, with Turkish forces throwing 70,000 artillery shells at Fort Saint Elmo and the fortified peninsulas of Senglea and Birgu. The defense was led by the Grand Master of the Order, Jean de la Valette, who like his arch enemy Suleyman was over seventy. A man of superhuman toughness, Valette outthought, outfought, and outlasted the Turks, who finally slunk home in defeat.

Two hundred and fifty years after the Great Siege, Voltaire said it was the most spectacular event in the history of mankind. With some prodding, he was persuaded to add, since the birth of Christ.

Riches poured into Malta from grateful kings all over Europe. Valette, anticipating another attack, used the money to build an impregnable series of fortifications. Suleyman got tied up conquering Hungary and never renewed the assault. Zammit's ancestor John had been one of the knights who fought in the defense, and it was his suit of armor that was in Zammit's Seattle apartment.

"That's ancient history, Julia," said Mike Zammit. "Turkey's a democracy now, just like this country. Time to kiss and make up."

Julia snorted. "Your ancestors fought the Turks, and don't ever forget it. Fought them and beat them. You're a knight of the Order as well. That toughness is in your blood. You'll need it someday."

"Ancient history," repeated Zammit. "The knights don't fight anymore, remember? We do good works."

The thunderous look on her face gave him some idea what the Turks might have faced during the siege of 1565. "Lighten up," he protested. "Remember when the Turkish ambassador visited a few years ago and was given a tour of Fort Saint Elmo? They took him down into the depths, where the knights had tended their wounded. He looked around and said, 'I am humbled to realize I am the first Turk in history ever to enter this place.' He was graceful about the fact that we'd beaten the crap out of them."

He opened the fridge again and grabbed a bottle of ice cold Marsovin Special Reserve. As he opened it he said, "I'm going to have a look at the microlab. Call me when Stavros and Rocco get back."

He leaned over a pile of fish on the counter. "So, what's everyone else going to have for supper?" Julia grinned and pushed him toward the door.

 To loosen muscles stiff from hours of air travel, Zammit bounded up the worn steps two at a time to the top of the three-story fortress. He walked down the hall, passed his bedroom, and went into the next room. Panting from exertion and the heat, he drank from the bottle, already beaded with moisture. Setting it on a stone bench, he fetched the lab and carefully opened the case. He smiled fondly at the array of gleaming glass and metal and said under his breath, "Honey, I shrunk the lab."

He'd been working on this for a long time. The size of a suitcase, it contained tiny factories, labs, and micromachines. The first set of shelving held glass wafers the size of credit cards. Chemical etching techniques allowed him to use hydrofluoric acid to sculpt hundreds of tiny channels less than half the width of a human hair to produce a microscopic network of capillaries. These tiny molecular labs could detect concentrations equivalent to an aspirin tablet dissolved in twelve Olympic-sized swimming pools.

The second set of shelves held silicon wafers, tiny factories complete with conveyor belts, mixing vats, and separation systems. The mixers and movers in the miniature factories used a phenomenon called dielectrophoresis to harness the small electrical charges generated by every living thing. Dielectrophoresis relies on the fact that the capacitance and resistance of a microorganism's cells determine how it responds in an electric field, and it allowed him to work with samples 100,000 times smaller than normal and to perform an analysis in five minutes rather than five days.

The third component was the newest. Frankie Richards, who had come up with the idea, called them "disease dipsticks." Glass wafers coated with a plastic polymer called polydiacetylene film were able to target different microorganisms and their toxins. Depending on the toxin, the film simply changed color like an old-fashioned piece of litmus paper.

Finally, there was a miniature gas chromatograph mass spectrometer. It was very fast, required only minute samples, and was preprogrammed with the spectrums of tens of thousands of known compounds.

When it was hooked up to a properly programmed laptop and

a satellite link, Zammit expected the lab to be the latest in environmental science technology. Soon it would get its first real field test. He sat down on the bench, drank some more wine, and contemplated the lab. So much money, time, and effort invested in this project. He went to the bedroom to fetch his laptop so he could conduct a final test, but seeing the two suitcases on his bed, he decided to spend a couple of minutes hanging up his clothes.

After emptying the first suitcase, he bent to open the second. He dialed the combination, threw back the lid, and pulled out the top two shirts.

In a convulsive reflex, Zammit jumped back so far he crashed into the antique armoire in the corner. Eyes closed, breathing hard, he counted to five. Wiping his sweaty forehead, he walked over and gazed into his suitcase.

Catula.

The insectoid was motionless on top of a pile of clothing and its eyes were blank. Following the second command to hide itself, it had obviously gotten into his luggage after he had packed but before he'd closed the lid and locked it. Unable to feed during its long imprisonment, it had run down and was now asleep. Gingerly Zammit took it out with both hands. He had never picked it up before and it was surprisingly light. Asleep, its tentacles hung down like an octopus's. He half expected it to be warm like a living creature, or to suddenly start thrashing its eight legs. He didn't like this thought at all and quickly knelt to lay it on the stone floor. As he spread it out, the articulated metal tentacles made a series of tiny clicks as the weight of the body settled.

What the hell am I going to do with this? thought Zammit. As he considered whether or not to plug it in and revive it, he heard quick footsteps coming up the stairs, and Aunt Julia appeared in the doorway. "Michael, it's His Highness, the Prince Grand Master. He's dropped by for a visit. I ran into him at the market yesterday in Valletta and mentioned you were coming. If you could give him a few minutes—he thinks so highly of you. He—"

Her eyes fell to the floor. She clutched both hands to her mouth. "No. Please."

Zammit moved quickly toward her but not fast enough and flinched as she let out a piercing scream. "It's all right," he said soothingly. "It's just an experiment. It's asleep."

"Asleep? You mean it's *alive*?" Her voice rose like a jet engine preparing for takeoff. "You bring something that looks like that into this house? Are you *pazzo*?" Zammit never liked it when people shouted, much less screamed, and he wondered if the visitor could hear it. He took her by the shoulders and explained about Dikka and her insect robots. "I didn't intend to bring it," he concluded. "Honest. It just crawled into my luggage."

Wildly her eyes searched his. "It *crawls* into places? Well, you are certainly taking it with you when you leave tomorrow. There it can crawl around all it wants. Let it make the Turks *pazzo*!"

"Julia, I don't need it in Turkey. I want to leave it—"

"No! That malevolent creature is not staying in this house!"

"Julia, it's not malevolent, because it's not alive." Zammit glanced over at the robot and sighed. "It just looks malevolent. It's asleep, and you can simply lock it up somewhere until I come back." Suddenly it occurred to him that it would be just like Dikka to install a small battery to jump-start the thing awake after a certain length of time, just enough power so it could drag itself to an energy source. He remembered his own explosive terror at three in the morning and figured that in a similar situation, Julia would have a stroke. What was it he'd read somewhere? All human beings have an instinctive aversion to snakes, centipedes, and spiders.

They both turned as they heard the scrape of hesitant footsteps on the stairs. A tall elderly man of ascetic features and spindly build appeared in the doorway and bowed slightly, with the elegance of long practice. He had always reminded Zammit of a kindly praying mantis. His jet black hair, dyed through vanity, was combed straight back. His eyebrows were dyed the same color and made his already pale face look paper white. Replace the expensive navy blazer, aqua-blue shirt, blue and gold tie, and green slacks with a crimson-lined cloak, thought Zammit, and you had a benevolent Dracula. In contrast with his physique, his baritone voice was fat with wine, grappa, and good cigars.

"*Con permesso*. Ordinarily I would never dream of intruding, but I heard this ghastly scream . . ." His eyes fell to the floor. He stepped back a pace. "*Madonna*!" Hesitantly he leaned forward and peered, then smiled beatifically at Zammit. "Some sort of experiment, I suppose? Science and all that? Fascinating."

"Hello, sir. I thought you were usually in Rome at this time of year," said Zammit. Damn, he thought, I don't have time for this.

Fra Angelo Fortucci, Grand Master of the Knights of Malta, entered the room and they shook hands. The old man's pale eyes were keen as they searched the scientist's face, and he knew they could see the discomfort there. "I'm here only briefly. As you know, we are completing the computerized cataloging and indexing of the Order's archives. The Jerusalem section has some inexplicable gaps in the 12th century. Also, there is the annual homage to prepare for." Zammit nodded as he remembered. September 8 would be the 438th anniversary of the raising of the Great Siege of 1565. Every year the knights gathered at the Conventual Cathedral of St. John to pay respect to the dead who had saved European civilization.

"Will you be attending his year?" inquired Fortucci.

"Probably not," replied Zammit. "I have some urgent work to do." He hadn't attended in a long time. He wondered if his black ceremonial robe with the white satin cuffs and stitched with the white Maltese cross was falling apart or covered with dust.

"That's a shame," said Fortucci. "I can't tell you how much we appreciated what you did in Venezuela after those mud slides devastated the tenements. Or how grateful we are for your very handsome annual donation. It is unusual for a Catholic knight to also be a scientist."

That's the problem, thought Zammit: I live in a divided house of faith and reason. The death of his parents had badly shaken his adolescent faith, which had never been strong in the first place, and the lingering, painful death of his wife had made him even more cynical. He thought of Adam Richards's disappearance and Frankie's anguish. He looked at Catula. Maybe God was a spider, weaving dense webs of destiny into which people blundered and became enmeshed, forever unable to free themselves. Yet there was the historic connection between his family and the Order, so he felt compelled to remain a member. Because the Order was wholly reliant on donations from its members, he assuaged his guilt with a large sum every year, and when asked helped the organization in its primary work, disaster relief. He remembered something his father had told him—how much the Lord hates hypocrites.

"I must say, that is a remarkably evil-looking creature," said Fortucci. Zammit realized that the old man had followed his gaze. "By design or by accident?"

"Design. The woman who made it likes them to look that way."

The elegant black eyebrows arched, and the Grand Master looked quickly around the room. "Them?" Once again Zammit explained about Spargo.

"I see. At least it has only the appearance of being evil. Have you thought any more about the problem of evil since our last discussion?"

"Yes. You remember Stavros Costopoulos?"

"Of course. A most interesting man. I'd like to speak with him more often."

Aunt Julia interrupted. "He's coming tonight. Why don't you have supper with us?"

"I would be both honored and delighted."

"I'll leave you to your discussions," said Julia as she left.

"What a lovely woman," said Fortucci. "You were saying?"

Zammit looked around his bedchamber with its single chair. "Why don't we go into the other room and sit down. Would you like a glass of wine?"

"Please."

He picked up Catula and placed the insectoid back in his suitcase because he didn't know where else to put it. From the bathroom he fetched a couple of clean glasses, and they walked down the hall to the adjoining room. Zammit poured the wine and they sat down. "*Sante*," he said as he clinked glasses with the old man. "To continue. A few weeks ago Stavros introduced me to a forensic psychologist who works for the FBI."

Fortucci raised an inquiring eyebrow.

"Someone who analyzes the criminal state of mind."

"Ah."

"This guy has made something of a specialty of serial killers, mass murderers, and the like. I remembered our discussion and asked him if he believed these people were mentally ill or evil. It was pretty obvious he'd thought about that question before."

Fortucci sipped his wine. "And?"

"He said he'd worked on a couple of hundred cases and that in his opinion almost all of them were mentally ill, as a result of organic brain damage, abuse, whatever. There was always evidence of a cause to explain the effect."

The old man's eyes were keen. "Go on."

"Except for two or three of them. He said they looked human and you could talk with them, but when you looked in their eyes there was nothing there. He'd studied one of the female members of the Charles Manson family because it's unusual to find a woman who's a mass killer."

"Go on," said Fortucci. "This is fascinating."

"This psychologist said her eyes were like that. They'd run tests and determined she wasn't schizophrenic. He said that if you gave this woman the opportunity to either say good morning to you or slit your throat, it's fifty-fifty which one she'd choose to do. She simply was not human in any important way he could recognize. She was morally insane, a psychopath. In his opinion, she was just plain evil."

The Grand Master nodded thoughtfully. "Do you agree with him?"

"I'm inclined to respect expert opinion."

"I don't know," said Fortucci. Zammit raised an eyebrow—he had taken it for granted that the old man would agree with the FBI psychologist. "Why not?" he asked.

"It sounds as if this woman functions as a sort of automaton. Does terrible things without forethought, out of some sort of compulsion. That spiderish thing of yours—it looks evil, but we know it isn't because it's just a machine. It sounds to me as if she can no more control her behavior than a robot, that her ability to make choices is severely impaired."

Zammit could tell where this was heading. "You mean she can't exercise free will."

"Precisely. The problem of evil is inseparable from the problem of free will. A truly evil person is one who is mentally sound but chooses to do bad things. It's the element of choice that counts. I think true evil is actually very rare. Then again, believers in determinism won't accept that there is such a thing as free will."

Zammit shrugged, suddenly bored. "I *know* my will is free, and that's the end of the debate, as far as I'm concerned."

The Grand Master smiled. "A very commonsense approach."

They sat awkwardly for a couple of moments. Fortucci pointed at the lab. "What's that?" Zammit explained briefly. The old man shook his head. "Amazing." Once again, the keen gaze. "You like your machines, don't you?"

"Yes. I have a lot of faith in them."

"More faith than you have in your faith, if I may put it that way?"

Zammit didn't want to lie. "Yes," he said bluntly.

Fortucci didn't seem surprised.

"I'm a practical man who does practical things, not a meta-physician," Zammit continued. "Someone once defined meta-physics as a blind man in a dark room looking for a black cat that isn't there. I guess that's where faith comes in: You say to yourself, I just know that cat's in here somewhere. Personally I can't bring myself to believe it's there at all."

"The question of faith is important, but we were talking about evil. It does exist, and we have always fought it."

Another awkward silence, as the Grand Master nodded slowly, formulating another thought. Zammit glanced at his watch, knowing the old man could talk about this kind of thing for hours. *Basta*—enough. Before Fortucci could say anything more, Zammit said, "Look sir, I have to test that microlab before I leave tomorrow morning. I want to do it before Costopoulos gets here."

The old man put down his glass and rose to his feet. "Of course. I've been wasting your time." Before Zammit could say, No, that's not what I meant, Fortucci spoke again as he walked to the door. "Perhaps as a man of science, you'll listen to another man of science. At the end of his life the British physicist Sir James Jeans said, 'I've always thought the universe is a great machine, and now I realize it is a great thought.' "

Before Zammit could reply, the Grand Master was out the door and down the hall. His deep voice echoed back. "Always a pleasure talking to you, my son. I'll keep your aunt company until dinner."

Zammit spent almost an hour checking the equipment and the computer until he was satisfied everything was functional.

He sat on the stone bench by the window and finished his wine, staring unseeingly at the microlab. The computer monotonously spitting out the same impossible scenario—but it simply wasn't possible for any kind of organism to exist in the reservoir in such huge amounts. The e-mail message. He pulled the tattered piece of paper from his pocket and read it again. Who had sent it, and why? He was filled with a sense of terrible foreboding. He couldn't shake the suspicion that what was happening at the Ataturk Dam wasn't natural.

Abdul Jamal lifted his heavy gold fork and took another mouthful of Veal Foyot. He'd tasted the real thing many times at the old Hotel Foyot in Paris, and this greasy mess didn't even come close. Where was their chef from, Albania? He sipped quickly from the gold-rimmed wine goblet. At least they couldn't ruin Leroy Chambertin 1983.

"Pretty good, huh?" asked Ivan Popov, president of Tuvanistan. "Nothing but the best. The *best*."

Jamal smiled politely. "I assure you, it is absolutely extraordinary."

Popov beamed with satisfaction.

For the time being he had to be polite. They could do what they wanted because they had their own country. Once he had his own country he could do what he wanted as well. He looked at Ivan, the huge head, the hairline that started two inches above his eyebrows, the ferrety eyes, weak chin, and wet lips. He was perfumed like a woman, sported a diamond pinkie ring and a cabochon ruby, and wore lifts in his shoes to appear taller than his five feet six inches. Perhaps once he had his own country he could start a war with theirs. The thought cheered him.

He picked at the congealed cabbage dumplings that accompanied his flabby veal, then gave up. For a gourmet this meal was the culinary equivalent of first-degree murder. He watched as Anastasia wolfed down her food. Her huge breasts threatened to tumble out of her garish red dress, which was precisely the wrong color for someone with orange hennaed hair. She had once been attractive, in a coarse, peep-show sort of way, but she had gone to fat, and her hips bounced like saddlebags on an overweight mare. In contrast, her face had the sleek, tight, wind-tunnel look of someone who had face-lifts almost as often as they bathed. Her eyes were a brilliant, unnatural turquoise—obviously colored contact lenses.

To avoid the sight, Jamal looked around the vast banquet hall. Financed by Tuvanistan's oil revenues, the Popovs had spared no expense on this enormous vulgar palace. He knew all about the Popovs from the research he had done before approaching them for refuge, and idly ran through some of the details.

Ivan was rumored to have started his career as a paid police spy who specialized in luring "degenerates" into homosexual encounters in public washrooms. Anastasia had started hers as a stripper and prostitute, although it was worth the life of any Tuvanian to so much as hint at the fact. Their respective beginnings as whores led naturally to success in Soviet-era politics, and both rose to occupy prominent positions as party apparatchiks. With the demise of the Soviet Union, Tuvanistan had voted for independence and held its first and last democratic election. Presidential candidate Ivan Popov had stolen a narrow victory, which he promptly consolidated by murdering his opponents and declaring a temporary period of martial law. This suspension of the constitution had now lasted for ten years.

The Popovs' primary preoccupation was money. They were determined to have more of it than anyone else. To this end they treated their oil-field workers as virtual serfs, forcing them to work eighteen-hour shifts in health and safety conditions that would not have been unfamiliar to a 19th-century coal miner. They had a complete list of all the world's 385 billionaires and their assets and were determined to move up from their present ranking of number 137. Jamal had been careful to avoid any discussion of his own wealth, but he also liked to keep score, even though, as a fugitive, he was not on the list. He estimated that he was number 131. The very mention of the world's two richest men, the Sultan of Brunei and Bill Gates, was enough to send Anastasia into paroxysms of jealous rage. Jamal liked mentioning their names as often as possible without being too obvious about it. Everyone knew she was the brains of the two.

But not all the money in the world could buy taste or class. He looked at the giant picture facing him above the priceless 15th-century gilt Venetian mirror. Painted on aquamarine velvet, a portrait of Anastasia's favorite white Persian cat stared at him with eyes made of genuine sapphires. He suppressed a shudder.

"Abdul, would you like more food? More wine?" asked Ivan.

"No more food, my friend. I must watch my weight. But the wine is excellent."

Ivan clapped his hands and shouted. A cringing servant in bright yellow livery peeled himself from the wall to pour more Burgundy into Jamal's glass.

Jamal watched the little man play with his diamond pinkie ring. It was the sort of gaudy thing he'd seen before only in Las Vegas. "You know how much of that wine I have?" asked Popov. "Fifty cases. Cost a fortune. It is the best. One evening I drank three bottles of it. Next morning, no headache at all. The *best*."

Jamal sipped as Ivan continued, "It is not often a Muslim drinks wine, is it?"

He concentrated on replying coolly but courteously. "There are different kinds of Muslims as there are different kinds of Christians. Some drink alcohol. But I think very carefully before cracking open a bottle of cognac in front of the faithful."

"Of course, of course. I didn't mean to offend," said Popov hastily. He changed the subject. "I notice you are taking advantage of the palace's communications system. It is the best. The *best*."

"Yes it is," agreed Jamal. It was state-of-the-art, and they allowed him unlimited access to the control room. But he always made sure to scan the room first electronically to ensure he couldn't be filmed or recorded by hidden cameras or microphones. And he changed his encryption protocols twice a day.

"So, business is good as well as brisk?" probed Anastasia, dabbing at her greasy mouth and removing a lot of her bright red lipstick in the process.

"I have some deals under way," said Jamal carefully. This was delicate. The Popovs tried to pump him for information about his businesses and made unsubtle hints about forming partnerships. That was the last thing he wanted. His family had been merchants in Oman for 500 years and had developed an enviable reputation. Of Jamal's father it was said that when you shook hands with him on a deal, you'd better count your fingers afterward. Like virtually all former Communists, the Popovs had about as much understanding of finance as a Mongolian yak herder. They were looters and gangsters, not businesspeople, and he had no intention of letting them form part of his plans. He was here only because it was a refuge, not because he liked it. Or them.

He watched Anastasia smear a coin-sized bit of toast with truffle and cognac paté imported from Fauchon in Paris. He felt a sudden stab of nostalgia for the city where he had spent his youth, and which he could never visit again.

"With Anwar Hussein?" she asked craftily.

Jamal acknowledged the hit with a tilt of his head. He hated being surprised. Were they monitoring his communications after all? He had assumed they weren't clever enough and made a mental note to double-check. "A valued client. The Iraqi economy has still not recovered from the oil embargo and UN sanctions over weapons of mass destruction. And it is the right of every sovereign nation to defend itself."

"A weapon is defensive or offensive depending on whether you are in front of it or behind it," sneered Anastasia.

Jamal felt a surge of rage at her tone. Maybe I'll kill her one day, he thought. But he smiled and replied, "What they do with their armaments is not my concern."

Ivan Popov interrupted. "Speaking of business, are you still into pharmaceuticals? I hear there's a lot of money in these new drugs, the ones that can be put into water supplies and such."

Popov was rarely subtle, and even Anastasia winced. He'd brought the subject up before. He wanted something he could administer to his people en masse to turn them into docile zombies. It might be a valuable source of income in the future, but it was a mistake to give anything away now.

"There are such substances. It might be possible to obtain them." He shrugged and lied. "But as always, the mainstays of my business are the more traditional drugs."

There was a clatter of footsteps and a troop of palace guards burst in.

"Protector of the Fatherland, Genius of the Caucasus," panted the leader, "the oil workers are marching on the palace." Dimly Jamal heard the rattle of gunfire.

Ivan Popov's eyes bulged and his tongue flicked wetly.

"What are you waiting for?" screamed Anastasia. The turquoise eyes blazed like a viper's in the suddenly reptilian face. "Kill them all or be killed yourselves!"

The three turned and fled. Abdul Jamal rose to his feet just as Wurban Ice entered the room with his heavy measured tread. He felt Ice's hot breath on his ear as he whispered his report. "Poorly armed, badly led. Hundreds were electrocuted as they tried to swarm the fence. When it shorted out I killed two of the guards as they turned to flee, to make the others stand their ground. It is under control, but some of the workers made it into the palace."

Jamal nodded. "Go immediately to the control room and protect the communications equipment. I'll follow. The only people you do not have my permission to kill are the Popovs."

Ice turned and jogged heavily from the room, unholstering his 9 mm pistol. Jamal followed, reaching for his own weapon, a small silver Beretta. In the hallway Ivan wrung his hands as Anastasia shrieked orders to a milling throng of servants and troops.

Jamal frowned. He was sensitive to political atmosphere, and this place stank of incompetence, cruelty, and the very real possibility of revolution. As always when something occurred that he could not control, a feral snarl transformed his handsome face into something frightening. The Popovs were idiots. They had their own country, oil fields, a virtual license to print money, and they were throwing it all away. You could build yourself a throne of bayonets but you couldn't sit on it for long. Not without something more.

As he neared the control room he saw a sudden movement out of the corner of his left eye. Instantly he pivoted and fired three times.

It was an oil-field worker in filthy overalls. Two of the shots had passed through his throat and the third had drilled him through the forehead. He was dead and staring.

Jamal heard Ice thudding back down the hallway and waved impatiently to tell him to make for the communications center. Jamal turned and continued walking. Although alert to his surroundings, he was thinking hard.

He made a mental note of whom to contact as soon as the palace was secure. He could not stay here much longer. Time was of the essence. Men most fear in others the motives they feel predominant in themselves, and most of all Jamal wanted to avoid being the victim of treachery before he could betray his partners.

" 'It is good to trust, but it is better not to trust,' " quoted Dr. Stavros Vyronos Costopoulos. "An old Roman proverb. Especially when it's a computer program. More wine?"

Zammit and Costopoulos lounged on the roof of the Lascaris fort next to the satellite dish, gazing out over Ramla Bay. The night sky arched over them, strewn with stars like diamonds from the hand of a celestial benevolent. A fat Mediterranean moon glimmered on the surging sea far below the towering cliffs.

The scientist studied Costopoulos's hawkish profile with affection. Forty-eight years old, five foot ten, and a trim 160 pounds, the Greek was built like a middleweight fighter, even though he didn't like exercise. He reminded Zammit of the portrait of a man found in the ruins of Pompeii—thinning black hair combed forward like Julius Caesar's over a bulging forehead, as if the skull were too small to contain the overactive brain, a thin impatient line of a mouth softened by the expression of thoughtfulness in the big brown eyes. They had met at a conference in Helsinki, had a tremendous argument about something he couldn't even remember, gone out drinking to continue the argument, and become fast friends.

Because it was too hot to eat on the roof of the fort, they dined in the old banquet hall. The long table was made of blackened timbers taken from the hull of a 16th-century ship that had foundered on Malta's rocks. The table was strewn with silver utensils, traditional Maltese earthenware, and lit by a dozen candles. Zammit loved candlelight. He breathed the smell of hot wax and old cold stone and enjoyed the way the candles threw everyone's faces into sharp relief, planes of light and dark, like a painting by Rembrandt.

Supper had been wonderful, as always. Julia had outdone herself with traditional Maltese delicacies. The most spectacular dish was a scorpion fish. Its flesh was so fine it was impossible to fry because it would disintegrate. Instead the whole fish was steamed over boiling water in which a few fennel seeds had been strewn.

The snow white mouthfuls reminded Zammit of eating a delicately scented cloud. The Grand Master and Costopoulos received the choicest delicacies, the gills. They also had roast lamb with garlic and oregano, tomatoes fried in virgin olive oil with onion, garlic, and eggplant, and the cheese pastries known as *pastizzi*.

Fortucci drained his wine and sighed. "Julia, you have surpassed yourself. If I ate like this every day I'd put on a hundred pounds."

Costopoulos grinned. "I agree. I shouldn't have had that third helping. But one must soldier on. What's for dessert?"

"*Mqaret*," said a blushing Julia, fetching a tray from an antique sideboard.

They each had several of the diamond-shaped pastry shells filled with dates mixed with sugar and flavored with aniseed. Julia served espresso coffee and thimbles of fiery grappa.

The Grand Master was always inquisitive. "Stavros, I've never known your full name before tonight. Your middle name is Vyronos. I've never encountered it in the classical literature."

Costopoulos sipped his grappa. "Because it isn't there. I'm named after Lordos Vyronos. That's Greek for Lord Byron, the poet. We've always appreciated the fact that he fought with us in our war of independence against the Turks in the 1820s. Vyronos is still a common boy's name."

"Fascinating." Then Fortucci got onto one of his favorite topics. "Are you an active member of the Greek Orthodox Church, or do you have the good fortune to be Catholic?"

Stavros smiled. "Let's just say I am amiably agnostic. Ever heard the story about the philosopher and mathematician Lord Bertrand Russell? He was a pacifist during World War I, and as a result was arrested. The jailer had to fill out a form. He asked Russell his religion, and Russell replied, 'Agnostic.' The jailer stared at him for a moment, sighed, asked how to spell agnostic and then said, 'Oh, well. At least we all worship the same God.' Russell said that as he sat in his cell, this remark kept him cheerful for a week."

Fortucci threw his head back and laughed. "Marvelous."

Costopoulos continued, "I do believe there is an ordering intelligence in the universe, but what it is, I don't know. As far as organized religion goes, what's the definition of a cult?"

Zammit had heard this one before. "The church down the street from yours."

Stavros went on, "I don't like this business of encouraging people to buy their way into heaven. A few years ago I talked to this old man, a Greek. A terrible reprobate, a cheat and a liar. Ninety years old and he's just given $50,000 to the Orthodox Church. I reminded him that the only time he was in church his whole life was when he was baptized. His whole life, nothing but drinking, gambling, and whores. I asked how he could do such a thing. With tears in his eyes he told me he didn't want to go to hell. I told him he was thinking like a peasant, that God is like a headwaiter in a restaurant, you slip him a few bucks to make sure you don't get a bad table and he's going to make everything OK. He cried, 'But Stavros, I don't want to go to hell.' What can you do with such people?"

After more banter, the Grand Master said his farewell and disappeared into the warm blue velvet night, waving a thin praying mantis arm and smoking a Sobranie Black Russian in an amber holder. Julia and Rocco began clearing the dishes, Zammit took a bottle of wine, and he and Costopoulos climbed to the roof to have a talk.

The distant surf sounded like the beat of some ancient heart as Zammit finished briefing the Greek scholar. Costopoulos looked thoughtful as he filled their glasses with strong Gozitan wine.

Stavros had many talents. Fluent in over a dozen languages, he was also an expert in the arcane field of cognitive anthropology. INERT often worked in different cultures to investigate environmentally harmful practices that might be age-old. Understanding how people thought about those problems was vital, so the skeptical Greek's expertise in the history of thought and human psychology was useful. He was defiantly low-tech, loathing television and computers. "The day I need machines to help me see and think is the day I blow my brains out," he'd once said. Like his intellectual ancestor Plato, he loved theory and abstract thought but didn't have much use for practical, applied science. Zammit found that their different ways of looking at the world complemented each other, so when Costopoulos spoke, he listened.

Stavros spoke now. "Based on what you've said, there are two theories."

"Which are?"

Costopoulos shrugged. "You're the field scientist. You tell me."

Zammit sipped his wine. "Environmental degradation leading to some sort of bizarre organic contamination. It's happened before. There have been water problems in the region for thousands of years. That parched desert was once crammed with people, filled with the richest cities in the world. The ancient chronicles are full of stories about mysterious outbreaks of plague and waterborne diseases. Then the barbarians came and wrecked everything for good."

"And the problem with this theory is?" probed the Greek. Stavros was addicted to the Socratic method of patient questioning to elicit understanding.

"Contamination of that nature, whether it's red tides or whatever, always has an identifiable cause, usually pollution, overpopulation, or dramatic climatic changes. In this case, there's no industry, no population pressure, and even though this drought is the worst ever, it's still part of a cycle as old as civilization itself. So the environmental theory is out."

Costopoulos nodded as his mind made one of those lizardlike dodges that many people found disconcerting. "You know, I love reading the old Greek poets—nymphs, green leafy places, and water. Always water. A lot of Greece is now sun-bleached rock. It's like the old gods dried up and blew away. The ancient Greeks destroyed their environment."

Zammit stood and stretched. "Just like these islands. World headquarters of the Mother Goddess cult for thousands of years. More than thirty megalithic temples, far older than Stonehenge. There used to be dwarf rhinoceroses here, so it must have been a verdant, watery paradise. My great grandfather was Sir Themistocles Zammit. He developed a theory that what destroyed the culture was environmental exhaustion."

Costopoulos filled his glass. "I've always meant to ask you more about Sir Themistocles. I know he excavated many of those megaliths. Did he actually find the Hypogeum?"

Zammit shook his head. "It was 1902. Someone was excavating the foundation of a house and hit big rock. Tried to dig it out and crashed through the dome of the Hypogeum. That's when they called him in. A big underground Neolithic cathedral. Looks eerily modern even today."

The Greek gazed out to sea. "That's what fascinates me about cognitive anthropology. Look at all the temples here. So many of them, a fantastic exertion for a Neolithic people with stone tools.

Why did they do it? What did they *think* they were doing? I've spent my whole life trying to figure out such things. People always have a reason for doing something, however bizarre it may seem."

He looked at Zammit, pacing along the battlements. "Which brings us, I believe, to theory number two."

Zammit sighed. "Are you thinking what I'm thinking?"

"Frankly, I've been waiting for this for years. The e-mail message is the clincher. But it still isn't physically possible, at least according to those damn machines of yours."

"They're just machines. As a detective, I appreciate what Sherlock Holmes said—when you've eliminated every possible explanation, whatever is left, however improbable, must be the truth." Zammit looked at his watch. "It's midnight. I have to call Cairo."

"I'm not going anywhere. Do you have anything to read?"

"I'll meet you in the library. I have to do some work tonight anyway."

In the small communications room, the connection came through almost instantly. "Cairo. Any news?" asked Zammit.

"Yeah. All bad. The Turkish air force shot down four Iraqi MiGs that violated their airspace on a flight path toward the Ataturk Dam. Anwar is moving troops to the border. Assad in Syria hasn't said a word, which is a bad sign. To top it all off, the Russians and Ukrainians have started full-scale military and naval maneuvers along the north coast of the Black Sea. The Turks are upset they weren't notified. The president can't get an explanation from the Kremlin or Kiev about what the hell is going on. Mike, you don't have a lot of time."

Zammit briefed Cairo on his discussions with Stavros Costopoulos. There was a long silence at the other end of the line.

"Damn," said Jackson finally. "When do you leave?"

"Early this morning. I want you to contact Lloyd Lavender. Who else am I meeting at Urfa?"

"Colonel Hakim Yildiz, Turkish Chief of Intelligence. Expert in counterinsurgency. Supposed to be smart."

"Do I see Prime Minister Amurkhan?"

"No. She's fighting for her political life against the fundamentalists.

Zammit rubbed his face. "Have you heard anything at all from Connie?"

"Yeah. A few minutes ago. Apparently something went wrong with the refrigeration facilities at Urfa and the samples are useless."

Zammit thought quickly. "I don't want any more mistakes. Tell Lavender and Yildiz I want to go directly to the dam instead."

"OK."

"Anything else?"

"Yes. Remember you asked me to look into that New Age fake Edward Pompo and his two Irish goons?"

"I'd forgotten all about it. It's not important now."

"I wouldn't be too sure. Checked with the FBI and the CIA. Very interesting. Pompo makes a fortune off of other people's gullibility, but apparently he really does believe all that crap about post-industrial society and the rest. I doubt his two goons do. Fergus Cronin and Roy Dool, ex-IRA turned freelance bodyguards because they've been terrorists for so long they're unfit for any other kind of work. And guess what? Pompo's institute, the Spiritual Brotherhood of the Shit-Eaters or whatever it's called, is international. He does a lot of work in Ireland, where I guess he picked up Cronin and Dool. Also, he's apparently been doing business in Russia, of all places. In fact, he's there now. I understand his institute's emphasis on shamanism, prayer, faith healing, and back-to-the-landism strikes some sort of chord with the Russkies. He left for St. Petersburg right after you made him look like a fool on the Molly Katz show."

Surprised, Zammit tried to digest this information, which seemed significant in some way he couldn't put his finger on.

"Mike, you still there?" asked Jackson.

"Yes." Zammit abandoned his attempt at analysis. Stop being compulsive, he berated himself. Despite their increasing frequency, he was always surprised by the synchronicities that occurred as a result of the increasing globalization of the world's economy and the ease with which people, industries, and ideas moved around the planet. All of what Cairo had just said had to be mere coincidence. Irritably he shrugged off his original suspicion that it was more than chance. You could spend your life in a fog of paranoia if you let yourself worry about such things.

"So now we know the Russians are as gullible as Americans.

Why am I not surprised. What about the Ataturk Dam and reservoir? Any more deaths?"

"No. The whole thing is shut down. Syria and Iraq aren't getting a drop of water. Reuters and Associated Press stringers have been sniffing around, and the Turkish military has put them in detention. With their arrest, the downing of the fighter planes, and the rhetoric from Iraq, pretty soon the media is going to be on this big time."

After a few more terse words Zammit rang off and went into the library.

The Greek looked up from a leather-bound volume and listened as Zammit summarized what he'd learned from Cairo Jackson. "Stav, you might as well go to bed. As a result of our discussion I'm going to run through this again."

Costopoulos looked at the computer in distaste as he left the room.

Far into the night, as waves crashed on the rocks and threw tangy, sea-scented spray into the perfumed air, Mike Zammit traveled back through time to the cradle of civilization, Mesopotamia, and its lifeblood, the rivers of Babylon. Alternating between glowing screen and musty books, he sifted through all the information at his command. As he read, it seemed that thin shapes formed and moved in the deep shadows of the great room. Ghostly armored soldiers refought desperate battles now known only to scholars, faint voices shouted in fear and rage, empires secular and religious came and went. Clouds of dust marked the passage of mythic armies, themselves now nothing but myth and dust. And old gods died, and new ones were born.

As the huge black helicopter thundered over the Ataturk Dam, Mike Zammit wished the sound weren't so loud. He'd drunk too much wine the previous evening and he was short of sleep. He stared out the window. He'd seen pictures of what it was supposed to look like, but nothing had prepared him for this sight.

The acronym DSi was displayed on the gray face of the giant dam in huge white letters—the Turkish abbreviation for the Southeastern Anatolia Development Project's builder, the State Hydraulic Works. On one side of the dam, where there should have been sky-blue water, there was a lumpy greenish mat. As he tried to ignore his queasy stomach, it struck Zammit that the reservoir looked like a colossal toilet bowl filled with green vomit. On the other side, nothing but parched riverbed and aimless eddies of dust.

Connie Palaeov tapped his shoulder and pointed. Below them was the helicopter pad. Whirling blades slashed the hot air as they descended into a melee of tense-looking engineers and shouting soldiers.

After landing at Urfa airport, Zammit and Costopoulos had gotten a briefing from Palaeov and Lloyd Lavender. Connie said the samples had been stored in refrigeration units whose power supply failed before he could start testing. According to Lavender, such a failure was a common occurrence, especially during the summer, although the Turks angrily denied such a thing was possible at their facility.

As they stepped from the helicopter, Lavender and Palaeov helped Zammit lift the padded cases that contained the microlab and other equipment onto the tarmac. Ripples of superheated air shimmered on the asphalt. The smell of fear was pervasive, as was the smell of something else.

"Christ Almighty," said Lavender, blinking sandy lashes over opaque blue eyes as he squinted in distaste. "Stinks like a Marseilles sewer in July." The fetid stench was everywhere, and Zammit could already feel it penetrating his clothing. He swallowed hard and tried not to think about his queasy stomach. Definitely too much wine.

There was something familiar about the appearance and smell of the greenish mat. He tried to remember. Another body of water somewhere, long ago. Suddenly he had it. Twenty-one, the scientific member of a hotshot forest fire fighting crew in northern Canada, investigating the effect of random burn patterns on boreal forest wildlife. Cut off from his crew, forced to the edge of a lake by a wall of fire, he had leapt into the water, penetrating a layer of blue-green slime and ingesting a fair amount of it as he thrashed around, struggling to remove his heavy boots and flak jacket before they pulled him under. It had smelled a little like this, and he'd been ill for several days afterward. Itched like hell too. What had it been? Some sort of algae. No, that wasn't quite right. He couldn't recall anything more. Was it algae in the Ataturk reservoir? If so, what species could be so lethal and grow so fast in an environment with virtually no nutrients?

A stocky man of medium height approached them as they ducked under the helicopter blades and away from the turbulence. The gold braided military cap and immaculate dark blue uniform contrasted strangely with the cigarette that stuck rakishly from the corner of his mouth.

Lloyd Lavender shouted in Zammit's ear, "Colonel Hakim Yildiz, Turkish Chief of Intelligence. He speaks English."

Yildiz's dry firm grip was different from the usual limp Middle Eastern handshake, which was like squeezing a damp rubber glove half-full of warm water and made you want to wipe your hand on your pants. Zammit stared into a swarthy face with a thick black moustache and big sad brown eyes beneath eyebrows as heavy as black caterpillars. He saw an intelligent but worried man.

"Did anyone ever tell you that you look like Omar Sharif?"

"Often," replied Yildiz sardonically. "I even play bridge."

Zammit grinned in spite of himself. This guy was quick. He introduced Connie and Stavros. "*Merhaba*," Costopoulos greeted the soldier in Turkish.

Yildiz's eyes were suddenly hard and appraising. "I don't wish to be rude, but no one told me there would be a Greek coming. This is a restricted facility, and for reasons of national security I'll have to ask—"

Zammit had anticipated something like this. Greeks and Turks mixed like oil and water. They had fought several wars in the past hundred years and were still feuding over the island of Cyprus.

"He's with me," he interrupted. "And he stays with me. If he goes, I go, and you can deal with this mess on your own."

Yildiz finally shrugged. "Russians, Americans, Greeks." He flicked his cigarette onto the hot tarmac. "So much for security."

He turned and gestured for them to follow. Soon they stood 600 feet in the air on the narrow walkway of the dam's crest, more than a mile long. Zammit looked out over the wrinkled, fetid green carpet of contamination in the reservoir far below him, imprisoned behind the concrete wall of the Ataturk Dam. Then he walked a few feet to the other side and stared at the dry riverbed of the Euphrates, meandering toward the horizon, Syria, and Iraq. The poison's only outlet. He frowned. He lifted his arm and pointed his index finger at the horizon along the track of the dry riverbed, then jerked his finger as if pulling the trigger of a gun.

"What are you doing?" demanded Colonel Hakim Yildiz.

"Thinking. Remembering." Zammit turned away.

They descended to the control room. The silence was eerie—the thrum that would ordinarily have filled the facility was gone. Colonel Yildiz waved at the array of blinking monitors and panels. "As you can see, the complex is completely closed down. The turbines are not running, and no water is being released."

"Have you tried filtering the organic material and the poison from the water?" asked Lavender.

The Turk gestured irritably. "Of course. The filtration system can remove occasional debris. It could even remove the organic material, given time. But not the poison it secretes. This is a dam, not a water treatment facility."

He turned to Zammit. "I have been instructed by the prime minister to give you every assistance. How do you wish to proceed?"

"I want to collect some samples from the reservoir directly."

"But we have been collecting them ourselves. We have several large tanks filled with both water and organic material, and we have laboratory equipment."

A few quick questions were enough to determine that the samples were old enough to have decayed significantly. Besides, Zammit had his own agenda, which he had worked out with Costopoulos on the way to Urfa.

After explaining the purpose of the microlab and how fast it could complete an analysis, he said, "But there's no reason not to test your samples as well. Connie, you and Stavros check out those tanks. I'll get suited up for a trip to the water's edge." The two nodded and were escorted from the control room.

Zammit turned to Yildiz and asked a question, hoping for a negative answer. "Any more deaths by inhalation?"

The Turk shook his head. "We have been very careful. That terrible stink is everywhere, and many of the personnel have come down with headaches and other maladies, but no one else has died. The stench is worst near the water's edge, and whenever anyone ventures near they wear oxygen equipment."

"Have you completed the autopsy on the soldier who died?"

"No. But we should have the results today."

Zammit nodded. "Any more ventures into your airspace by the Iraqis?"

"No. And there better not be," he said grimly. He turned to Lloyd Lavender. "I understand we have some strategy to discuss?"

Lavender nodded. "The White House and the Pentagon have researched several probable scenarios. I'd like to brief you as soon as possible."

"Do it while I'm running the tests," said Zammit. "Where can I change?"

Yildiz escorted the two of them to the locker room and Zammit opened his equipment bag. He took out the orange protective suit and began checking the seams and breathing apparatus as Yildiz lit another cigarette. He held the pack of extra-strong Birincis out to Zammit, eyes alert through the pungent blue cloud of Turkish tobacco smoke.

"No thanks." The Turks were among the world's heaviest smokers and proud of their most famous product.

"Why not?" said Lavender. "I quit months ago, but I'd rather inhale cigarette smoke than that godawful stench."

As Lavender accepted a light from Yildiz, Zammit said, "Tell me a story, colonel."

"What kind of story?"

"About this dam. About that stinking green muck out there. You must have a few theories."

As he pocketed his lighter, Yildiz blew two columns of smoke from his nostrils like a sad-eyed dragon. "You have to remember what we have been through with this project. More than thirty years of planning and hard work. No other country, no bank syndicate, not even the World Bank, would lend us any money. We had to finance the whole thing ourselves, all 32 billion dollars. The government sold bonds and the people bought them, like financing a war. Only it was a war of economic development. Every Turkish citizen feels they have a stake in this, that they own it."

"Why wouldn't they lend you the money?"

"Because they think we're a Third World country, that the project is too big for us. That it will cause environmental damage. Because of threats from Syria and Iraq."

"And the Kurdish problem too," said Lavender, as he transferred the Birinci cigarette to his left hand and ran his right through suddenly damp strawberry blond hair. Zammit noticed that he was even paler than before and sweat was beading on his upper lip. Dizzy from the unaccustomed powerful tobacco.

Yildiz raised his shoulders toward his ears and his eyebrows toward the ceiling. "Officially, there is no ethnic group called Kurds. Officially, they are called Mountain Turks."

"Name games aside," replied Zammit, "as I recall from my briefings, you're an expert in counterinsurgency?"

Yildiz nodded as he watched Zammit program his cell phone. "That's why I know this area so well. Half our army, almost 300,000 men, is tied down in this part of the country trying to keep things under control. It costs us 6 billion dollars a year."

"They want their own country, right? Kurdistan?" asked Lavender, stubbing out his half-finished smoke. "I understand the Kurds are the largest ethnic group in the world without their own nation."

"Yes, they want their own country. It would mean taking most of this area, southeastern Anatolia, and part of northern Iraq, as well as chunks of Iran, Syria, and Azerbaijan. The area known as the Kharkurk Triangle." He inhaled moodily. "It is like your Bermuda Triangle. Every year we launch a cross-border offensive at their base camps, and every year all we do is make the Iraqis and Iranians furious and watch thousands of troops and billions of dollars disappear. The Kurdish population is spread over all five nations. But they can't have their own country."

"Why not?" asked Zammit.

Yildiz sighed. "Turkey was founded in 1923 from the shattered remnants of the Ottoman Empire. There are dozens of ethnic groups—should we let them all have their own country? We must concentrate on making a Turkish identity. We are surrounded by hostile nations. The Kurds live in a political entity called the Republic of Turkey, and they must *be* Turks. That is one of the reasons we have such high hopes for this project. We will turn the Plain of Harran into an agricultural Eden, what this part of the world was 4,000 years ago. Prosperity for everyone, including the Kurds. Maybe wealth will make them forget this nonsense about nationhood."

"Somehow I doubt it," said Zammit. "Based on what I've heard, what they'll remember is that you've forced the evacuation of thousands of their villages, all of which will be drowned when the drought ends and the reservoir finally starts filling to capacity."

Yildiz shrugged. "It was necessary. You can't break an omelet without making waves."

"What?" asked Lavender.

The Turk frowned. "It is not correct? American slang is very hard to keep straight."

"Never mind," said Zammit, suppressing a smile. "Tell me more about the Kurdish problem."

"It is like a fight within a family. I seem to remember a similar situation in America. Some states wanted independence, their own government and country, and there was a terrible war."

"The Civil War."

"That's it. I don't know how many Americans wanted to leave, but there are more than 25 million Kurds in total, and they make up almost twenty percent of the Turkish population. It's not like they are some tiny minority." He sighed. "I'm half-Kurdish myself." Zammit looked at him, surprised. "So is the deputy prime minister. Just like your American Civil War, this war is like a fight within a family. It's horrible."

"What about the green muck and the poison? You must have some theories, some suspicions."

Yildiz blew a smoke ring. "I suspect everyone. It's my job." His gaze was appraising.

Zammit didn't like the look. "Even us?"

Yildiz shrugged. "Even though you are an American, I have been briefed. Historically, the Maltese and the Turks have not exactly been the best of friends."

Lavender cleared his throat nervously to defuse the tension. "You don't have to worry about us. Who else do you suspect?"

"Kurds. Iraqis. Syrians. Greeks. Martians. Everyone."

Zammit stepped into the orange suit and tucked the helmet under his arm. "I wish this had an air-conditioning unit built into it." He punched a button on the phone. "Just testing, Stav. I'm heading outside. Anything interesting in those tanks?"

He listened. "I didn't think so. Keep at it anyway." As he slipped the phone into its holster he said, "I'll relay data to my headquarters back in Seattle via satellite link." He picked up the microlab and paused by the door.

"I'll meet you back in the control room," Yildiz said to Lavender. Graves's man nodded and left.

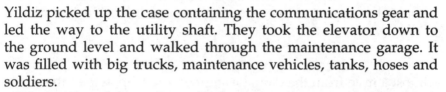

Yildiz picked up the case containing the communications gear and led the way to the utility shaft. They took the elevator down to the ground level and walked through the maintenance garage. It was filled with big trucks, maintenance vehicles, tanks, hoses and soldiers.

They stopped by a Jeep. "You want an escort of soldiers? A driver, at least?" asked Yildiz.

"No thanks. I'm the only one who can do this, and watching me perform the tests is about as exciting as watching water evaporate. I won't be long."

Yildiz frowned suspiciously. "Why don't you get the samples and come back here to do your analysis and transmission instead of carrying all this equipment?"

Zammit thought fast. He didn't want to explain his theories just yet, and depending on what he found in the reservoir, he didn't want Yildiz listening in on his conversation with Frankie Richards.

"This is the first field test for this equipment. I want to see how it performs in the wild, so to speak. As for the transmission, this facility is crammed with electronics, and there might be interference. It's best if I do it out there."

Yildiz shrugged as Zammit put the microlab and communications gear into the rear and climbed behind the wheel of the Jeep, his suit making it awkward. He put the orange helmet on the seat beside him and turned the ignition. "Showtime."

Yildiz thrust his arm in front of Zammit's face. The scientist stared at the watch for a moment, then grinned. There was no doubt the colonel's command of American slang left something to be desired.

"Thanks. I'll be back before you can say crackerjack." As the Turk's heavy eyebrows contracted, Zammit engaged the gears and drove out of the garage and onto the maintenance road that accessed the reservoir. While on the dam's crest he had decided where he was going to take his samples. He squinted up into the sky, glowing like an inverted enamel blue bowl.

In the distance he saw a couple of squat hills with shaved-off tops through a shimmering smoky heat haze, quite unlike the rolling hillocks that characterized most of the brown and dusty landscape. He knew they were ancient settlements or cities, untouched by any archaeologist. There were hundreds of them throughout southeastern Turkey, once the richest part of the Roman Empire before it had reverted to desert with the coming of the barbarians.

Almost a mile from the dam, he stopped the Jeep, wiped the sweat from his face, put on his helmet, and adjusted the flow of oxygen. Then he drove down the service road to the edge and stopped. Leaning his muscular forearms on the wheel, he frowned at the blanket of green muck and the strange greenish-black bulbs growing from its surface. Underneath the orange suit, he wore a collarless, long-sleeved black Gore-Tex shirt and black slacks of the same fabric. A trickle of sweat down his spine again reminded him of the searing heat. He looked around as he got out of the Jeep. Apart from a patrol of soldiers a hundred yards away, there was no one in sight. He carried the two cases to the top of the slight rise, set them down, and gazed at the brown desolation that stretched to the horizon.

Zammit opened the communications suitcase and contemplated its contents. As usual he'd brought too much stuff, but then he never knew what conditions he might have to work in.

He removed the dual-mode satellite adapter, the size and shape of a sniper's scope, and snapped it into the Qualcomm-made multimode cell telephone. Now he could communicate anywhere on earth through the Globalstar Satellite Communications System, a series of geosynchronous satellites orbiting the earth.

Now the lab.

Zammit intended to perform several tests. He wanted to determine the morphology of the organic material through visual examination under the microscope as well as conduct some basic DNA sequencing. Then the molecular labs, disease dipsticks, and GC mass spectrometer would help him identify the toxin in the water. Or so he hoped.

He tore the plastic wrap off an empty specimen container and tucked it under his arm as he prepared the underwater sample retrieval device. He fitted a sterilized reinforced glass ampoule to the end of a syringe. After plugging it into the barrel of the gas handgun, he inserted a gas cartridge into the butt. It took only a few moments to program the gun to detect resistance so that the ampoule would come to rest in the water once it had penetrated the layer of green muck. He selected a container of distilled water, snapped the seal off the spout, and walked down the slope to the water's edge.

For a few moments he contemplated the foul green carpet that spread before him, gleaming under the bright sun as if it were coated with oil. Then he knelt and scooped a containerful of the green muck. It was slimy and dense, the color and consistency of thick green oil paint but heavier. He carefully sealed the container, rinsed it and his glove with distilled water to clean off the residual contamination, then laid it on the ground.

He aimed the gas handgun. Knowing the recoil was terrific, he used both hands to fire the projectile into the muck at an angle of thirty degrees. After a few seconds the wire securing the syringe to the gun was taut. He looked at the gauge and whistled softly. Twenty feet. What was this stuff? He thumbed the button to open the syringe and obtain a sample of the water underneath the green slime, then pushed the retrieve button. He watched as the wire respooled and brought the ampoule back to the surface. Holding it at arm's length, he rinsed it, then picked up the container of green muck and walked back up the rise to where he had left his gear.

From the microlab he removed the equipment he needed for the moment. Reaching into a coverall pocket, he took out what looked like a slab of metal. He unfolded it and laid it over the microlab. He'd figured that when working in a desert, it would be wise to place an aluminum sheet over the equipment to reflect sunlight so it didn't overheat and incapacitate the miniature systems in the lab, perhaps by melting the plastic film on the disease dipsticks. Miniaturization was always a tradeoff—small and fast was great, but the price was fragility and vulnerability.

Zammit knew he'd have to work quickly. He held up the container of slimy green organic material. "You first, you nasty bit of whatever-you-are."

He took a small amount and mixed it in another container with distilled water to obtain a dilute solution, then smeared some on a sterile slide. Using a clean glass pipette, he added purple dye to make the cells stand out from the gelatinous mucous sheath surrounding them and covered the slide with another thin glass sheet to prevent the sample from drying out. He examined the slide under the miniature microscope, then started keying information into the laptop.

Ten minutes later he stopped, frowning at the image on the screen. It matched the image under the microscope almost exactly. "Impossible." He stared out over the expanse of fetid green muck that stretched to the horizon. "But there it is."

He loaded some of the water sample into the receptor ends of the glass slides and silicon wafers that made up the miniature molecular labs. As the analysis proceeded, he took one of the disease dipsticks and immersed it in the water sample as well. Next he used a pipette to load a sample into the spectrometer. All three tests worked perfectly and he had the results in less than five minutes.

Zammit stood. He reached up, disengaged the oxygen unit, and pulled off his orange helmet. He lifted his face toward the scorching sky. He could feel the sun drying the moisture on his brow. The putrid flesh smell was so powerful he could taste it as well as smell it. He felt his gorge rise and swallowed. It might stink, but breathing it wouldn't kill you.

He felt a vibration and pulled the phone from its holster. "Stav?"

"Mike, the results just came in from the autopsy on the corporal. He had an aortic aneurysm, one of those silent congenital defects. The violent vomiting caused by the foul smell triggered a heart attack. I assume a healthy person can't die by inhalation."

"I figured that out already."

Zammit threw his helmet on the ground, thinking furiously. It was the only possible explanation, and based on his research it was certainly plausible. He spoke again into the phone. "Is Colonel Yildiz there? Good. Ask if the Turkish army has ever used organophosphate chemical weapons against the Kurds in this area. And inform him as nicely as possible that if he lies to me I'll shove his cigarettes up his ass."

He had to wait only a few moments. "No? Is he telling the truth?"

He sighed. "OK. If you think so, I trust your assessment. Don't say anything more. I've got an approximate structural identification and a toxin verification as well. Also, there are some odd compounds in the water. The probability of all this stuff being here naturally is about as great as finding a McDonald's on the moon. I'm going to transmit the data to Frankie in Seattle, then drive back. We have an ugly problem here, and I want to be sure about our results before we tell the Turks anything." He ended the transmission.

He unplugged the laptop from the microlab and stood the case up on one end to minimize contact with the hot soil. Draping the aluminum sheet over it, he put the satellite phone on top of the case, punched a button to dial, then hit the speaker function and wearily sat down on the ground.

"Mike?"

"Frankie, I hope you're alert as well as awake. I've got a poison ID. The concentration is incredibly high and climbing. It's an endotoxin, an alkaloid with a chemical signature similar to cocaine."

"Anything more?"

"Not about the toxin. The detailed analysis is up to you. But that's not the weird part. I remembered something that happened to me years ago when I was fighting forest fires in Canada. I jumped into a lake filled with blue-green algae. Using that experience, I was able to do a very directed investigation. The organic material that generates the Ataturk contamination is a massive bloom of cyanobacteria. Appears to be stromatolites, believe it or not. Ring a bell?"

"Yes," said Frankie. "Wait a sec, I'm doing a search. Here it is. Until 30 years ago cyanobacteria were called blue-green algae. It's one of the most ancient life forms on the planet, originating more than 3 billion years ago. The name change was the result of the discovery that it isn't really algae at all but a weird intermediate life form, one of the earliest rungs on the evolutionary ladder. A type of bacteria that, like a plant, uses photosynthesis to thrive."

"As I recall, there are several species. Cyanobacteria can survive anywhere, from the tropics to the Antarctic. But I've never heard of anything that kills on this scale."

Frankie Richards continued. "Ordinary pond or lake scum is often cyanobacteria. It's relatively harmless, if unsightly and smelly. But you say they're stromatolites? They're the most ancient of all cyanobacteria, found in very few places. Billions of years ago, stromatolites slowly began filling the young Earth's atmosphere with oxygen. Without stromatolites and the oxygen they produced, the Earth would be barren of all oxygen-based life forms. But some species produce nasty toxins."

"So," said Zammit, "they gave life, and they can take it away. But what's the stuff we're dealing with here? I can't do a lot of DNA sequencing with this equipment, but I did a little. A lot of the base pairs don't line up at all with any known species of cyanobacteria. This thing is really strange."

"May I suggest a next step?" Lots of static.

"Frankie, this transmission is breaking up. Make it quick."

"Transmit your data to me, so I can determine what kind of cyanobacteria it is and the toxin it generates. But we also have to figure out how to kill it."

"I agree," said Zammit. "And although we've got an ID, we still need an MO—how the hell did it get here? Incidentally, I've figured out part of that e-mail message. . . ."

Suddenly Zammit noticed movement out of the corner of his eye. The drape of the aluminum sheet reflected distorted images like a funhouse mirror, and the shapes moving up behind him didn't look like anything he wanted to see.

Without turning around, he said, "Got trouble. Transmitting now."

"Mike, what's wrong? Are you OK?"

He quickly plugged the laptop into the satellite phone. He typed fast, trying to keep one eye on the monstrous shapes approaching him. They halted briefly, and he heard a word barked in a language he didn't understand. Pretending not to hear, he typed commands as fast as he could. He forced himself to concentrate on what he was doing, forced himself not to look at the looming danger.

Another barked order as a giant shadow suddenly darkened over him. He hit the transmit key just as something very hard hit the base of his skull. And then all was night.

It was still night when he awoke, only it was starry night. It took him several moments to realize that the stars were in his eyes.

The back of his head ached. He rolled over onto his side, suddenly stopped by a wave of nausea. In front of him he could dimly see the orange sleeve of his right arm. He managed to raise himself on one elbow and looked groggily around.

He seemed to be buried alive.

The chamber in which he lay was the size of a suburban bedroom but made entirely of some strange white rock that glowed eerily. A lantern on the floor cast a dim light. A shadowy silhouette in the doorway called someone, his voice echoing hollowly. Zammit closed his eyes and lay back again.

He was roused by a blinding light. He tried to shield his eyes from the flashlight's beam. As it dimmed he became aware of several people around him. A woman knelt at his side. Her jaw was square and set. Short ebony hair framed unfriendly pale gray eyes. She was about thirty years old, with a badly broken nose and a long scar on her left cheek. She was pointing a .45 automatic at his groin. She said something guttural in a voice of command.

Zammit replied, "Think of me as a dog. I only follow orders I can understand given by someone I know."

The pale gray eyes appraised him. "You speak English. You are not a Turk?"

"No. American."

"Lucky for you. If you were a Turk we'd kill you." She jabbed his leg with the gun. "Where does that filth in the reservoir come from? Did you put it there?"

"I don't know where it comes from, and I didn't put it there."

"Did the Turks put it there?"

"No."

She gestured at the microlab and the communications suitcase, half-hidden in a gloomy corner. "What are those?"

Zammit didn't like her attitude. "I'm a traveling salesman. I must say the markets here suck."

She swatted him across the face with the pistol barrel. When he could raise his head again, she was across the room, removing her quilted jacket. After tossing it in a corner she strode back toward him. She was heavily muscled for a woman, the kind of long lean muscles that mean hours of training and that spell power. She wore heavy black combat boots, a sleeveless green tank top, and khaki combat pants. Her arms, on the inside elbows, were heavily scarred with crazed slashes everywhere. As if she had tried to commit suicide with a razor and wanted to die so badly she couldn't wait.

"Failed your correspondence course in home surgery, I see."

She lifted the pistol again and he braced himself. Nothing. He opened his eyes. She was looking at him intently. The others in the room were all men. Two wore camouflage, the others the flowing trousers, bomber jackets, wide sashes, and coiled turbans he recognized as traditional Kurdish dress. The two men pointing AK-47 Kalashnikovs at him had wild, romantic countenances, with hooked noses, great shocks of long black hair, and dark, intense eyes.

The effort of holding his head up to talk to her was making him giddy. "A pirate movie. Where's Errol Flynn?"

"Shut up."

"Mind if I get up?" She pointed the .45 at his forehead. "Whatever you say."

"What is your name?"

"Michael Zammit."

"What is your profession?"

"Environmental investigator." She nodded thoughtfully.

"And your name?"

"You may call me Sultana."

"And your profession?"

"Freedom fighter." Her gray eyes were as cold as dirty ice.

"You're a Kurd?"

She nodded. "I am a member of the Kurdish Workers' Party."

Zammit gingerly touched his face. The skin wasn't broken. "The PKK. You're one of the Kurdish guerrilla groups keeping half the Turkish army tied down." He looked around the ancient stone room. "I like your ultramodern headquarters. Got a fax machine I can use?"

"Your sense of humor is very tiresome," said Sultana.

"And your English is very good."

"I was educated in the United States. I came back here as a

teacher to help my people by working in the more remote villages. I realized it wasn't enough to do good works. Then I ran into . . . some troubles. It made me hard, and I joined the PKK."

Zammit glanced again at the broken nose, the facial scar, the slashed arms. "I'm sorry about your troubles."

She stared at him for a moment, then started pacing. "I recognize your name from when I was in America. Beluga whales in the St. Lawrence Seaway, their carcasses so filled with industrial chemicals they had to be classified as toxic waste."

"You have quite a memory."

"What are you doing here?"

"There's poison in the reservoir, generated by the green slime. It's killing people downstream. The Syrians and Iraqis are angry. The Turks asked me to investigate."

"Most of those killed downstream are my people." Her gray eyes smoked like banked fires. "The Turks can try to find us. We will cut their balls off."

"Have the Turks used chemical weapons against your people?"

"No. The Iraqis have, several hundred miles away, but not the Turks. Why?"

"There are high concentrations of organophosphates in the reservoir water, as well as poison. If there was intensive agriculture in this area and lots of pesticides being used, that might account for it. Or if the Turks were using chemical weapons, it's just possible it could be a natural phenomenon. Otherwise, such material just can't be there."

"Unless someone put it there," said Sultana.

"Unless someone put it there," agreed Zammit.

She knelt beside him. "What if I told you the Iraqis did it?"

He gazed up into her battered face. "Look, do you mind if I get up?"

She held out her hand. He grasped it, and with surprising strength she heaved him to his feet. He felt the blood drain from his face and swayed dizzily. Three of the men braced the muzzles of their rifles against his body.

"It's OK, guys. I promise not to fall down."

Sultana said something and they backed away. Zammit turned to face her. "Everyone knows the Iraqis have chemical weapons. They're not shy about using them. But why would they poison their own water supply? And how would they get the stuff into the reservoir? I understand this part of the country is sealed up so tight a Kurd can't walk out of his tent at night to take a leak without the Turks knowing about it."

She crossed her muscled arms across her chest. "How they would plant it in the reservoir, I don't know. And if the Turks have this area sealed up so tight, how are we able to keep fighting, and abduct you from right under their noses in broad daylight?"

"I concede the point," admitted Zammit.

"Everyone knows Anwar Hussein hates the Turks. And since when has the welfare of his own people ever kept him awake at night?"

"Once again, good point. But does he strike you as an e-mail kind of guy?"

As she stared, Zammit said, "Never mind."

"We know it's the Iraqis," she continued. "They were moving troops and armor to the border even before people started dying downstream. They tell UN monitors it's to combat us, but it's a lie. They *knew* the water was going to be poisoned. We shot down one of their aircraft right on the border. One of the passengers was a top general. We interrogated him. He didn't tell us much before he died, but he confirmed what our spies already told us. Something big is being prepared."

"He can't possibly be thinking of invading. Half the Turkish army is here. It'd be no contest. And it still doesn't answer the question why Anwar would poison his own water supply."

"There's something else," said Sultana. "Several weeks ago we were approached by representatives of the Resistance Army of Allah. They asked if we wish to participate in the liberation of Turkey from the corruption of Westernism. They seem to think the government will be overthrown soon."

"Aren't they behind the riots against Prime Minister Amurkhan?"

Sultana nodded. "Fundamentalists. They specialize in bombings, mostly in Istanbul and Ankara. They also assassinate Turkish diplomats abroad. What were they doing here, where they've never operated before?"

"What did you tell them?"

"Not interested. We're political fighters for Kurdistan, not religious zealots. It is a known fact that Anwar has been cultivating them for his own purposes, whatever they may be."

Zammit shook his head. "It still doesn't make sense."

"There's more. Other people have been observed in the area. I don't know who they are. They ignore us, so we ignore them. They are heavily armed, stealing antiquities."

"Antiquities? Where?"

Sultana gestured at the cool dim stone room. "Places like this. The whole area is filled with ancient cities and temples, most never excavated. This was once the richest part of the world, and treasures are buried everywhere. The geology is mainly limestone, so there are miles of caverns and tunnels. But this is the only underground temple we have found."

"Underground?"

"Yes. I believe it was a Hittite temple, probably to the moon goddess, Sin, carved out of the rock thousands of years ago. It is well hidden and close to the dam, so we use it as a staging area. We found it by accident and haven't even explored the full extent of it. It goes on for miles. There is a huge treasure here. We're not sure what to do with it."

"What kind of treasure?"

"Statues in gold, silver, electrum, and bronze. Big blocks of coins. In temple complexes worshipers used to throw coins and other precious objects into the fountains that always played around the statues. After centuries they fuse together. It's an amazing sight."

A Kurd came into the room and whispered something to Sultana, who said to Zammit, "The Turks are looking for you. Helicopters and armored cars everywhere. We must warn our comrades of this intensified activity."

"Since you know I'm a good guy, I take it I'm free to leave?"

"No. Perhaps you are not who you say you are. Perhaps you are in league with the Turks. Perhaps you were awake when you came here and remember the location."

"Out cold."

Sultana spoke briefly with the men. She was obviously the leader of the group. "You'll stay here for the time being. I must check with our regional commander."

Zammit thought quickly, wondering if the data he'd transmitted to Frankie Richards had arrived at INERT headquarters. "Look, there's a political and environmental catastrophe happening out there. I may be the only person on earth who knows what's in the reservoir."

"Later. Anything that causes discomfort for the Turks is good for us." She gave an order to her men. "We will take you across the hall and restrain you. Ordinarily we would post a guard, but we have a skeleton crew, and everyone will be needed."

A Kurd started to say something and she snapped at him. "Despite what he thinks, you can't possibly escape. This corridor is a dead end with only one way out, and that's through us, at the end of the hall. And after all, you're just a scientist, aren't you? Even if you free yourself, we are deep underground. This labyrinth was designed to kill intruders. Without us as guides, you could never find your way out. You'd get lost, and a thousand years from now someone would find your skeleton." She smiled thinly. "And wonder why the ancients wore orange polyester."

"Look—"

She gave an order, and three of the men seized his arms and dragged him to the room across the corridor. He just had time to glance quickly right and left. To the right was a rough-hewn corridor, a narrow hallway the shape of a very long keyhole. There were lights at the end, where the PKK guerrillas were staying. To his left the corridor ended a few feet away in solid rock.

Across the corridor there was an even smaller room made of the same glowing white stone, where he was thrown to the floor, hands bound behind his back and ankles tied together.

"I'm not a rodeo calf," grunted Zammit. "Not so tight. You think I'm Houdini?"

As they trooped out of the room, Sultana raised a muscular arm in mocking salute. "Save the whales."

Zammit could hear them talking as they headed down the corridor. The only illumination was from the lights at the end of the hall almost fifty yards away and the strange soft glow from the white rock walls. They'd taken his phone, but underground it wouldn't work anyway. He fanned through his options and decided.

He rolled onto his side, arched his spine, and bent his knees so his bound hands touched his feet. They had obviously searched him while he was unconscious, but how thorough had they been? There were a lot of pockets in the protective suit, including two small ones around his ankles. His straining fingers grasped the edge of the Velcro flap on his left ankle and tugged. A faint rip.

The tiny pocket opened. He rolled as much onto his back as he could, lifted his bound legs in the air and shook them. A tiny tinkle on the stone floor told him the body search had not been thorough enough.

Suddenly a weird yellow glow appeared on the wall of the room across the corridor. The glow moved along the wall and disappeared. Must be a PKK patrol with a flashlight. He realized the underground complex was like a buried building with rooms and corridors. But how could light be seen through a rock wall?

He scraped along the floor, squinting, trying to see the flat two-inch-long half-moon of orange plastic. He fumbled blindly with rapidly numbing fingers until he finally grasped it, then felt along the small object until he found the tiny black plastic slide on the side of the orange casing. He pressed the slide with his thumb.

The half-inch-long rectangular razor contained in the little OLFA Touch-Knife was incredibly sharp. He always carried one around for cutting pages from magazines or sectioning specimens. Or cutting ropes in underground prisons. He sawed the tiny blade back and forth against the rope. It parted in less than a minute. He shook his hands free and sawed at the rope binding his ankles.

Then he stood, rubbing his wrists and ankles to restore circulation. Slipping to the doorway, he looked carefully down the corridor. Empty. He'd have to work fast. If they did regular patrols, it was certain they would check on him.

He unzipped the orange suit and laid it on the floor. In his black garments he was now virtually invisible in the shadowy gloom.

He peered around the corner again and quickly ducked back. One of the Kurds in traditional dress, carrying a Kalashnikov and a flashlight, had turned the corner from the main room and was heading his way.

As the guerrilla entered the room, Zammit snatched the flashlight from his hand and cracked it over his head. He had not foreseen the cushioning effect of the turban and had to hit him again. He laid the unconscious Kurd on the floor and checked the rifle's magazine. How much noise had he made? Everything was still.

He darted across the corridor to the other room. A soft snick as he opened the latches of the microlab. He flipped the switch that activated the interior light. A quick search and he found what he wanted. As he slipped back across the corridor he saw the Kurd's right leg slowly scraping across the floor. Damn. The guy's skull must be two inches thick. He didn't want to hit him again. Zammit seized one of the sleeves of the orange uniform and hacked off a scrap of cloth with the razor. He popped open the plastic container, poured some liquid onto the cloth, knelt, and pressed it over the Kurd's nose and mouth. He wasn't sure how long he could apply the poisonous liquid without inducing cardiac arrest and wished he had chloroform instead of formaldehyde. After fifteen seconds the man's body went rigid, then relaxed. Zammit checked his pulse. Still alive.

He slipped the container and cloth into his pocket, dragged the Kurd over to the orange uniform, and began undressing him. Within two minutes the Kurd was zippered into the orange suit, bound, and gagged, and Zammit wore the guerrilla's clothes. They were tight—he still had his black garments on underneath, and the Kurd was smaller than he was. He hoped he'd coiled the turban in a plausible manner.

He looked down at the flowing trousers. *Très chic*. He patted a bulge in the tight bomber jacket and opened the pocket. Cigarettes and a lighter. As he picked up the Kalashnikov, he heard faint voices at the end of the corridor.

As Sultana rounded the far corner, Mike Zammit slouched casually against the stone door frame, knees slightly bent to reduce his height, lighting a cigarette. He shone the flashlight down the hall so she was momentarily blinded. Lowering it, he allowed three seconds to let her eyes partially readjust to the dimness, then hefted the gun on his shoulder and exhaled slowly, wreathing himself in a cloud of smoke to obscure his appearance. He gave a small wave—having no idea whether Kurdish body language was expansive or repressed, he figured less was best. She stopped and called something softly. He nodded, desperately hoping the ruse would work so he wouldn't have to shoot her.

She turned and walked back up the corridor. Zammit blew a plume of smoke in relief, then crushed out the cigarette. He checked the Kurd. Still out, breathing shallowly. He slipped across the corridor and propped the rifle in the corner. He turned the flashlight off so that no one from the end of the hall would see the beam moving around and wonder what was going on. His heart sank as he opened the communications suitcase. All the phone equipment was missing, even the antennas, high-capacity batteries, and his pager. The compass and laptop were gone. The computer didn't matter because the database information would be destroyed the instant anyone tried to hack it. He just hoped the information had gotten to Frankie Richards.

No satellite phone. No means of communication at all.

For the first time, he was thankful he'd brought too much gear. He fetched the flashlight again, but now it didn't work—he must have damaged it when he whacked the Kurd. He rummaged through the case and finally found the secret tab that allowed him to lift the panel separating the bottom compartment from the top. He smiled—they hadn't found it. He slipped the MPR SATFIND personal locator beacon into his Kurdish sash and wrapped the Generation IV ITT Night Mariner goggles around his neck. He remembered what Sultana had said and tucked the miniature metal detector into the sash.

He had to move fast, and he didn't want to move against a hail of bullets.

He walked over to the rock wall, where he'd seen the glow of the flashlight through the stone, and placed his hands on it. The rock was pure white, finely grained, and strangely translucent. He scratched it with his fingernail and it left a cloudy white mark. He closed his eyes and tried to recall his college courses in geology. Finally it came to him. A form of gypsum, a hydrous calcium sulfate formed by the drying of bedded deposits precipitated from evaporating ancient seas.

Alabaster.

His eyes searched the white stone room. No wonder the Hittites had decided to carve their underground temple here. A giant deposit of alabaster was about as easy a stone to work as you could find. For thousands of years used mainly for statuary, it was soft and easily broken. A sheet of alabaster could be carved so thin you could read a newspaper through it.

With all his weight Zammit pressed hard against the wall. It was thin enough to see a strong light through but too thick to be broken by muscle power alone. He thought for a moment, then returned to the microlab. He removed two suction cups, a glass container, a plastic container, and an atomizer. From the microtome next to the microscope he carefully removed the supersharp steel blade used for sectioning specimens.

Back at the wall, a quick inspection told him it was carved in a concave fashion, thinnest in the middle and thickening toward the edges. He adjusted the nozzle of the atomizer to deliver a thin sharp stream. Carefully he removed the cap from the glass container and poured the contents into the atomizer. He uncoiled part of the turban from his head, pressed it over his mouth and nose, and held the atomizer at arm's length, the nozzle four inches from the middle of the alabaster wall.

He sprayed quickly, a three-by-four-foot rectangle. Acrid white vapor hissed on the wall as the hydrofluoric acid ate through the soft calcareous stone. He waited a few moments, then sprayed the rapidly deepening furrows with distilled water to dilute the acid. When the vapor dissipated, he seized the microtome knife and started hacking at the etched furrows. He was surprised at how little time it took.

He picked up the two suction cups and pressed them against the stone section framed by the acid furrows. Once they were secure he finished cutting through most of the stone, leaving just four thin connecting pieces on each side to hold the cut-out section in place. Firmly grasping the handles of the suction cups, he heaved against the stone. There was a crunching sound and a few rock splinters pattered on the floor. He lifted the heavy slab of alabaster and leaned it against the wall.

Nothing like seizing a window of opportunity.

He leaned out of the newly created exit into the corridor. No one. He quickly replaced everything in the microlab and heaved it through the window. He'd taken everything useful from the communications suitcase, but the lab was his baby and he wasn't going to leave it behind. He contemplated taking the rifle. Too much to carry. Besides, with a head start he wouldn't need it.

He carefully wiped the bottom frame of the window to remove any residual acid and swung his legs over. He pulled the Night Mariner goggles over his eyes and adjusted the gain control on the image intensifier. The unit had a tiny infrared light source, invisible to the human eye but within the range suitable for light amplification of the image intensifier. The goggles magnified available light 500,000 times.

"Just a scientist," he whispered as he grabbed the microlab and headed down the glowing stone corridor.

Frankie Richards stared at the screen. Her lab door was closed and locked. Cat was with Kitson Kang, and she'd ordered Dikka to put all the robots to sleep. Solitude and silence. Concentrate.

She thought, God, I wish I had samples. Zammit's data from the Ataturk reservoir was workable, but PCR would be so much faster. She typed an equation. The elusiveness was maddening, like a Rubik's cube—everything neatly aligned except for one annoying little section. Why can't I find it? Please line up. But the DNA base pairs did not line up. She pulled all the information she had on cyanobacteria, then compared it with Zammit's data. Nothing made sense.

She walked to the greenhouse, opened the door, closed it, breathed the humidity and the scent. It always relaxed her, allowed her thoughts to free-associate.

The transmission from Zammit had ended so abruptly. What happened? He said he had trouble. The shouts, that awful crunching sound, then silence and static. She put her hands over her face. No time to think about that. The thought of Adam's disappearance intruded on her thoughts like a nightmare.

Concentrate. She gazed at her bizzare collection of plants. She thought of Cat and the ruin of her recent experiment because of Catula. Natural versus artificial creation.

She had it.

She left the greenhouse, returned to the computer, checked the data again. It was the only answer.

She got on the intercom. "Has Cairo left for Turkey yet?" When Zammit had disappeared in midtransmission, the big guy had insisted on going to help with the search. "No? Good. I have to talk with him."

She waited a few moments until he came on the line. "Cairo, come to my lab. I've figured something out. We have a problem. A big, big problem."

 It seemed to Zammit that he'd been walking for hours.

They'd taken his chronometer. He didn't know how long he'd been unconscious, the date, or the time. The microlab was heavy, and the Night Mariner goggles gave him a crashing headache.

He activated the MPR SATFIND personal locator beacon, but since the Turkish army didn't arrive, he concluded that it didn't work below ground. He turned it off to conserve the batteries. He looked at the metal detector. When Sultana had described the underground temple as a labyrinth designed to kill intruders, she had not exaggerated.

The complex was built in layers, like an anthill. There were winding stone staircases that led up or down to other corridors. Corridors branched off into other hallways that turned out to be dead ends. Although the corridors were narrow, they were high. And extremely dangerous. As he crept along in the crepuscular gloom, there'd suddenly be a hole in the floor big enough for a man to fall through. There was no predictable pattern to their location. Given the height of the corridors, a fall onto the hard stone floor of the corridor below would be enough to break your leg or spine.

It was like walking through an enormous booby trap. Zammit had a good idea who the booby was.

The place was stifling. But occasionally there would be a strong blast of sweet fresh air from some hidden access to the outside world. The blasts of air must be for ventilation, probably narrow pipes to the surface. The gusts always occurred just before or after one of the holes in the floor. He felt queasy as he realized how devilishly clever it was.

When the complex had been built thousands of years before, the only light available to someone walking through the darkness in either direction would have been a flaming torch made of rushes and bitumen. If that someone was an unwelcome intruder who did not know the plan of the complex and the placement of the vents and holes, the blasts of air would unexpectedly extinguish his torch. Trapped in impenetrable blackness, the intruder would then fall through the floor, and there he would lie with broken bones until he died of shock or thirst.

The only saving grace, apart from the Night Mariner goggles, was the metal detector. Sultana had said there was an enormous mass of treasure somewhere in this complex, and he knew he was heading toward it. Unfortunately, he couldn't head for it as the crow flies but had to follow the looping hallways. All he could rely on was his knowledge of how temples had been built on Malta. His great grandfather Sir Themistocles Zammit had discovered that all ancient temple complexes had the god or goddess shrine at the center, with pathways leading from there to the outside world. If he could find the center, he could find a way out. Presumably there were multiple entrances and exits, and that would make it easier.

Suddenly he heard an echo, the sound of booted feet above his head, then voices. He looked up and saw one of the deadly corridor holes right above his head and the crazy flitting beams of flashlights being swung around.

Somehow they were on his trail. And very close.

He adjusted the image intensifier and peered at the end of the corridor. A winding staircase. Someone was coming down it. The light from their flashlight was blinding. He tore off the goggles and ducked into a side corridor. He blinked to get the stars out of his eyes. He should've brought the Kalashnikov.

The booted steps sounded along the stone floor to where he was hidden. It was obvious the person was shining the torch down every intersection. Before he could be blinded again Zammit sprang around the corner.

It was Sultana.

He knocked the pistol from her hand and grabbed her. She dropped the flashlight, and he heard a tinkle as the lens shattered and it rolled to the edge of the corridor. He spun her around, pressing his chest against her back, his arms locked around her, grasping her wrists. He was confident his strength would hold her tight.

He was wrong.

At the touch of his body she twisted like an elemental force of nature. He knew she was strong, but this was incredible. A right elbow slammed into his belly, followed by a left that almost dislocated his shoulder. When he grunted with pain it seemed to madden her even more.

The flashlight's beam threw their monstrous black shadows on the wall as he tried to parry a series of backward blows while hanging on to her. Her hands tore at his clothing as she suddenly shifted her weight. Just as her heavy boot kicked up, aiming for his groin, he threw his entire weight up and forward. Strong though she was, she pitched slowly forward and collapsed to the floor. Zammit slipped his arms under hers so she was helpless in a full nelson. She wept as she struggled.

"I don't want to hurt you," he whispered. "I'm just trying to get out of here."

She thrashed and kicked. Low moaning noises told him she was not susceptible to logic and still extremely dangerous. He slipped his right arm from underneath hers and wrapped it around her neck so that the V formed by his biceps and forearm pressed against both the arteries that fed blood to her brain. Choke hold.

As she struggled Zammit hissed, "Listen to me! I'm going to render you unconscious. Nothing more. You understand? Nothing more!"

Finally she was still. He rolled off, panting, and turned her on her back. No sound from the corridor above. By the light of her damaged flashlight he leaned over and gazed at her battered face, the scarred flesh inside her elbows. Softly he said, "I hope whoever the bastard was, you find him someday. And make him pay."

He took off his turban, tore it into strips, and bound her. He considered a gag but didn't know how well she could breathe through her broken nose. From underneath his Kurdish clothes he took the strip of orange cloth and the formaldehyde and administered a fifteen-second dose. He left the flashlight on and by her side so the other Kurds could find her. He put on the goggles, looked at the metal detector, and slipped away.

It might take them two minutes to find her or two hours. Got to hurry. He shifted the microlab from one aching arm to the other. With alarm he noticed that his sense of balance and distance was deteriorating from exhaustion and the mounting confusion in his brain, unused to analyzing glowing green artificially enhanced images for hours on end.

He still tried to hurry. He looked at the metal detector just as he rounded a sharp corner.

And then he was falling. He managed to heave the microlab around and slam it on the floor as he fell through the hole. The lab was heavy enough to act as a counterweight, and he hung

suspended, his rib cage jammed against the hole's stone lip. Blearily he looked straight ahead and saw the lab caught behind a bump
on the floor. The protrusion barely held the lab—and him—in
place. Zammit gritted his teeth as he saw the handle slowly turn,
saw the end of the lab start to rise off the floor. Once it got high
enough, it would slide over the protrusion and he would fall. He
kicked and lunged forward. The lab dropped. He looked down to
the corridor beneath him. A fall of at least twenty feet. He would
fall backward, landing on the stone floor as a V, shattering his
pelvis, or flat on his back, an X, crushing the base of his skull.

What a stupid way to die.

He scrabbled desperately. Once again the base of the case started
to rise from the floor. With a convulsive effort he managed to get
his left leg over the edge of the rim. He thrust powerfully against
the stone floor and out of the hole, just as the lab slipped over the
protrusion. He rolled over onto his back, pulled off the goggles,
and laid them on his heaving chest. Dancing green auroras spun
through his retinas.

Blackness.

When he awoke, he didn't know how long he'd been unconscious
or where he was. The sensation of being stifled reminded him. He
still clutched the goggles to his chest. They were important, he
thought vaguely. Slowly he put them on again, his arms leaden.
There'd been a hole in the floor. He felt for the wall and painfully
rose. He picked up the microlab and metal detector and stumbled
down the corridor, slowly this time, his hand scraping against the
wall to help him stay on his feet.

Twenty minutes later the corridor suddenly widened into a
yawning space of rough-hewn yellow stone. A vault rose into the
gloom, like some primeval cathedral, with crude oblong niches
hacked in the rock.

Zammit started as he saw two eyes staring at him from a face
of timeless beauty. It took a few moments to realize that it was a
statue, a naked woman, her weight resting gracefully on her left
hip as she gazed sightlessly at him. He walked closer to the bronze
figure and noticed that the whites of the eyes were of alabaster,
the irises made of emerald or jade. Classical Greek or Roman.

There were other statues in the room. Blocks of fused coins littered the floor. The room had obviously been used as a repository for antiquities gathered from a variety of places, perhaps by some long-dead treasure hunter who never survived to haul away his loot.

While looking around he noticed that the walls were no longer as white. They were yellowish and lacked the smoothness and finish of alabaster. The Hittites had found this stone more difficult to work.

A large square niche at the far end of the room was identical to the one in the Hypogeum on Malta. The priestly oracle would have spoken from it during religious ceremonies, and the acoustical properties of the circular temple would have served to echo his voice. Zammit wondered if the niche had the same acoustical properties as the one on Malta.

All around the circular vaulted room, doorways framed with pillars and lintels had been carved out of the living rock. He was at the center of the complex, and the pathways would lead to the outside world. But which ones?

He stood in the door frame of one of the exits and thought. He didn't want to get lost again. He opened the microlab, removing the fluorescent red felt-tipped marker he used to identify glass slides in the field. With the OLFA razor he trimmed the nib to make it broader and flatter. He drew an arrow on the yellow stone above his head. The red mark was easily visible if you knew where to look.

Pen in one hand, microlab in the other, Zammit headed down the stone corridor. Every few feet he reached up and made an arrow mark, always on the wall to his right. If this exit from the temple led further underground or ended abruptly, he'd be able to find his way back and start over.

There was no sound except his labored breathing and the scraping of his feet. Several times he almost plunged through holes in the floor. They were ingeniously carved so that you couldn't see them until you were almost on top of them.

Suddenly he inhaled a lungful of sweet fresh air. He paused and breathed deeply. The corridor began slanting steeply upward. Keeping a keen eye on the floor, he walked faster. Ahead, a dim light illuminated a set of carved stone stairs. They divided at the top, with a broad set of steps angling around to the right and out of sight, while the other set was narrow, crudely carved, and twisted away to the left, appearing to vanish into nothingness.

The smell of fresh air was almost intoxicating. He quickly

mounted the stairs. Where they divided he chose the broad set of steps that wound to the right. Just as he was about to bound around the sharp corner, he stopped in midstride. He stared at the steps curving out of his sight, then looked back over his shoulder at the narrow, uneven, uninviting ones that angled sharply to the left and seemed to disappear into darkness.

He'd seen this before. Just like the oracle niche, in the Hypogeum.

Returning to the bottom, he set the microlab at the base of the stairs. Slowly he walked back up the broad steps that spiraled to the right. Where they rounded the corner, he stopped and peered carefully around the rock wall.

Into nothingness. There was a sheer drop into a narrow, smooth-walled rock chamber. He couldn't see the bottom. It looked like the opening of a very deep coffin.

Which was exactly what it was.

Next he cautiously mounted the narrow, dangerous steps that spiraled to the left. They rose higher and higher and wound around the central pillar of living rock until they connected with another broad flight of inviting steps leading downward to his left.

Suddenly he realized how ingenious it was. If a thief found this entrance to the underground temple, the prospect of riches would ensure that he was hurrying. If he was descending, he would take the broad inviting set of stairs that wound down to the right. And fall straight into the stone crypt, from which it would be impossible to escape. If the intruder had somehow made it into the temple through another entrance and was trying to exit through this one, he would also take the broad set of steps, falling into the trap.

Zammit felt an icy finger slowly trace a trail down his spine at the sheer ingenuity of it. Anyone would choose the broad, well-carved steps. And it was a nice touch to have them winding to the right—most people were right-handed, and if the inviting nature of the stairs didn't ensure that they were chosen, the victim's natural handedness would.

Zammit picked up a rock. As he leaned over the entrance to the narrow crypt, he noticed a thick stone lid propped against the wall. Of course. You wouldn't want the stink from an intruder's decaying corpse to pollute the air.

He dropped the rock into the crypt. Silence for a couple of seconds. Then, instead of the sound of stone against stone, a rustling thud, the sound of stone hitting a carpet of bones and clothing.

How many bodies had the crypt claimed in the past four thousand years?

Seizing the microlab, he edged his way around the left-hand staircase, feeling stone underfoot at every step. Finally he reached the top. He edged around a stone slab and walked into the desert air, the coolness wonderful against his clammy skin. He took off the goggles and looked up at the full moon and the star-studded night sky. The brown, boulder-littered landscape was featureless, inhabited only by knife-edged black shadows. No tire tracks or footprints to indicate that this entrance to the temple had been recently used. If the PKK hadn't explored the entire complex, they might not know this entrance existed. He turned around, seeing a pile of boulders and stone slabs and nothing to show they were anything other than a natural formation.

Zammit gazed at the metal detector in his hand. There was one final service it could render. He trudged back to the rock formation and jammed it into a crevice. With the right equipment, even a dying signal from the device would enable him to locate it again.

He had no idea where he was. He was desperately thirsty, hungry, and exhausted, but he had to keep moving in case of pursuit. He started walking but after 200 yards couldn't continue. Staggering down a slope into a depression in the ground, he stiffly sat down. He ran his tongue over his cracked lips as he opened the microlab, removed a container of distilled water, snapped off the spout, and drank deeply until it was empty. He opened another, his last, still feeling weak. He'd sweated away a lot of salt and minerals, and in distilled water there weren't any. A painful growl from his stomach told him that even more than replenishing his body's supply of electrolytes, he needed some calories to give him energy. But there was nothing to eat.

He opened the bottle of pure ethanol he carried in the microlab to sterilize equipment. Alcohol had calories. He drank most of the second container of distilled water, poured in some ethanol, and shook it like a cocktail shaker. He sipped like a connoisseur. It wasn't bourbon, but it wasn't kerosene, either. He'd sampled Russian moonshine, *samogon*, that tasted a lot worse than this. He held up the container and proposed a toast to the fat moon, beaming as if it was glad he was free. "You're awfully good-looking, but I don't care much for your taste in architecture."

He drank deeply, laid the container on the ground, and within moments was fast asleep.

"There he is!" shouted Cairo Jackson. He pointed out the side door of the Turkish air force helicopter, a Boeing CH-47D Chinook especially designed for search and rescue missions.

Striding through the desolate landscape in the brilliant dawn light, the tiny figure far below looked incongruous in flowing trousers and a sash, carrying a large white plastic suitcase, like a tourist on Mars convinced there was a space port nearby.

Zammit had awakened with the dawn. Deciding to walk toward the sun rising in the east, he activated the MPR SATFIND personal locator beacon that the Turkish helicopter was now homing in on. When he saw the chopper, he stopped and waited as it descended, whipping up swirls of powdery dust.

Cairo Jackson leapt to the ground, followed by Stavros Costopoulos and Dikka Spargo. Jackson stood with his hands on his hips. "Sorry, I thought you were Mike Zammit, not Aladdin."

"I hate to break it to you, boss, but they finished filming Lawrence of Arabia some time ago," said Dikka.

"Fetching," said Costopoulos. "The latest from Armani?"

Jackson noticed the rips in Zammit's Kurdish clothing. "Get into an argument with a cougar?"

"Something like that," Zammit smiled. "And I'm glad to see you too."

Cairo leaned and sniffed. "Where the hell did you find a saloon in this wilderness?"

"Wandering the desert wastes like a biblical prophet is thirsty work. Couldn't find honey, but at least I didn't have to eat any locusts."

"Speaking of bees," said Costopoulos, "you were on a beeline away from the dam, headed straight toward Iraq. It's a good thing we found you before you hit the border and got your head shot off."

After piling into the helicopter, it was a thirty-minute flight back to the Ataturk Dam. The pilot radioed ahead with the news that Zammit had been found. Although it was too noisy to do much talking in the chopper, Zammit learned he'd been missing for almost forty-eight hours and that Cairo Jackson had left Seattle to help in the search when he had disappeared. Frankie Richards and Kitson Kang were still in Seattle analyzing the data he had sent. Jackson's eyes watched Zammit's as he leaned over and shouted, "Frankie said all she heard was you typing, someone yelling, and then a sound like a watermelon being clubbed with a baseball bat. She was beside herself!"

When they landed at the dam, Dikka Spargo headed off to help Connie Palaeov. Zammit told her to make sure they collected several of the fleshy bulbs growing so quickly on the surface of the green mat. As Cairo and Stavros accompanied him to the facility's infirmary, they were informed that Colonel Hakim Yildiz was on a conference call with Prime Minister Thamar Amurkhan. Once finished, he wanted to see Zammit as soon as possible.

The infirmary's physician determined that Zammit's head was not badly hurt and that apart from a few bruises he was fine. A medic applied a heat pad to loosen the muscles of his aching back. He showered, shaved, and changed his clothes, then wolfed down a couple of sandwiches as he quickly filled Cairo and Stavros in on what had happened.

"Underground," said Jackson. "No wonder it was like you vanished into the ether. All we found was the orange helmet and some tire tracks from the Jeep that petered out in the desert in the middle of nowhere."

"I'm glad you got the information I transmitted," Zammit said. "What has Frankie found?"

"She confirms the poison is an endotoxin. *Anabaena toxin*, to be precise. And the massive bloom of cyanobacteria that generates the toxin is in fact damn strange."

"Has she determined the species?"

"*Anabaena flos-aquae*. With a caveat."

Zammit shrugged. "Never heard of it. What's the caveat?"

Jackson flipped through a sheaf of printouts. "*Anabaena* is extremely poisonous. The toxin it generates attacks the liver. It grows primarily in stagnant water during hot weather, so this climate is perfect for it. The problem is that this particular strain is something new. In its natural form, it's just a stinky thin green film that secretes toxin. It does not form those dense thick carpets, which are called stromatolites, or the big fleshy bulbs growing on the surface."

"How can it be new?" objected Zammit. "This stuff has been around for almost 4 billion years and it hasn't evolved at all. It's the Methuselah of biological organisms."

"Frankie says it *appears* to be *anabaena*, but it also has some weird genetic bits—the mismatching DNA base pairs you mentioned, which might account for the stromatolites and the bulbs," replied Cairo. "It seems to be some sort of mutation, or perhaps a hybrid. In addition to attacking the liver and the gut, the toxin also depresses respiratory function. When the concentration in drinking water is over one milligram per kilo of body weight, you're dead in less than an hour. And there's enough *anabaena toxin* in that reservoir to kill every human being on earth."

"Mutation? After 4 billion years it's decided to mutate?"

"Apparently. Frankie says this particular strain pumps out industrial strength toxin at a fantastic rate and grows so fast you can actually see it multiplying with the naked eye."

"Still," protested Zammit, "bacteria of this type can be killed with algaecide."

"Afraid not. Frankie says the only thing that would work on this stuff is copper sulfate and you'd need a million tons of it. And too much copper is poisonous for drinking water and agriculture. You'd be exchanging one toxin for another."

"All right then. Antibiotics."

Cairo Jackson shook his head emphatically. "Not this stuff. *Nothing* kills it. When I arrived here with Dikka, we started working with Connie based on what Frankie had figured out. We've tried every treatment, including antibiotics. Penicillin, ampicillin, neomycin, vancomycin, even ciprofloxacin, you name it. This stuff is immune to every antidote known to science."

"That is impossible," said Zammit flatly.

Jackson shrugged. "Them's the facts. There are millions of cubic yards of the stuff. According to Frankie, even if we found an antidote that would kill the cyanobacteria—assuming we can do it, given that we have very little time—we'd need thousands of tons of it. How would we manufacture so much of it so fast? And the reservoir would still be full of toxin. How do we deal with that? We don't have an antidote for that either. We don't have one crisis, we have two—the green stuff and the poison."

Zammit rubbed his face. "Every living thing has to eat something. Cyanobacteria eat nitrogen and phosphorus. This stuff is growing so fantastically because of the high concentrations of organophosphates in the water."

"True. But Frankie says the stuff grows like gangbusters on very little nutrition. It's like finding a ten-foot-tall gorilla that can break concrete slabs in half but is happy and healthy on a diet of lettuce leaves."

"Where do the organophosphates come from?"

Jackson shook his head. "Not a clue. The only possible source would be huge quantities of agricultural fertilizer, and there's no agriculture here except at the Plain of Harran, and it's miles away."

Stavros Costopoulos interrupted. "Which of course is why your original computer simulations kept identifying this particular scenario as impossible. So if it can't be a naturally occurring phenomenon, that leaves us with theory number two, as we discussed on Malta."

Zammit remembered as well what Sultana had said. "Somebody put it there."

He said to Jackson, "Before I was kidnapped I started to tell Frankie that I'd figured out the e-mail message. Back in Seattle, you asked how you can threaten someone with primordial soup. Well, you can if it's a lethal bacterial soup from the dawn of time."

"I'm glad we're finally discussing something I can understand," said Costopoulos. "I don't know this bug stuff, but I do know psychology, and the psychology here is fascinating. Do you have any idea who might have sent you that message?"

"Yeah," said Jackson. "Have you pissed anybody off lately?"

"What do you mean, psychology?" asked Zammit.

Suddenly a Turkish soldier stuck his head in the door and said something. Costopoulos nodded as he listened. "Colonel Yildiz wants to see you. How much do you want to tell him?"

Zammit replied, "I'm not going to mention a couple of things. The cyanobacteria and organophosphates got in that water somehow, and it's possible someone here at the dam was involved. I doubt if it's Yildiz, but until we know for sure, I'd rather keep certain things quiet."

Zammit was pondering other considerations as well. He thought of Sultana and her battered face, her horribly scarred arms, the troubles she had mentioned. He knew the Turks weren't gentle with dissidents. Perhaps she'd been beaten up, imprisoned, and possibly raped by Turkish soldiers or security. He remembered her frantic struggles and didn't feel like giving any information that would allow the Turks to find her. And her reference to good works rang a strong bell in connection with his own reluctant membership in the Knights of Malta.

Crammed with filing cabinets and stacks of paper, Colonel Yildiz's windowless, stuffy office was painted a sickly institutional green and reeked of stale tobacco smoke. Zammit faced a barrage of questions. He told the chain-smoking Turk everything about his capture and escape except the fact that the place he'd been detained was an underground temple—he described it simply as a series of interconnected caverns. He also didn't mention that he'd planted the metal detector, and the theft of antiquities was irrelevant.

"You don't remember at all where you were held?" frowned Yildiz, plucking at one of his caterpillar-like eyebrows.

Zammit shrugged. "It was dark, and I didn't have a compass. The landscape is featureless. I got away as fast as I could in case they were on my trail."

"I'm in a great deal of trouble," said Yildiz, savagely stubbing out his cigarette in an already overflowing ashtray. "To have someone like you abducted from this facility in broad daylight is bad enough. Not to be able to find you for almost forty-eight hours is worse. And not being able to punish the PKK is the worst of all. The prime minister is furious, and Lloyd Lavender and your Colonel Graves have been making my life a misery."

"I'm sorry to hear that, colonel. It wasn't your fault—I'm the one who refused an escort when I went out to get the samples. Maybe it'll help when you tell them we've identified what's in the reservoir."

He briefed Yildiz on what they had discovered about the toxin, and their suspicions that the cyanobacteria had been deliberately planted. Hakim Yildiz became more and more agitated as Zammit spoke. When Zammit told him what Sultana had said, he suddenly slammed his fist on the table, stood, and started pacing furiously.

"You are sure it isn't the PKK guerrillas who put the material in the reservoir? Or the Resistance Army of Allah?"

"Positive," said Zammit. "Where would they get it from? They have no facilities for breeding this kind of biological warfare agent."

Yildiz suddenly stopped pacing. "Warfare agent?"

Zammit nodded. "You have the dubious honor, colonel, of witnessing history's first use of a genetically modified organism as a biological weapon."

26 Even with outriders of soldiers and police on motorcycles, they made slow headway in Istanbul's teeming morning traffic. The city's air was blue with diesel exhaust, and the fumes of leaded gasoline hung heavily in the brilliant morning sunlight. The cacophony of horns in the metropolis of 6 million people was deafening, penetrating the interior of the armored official limousine. They had flown directly from the dam, landing at the Ataturk Airport at Yesilkoy, an hour's drive west of the city.

Mike Zammit gazed at the glittering waters of the Sea of Marmara. They were driving east along Kennedy Cadessi, a broad avenue named after JFK. The sea was the color of new denim. Huge tankers and merchant ships plied the waters in the brilliant sunlight. Far off in the heat haze he could see a gray battleship of the Turkish navy. He turned to Colonel Yildiz. "Are we going through Askaray district or around Sultanahmet?" He wanted the Turk to say Sultanahmet so they could follow the curve of the peninsula and see water all the way.

"Sultanahmet." Yildiz was surprised. "You know this city?"

"I did the backpacking thing during college. Stayed in an old place in the university area, near the Blue Mosque and Hagia Sophia, ate at those cheap little restaurants called *locantas*. A buck a plate for great food."

Zammit pointed at a ferry, one of the many that plied the Sea of Marmara, the Bosphorus, and the Golden Horn a dozen times a day, a necessity in a city divided by water. "Before sunset I'd always catch one of the evening boats at Eminonu, travel up the Bosphorus to Bekistas, then back again. Round trip, about an hour and a half. Never got tired of it. From the water this city is as beautiful as Venice. And the sunsets are spectacular."

The Turk's eyes were shrewd, as if he had learned something unexpected. "If I may say so, Doctor, you don't strike me as a romantic, or a connoisseur of sunsets."

Zammit shrugged. "I was nineteen years old." He didn't know what else to say. He wondered what the eager adolescent he had once been would think of the man he had become. Did anyone at that age think they'd end up alone, angry, and full of scars, physical and emotional? No, at that age you were convinced such things only happened to other people, and that maybe they kind of deserved it, hadn't done things right, hadn't planned properly, maybe were a little stupid. He looked in the mirror every day, and the hardness around his eyes and mouth told him the bitter truth. He remembered his father telling him as a boy that people always ended up with the faces they deserved. He tried to recall that colt-ish, trusting, long-dead youth and couldn't—he was a stranger now. It occurred to him that if he could somehow meet his younger self, he wouldn't be able to resist the urge to slap him around, tell him to pay attention, that life is filled with treachery and disap-pointment. You started your journey through adulthood with a lot of energy, a lot of hope—far more pluses than minuses. But the older you got, the more the minuses multiplied until, in the end, you were left with zero.

As they rounded the peninsula he could see the Galata Bridge spanning the Golden Horn. Then again, maybe he wouldn't slap his younger self around. Instead, take him out for dinner, let him talk about his big dreams. Let him enjoy his innocence. The kid would find out soon enough.

He spoke again. "During the ferry ride I'd stand at the railing, drink Turkish tea and eat pistachios the whole time. What's the name for Turkish tea?"

"Çay." (Pronounced *chai*.)

Zammit nodded as he remembered. "I loved that stuff." He looked to his left, at the glittering office buildings, incongruous amid the red tiled roofs of the older houses. A forest of slender minarets stabbed toward the sky through the round, breastlike domes of the mosques. As they crossed the bridge, he knew they were leaving the old part of the city, located in Europe, and head-ing toward the new part, located in Asia. The only city in the world that straddled two continents.

A question suddenly occurred to him. "Colonel, when did the name change?"

"The name of what?"

"This city. Originally called Byzantium. Then in the 4th century the capital of the Roman Empire moved from Rome to here, and it was renamed Constantinople."

Yildiz nodded. "It became Istanbul in 1930 as part of the effort to create a Turkish identity, a Turkish nation."

"Does the name mean anything?"

The Turk frowned. "Istanbul is a corruption of the Greek *eis tin polis,* which means 'to the city.' " Yildiz looked broodingly out the limousine window, as if reflecting on the unfairness of owing anything to the Greeks.

"Thanks." Zammit wondered if Costopoulos knew this. Probably. A few moments later they passed the Tophane Fountain. "Where are we meeting with Prime Minister Amurkhan?"

Yildiz still looked glum. "The Dolmabahçe Palace, residence of the last sultans. We're meeting there because it's close to Taksim Square. The prime minister has to attend a political rally there early this afternoon and it can't be rescheduled. You'll have to be brief."

"Did you tell her about the Resistance Army of Allah? Their belief that the overthrow of the government is imminent?"

Yildiz nodded. "Personally I don't think there's anything to it, but we can't take chances. I'd be a lot happier if we were meeting in Ankara instead of trying to organize security in this chaos. But this is where the votes are, so she has to be here."

The palace was right on the banks of the Bosphorus and overlooked the sparkling blue strait. As they got out of the car, they were instantly surrounded by soldiers and security men. Zammit spotted Costopoulos and Jackson. They were in the same car as Colonel Graves, who had flown from Washington after conferring with the president. A fleet of big black limousines told him Amurkhan had already arrived.

Although he had seen it before on his ferry rides, Zammit had never been inside the ornate building. "It's always a shock to see this French palace in the middle of Istanbul. What does 'Dol-ma-batch-eh' mean?"

" 'Filled-in garden,' " replied Yildiz. "In a fit of petulance one of the last sultans decided he wanted to imitate Versailles, so he bankrupted the Ottoman Empire to build this place. The world's only palace with a staircase made of Baccarat crystal."

"I see. A man of moderation and taste."

Colonel Yildiz led the way into the building. "Apparently we're meeting in the throne room."

A riot of color, with red, green, and purple marbles and red silk wallpaper, as well as velvet and rococo gilding, covered every surface and piece of furniture. There was the cold musty smell peculiar to museums all over the world, and their footsteps echoed on the marble floors. "Louis XIV would've felt right at home," remarked Zammit as they mounted the sparkling transparent crystal staircase. He pointed to an ornate clock on the wall. "It's ten in the morning. That says 9:05."

"The founder of modern Turkey was General Kemal Ataturk," replied the colonel. "He kicked out the degenerate sultans and caliphs in the 1920s and transformed the nation from a medieval autocracy into a modern democracy, even gave women the vote. He died in this palace at that time on November 10, 1938. Every year the entire nation comes to a halt in respect."

The throne room was spectacular. Zammit halted and stared at the colossal chandelier spreading and sparkling like a giant crystal flower above the long gleaming conference table, set with microphones, pitchers of water, and glasses.

Yildiz noticed and grunted. "Weighs 10,000 pounds. Biggest in the world. Another bloody sultan."

Prime Minister Thamar Amurkhan, elegant in her trademark white skirt and jacket with her sunglasses tucked into one of the pockets, walked up with a smile. Zammit shook hands, trying not to notice the resemblance to Sophia Loren. "Good to see you again. How goes the campaign?"

Her voice had the slightly nasal singsong typical of Turkish women, and she spoke English with just a trace of an accent. Zammit liked the sound. "If I'd been able to do more with the economy it would be no contest. Voters don't like an annual inflation rate of eighty percent."

He noted the dark circles of exhaustion under her almond-shaped pale green eyes as she leaned forward and spoke in a low voice. He could smell Chanel from her short cinnamon-colored hair. "This poisoning of the reservoir could kill millions and cause the entire Middle East to erupt. Not to mention costing me the election."

Zammit spoke with a confidence he did not feel. "We're working on it."

An aide rushed up and whispered, tapping his watch. Amurkhan nodded and took Zammit's arm. As she escorted him to the ornate chair by the microphone at the head of the table, he whispered urgently in her ear. She listened for a moment, then to his relief began nodding. As they walked he noticed, in addition to secret service men and political advisers, several preoccupied-looking senior military men. He knew they were members of Turkey's National Security Council, a body of five senior army commanders and four civilian ministers empowered under Article 118 of the constitution to take any action necessary to preserve "the independence of the state" and "the peace and security of society." They saw their role as that of safeguarding the republic in the event of a crisis, and they had a reputation for moving fast and brutally. He quickly set up the audiovisual unit, opening the two-by-three-foot flat display panel.

He was about to begin speaking when he noticed Graves pointing to his own ear, in which there was a plug with a wire trailing to a laptop-sized black box. Of course. They all gazed at Zammit expectantly as he inserted the earpiece of the Universal Translator. The computer would automatically translate any question or comment from a foreign language into English. He checked the device—Turkish was preselected. Several of the people around the table had similar earplugs, their translators tuned to English. Yildiz was already chewing his nails because smoking was forbidden. Colonel Graves nodded, encouraging him to begin.

On the plane Zammit had rehearsed his presentation. He began to speak, without notes. "The oldest organized municipality in the world is Catalhoyok, not far from here, founded some 10,000 years ago. In addition to being the cradle of civilization, this country was once the heartland of the classical world. The richest and most sophisticated cities on earth were here. And then the barbarians came and wrecked it all."

Amurkhan looked puzzled. Graves pointed at his watch.

Zammit didn't want to be rushed. They had to understand what was going on. "I assure you this brief history lesson is relevant to the present crisis. A desert-based civilization relies for its survival on water and everything that goes with it—pipes, aqueducts, irrigation canals, dams, and reservoirs. It's as true today as it was two thousand years ago. What does such a civilization have to fear most?"

An expectant silence.

"A barbarian with a pickax. In this case, a biological pickax."

He turned to the flat display panel and aimed the remote control. A multicolored three-dimensional model of *anabaena's* altered genetic structure rotated on the screen.

"A couple of millennia ago it was real pickaxes that killed those ancient civilizations by destroying their water supply infrastructure. You're looking at today's pickax, a GMO."

"A what?" asked one of the soldiers, in heavily accented English.

"Genetically modified organism. GMOs of this type are collectively referred to as the Fifth Horseman of the Apocalypse, to accompany the traditional four mentioned in the Book of Revelation." He saw the blank look on the Muslim's face and added, "The last book of the Christian Bible. The Four Horsemen are death, war, famine, and pestilence." He continued, "Of all the horsemen, this one is the worst because it's not natural and because of its enormous destructive potential."

Briefly Zammit explained what they had discovered about the cyanobacterial stromatolites, the organism's altered genetic structure, the lethal toxin it generated, its immunity to any treatment, and their conclusions. Dead silence.

"Legitimate GMOs have been around now for a long time in the agribusiness and food processing industry, particularly in America, although some European countries still ban or try to regulate them. Genes from one plant or animal are inserted into another to convey some sort of advantage. Many people don't trust GMOs because they believe they might interbreed with natural organisms, with harmful or at least unforeseeable effects."

"You mean the contamination in the Ataturk reservoir is the result of an agricultural experiment gone wrong?" asked Amurkhan.

"No. What we're dealing with cannot possibly be a commercial product. It must be the result of a sophisticated and expensive biological weapons research program."

Zammit took a sip of water. "Poison weapons have been around for a long time. By poison I mean both chemical and biological weapons. They have always been universally condemned, and sometimes banned by law—the first legislation was passed in India around 500 B.C." He'd gotten all of this historical information from Costopoulos. "There have been isolated incidents of biological warfare—in the 14th century the Mongols catapulted plague-infected corpses over the walls of Kaffa, in the Crimea, not far from here. A British officer in early colonial America gave smallpox-infected blankets to Indians. The only instance in the last century was Japan's use of plague and other bacteria against the Chinese during their invasion of Manchuria. Chemical warfare is a little different. The use of poison gas during the First World War was so horrific that the Geneva Protocol was passed in 1925, banning the practice. Even Adolf Hitler respected this prohibition, although Saddam Hussein was not as scrupulous, and neither is his son Anwar. However, chemical weapons are not our concern here, and I will now concentrate on bioweapons."

Zammit pointed at the display screen and the image of the altered *anabaena*. "Both plague and smallpox are horrible diseases, but at least they are naturally occurring organisms. Plague can be treated with vaccines and antibiotics, although some resistant strains are now appearing. No cure has ever been found for smallpox, which terrorized mankind for 10,000 years, but it doesn't exist anymore except under lock and key in a couple of isolation containment labs."

He heard a tinny, robotic voice in his ear and searched the table to identify the speaker. "Why don't they just destroy it?" A heavy-set Turk in a blue suit was speaking.

Zammit thought for a moment. "For the same reasons you don't want any other organism to become extinct—you reduce the planet's genetic diversity. There's always the chance it might prove useful. There have been plans in place for years to have a sort of symbolic bonfire to destroy the last remaining smallpox samples. A bonfire, since smallpox was known as the Great Fire— it burns you up from within, dissolving your internal organs. It's the most destructive disease in the history of mankind, even worse than the Black Death. It killed 300 million people in the 20th century alone. It is estimated that 1 out of every 10 people who ever lived has been killed or disfigured by smallpox. The plans involve taking the last remaining vials—there are a couple of hundred—and inserting them in a 1200-degree Celsius incinerator. They'll probably vaporize instantly, but just to make absolutely sure, they're going to run the burn for twenty minutes. You don't take any chances with this stuff. They haven't done it yet because what if it turns out that something in a smallpox virus is vital in a cure for cancer?"

"I see," said the tinny voice. "Please continue."

"What makes weapons-grade GMOs so terrifying is that no human being on earth has any resistance to them because they're *new*. Also, because they're new we don't have any vaccines or antibiotics that will fight them."

A Turkish general interrupted. "I don't understand. You say this is a biological weapon. War is about strategy and tactics, minimizing your own losses while maximizing the enemy's. With this, everyone loses."

Zammit nodded. "An excellent point. We know what's in the reservoir and the poison it's generating. Why is it there?"

Zammit gazed at Stavros Costopoulos, listening attentively a few seats away. "Everyone has a motive for doing something. I am a scientist and I believe everything happens for a reason. Take the present situation. No one in history has ever used bioweapons on a large scale, because the disadvantages far outweigh the advantages."

Yildiz interrupted. "How?"

Zammit pointed at him as if aiming an imaginary gun. "Let's say you and I were sitting in a restaurant here in Istanbul and I wanted to kill you. I could use a directed weapon, like a gun. I point it at you, pull the trigger, and kill you and only you. Or I could use a bioweapon, which is indiscriminate. I'd kill you, but I'd also kill myself, every other person in the restaurant, and half the population of Central Anatolia. That's why no one has ever been crazy enough to use a naturally occurring bioweapon, much less a genetically altered one. There's also the risk that if you deploy a bioweapon, it's permanently deployed, because it's alive—it might survive and reproduce in the environment forever. It's like deciding to squeeze toothpaste from the tube—once it's out, it's out."

He turned back to the screen. It now displayed a satellite photo of the Ataturk Dam and reservoir. "But this bioweapon has been well chosen. All the evidence shows that a great deal of thought has been put into it. That it is, in fact, a directed weapon."

He pointed at the image. "The poison is in the concrete prison of the Ataturk reservoir. That reservoir has only one outlet—downstream to Syria and Iraq. It is unthinkable, from a terrorist's logic, that such a bioweapon would be deployed in a sparsely populated area. What's the point? You can't terrorize a wilderness. There's also the fact that most biological weapons are lethal through inhalation or skin contact. Delivering a toxin through a water medium is always inefficient, but particularly so in this case. You just close off the water supply."

Zammit made a temple of his fingers and tucked it under his chin, thinking hard. "So what's going on? If a terrorist wanted to kill millions of people, he'd use something he could release in the air, something that could be inhaled. And he'd choose something small and portable." He held up a pen. "For example, a piece of crystallized polio the size of this pen nib contains enough virus to annihilate everyone on earth."

Gazing at the grim faces around the table, he continued. "And if someone just wanted to contaminate this particular water source, it would be much easier to dump plutonium into the reservoir. And plutonium, even though you can't buy it at your local supermarket, would still be easier to come by than genetically modified cyanobacteria and much easier to plant. It also doesn't have to eat."

Zammit displayed four satellite photos showing how fast the infestation had grown in the reservoir. "This GMO had to be introduced. To introduce so much of it so fast by conventional means, you'd need supertanker loads. The reservoir is in the middle of a virtual war zone monitored by the Turkish army and space satellites. And cyanobacteria eat organophosphates, which also had to be introduced in significant quantities."

Zammit faced Yildiz. "Since we are assured that during the last month a convoy of trucks with Bio-War: We Deliver painted on the sides didn't pull up to the reservoir, it's safe to assume that everything started at the dam itself. Using a delivery system we don't yet understand."

Yildiz was pale. "Ridiculous," he snapped.

"You have a wide variety of equipment and supplies at the dam?"

"Yes."

"And a wide variety of suppliers?"

"We purchase supplies from all over the world."

"I'd like to go back to the dam and have a look at some of your supplies. And get the names of your suppliers."

"Of course," said Amurkhan. "Today, if possible."

Cairo Jackson waved a huge hand.

"Cairo?"

"May I point out something the technologically inclined gentlemen here have overlooked?"

"Go ahead."

"You mentioned earlier a barbarian with a pickax. All we've talked about is the pickax. Who is the barbarian wielding it?"

Zammit smiled as the others around the table looked at each other, coughed, and shuffled. "Good point. Anything else?"

Stavros Costopoulos spoke. "The identity of the barbarian is of course very significant to this whole crisis, as is his psychology. The whole thing is just so, so . . . *elaborate*. It's hard to explain."

One of the generals interrupted impatiently. "We all agree it's a good point, but I don't think psychology is our primary concern here. Who are the candidates for barbarian?"

Mike Zammit turned to Graves. "Colonel?"

Graves fiddled with his earplug and cleared his throat. "According to our Office of Technology Assessment, there are at least twenty-five countries that either have or are developing biochemical warfare capability."

"What about America?" asked another general.

Graves's gaze was icy. "I'm afraid I am unable to comment, sir." So, thought Zammit. We're players in this nasty little game too.

The colonel continued. "Since 1972 some 140 nations have ratified the Geneva Biological and Toxin Weapons Convention, a treaty that bans their development and use. Unfortunately, the convention has no provisions for verifying compliance, which for all practical purposes means it's useless. We also worked hard to establish the Chemical Weapons Convention, which went into effect in 1997 with over 160 signatories. Same problem—no adequate verification procedures."

Amurkhan interjected. "Just how hard is it to develop a bioweapon?"

Graves waved at Zammit. The scientist shrugged. "It's not hard at all. Anyone with a kit for brewing beer in his basement can do it with relative safety, so long as you take precautions to make sure you don't end up poisoning yourself. It also doesn't take very long. Let's say a single bacterium divides every twenty minutes. The growth is exponential—2, 4, 16, 256, 65,000 plus, and so on. Within ten hours that single bacterium will produce over a billion more. At the end of a week . . ."

Stunned silence. One of the generals muttered, "Allah," and in his earpiece Zammit heard a faint, metallic "God."

"There is no point in continuing this discussion," interrupted another military man. "As the PKK told Dr. Zammit, it's the Iraqis. They have biochemical weapons factories, and Anwar hates us. And as Mr. Jackson says, there must be a barbarian. It must be them."

He turned to Costopoulos. "Where psychology is concerned, we all know Anwar is insane, and this is an insane thing to do. Everything fits perfectly. Madam Prime Minister, I advise that we attack immediately."

"And there goes the election!" snapped Amurkhan. She and the general glared at each other with open hostility. "The fundamentalists support Iraq, and they'd use it against me."

Zammit interrupted before this exchange could escalate. "I don't think it's a good idea either, but for a different reason. Despite all the evidence, I don't think it's the Iraqis. It took some skillful genetic engineering to produce this GMO, and if Anwar has that capability, I'll eat this table."

"So who does?" demanded Amurkhan.

"We do," said Zammit, gazing at Colonel Graves, who gazed impassively back. "The Russians do. Or did."

"It has to be the Iraqis," insisted the general. "America is our ally and has nothing to gain from this, and neither do the Russians. You said the PKK told you Anwar had foreknowledge that this was going to happen. It's obvious. We must attack immediately."

Zammit was about to reply when Thamar Amurkhan's words rang out over the rising chorus of angry male voices. "I'm sure we all want to know who is responsible for this crisis and punish them. But there is the crisis itself, which will soon turn into a full-fledged disaster. We have international agreements to supply water to Syria and Iraq, and we are not doing it. In a short time millions of people will begin to die of thirst, as well as their crops, so there will be starvation too. The first task is to find a solution to this contamination. We can punish the perpetrators later. Dr. Zammit, what do you suggest?"

"My people are trying to find out how to kill the cyanobacteria and destroy or neutralize the toxin. I want to go back to the dam. Finding out how the bacteria got there in the first place will give us vital clues."

"Very well. Keep me informed through Colonel Yildiz."

As everyone left the room, Colonel Graves pulled Zammit, Jackson, and Costopoulos aside. "How long?"

"I don't know. We're working as fast as we can," replied Zammit.

"Work faster. Turkey has a history of military coups. The army has taken over four times in the last forty years. They only step into certain situations—civil disorder, political corruption, or an outside threat they feel a civilian government can't handle. A situation just like this one."

"I know," said Zammit. "Article 118 of the constitution."

Graves glanced around to make sure no one was listening. "The problem is, fundamentalist factions have succeeded in infiltrating the Turkish military, perhaps even at the highest levels. That's bad enough, but you also saw how the National Security Council members are itching for a fight. Most of these guys, even if they are in favor of democracy, are still Muslims. They think Thamar Amurkhan should be at home cooking meals and making babies."

Zammit nodded. "Tell Yildiz and Amurkhan about fundamentalists in the military. It could tie in with the Resistance Army of Allah's confidence in the imminent overthrow of the government."

"Good idea," said Graves. "And for God's sake, work as fast as you can."

He tried to imagine what it had looked like before it was desecrated.

Virtually alone in the early evening light, he walked through the massive structure. Dedicated by the Byzantine Emperor Justinian in A.D. 537, shaken and damaged by earthquakes and scorched by fire, the rose-red church still stood after more than 1400 years.

Justinian, heir to the Roman Empire after the fall of the West, had wanted the greatest building in the world and he had gotten it, from his Greek architects Anthemios and Isidoros. When it was finished, Justinian, astounded, had held his arms to heaven and cried, "O Solomon, I have outdone thee!" And indeed, the building was rumored to surpass Solomon's temple in size, beauty of proportion, and richness of decoration.

No mortar held it together—a secret combination of limestone and melted lead had been used to fuse the stones forever. Twenty-four tons of twenty-four-carat gold had been used to make the 18,000 square yards of golden mosaics. The sanctuary, which only the priests could enter, contained twenty tons of silver.

He remembered what he had been taught. Someone had said that all the world fears Time, but Time fears the pyramids. As he walked slowly through the ancient building, he thought that perhaps the pyramids feared this church. Centuries after it had been built, the Venetians, arrogant in the safety of their lagoon, proud of their independence and originality, of their vast material wealth, which was matched by the genius of their artists, had, when they came to build Saint Mark's Church, meekly copied the design of this church, knowing that no greater could be found.

He stopped at the cavernous entrance of the Orea Porta, the Beautiful Gate. It led, through a cool darkness still spicy with 900 years of incense, to the inner Imperial Gate, through which the emperor had traditionally entered the nave.

Through which his ancestors had entered the nave.

He noticed deep grooves worn into the hard stone pavement. Over nine centuries of bored imperial chamberlains shuffling their aching feet as they fought to stay awake during the interminable ceremonies of Greek Orthodoxy. The worn stone gave mute but eloquent witness to the immense age of the place.

Then, in 1453, the ceremonies had ended. Soon they would begin again.

The vast airy space that stretched away on all sides seemed as large as the universe but more grand. Shot with veins of sunlight that poured through forty windows, it was contained under a dome that seemed to float, as if suspended in the air by a golden chain that descended from the very anchor of heaven itself.

The huge marble columns that marched away into the gloom on either side were from the lost Temple of Artemis at Ephesus, one of the Seven Wonders of the ancient world; from the Egyptian Temple of the Sun at Heliopolis; even from the Babylonian Temple of Baalbek. The marble varied: deep green porphyry from Sparta, rose-red Phrygian from Synnada; Iassian, with blood-red veins on livid white.

Once again he ran through the list fixed in his mind, a list of the work that would be necessary to restore the building to its original appearance and function. He gazed reverently at the glistening mosaics of saints, emperors, and Jesus Christ. The Messiah of the Orthodox was no gentle American Jesus, meek and mild in a pink nightgown, eyes soulfully upcast, ready to be sacrificed as the lamb of the Lord, already floating to heaven on a cottony cloud. The Messiah of the Orthodox was Christ Pantocrator, an emperor, not a shepherd. Grim, humorless, and determined, lord and master of the universe, he was as hard and glittering as the gold and black mosaics that portrayed him.

He remembered what he had been taught. Many mosaic images of the saints had been gouged out over the centuries. The metal cross on the dome had been replaced with Islam's crescent moon, covered with 50,000 fused gold coins in a futile attempt to compete with the solid gold lining of the dome. The Muslims had found it impossible to lift the giant building physically and turn it toward Mecca. Instead they had built a mimbar and a mihrab for prayer, located at a thirty-degree angle to the Christian altar, slanted across the general floor plan, so they would both face the distant holy city of Mecca.

They had taken the greatest Christian building in the world and turned it into a mosque. Kemal Ataturk had turned it into a museum but left it looking like a mosque. And now Turkey's fundamentalists said they would turn it into an active place of Islamic worship once more.

As he looked at the huge disks that hung from what should have been a Christian dome, Muslim green gilded with gold Arabic characters, he wanted to spit on the floor.

His eyes closed in ecstasy as he imagined what it would soon be like. A thousand candles and lamps glimmering beneath the vast dome. The images of Christ and His saints and of the emperors and empresses of Byzantium, his ancestors, being carried through the adoring mob. The bishops with their miters and white satin robes picked out with gems and pearls, holding aloft the most precious relics of their religion, the golden caskets and jeweled icons, as they glided chanting through the supplicating crowds . . .

Suddenly he heard two men speaking Turkish. They were giggling, eating baklava from paper napkins, and sneaking cigarettes in defiance of the posted signs.

Shaking with fury, the Holy Chosen One turned on his heel and walked out of Hagia Sophia, the rose-red Church of Holy Wisdom.

 The storage warehouse of the Ataturk Dam was cavernous, swarming with soldiers, technicians, and maintenance staff. It smelled of oil and gasoline, solvents and hot metal. Mike Zammit walked through it accompanied by Colonel Hakim Yildiz. They'd arrived at two in the afternoon, flying back to the dam from Istanbul after the meeting with Amurkhan. It was almost five-thirty—they'd spent more than three hours checking everything. And finding nothing.

Costopoulos had stayed in Istanbul with Connie Palaeov to confer with Colonel Graves, and Jackson and Spargo were in Yildiz's office with Lloyd Lavender. No further information had come in from Frankie Richards and Kitson Kang in Seattle.

"I see what you mean about getting supplies from all over the world," remarked Zammit, leafing through a list of the dam's suppliers and equipment. "I presume you inspect everything that comes in?"

Yildiz shrugged. "Security is what you would expect at an industrial facility in the middle of a desert. It's not like we're running a nuclear reactor. We buy standard industrial equipment and chemicals."

"What are these?"

The colonel peered. "Bill of lading. Materials inspected and signed for by the appropriate individual." He pointed at another document. "Hazardous materials manifest. Same thing."

Zammit gazed around, feeling the low swell of frustration. "This could take days. We don't have days."

He began to pace rapidly, and the stocky Turk had to scurry to keep up. "In Istanbul I talked about the ineffectiveness of delivering a bioweapon through water. There aren't a lot of options. You said the only planes that fly over here are Turkish air force jets or cargo planes and they never do aerial spraying."

"Correct."

"And you don't use organophosphate chemical weapons."

"Correct."

"And convoys of trucks don't dump anything in the reservoir."

"Correct. However, now that you mention it, there was an accident a couple of months ago. Two supply trucks ran into each other, and they both ended up in the reservoir. The containers they were carrying were lost."

Zammit halted. "Did you recover them?"

Yildiz saw where this line of questioning was headed and his brown eyes flickered. "No. We don't have salvage equipment. They were just empty tanks."

"How do you know they were empty?"

"We examined the bill of lading and the manifest. Both said they were standard black metal tanks used for taking water samples for analysis."

"So the tanks themselves were never inspected?"

"No. They fell into the reservoir before they reached the warehouse. As far as I know, no one even saw them."

"Where were the tanks from?"

"A regular supplier in Russia."

"Are there any routine procedures at the dam or reservoir that would take employees down to the water with large pieces of equipment?"

"Of course. We routinely sample the water as a precaution."

"Using the same types of tanks?"

"Yes."

"Where are they kept?"

They walked to the tank storage area as Yildiz pointed out the great coils of hose and explained how the samples were taken from the reservoir. "So the samples are sent to Urfa for testing?" asked Zammit.

"Yes. It is strictly routine. We've never found anything."

"But the tanks stay here?"

"Yes. To be used again."

At the storage area, Mike Zammit contemplated the huge black metal tanks. "Who actually does the sampling?"

Yildiz conferred with a tall Turk in a white lab coat as Zammit ran his hands over the tanks nearest him.

The colonel returned. "The sampling is done by the chief sampling protocol technician. He does it himself—the procedure is fully automated. He is also the person who signs bills of lading and manifests whenever the tanks are delivered."

"In other words," said Zammit, "he would've signed the documents certifying that the lost tanks were standard tanks and empty, right? Even though he never saw or examined them?"

Yildiz opened his mouth to argue, then realized there was nothing to say. "Yes."

"Colonel, I want the lids taken off these tanks so I can examine the interiors."

The Turkish colonel protested. "Why these? I thought you were concerned about the ones that fell into the water."

"I'm concerned about them all."

"But they've been cleaned."

"Believe me, that doesn't matter."

"Very well. And the name of the chief sampling protocol technician is Ruslan Glinka."

"You have a Russian technician working here?"

"GAP has twenty-two dams and nineteen power stations. It's one of the biggest projects of its kind in history and it takes a lot of people to run it. As well as getting supplies from all over the world, we hire from all over the world."

"Do you check your personnel as carefully as you check your suppliers?"

Yildiz colored. "Of course. References, recommendations, everything. Everyone is thoroughly investigated."

"I want to check the tanks first. Then I want to talk to Glinka."

Working with a team of technicians and maintenance staff as Yildiz watched, Zammit examined the interior of the tanks visually. They were empty, but they had recently been rinsed and were still damp. He opened the microlab as Yildiz peered over his shoulder, fascinated. "What are you going to do? Please explain."

"This won't take long," replied Zammit. He pointed to the silicon wafer factories, the disease dipsticks, and the miniature GC mass spectrometer. "We don't need these. The rectangular thing is the spectrometer, preloaded with the spectrums of tens of thousands of known compounds. These wafers are miniature factories that measure dielectrophoresis, the minute electrical charges generated by all living creatures. Same with these glass slides— disease dipsticks. They're coated with a special film—they identify different microorganisms and their toxins. But we're not looking for an organism, we're searching for a chemical."

He held up a glass wafer the size of a credit card. "A molecular lab that can detect incredibly minute chemical concentrations. Including the one we're looking for."

Zammit put on latex gloves and took swabs from the damp

interiors of ten tanks chosen at random. For each one he wrung out the residual liquid into a container, then used a special syringe to load the liquid into the silicon wafer factories. The process took ten minutes. He hooked up the laptop and started typing. Three minutes later he said, "Well, that was easy. Five are clean, five show unmistakable traces of organophosphates at high concentrations, even though the drums have been rinsed."

The Turk's eyes went as cold as the surface of Pluto.

"Colonel, I think we should have a chat with Ruslan Glinka, in your office. Try to make the invitation sound casual so he doesn't become alarmed. Having soldiers nearby might be a good idea."

Yildiz barked orders as Zammit cleaned up the microlab and saw to its safe storage.

They went up to the colonel's office and briefed Jackson, Spargo, and Lavender.

Jackson spoke first. "So that's how nutrients were fed to the cyanobacteria. What about those tanks still in the water?"

"I bet they contain, or rather contained, the original culture of the cyanobacteria. Probably some sort of time release mechanism on the tanks. We won't know for sure until we retrieve them. We'll ask Colonel Graves to supply the equipment."

"But there's millions of cubic yards of the stuff out there. It all came from a few tanks?" protested Spargo.

Zammit nodded thoughtfully. "The genetic engineering on the stuff is very sophisticated. We already know it breeds incredibly fast. Whoever developed it might have had some way of drying it or otherwise treating it so it's superconcentrated. Once in the water, in contact with ideal environmental conditions and concentrated nutrients, it would start growing explosively."

There was a knock on the door. A senior staff member with a large purple bruise on his cheek entered the room. "We found him. He was on the telephone with someone when he saw us and immediately tried to run. The soldiers helped subdue him."

Soldiers dragged Ruslan Glinka into the room. He was disheveled, with a bloody nose and torn clothing. "Do you speak English?" Zammit asked. Glinka didn't answer.

"He does," said Yildiz, his face a mask of anger.

Zammit hitched his hip onto the edge of the desk. "So you're the waiter who delivers meals to that poisonous muck out there. Who's the chef?"

Glinka was defiant, a strange glint in his eyes. "Jew!"

"Sorry to disappoint you. Interesting turn to the conversation, though."

The Russian's head swayed back and forth like a cobra about to strike. "Satan!" he hissed.

"He couldn't make it," said Zammit, wondering what was going on. "Maybe next time."

Glinka's body suddenly went rigid, and he began to struggle in the soldiers' grip. He screamed, flecks of spittle mottling his lips. "*Derzhava*! A strong Russia! *Sobornost*! A spiritual Russia!"

"I couldn't agree more," said Zammit, baffled. "But you're not answering my question."

Convulsively Glinka broke partially free and bit his wrist before he could be restrained. Again he went rigid. Two seconds later blood poured from his mouth, ears, eyes, and nose in a crimson torrent. He collapsed to the floor like an emptying bag of hospital blood and thrashed, leaving slimy orange-red smears as his legs scissored back and forth. Then, just as suddenly, he was still.

"Holy fuck," said Cairo Jackson.

"I'm going to be sick," gagged Dikka as she darted from the room. Lavender was pale, the soldiers and Yildiz stunned with shock.

Mike Zammit stared at the spreading red lake on the yellow linoleum floor. Irrationally he thought, Don't get any on your shoes. His nostrils prickled with the never-to-be-forgotten rusted-iron odor of cooling human blood.

There was a thick newspaper on the desk. Zammit separated the sections and threw them on the floor over the pool of blood to make a path to the body. He walked gingerly over the paper, knelt, and lifted Glinka's wrist. He looked closely. "His watch. The lens is shattered and there's some residual liquid."

"Obviously it didn't contain vitamins," said Jackson.

Zammit was about to put the limp hand back on the floor when he noticed something. He checked Glinka's other hand and wrist as well, frowning. As he looked under the dead man's hairline, he said, "Cairo, take off this guy's shoes and socks." Jackson wrapped his hands in newspaper and pulled off the loafers and socks. Zammit checked the dead man's feet.

"What on earth are you doing?" demanded Lavender.

Zammit knelt by the body as Yildiz handed him a box of Kleenex so he could wipe his bloody hands.

"I know it sounds incredible, but at some time in the course of this man's life, he was *crucified*!"

Navy Seal Peter Morris, in scuba gear, stared dubiously at the fetid, oily green slime a few yards away, holding an oxygen mask over his face. He squinted up into the scorching blue sky. Holding his breath, he removed the mask and quickly exhaled the question to avoid inhaling the stench.

"Sir, tell me again why you thought I might have to dive into this crap?" He put the mask back on.

Bursting with impatience, Mike Zammit stood at the edge of the reservoir shielding his eyes from the glare as he watched what was happening a hundred yards away. It was noon, some forty-three hours since Glinka had committed suicide. The modular components of two vessels were being assembled by a swarm of technicians, half-hidden in sprays of sparks from welding torches, with the ease and speed of a couple of giant Meccano toys. One was the U.S. Navy vessel *Alliant,* an experimental craft being tested by the technicians and crew of the *USS Carl Vinson* in the Arabian Gulf. After hearing about Glinka and the lost tanks, Colonel Graves had arranged to have the ship dismantled and flown directly from the *Vinson* to the dam. The second vessel was the state-of-the-art salvage ship *DeepFind*, owned by the Welsh company Deep Redeemer Inc. *DeepFind* was searching for treasure in the Mediterranean when the vessel's owners were contacted. The U.S. government agreed to pay a hefty fee to borrow the ship and crew and fly them to the Ataturk Dam.

Zammit wiped sweat from his brow as he turned to Peter Morris, who was from the *Vinson* as well. "We have to find out what's happening underneath. This stuff is growing downward. It's only a matter of time before it reaches the bottom. Because it's genetically altered, we can only guess at its life cycle. We've stopped feeding it, but it's still producing toxin. We need a visual examination and assumed it would have to be done by a diver. Then we found out about those two vessels. They'll do it instead."

Morris looked grateful. "Sir, this stuff is really thick. It'd be like swimming through liquid concrete. Once I reached the water underneath there'd be no light at all. You'd get disoriented pretty quick."

Zammit wondered whether to tell Morris about the toxin but decided against it. If anything went wrong with the two ships and they had to use the kid, he'd tell him then.

"Apart from examining the underside of this crap, what else was I supposed to be looking for?"

"Metal canisters. They used to contain this stuff."

Morris looked incredulous. "All of it?"

"No," said Zammit. "A concentrate of some sort."

He had used the microlab to analyze Glinka's watch and the residual poison it contained. The lens, instead of being crystal, was a hard crystalline sugar designed to dissolve instantly when it came in contact with certain enzymes found only in human saliva—not even salt water, tears, or blood would melt it. Since people never licked their watch lenses, it was a foolproof containment for the poison. "Something I've never seen or heard of before," he explained to Yildiz. "Seems designed to cause an instantaneous and catastrophic rise in blood pressure. Its only use would be as a suicide weapon."

Now, in brilliant sunshine fouled by stink, he frowned as he remembered. A biological weapon he'd never seen or heard of before. A suicide drug he'd never seen or heard of before. Used by a Russian technician of considerable education and with impeccable references, none of whom mentioned that he hated Jews, had an obsession with Satan, and just happened to have been crucified and somehow recovered.

What was going on?

His reverie was broken by Peter Morris. "Sir, how are those two ships supposed to work together? I've heard a little about the *Alliant* but not much. What's happening?"

Zammit reviewed the plan in his mind. If it worked, it was going to be a masterpiece of improvisation, something that might prove useful for decades to come.

"In the Arabian Gulf, the experimental craft *Alliant* is testing a new type of sonar equipment called synthetic aperture sonar, or SAS," he explained to Morris. "The technology has the potential to produce pictures of the sea floor showing detail with a resolution twenty times finer than conventional sonar."

"What kind of detail?" asked Morris.

"In conditions where conventional sonar might locate an object the size of a ship's hull, SAS can find something as small as a teapot. Current sonar devices are essentially bolted to the ship that carries them, but the *Alliant* tows a flexible array of sonar pods, each packed with electronics, beneath and behind its hull."

"Man," said Morris, "I've never heard of that before."

Zammit recalled his briefing session. "The pods can be lowered to depths of many feet to avoid surface and subsurface turbulence—or, in this case, a carpet of green slime that floats on the water. As they move beneath the water, each pod takes simultaneous sonar readings—acoustic snapshots—of the sea floor. *Alliant's* on-board computers then combine the data from each pod, compensating for the range and the Doppler effect."

"The Doppler what?"

"The pod is moving. The sea floor is stationary. The result is that you get different readings from the sonar waves depending on whether you're moving toward an object or away from it. That wave distortion—the Doppler effect—means you can't locate something accurately unless you use a mathematical equation to compensate."

Seeing the confusion on Morris's face, Zammit said, "Never mind. Anyway, the ship's computers produce a high-resolution image of whatever is on the bottom. I expect the *Alliant* to pinpoint the location of the canisters easily, but that doesn't solve the other problem."

"What's that, sir?"

"Retrieving the things. *Alliant* can't bring them to the surface. Enter the other vessel, *DeepFind*. It's a salvage ship that will use its hydraulic grab, a giant six-fingered claw with a four-yard span that can lift three tons at a time."

"Jesus," said Morris. "Can I stay and watch?"

Zammit grinned. "Sure. The grab is equipped with underwater lights and a series of low-light video cameras. It's suspended from the mother ship by an umbilical cord loaded with electronics. The grab brings the canisters to the surface and stores them in the cargo hold after they've been disinfected. Then they come ashore. At least that's how we hope it'll work."

Designed to function in deep water where no diver could go, the *DeepFind* should have no problem hauling up the empty canisters from the shallow depths of the reservoir. But Zammit was still worried.

"Fiendish," grinned Peter Morris.

Cairo Jackson jogged up, panting in the broiling sun. "Gotta spend more time in the gym. They're ready. Good thing they were both designed to be modular and can be taken apart and put together again quickly."

"What about the modifications?"

Jackson wiped his face with a damp handkerchief. "All in place. We've installed decontamination facilities on each vessel—both antiseptic rinse and ultraviolet light array, just to be sure. The big problem turned out to be modifying the video cameras and low-light array on the grab so they could be swiveled upward from the claw. Fooling around with fundamental design is tricky. The builders never considered the possibility of looking up instead of down."

Zammit nodded. To avoid risking Peter Morris's life, the cameras and lights had to be able to look upward so that they could illuminate and film the underside of the cyanobacteria. "Let's go."

It took the *Alliant* an hour to find all the containers. There were 112 of them scattered on the reservoir floor within 200 yards of each other—they had obviously rolled down the incline that led from the water's edge to the reservoir floor. It then took another two hours to transfer the location data from the navy ship's computers to the salvage vessel's, which were different. By the time the appropriate computer language translations were done and the links tested, it was almost evening. It took another five hours for *DeepFind* to retrieve the containers. By the time the task was done, it was dark.

They worked under a huge black sky so filled with stars that they cast a ghostly blue light. Because of the darkness they rigged floodlights on *DeepFind* and on the reservoir shore so the salvage vessel could do its job. Once the containers were decontaminated and unloaded, it took Zammit two hours under the blinding floodlights on the shore to examine the canisters and pry off the lids, grimly wondering what might be left for him to test, given the length of time they'd been in the water and the fact that they had been subjected to antiseptic rinse and ultraviolet light.

Nothing. Not even residual traces of what they had once contained. He felt a deadening sense of defeat. He also realized the microlab was running out of slides and reagents.

Then, in the last group of five, he found himself staring at the only tank with an intact lid. He grinned. The only tank whose time release mechanism had failed. He opened it carefully and began analyzing its contents with the microlab. Fifteen minutes later, he was done.

Back in the control room he stared at the results, feeling a rising sense of frustration at his inability to figure out what was going on. He waited as Colonel Yildiz patched through an audio-video feed to Colonel Graves in Istanbul.

"Mike, what have you found?"

"The canisters. A hundred and twelve of them. All have time release mechanisms. One failed, so I was able to test the contents. Like I figured, all of them once contained a superconcentrated form of the cyanobacteria. It was dried."

"You mean freeze-dried?"

"No. You can't freeze-dry a living organism without killing it. Freezing creates ice, ice expands, the cell wall ruptures, and it dies. It was dried using a desiccant, a sugar called trehalose. The sugar dries and shrinks the living organism into a powder that looks like green coffee creamer. Each grain of the powder is a tiny crystalline sugar bead. The process also achieves a fantastic concentration. The bacteria could stay viable for hundreds of years. Just mix it with water and the right nutrients, and it's alive again."

"Where would this come from? Who's the barbarian?"

"It's definitely not off-the-shelf technology, and there's no way the Iraqis could do it."

"Any word on a solution?"

"No. I'm sending a container of it back to the lab in Seattle. Also, Frankie Richards is examining the contents of those bulbs that are growing so rapidly on the surface. There might be something there. I've done everything I can do at the moment. Colonel Yildiz, your opinion?"

The Turk's immaculate uniform was losing its knife-edge crease and he had loosened his collar. "You do what you think best. Immediately advise me of any new developments. I must go to Istanbul and brief the prime minister."

As Yildiz turned away, Zammit said, "I trust you're taking precautions, as I advised? You might not take the Resistance Army of Allah stuff seriously, but I do."

The colonel nodded curtly. "I will meet secretly with Amurkhan at the Hilton on the banks of the Bosphorus instead of at the usual ministries. No one can possibly know."

Zammit rubbed his eyes as Yildiz left the room. He turned back to the screen.

Graves nodded. "Get some sleep. Tomorrow we go to the Crimea."

Zammit felt a sudden sense of psychic dislocation. "What?"

"The president's assistant, Randy Berkowitz, got a package from a buddy of his. It was marked urgent. The guy ignored channels and he's going to get his ass reamed out, but it's a good thing he did because otherwise the report would've sat for days before anyone looked at it. One of our people in Sevastopol. A CIA analyst named Jack Morgan."

Gazing at the bowl of green-tufted rocky hills that cupped the bay, the amethyst sea, the palm trees, colored parasols, and browning bodies lounging on beaches, Mike Zammit knew he was on the same latitude as Nice. It was almost possible to think he was on the French Riviera.

What gave it away was the cheap clothing worn by the many in contrast to the expensive clothing worn by the haughty few, the Mongol features of many people on the streets, the signs in the Cyrillic alphabet on seedy-looking buildings, and the huge concrete block apartments. There was no mistaking the tidal-flat mud color of Soviet concrete.

As they drove in the black Volga limousine along the beachfront boulevard of the Crimean peninsula's premier city, a famous resort and naval base, Zammit asked, "Where are we going?"

Graves rolled down the window to smell the sea air. "Morgan's downtown. Ah, the sweet smell of raw sewage."

"Why are you keeping us in suspense?" asked Costopoulos. Zammit had told Graves he wanted to bring the Greek along, and the colonel had agreed.

"I don't know the whole story, and we should all hear it from the horse's mouth."

The limo let them off on a street of run-down villas painted in lemon yellow, ochre, pale pink, baby blue, and peppermint green. All had white slatted shutters. Their destination was a pink one, in need of a new paint job. Obviously pre-Revolution, it had an air of neglect and decay, its facade mottled with discolored white patches where the plaster had fallen away. The entrance was filthy. The elevator was out of order, so they trudged up the grand staircase, littered with garbage, to the third floor and a brass plaque that said AmeriSlav Import-Export Company in both Ukrainian and English.

A tense-looking aide let them in. The suite of rooms wore a look of shabby gentility. Zammit imagined that it was once the home of a minor aristocrat who could no longer stand the harsh winters in Moscow. The modern desks and office chairs didn't fit with the antique furniture along the walls. In the middle of the room, across from the fireplace, a low round conference table sat surrounded by an overstuffed sofa and easy chairs. The aide reappeared through one of the doors followed by a short round reddish-yellow man and a tall lanky one with the all-American good looks of a college football quarterback. After they were introduced, the man identified as Lance Yarham dismissed the aide, who seemed only too glad to escape into the next room and close the door.

Hands on his hips, belly thrust forward, Yarham was obviously angry. Zammit appraised the yellowish skin, reddish hair, round face and belly, and thought the man looked like a decaying orange. Jack Morgan looked as if he knew why Yarham was angry and didn't care.

"Coffee? Tea? Something stronger?" asked Morgan. "I think I'll have something stronger."

"OK," said Mike Zammit.

A small smile creased Morgan's face. "I've heard about you. Not often you meet a tough-guy scientist. Slivovitz all right?" He pulled the cork out of a bottle and a sharp sting filled the air. Zammit thought, What does this smell like? He remembered. Ozone. Mixed with varsol.

"It's rocket fuel," apologized Morgan.

"I've had it before," said Zammit. "Plum brandy. If you want a real treat, buy a jar of plums preserved in slivovitz, pour it over vanilla ice cream, then set fire to it."

"Set fire to it?"

"Yeah," said Zammit. "Slivovitz burns with an electric-blue flame. If you do it in a darkened room it'll impress the hell out of your girlfriend."

"I'll have the same, if you don't mind," said Costopoulos. "Minus the ice cream, the girlfriend, and the fire."

"Coffee," said Yarham curtly.

"Nothing for me," said Graves, raising a bushy gray eyebrow at Zammit.

They sat around the conference table, stained with rings from years of wet glasses and coffee cups. The tension was thick. "So," said Graves. "You sent some information to Randy Berkowitz at the White House."

"Goddamn it!" shouted Yarham. "There are procedures around here! If you don't follow procedures, everything's as organized as a bunch of guys fleeing from a burning building!"

Morgan sipped his drink and stared at the floor. "It's called initiative, sir. You said you liked it when we showed some. I did try to explain."

"I told you it was bullshit!"

"I disagree," said Morgan softly.

"And of course I can't touch you because you're best buddies with—"

Colonel Graves's voice sounded like a ton of coal rumbling down a chute. "Stop shouting. You know we have a crisis at the Ataturk Dam?"

Yarham shrugged irritably. "You've just stated everything I know about it. Nobody's telling us fuck-all." He tilted an aggressive chin at Zammit. "The only other thing I know is that wonder boy here was supposed to have it solved by now."

It was obvious the old CIA agent intended his presence to be obstructive rather than helpful. Zammit put his glass on the table and stood. "I want you to leave."

"I'm the senior officer at this station. I'm in charge. I—"

"Out," said Zammit.

"Out," said Graves.

Costopoulos waved good-bye as Yarham slammed the door.

Graves leaned toward Morgan. "That still doesn't mean what you did was acceptable. You'll answer to Langley."

"I know," said Morgan. "Do you have any idea how frustrating it is to deal with these complacent old farts?"

"Take it easy, Jack," said Zammit. "If you have anything, give."

Morgan nodded. "What I sent Randy was a copy, with a translation. I've got duplicates here." He reached into his briefcase and pulled out a pile of folders bound with elastic bands.

"Begin at the beginning," said Graves. "Don't leave anything out."

Morgan took a long pull on his slivovitz. "I have a lot of contacts. One of them was the editor of a local paper called the *Glory of Sevastopol*. Boris Kazov. Investigative journalism." He gave a mirthless smile. "In this country, the surest way to an early grave, apart from a firing squad. But Boris was very serious, and once he was onto something, he wouldn't let go."

Zammit nodded. "Go on."

"We'd get together secretly. I'd feed him stuff, he'd feed me stuff, the usual routine. I liked the guy. He was working on something big but wouldn't say what. Said he could be killed at any time. If he thought he was in danger he'd send me a package."

Morgan held up the sheaf of documents. "He sent me this the day he died."

"How did he die?" asked Zammit.

Morgan's eyes flickered. "I'd like to ask a favor."

Graves was impassive. "Depends what it is."

The young CIA agent cleared his throat. "It's a little unorthodox. You know, outside channels."

"Don't make a habit of this," said Zammit. "You'll ruin your career."

"She worked with Kazov. Irina Markova. She knows everything."

Graves frowned. "A woman? A Russian woman sitting in on a meeting like this? Are you nuts?"

"Colonel," said Costopoulos, "I think we should meet this woman."

"I trust her, and it really is important," said Morgan.

"I agree," said Zammit.

Graves nodded reluctantly as Morgan pressed the speakerphone button. "Send her in," he said to the aide. "Where's Yarham?"

"Sulking in a bar down the street."

Irina Markova strode into the room, her walk as casually precise as a fashion model's. Her handshake was firm. Her slender frailty was belied by burning eyes that looked at Zammit as if she knew him. Her auburn hair was tied back in a short ponytail. She wore tight burgundy pants and a matching jacket over a bronze-colored blouse. As soon as she sat down, she crossed her long legs, rummaged in a handbag, and took out a pack of Marlboros. Her battered Zippo lighter produced a flame the size of Zammit's thumb, and she inhaled deeply.

"I want Boris avenged," she breathed, in heavily accented English.

"I'm afraid we're not in the avenging business," said Zammit.

Her pale violet eyes were appraising. "I have heard of you. Moscow. Mafia smuggling chlorofluorocarbons. People made jokes when you accepted that picture of Lenin."

"I'm a fossil collector."

Her broad smile revealed a gap between her two front teeth. She laughed a croaky, smoky laugh. "So, we start where?"

"Boris Kazov. Your editor. How did he die? And why?" asked Graves.

Her cheeks hollowed as she sucked the cigarette. "He was burned from within."

"No riddles, please," said Graves. "We don't have time."

"He had been sick for about two weeks. Went to the doctors, they didn't know. Hair falling out, bleeding everywhere, in agony."

She pointed at the bundle Jack Morgan held. "Because of that."

She lit a fresh cigarette from the half-smoked one. "His office was burgled about two weeks before he died. I think they were looking for those documents. But they were so important he always carried them with him, or hid them. He died the same day I brought them to Jack. Boris was tough. To die so fast, that way, was not natural."

As she said "not natural," Zammit's gaze slid over to Costopoulos. The Greek was already looking at him.

"How wasn't it natural?" asked Zammit.

"I am like Boris. Aggressive and persistent. I hounded medical staff at a local hospital. Found someone who had worked at the Chornobyl nuclear reactor. They recognized the symptoms. We called in specialists."

She crushed out her partially smoked cigarette and fumbled blindly for another as her violet eyes filled with tears. Zammit rose and filled a snifter with six ounces of Scotch whiskey. She smiled gratefully as he handed it to her.

"Crimean investigators come into the office with a Geiger counter. The counter is right off the scale. Finally they find it. Sewn into the back of his leather armchair, where he always worked."

"What?" asked Zammit, already dreading the answer.

She wiped her eyes. "A lead-sheathed rod of plutonium-239 salted with cobalt-60. With a tiny pinhole drilled in it. The pinhole ensured that the beam of radioactive particles emitted by the rod passed directly into his spine. He died of radiation poisoning."

There was silence. From his past experience with radioactivity, Zammit knew that plutonium-239 and cobalt-60 were two of the deadliest substances on the planet. Clean nuclear weapons—ones with relatively little fallout—were made with uranium or plutonium. Other radioactive elements were added to make weapons that were dirty, with lots of fallout. And the dirtiest nuclear weapons of all were made with cobalt-60.

"Tell them the story he was working on," urged Morgan.

"There is a cult operating throughout Crimea, throughout the former Soviet Union. That monk who raises the dead."

Zammit nodded. "Lazar Smegyev. But there are hundreds of cults here. In America too. You think a bunch of religious nuts killed Kazov?"

Her eyes were troubled. "Yes and no. Boris found that Smegyev keeps his acolytes in line with strange narcotic drugs. Most of the cults around are ordinary people, ignorant people. In this one the acolytes are soldiers and sailors. And not just junior people. Senior staff too. There are scientists and government people who belong. Rumors of sophisticated machines and computers. That is how this cult is different."

Morgan interrupted. "I know Irina has more information, but I have to tell you that I was able for the first time ever to penetrate one of Smegyev's secret rituals. I speak the language, I had a uniform, fake ID, the whole thing."

Markova pointed her cigarette accusingly. "You never told me. Or Boris. It would make a great story."

"Sorry," said Morgan. "But I can't share everything I learn."

"Keep talking," said Graves.

"I not only saw Smegyev raise from the dead some guy they'd crucified, but I overheard a bizarre conversation. I reported it to Yarham, and he dismissed it. That's why I sent the package to Randy Berkowitz."

Zammit felt as if he were diving into a pool of crystal water with something horrible lurking at the bottom. "Someone crucified? And raised from the dead?"

Graves's bushy eyebrows were twitching. He looked at Zammit. "Glinka."

"What?" asked Morgan.

Graves leaned forward and stabbed a forefinger at Markova. "This is not a news conference, and everything we say here is off the record. If I get wind of any kind of story being prepared, young lady, they'll never find your body."

The reporter in Irina Markova was wide awake. Her eyes burned like violet laser beams through a plume of cigarette smoke, and she nodded reluctantly.

Quickly Zammit told them about Ruslan Glinka and what had happened at the dam. He would have told Morgan some details about the contamination itself, but not with Markova in the room.

The young agent frowned. "Committed suicide, huh? With a strange drug. I know these guys are fanatics, but man . . ."

"What's this Jew and Satan business?" Zammit asked Markova.

"Smegyev preaches the destiny of Mother Russia. He says that destiny will soon be fulfilled. The Holy Chosen One, a descendant of the last Byzantine emperor, will be revealed and rule once more in Constantinople. Russians have always believed in Jewish conspiracies—it was the tsar's secret police who forged the Protocols of the Elders of Zion to justify pogroms, the document that influenced Hitler so much. And Russians have always believed the rest of the world is in a satanic conspiracy to destroy them."

Zammit remembered his conversation with Grand Master Angelo Fortucci about Satan and evil. "Do you believe any of this?"

"Of course not. I was educated at Oxford. But Russians are a very spiritual people, with a strong mystical, fatalistic streak."

Costopoulos asked, "Does this Holy Chosen One actually exist? Anyone ever seen him?"

She shrugged. "I don't know. According to the legend, he must prove himself against a worthy opponent before he can be anointed emperor."

Zammit frowned. "Did Smegyev make all of this up? Like L. Ron Hubbard did with Scientology?"

"No. There is a historical basis." She pointed at Morgan's bundle of documents. "It's in there. A Russian monk named Nestor was in Constantinople the day the city fell. He survived and returned to Russia. Wrote a book called *The Secret Chronicle*. He claims the last emperor was not killed in battle but somehow escaped. He says he helped to spirit the emperor's treasures from the city, which is no doubt some sort of fantasy. It is very hysterical and mystical, but it is that book, and Nestor's prophecies about Russia's destiny, that Smegyev is using." She hesitated. "There is something else as well."

Zammit looked at her keenly. "What?"

She stubbed out her cigarette. "I do not think it is the nature of cults to form alliances."

"Alliances?" said Graves.

"*Da*. With other cults."

"That makes sense," said Zammit. "If your cult is a bunch of loonies who believe in Holy Chosen Ones and secret imperial treasures, you're unlikely to feel empathy for a cult that believes the Great Pyramid was built by aliens."

"But that is what is happening," said Markova.

"What are you talking about?" asked Morgan.

"Early in his career, Smegyev had contacts with a Japanese cult called Aum Shinrikyo—Supreme Truth. The ones who released nerve gas in the Tokyo subway in 1995. I cannot believe the two cults had anything in common. Except one thing. It was also a high-tech cult and used drugs on its members."

"Well," said Graves, "that could form the basis of an unholy alliance. Look at the Hitler-Stalin pact."

Irina Markova continued. "Smegyev is also in contact with an American group with a strange name. The Spiritual Brotherhood of the She-Manitou. What is a She-Manitou?"

As he stared at her, Zammit felt the pieces of the puzzle whirling in his brain, as if in a tornado, but everything was moving too fast and he couldn't put them together. Cults. Pompo, head of the Spiritual Brotherhood of the She-Manitou. A Japanese cult in contact with Smegyev's. A chemical weapon used by the Japanese cult. A biological weapon used at the Ataturk Dam. What possible . . . ? The others were staring at him. He filed the bits and pieces away with a sense of foreboding.

"It's a sort of forest-dwelling great spirit," said Zammit distractedly. He drained his glass and strode to the window, looking down at the streets of this half-oriental version of Monaco. "We can talk about other cults later. Let's concentrate on the problem at hand. Irina, you say Smegyev's cult is popular? Why?"

Costopoulos said something to Markova in Russian. Startled that he spoke the language, she nodded.

The Greek sipped his brandy. "The first Russian state was founded at Kiev in the 9th century by Viking mercenaries. Four hundred years later, they were conquered by the Mongols. The oppression of Russians by the Mongols was so brutal, so notorious, it was the origin of the English word *slave*."

Graves interrupted. "Interesting, Dr. Costopoulos, but I don't see—"

Zammit interjected, "Let him talk."

"That brutality entered their political system and the fabric of everyday life. They became a psychologically conflicted people, convinced of their greatness and yet always suspecting they were inferior to Europeans, who had not succumbed to the Mongols. The bulwark of their spiritual strength was religion, which dominated every aspect of life."

Costopoulos drained his glass. "Then along came a new religion, an economic one, preached by the Bolsheviks. Many believed it. But in 1991 the USSR collapsed under the weight of its own incompetence and corruption."

Markova interrupted. "It is true. First people were amazed and despairing, then angry and cynical."

Costopoulos nodded. "The Soviet myth they believed in turned out to be history's biggest bad joke. Once again they felt inferior to Europeans. Their money was worthless. Western businessmen, *bisnizmeny*, flooded in. War heroes stood on street corners, selling their medals for pennies. The Marxist myth destroyed, they cast about in despair, reaching far back into history, finding older myths. Thousands of churches were reopened, and cults began to proliferate."

"That's true," said Jack Morgan. "A lot of people go to church, and many listen to ranting peasant monks like Smegyev."

"For several reasons," said Costopoulos. "Russia has a long history of peasant holy men, Rasputin being the most notorious. When doctors could do nothing, Rasputin hypnotized the tsar's son to stop his hemophiliac bleeding. Smegyev crucifies his followers, then somehow resurrects them. Both are a form of show business. Smegyev is also popular because he takes an old myth about the Holy Chosen One and dresses it in new clothes. He offers certainty and greatness to an uncertain people who want to be great."

Graves spoke. "Well, he's going to be in trouble when he has to produce the Holy Chosen One and can't do it."

Zammit turned away from the window and began to pace. "So, Ruslan Glinka, a highly educated Russian technician, was a member of this cult. We know that because he was crucified. When he was caught he committed suicide, using one of the strange drugs Irina referred to. What does a Russian cult have to do with a Turkish reservoir?"

He turned to Markova. "Even in today's chaos, it can't be easy to get hold of a rod of plutonium salted with cobalt-60. Where is it?"

"The authorities confiscated it. But I was able to find out something important through my contacts at *Minatom*, the Ministry of Nuclear Energy." She lit another smoke. "There is an inventory system, so rods can be tracked. If one goes missing, they will know."

"How?"

"Each rod is numbered. The number is engraved into the lead casing. The system has broken down, and many rods have simply disappeared. But my contact told me the number of this particular rod and where it was stored before it disappeared."

"Where?"

"Penza-19."

Graves shook his head. "I don't understand."

Morgan replied, "It isn't commonly known, even within the intelligence community. I researched this during training at Langley. There is a network of secret cities all over Russia. Maybe sixteen or seventeen. All are sealed off with electrified fences and guard towers. The residents are scientists and technicians lured there by special privileges unavailable to ordinary citizens. But once they go into one of these installations they are never allowed out. They die there. At Penza-19 they do nuclear research. We believe this particular city has a population of over one hundred thousand, and the fenced-off area is over forty square miles. These cities never appear on any map, and officially they don't exist."

"What's the significance of the number?" asked Costopoulos.

Jack Morgan smiled grimly. "For decades Western intelligence agencies drove themselves crazy asking the same question. Where are the other eighteen Penzas? In the case of Krasnoyarsk-45, where are the other forty-four? It wasn't until recently we found out what the numbers mean."

"And?"

"It would be funny if we hadn't wasted so many resources on this over the last five decades. It's a postal code."

A brief silence. Zammit laughed. This was ludicrous. "Sorry," he said to Morgan. "But it *is* funny."

"Is it important to know where this rod came from?" asked Colonel Graves.

"At first I didn't think so," said Morgan. "Then I had a good look at Kazov's notes." He undid the elastic bands and opened a folder. He leafed through it, pulled out a photograph, and placed it on the table. Everyone craned to look.

It had been taken with a telephoto lens, then enlarged. A close-up of a face beneath the wide visor of a military cap. The face was square and meaty, and the hard pale eyes were slanted, Mongol style. The mouth was a brutal slit, compressed in anger, and the jaw, clenched in rage, bulged in tight knots of muscle.

"Crikey," said Colonel Graves. "Who's this gorilla?"

Morgan replied, "This is the only known photograph. General Vladimir Bled."

"So *that's* him," said Graves. "No one knows much about him, as I recall. Except that he's capable, hard as hell, and twice as mean. What's the tie-in?"

Jack Morgan leaned forward. "Smegyev's ritual, the one I got into. A big guy was there, in a general's uniform, drunk half out of his mind, talking about the Holy Chosen One being the new tsar enthroned in a rose-red church in Constantinople. He and Smegyev spoke briefly, about what I don't know. Then the big guy drank so much I thought he was going to die. He must have a liver made of asbestos."

Morgan stood and started pacing. "I didn't recognize him, and there were no pictures in the files. That's why Yarham didn't believe me."

He leaned over and tapped the photo. "It was him."

They heard the click of a cigarette lighter and turned to Irina Markova. She spoke, her husky voice full of whiskey and smoke. "And General Bled used to be in charge of security at Penza-19."

Dead silence.

"Wait a moment," said Zammit. "We're talking about one of the toughest, most capable soldiers in the former USSR, right? And he joins a cult like this?"

Costopoulos interrupted. "Bled must have believed in Marxism, or at least in the might of the Soviet state. Then it was proved to be a lie and a failure. For a proud and serious patriot, the humiliation would be almost unbearable. It's a process of transference. The intense conviction you felt for the idea that betrayed you is transferred, intact, to something else. If possible, its polar opposite."

Irina Markova looked thoughtful. "Humiliation. I heard a story. Bled and other military men were invited to meet with their NATO counterparts. Before the meeting, a German protocol staffer went to our soldiers and gave them a condescending lecture on how to behave—bathe, use deodorant, don't spit, don't bolt your food, don't get drunk and throw up. I heard Bled was so angry he destroyed an entire barracks with his bare hands and it took four units of military police to restrain him."

Costopoulos nodded. "Being made to feel inferior. And by a German."

Jack Morgan threw himself into a chair. "There's more. You know the Black Sea military and naval maneuvers going on? The ones nobody was told were going to happen?"

Mike Zammit was getting the picture. "Let me guess."

"That's right," said Morgan. "General Vladimir Bled. Drunk, religious fanatic, and commander of the Fourteenth Army Division. And a thief."

"What?" demanded Zammit.

"Bled is not only connected with the mad monk Smegyev, but the Russian mafia as well. That's the story Kazov was working on. If you wrote a novel about this, no one would believe you. I've got the details here."

"Do you have any more on this guy's background?" asked Zammit.

Morgan nodded. He opened another file and started to read. "Not much is known about his personal life, not even his date of birth. Wait a second, the career summary is in here somewhere."

Graves spoke as Morgan searched. "I remember. Brilliant tactician, brutal as hell but gets the job done. Wherever there's disaster looming, the Kremlin calls Bled. But he calls the shots."

"What do you mean?" asked Costopoulos.

"They sent him to Chechnya a few years ago. The Kremlin ordered him to bomb the capital city, Grozny, into surrender. Bled replied there were Russian troops held hostage and refused to bomb it."

"He disobeyed orders?" asked Zammit.

"Worse. He disobeyed a direct order from the president of Russia, his Commander-in-Chief. The way I heard it, he told Boris Yeltsin to go screw himself. There was nothing Yeltsin could do about it."

Zammit snorted. "Sure there was. It's called a court martial."

Graves shook his head. "Bled gets things done. In today's Russia, not a lot gets done. A guy like Bled knows he's indispensable. President Bugarin's stroke last year turned him into a zombie, and his underlings are duking it out in a power struggle. Under those conditions Bled, who is efficient and has the loyalty of his men, can function as an autonomous warlord. The Kremlin moves him around from post to post, trying to prevent him from consolidating a power base. They thought sending him as military liaison to the Ukraine, in charge of a single division, would cut him off at the knees. Obviously it hasn't. They always give him the tough jobs, hoping he'll screw up. But he never does, even though he's a notorious boozer."

"Wait a moment," said Zammit. "Bled is Russian. Sevastopol is in the Ukraine. The Ukraine declared independence from the former USSR in 1991. How can Bled have any influence here in the Crimea? This peninsula belongs to the Ukrainian Republic."

"Ah," said Graves, eyes keen over his half-moon spectacles. "That's what makes the post–Cold War world so interesting. Russia gave the Crimean peninsula to the Ukraine as a gift in 1954. The majority of the population is still Russian and they're agitating to rejoin Russia. But the Russians retained control of Sevastopol because it's a vital naval base. When the Ukraine declared independence, they said they would take Sevastopol as their own, and all the Russian ships harbored there too. The Russians said fuck you. They argued for years. Finally in 1997 they signed a deal. They divvied up the fleet, with the Russians getting four-fifths. The Russians also keep Sevastopol on a twenty-year lease, paying a hundred million dollars a year, while acknowledging that it is in fact Ukrainian territory. So the Kremlin has a lot of military and naval people here on the spot to keep an eye on things. Twenty thousand sailors, roughly the same number of soldiers, and the Forty-Third Missile Army Group of the Strategic Rocket Services guarding the nukes. That's Bled's current assignment."

"Here it is," said Morgan. He started to read Bled's career summary. "Graduate of the airborne training school in Ryazan. Served in Afghanistan with distinction. Made lieutenant-general. You already know about Chechnya and Penza-19. He was posted to Siberia a couple of years ago when things got tense with China over that border dispute. He was in charge of security for Biopreparat. Before that, he—"

"Wait a second," said Zammit. "Bio *what*?"

"Biopreparat. The old Soviet bio-war agency. We know almost nothing about it except that some of the secret cities do research for it. It's rumored they specialize in making biological warfare agents that are immune to Western antibiotics. Why, is it important?"

 An hour later, Mike Zammit stared in disbe-
lief as Jack Morgan shuffled together Kazov's
pile of documents. The picture of General
Bled still lay on the table.

Over a weak protest from Graves, Zammit
had provided a quick overview of what was
happening at the Ataturk Dam to explain the
significance of the fact that the cyanobacteria was genetically engineered to be immune to antibiotics. Then Morgan began reading
the material he'd translated from Kazov's notes.

At the end of Morgan's presentation, Zammit broke the silence
first as he began pacing the room. "So Kazov's best estimate is that
Bled has stolen at least $100 million in cash, weapons, and supplies
over the last three years?"

"The weapons and supplies are in addition to the money," cor-
rected Irina Markova. "To give an idea of scale, four months ago
1500 box cars, each carrying twenty tons of artillery ammunition,
went missing and were never found. And that was just in one
week."

"That's right," said Morgan. "The amount stolen by Bled in the
last twelve months alone is equal to four times the British army's
stored artillery. God knows how much these weapons and supplies
are worth, or where they are now."

"Or where all the money goes," said Markova. "I have tried to
find out, and I can't. I'm sure the Kremlin doesn't know either."

Zammit turned to Graves. "How is this possible?"

"The Soviet army was gigantic. And proud. Now the USSR is
gone, their currency is junk, and conscripts make less than twenty
dollars a month, if they get paid at all. Bled makes sure his soldiers
get paid."

"Boris doesn't get into it, but that's how this whole thing got
started," continued Morgan. "When Bled found out that post-
Soviet democracy couldn't pay the soldiers, he took charge. The
Kremlin liked it because it freed them of the obligation. If Bled
was in a particular post, whether it was Siberia or Chechnya, he
creamed the top of the local economy. The Kremlin turned a blind
eye. I bet they're regretting it now."

Markova interrupted. "None of that was news. But to extort

more money, he started using intermediaries. Mafia. He sold them supplies from the stockpiles because they need weapons."

"In effect," said Graves, "Bled has privatized his military command. He decides what his troops will or will not do and has made himself personally responsible for their welfare."

"Bled isn't the only commanding officer doing this," said Morgan, "but he does it on a gigantic scale, and he's untouchable, for the reasons we've already heard."

Zammit objected, "But this can't go on for long. The warlord gets stronger, makes powerful friends, sees how incompetent the Kremlin is, and thinks, Why not?"

Graves nodded. "Russia can overcome its past and become a successful democracy with a functional capitalist economy that isn't run by gangsters. Or it can turn into the world's biggest and coldest banana republic."

"Your opinion?" asked Zammit.

"I'm investing in banana futures."

"Why?" asked Costopoulos.

"Russia has always been an autocracy or a dictatorship. First it was the tsar, venerated as the embodiment of God's will. Then Lenin and Stalin, the embodiment of History's will. Russians *like* having such leaders. What they fear most is not a dictator but *bespredel,* anarchy. Today there is no strongman in charge, just underlings who think they could be one. Bugarin's stroke has made him unfit to govern."

"Surely there's a vice president to take over if the guy's incompetent?" protested Zammit.

Irina clawed tobacco off her tongue. "The last coup attempt was *led* by the vice president, so the office was abolished. Bugarin keeps all power for himself, appoints ambitious men to junior posts, and gives them overlapping responsibilities. They are so exhausted fighting among themselves they don't have time to plot against him."

"Is there *anyone* reliable in Bugarin's government?" asked Zammit.

Markova coughed. "Constitutionally, it should be the prime minister, but he has no power base. Here, if you don't have a power base among corrupt wealthy businessmen, the army and the mafia, it doesn't matter what your position is on paper. But there is the new national security advisor, Vyacheslav Radchuk.

Ukrainian. Military background. Just before Bugarin's stroke there was a power struggle. Radchuk got control of the Federal Security Service."

"Successor to the KGB," added Morgan.

"We have to find someone in the government we can trust. What's this guy like?" asked Zammit.

Irina shrugged. "Too early to tell. Supposed to be a democrat. Supposed to have integrity, whatever that means."

"Is Radchuk connected to Bled?" asked Graves.

"No," Morgan replied. "Apparently they hate each other's guts. That's one of the reasons Bugarin appointed him. He wasn't stupid enough to have a national security advisor who's bosom buddies with a guy like Bled."

As Irina reached for yet another cigarette, Zammit rubbed his face and coughed. "Good God, woman, are you trying to turn your lungs into bacon?" She slid it back in the pack.

Zammit threw himself on the couch. "So what do we have? First, a member of Smegyev's cult feeding the cyanobacteria."

Costopoulos nodded. "Second, General Bled is a member of the cult."

"Third," said Markova, "Bled was in charge at Penza-19, which is where the rod of plutonium salted with cobalt-60 came from, and at Biopreparat—"

"Where the cyanobacteria came from," agreed Zammit.

"He's heavily armed and has lots of money," said Graves.

"Without permission from either the Russian or Ukrainian governments, he is conducting military and naval maneuvers on the Black Sea," added Morgan.

"And," breathed Markova, "he found out Boris was doing a story on all of this and murdered him."

"Exactly," concluded Graves. "You don't have to be Sherlock Holmes to deduce that the mastermind behind this whole thing is General Vladimir Bled."

"It isn't," said Stavros Costopoulos.

Incredulous, Graves stared at the Greek scholar. "It's obvious! How can you say otherwise?"

Costopoulos shook his head. "Think. Boris Kazov. He's doing a story on you. You find out about it. You tell your partners, the mafia, whoever. You want him dead."

He stood and started pacing. "How do you kill him? If you're a military man, a soldier, you don't fool around. You shoot him down in the street as he walks to the café. You toss a grenade through his window."

He turned to Irina. "You say his office was burgled a couple of weeks before he died?" She nodded, transfixed. "And he was sick for two weeks before he died?" Another nod.

"Who brings a radioactive rod to an office burglary?" asked Costopoulos. "One with a pinhole already drilled in it?"

Absolute silence.

"Someone who knew that whatever was found in Boris's office, he was going to be murdered anyway. In a complicated way, using material hard to obtain. To ensure he died a lingering, agonizing death. It is well thought out. It is subtle. It is vicious. It is so, so . . ."

"*Elaborate*," said Zammit.

"Precisely. We have seen this psychological signature elsewhere, yes? At the dam."

Stavros walked over to the table and tapped his finger on the photo of General Bled. "This man is as subtle as a falling anvil. It can't be him."

"It isn't." Zammit rose to his feet. He pulled the tattered anonymous e-mail message from his pocket and held it aloft. "It's *him*!"

 **32** The sour, vinegary stink of old-fashioned printer's ink and solvent was almost as overpowering as the smell of stale tobacco smoke in the offices of the *Glory of Sevastopol*. A battered wooden desk covered with cigarette burns, a creaky credenza with a missing door, dented green filing cabinets, a picture of Stalin on the wall with an X drawn across it in felt-tip pen, a girlie calendar from 1995.

Frustrated that he didn't know Russian or Ukrainian, Zammit stood in the middle of the room as the others threw open every drawer in Kazov's desk and rummaged through filing cabinets and overflowing waste baskets. They'd had to break into the room through the seals Crimean investigators had placed on the door.

"How did he find anything in here?" panted Morgan. "Hire detectives?"

Zammit was thinking hard, trying to concentrate over the banging of drawers and the rustle of paper. He called to Markova. The cigarette in her hand was dangerously close to igniting a stack of yellowing newsprint on top of the filing cabinet she was searching. "In the two weeks between the burglary and Boris's death, you're sure he didn't mention any new information he'd uncovered? Nothing about Bled having another partner apart from the mafia?"

"*Nyet,*" she said curtly. "I didn't see much of him. He had me working on another assignment. Drug trafficking."

"Maybe the two stories were connected. The mafia controls billions in drug trafficking."

"*Nyet,*" she said distractedly, slamming the drawer shut and opening the last one in the last cabinet. "Small traffic. The mafia traffics in heroin, opium, cocaine. These are strange drugs, never seen before. Administered in unusual ways."

The pinwheeling of her fingers through the files became slower and slower, then abruptly stopped. Her violet eyes darted from side to side. A bead of sweat rolled down the face of a motionless Jack Morgan and he didn't brush it away. Graves was bent over with his hand in a wastebasket, staring. Costopoulos's head slowly rose as Zammit walked to the window and gazed out through the grimy glass.

"Ruslan Glinka committed suicide with a strange drug. Lazar Smegyev's cult uses strange drugs. Bled can't supply the cult with strange drugs, because the mafia doesn't have them and Biopreparat makes only biological weapons."

Zammit turned to face the others. "Which means the drugs come from another partner, someone who is working with Bled and Smegyev. That's why Boris Kazov had you working on that drug trafficking story. Where are your notes?"

Irina opened the door and disappeared into the main newsroom.

As they waited, Zammit noticed Costopoulos staring fixedly at the map of southern Russia, the Ukraine, and Turkey thumbtacked to the office wall. Slowly the Greek walked over to it and placed the tips of his fingers on the paper. His eyes searched the entire map. "National Geographic," he muttered distractedly. "Very good."

Idly at first, but with increasing intensity, he began tracing something with his forefinger. Graves was staring at the Greek as well.

"Michael," whispered Costopoulos. "Could you come here for a moment?"

Zammit and the other two men strode over. Zammit studied the hawkish profile, saw the gleam in the brown eyes, and knew he'd seen this before. Costopoulos had figured something out. He stared at the map, transfixed. Zammit knew he had to snap him out of it. "You want us all to hold our breath until we turn blue? What is it, Stav?"

Costopoulos scratched his cheek. "One thing we didn't talk about in our rush to get over here. Bled. The cult. The mafia. Stealing all that money, all those weapons. Unexplained military and naval maneuvers." He looked into Zammit's eyes. *"What for?"* he said. "Remember what the PKK told you? That Anwar Hussein knew about the contamination at the dam *before* it was discovered? Can you think of a better excuse for invading another country than having them cut off your water supply?"

Zammit suddenly understood. "Colonel, a country like Turkey is surrounded by hostile powers—Iran, Syria, Iraq, Georgia, Armenia, Tuvanistan, Russia, and so on. What does Turkey fear most?"

"A war on two fronts. So?"

Zammit pointed. "Anwar is in the southeast, being provocative, and actually having a good reason to do so. Half the Turkish army is there, trying to deal with the Kurds but keeping an eye on him too. Suppose he invades. I mean a *serious* invasion. Everything he's got."

Graves snorted. "Hello, slaughterhouse."

"But what if it's part of a wider scheme?" Zammit persisted.

"I'm a spy, not a military strategist. I don't understand," said Morgan.

Costopoulos pointed. "Anwar ties up the half of the Turkish army that's in the southeast. Once the Turks realize he's serious, the other half is also sent to the southeast to finish him off."

"Leaving the rest of the country virtually defenseless," said Zammit.

Stavros continued. "Most of the Russian and Ukrainian fleet is at the port of Sevastopol. General Bled, having ensured that maneuvers are under way, launches lightning air and naval strikes across the Black Sea."

Stavros did a rough measurement with his index finger. "The strikes capture the largest city, Istanbul, and Ankara, the capital. They are almost on the same latitude, about 400 miles from Sevastopol. He also seizes control of the sparsely populated 300-square-mile area between those two cities, control he can consolidate later. It's over before any of Turkey's NATO allies, or the Russians themselves, can even blink."

"But we'd retaliate and force him out," argued Morgan. "Just the way an international effort forced Saddam Hussein out of Kuwait in 1991. We already have aircraft carriers and fighters in the Arabian Gulf to patrol northern Iraq."

Zammit said, "Jack, Saddam didn't have nuclear weapons. Colonel, how many nukes does Bled have under his control?"

Graves's face was suddenly as white as his hair. Tonelessly he said, "A couple of hundred. Maybe more." He glanced at Jack Morgan. "And there aren't nearly as many troops, aircraft carriers, or planes in the Gulf as there used to be. It would take weeks to get a sizable strike force into the area."

"So," said Zammit, "once Bled has what he wants, who's going to take it away from him? Is Russia willing to get into a nuclear war with one of its own generals who knows everything about its strategy and contingency plans? Is the United States willing to risk nuclear war and possibly the incineration of the American heartland to save Turkey? Is either of them willing to nuke the Turkish people when they haven't done anything?"

"Oh, *man!*" Morgan moaned.

"But Bled isn't going to take and hold a country the size of Turkey with just the Fourteenth Army Division and the Forty-Third Missile Army Group," Graves protested.

Costopoulos interrupted. "I hardly think General Bled is the only senior army, navy, or air force commander who is a member of this cult. As Irina said, there are probably many more members of this conspiracy. It may even reach into the Kremlin itself."

Zammit nodded. "Besides, he probably doesn't want the whole country. He wants the port city Istanbul, formerly Constantinople. For almost 2,000 years it's been one of the most famous ports in the world. He also wants enough territory to make a new country that is agriculturally and industrially sustainable. Turkey is one of only seven countries on earth that is self-sufficient in agriculture. Most of that farming takes place in the area he's planning to capture between Istanbul and Ankara. Once he's got the cities and the farmland and can defend them with nukes, he's invulnerable."

"Excellent point," said Costopoulos. "He *can't* take the whole country, because the Iraqis have to get something out of this. Anwar probably gets most of southeastern Turkey—control of the major oil pipeline on Turkish soil, plus the Ataturk Dam, which will permanently secure his water supply. Bled has probably promised to protect him with nukes too."

"But it's not just the Turkish army and navy he has to defeat," argued Jack Morgan. "Turkey has a population of over 70 million. There would be riots all over the country."

"I know," said Zammit. He thought of the poisoning of the Ataturk reservoir and the deaths downstream. Did the conspirators intend to kill millions of people? "Maybe they have a way of dealing with that scenario."

Irina appeared in the doorway clutching a manila folder. They briefed her on their theories. She listened intently. "It sounds plausible, but don't you remember what happened in Chechnya? General Grachev described the Chechens as 'medieval savages' and said they would be defeated in a week. Instead they tore the army to pieces. The Russian military used to be fearsome. No more."

Zammit remembered the cringing conscripts assigned to guard him in Dzerzhinsk. "You may be right. The Russian army is as corrupt as the Tijuana police force and about as effective in an armed confrontation."

"Maybe we're jumping the gun," said Morgan hopefully.

Costopoulos still looked thoughtful. "Many of the troops will be members of the cult. Fanatics. And there are those drugs as well. What they could be for, I don't know."

He turned back to the map. "But something's missing. This has been so well thought out except for one thing."

"What?" asked Zammit.

"The poison in the dam, giving Anwar an excuse to invade. The timing, so it happens at the crucial stage of the election campaign. Making sure maneuvers are under way so Bled's strike will be lightning fast. It's brilliant. But it's like in Chechnya, with the Russian army running into so much trouble. They failed to take out the Chechen leadership beforehand. Chop off the head and the body dies . . ."

Pounding footsteps approached. Someone banged on the office door. Markova threw it open. A young newsman whispered urgently in her ear. She turned to the others, face ashen.

"Prime Minister Amurkhan has been assassinated."

Mike Zammit stared at the laptop computer on the steel desk and waited.

The white room, made of painted concrete blocks, had an antiseptic look and smell, a gray concrete floor, and no windows. Apart from the desk, an office chair, and a telephone, it was bare. The basement of the Istanbul offices of Turkish Intelligence was completely silent apart from the quiet whirring of the ventilation system. He assumed it was soundproof and tried not to think what sounds might be coming from the terrorist members of the Resistance Army of Allah as they were interrogated.

It had been six hours since he heard the news and flew with Costopoulos and Graves back to Istanbul from Sevastopol. Before they left, Irina Markova told him what she had learned while researching the story for Boris Kazov. He found the story so bizarre he could scarcely credit it, yet it had the odd little details that convinced him it was true. Besides, he increasingly liked and trusted Irina. He kept compulsively flipping it over in his mind, this bright coin of information, heads, tails, heads, tails. What did it mean?

Zammit contemplated the laptop. Flip the coin, flip the coin. The drugs must have come from another partner. But who was he, and what were they for?

He turned as he heard the door open. Relief washed over him. It was Kitson Kang and Frankie Richards, just in from Seattle.

"Hi, boss," said Kang. "Never seen riots before. Or so many police. I thought we'd be dragged from our armored cars and torn to pieces." He noticed the laptop. "That it?"

"Yes."

"Can I get started?" Kang was already moving toward the machine as fast as Catula toward Cat.

"Be careful," cautioned Zammit. "This is all we have. It may be nothing or turn out to be everything. We don't know what's in there, or how it's guarded."

Kang sat at the table and contemplated the computer, fingering his gold earring like Jackie Chan trying to figure out how to perform a particularly difficult stunt.

Richards was wearing charcoal palazzo slacks, a black blouse with silver stripes, and a black jacket.

"You ever been to Turkey before?"

"No."

"Don't go out alone. Turkish men are generally polite, but you'll be mobbed."

Frankie smiled. "I can take care of myself. But thanks for the advice. By the way, I'm really glad to see you're OK."

There was an awkward pause as she watched Kit open the machine, then turned to Zammit, all business. "What's happening? Cairo gave me a briefing, but it was a little hard to follow." She ticked the points off on her fingers. "Kidnapped by terrorists, an ancient underground temple, finding canisters in the reservoir, discovering what's in them, a mad monk who leads a cult, a renegade Russian general, a possible invasion of Turkey by both Iraq and said general, and something about a beautiful Russian journalist. Sounds to me like you're turning into Indiana Jones."

Zammit filled her in on the temple, his escape, and the recovery and analysis of the canisters. "The Russian is Irina Markova. Investigative journalist. Her murdered boss, Boris Kazov, had her working on a story about unusual drugs."

"Unusual how?"

"First, they're being manufactured illegally. They're also being tested illegally, sometimes with fatal results."

Impatiently Frankie said, "Specifics, please."

"According to her investigation, over the past couple of years a secret factory in Pakistan has been producing and testing, on an experimental basis, a wide range of odd drugs, both amphetamines and narcotics, in pill, liquid, and aerosol form."

"How did Markova get onto this?"

"Kazov assigned her to the story after learning that the mad monk Lazar Smegyev used drugs to keep his cult members in line," replied Zammit.

"Continue."

"Persons unknown were administering drugs to street people, derelicts, the desperately poor who for five dollars would take some 'medicine.' Boys, teens, those in the prime of life, the old— but always males, never females. Many died, and since autopsies weren't done on people like this, no one knew why. But some of the men who took the drugs went berserk."

"That's a pretty strong word. Give me an example," said Frankie.

Zammit pulled several pieces of paper from his pocket. "This is a summary of Irina's notes, in English." He flipped the pages until he found what he wanted. "The most spectacular case was a man, seventy-four years old, reportedly a gentle soul whose favorite recreation was dominoes. After swallowing a dose of something, the old man strangled his wife and three of his grandchildren, slashed his best friend to death with a saber, and went on a shooting rampage that killed twenty-two people. When police found him, he was clinging like a rock climber halfway up the rough walls of a medieval building, screaming curses. When they shot him, he fell to the ground, almost thirty feet, then got up and attacked the police. It took a dozen bullets to stop him, and even after he was stone dead his limbs twitched for five minutes."

"Jesus Christ," said Richards. "That's berserk, all right."

Zammit continued to read. "Intrigued by this bizarre episode, a visiting British pathologist volunteered to do an autopsy. Sections of the old man's brain were sent to Britain for analysis. No physiological abnormalities were found, but there was no serotonin in his brain at all, no beta-endorphin, and no trace of another substance, an enzyme called monoamine oxidase. Baffled, the police and the medical people finally gave up, but for a long time afterward there were periodic reports of similar occurrences, although never as violent. None of the drug dealers were caught." He put the papers back in his pocket. "That's it."

"What does it tell you?"

"The conspiracy involves the monk Smegyev, his acolyte General Bled, and Anwar Hussein. But none of them has the expertise to make drugs like these, so there has to be another partner, who is supplying them."

"Any idea who it could be?"

"Not a clue."

Zammit watched Kang clenching and unclenching his fingers, like a concert pianist about to tackle a Rachmaninoff piano concerto.

"What happened to Amurkhan? The news reports are garbled."

Zammit shrugged. "Amurkhan got to the back entrance of the Hilton, a meeting place no one was supposed to know about. A kid ten or eleven years old recognized her and asked for an autograph. She said sure, then all hell broke loose."

"How?"

"The kid had a small weapon in his hand, like a derringer, only plastic and loaded with dum-dum bullets. One of Amurkhan's security men saw it and lunged, but the kid shot her in the heart before he could get there. Then five other assassins came out of nowhere. Half a dozen of her security people were killed, along with some unfortunates who just happened to be in the alley. The little assassin was killed too. Several of the killers were captured. Apparently they're Islamic fundamentalists, members of the Resistance Army of Allah. I think bad things are happening to them right here in this building."

Richards grimaced. "What now?"

Zammit shrugged. "Who knows? But it could have been worse."

Her sardonic green eyes narrowed. "It could have been worse? I thought you liked Amurkhan. The prime minister of Turkey is dead and you . . ." Her eyes were suddenly shrewd. " 'Could *have been* worse?' " she quoted. "That's an odd verb tense to use. You're not telling me something."

This woman is extremely clever, thought Zammit, filled with a peculiar sense of pride, as if her intelligence reflected on him. "I've been sworn to secrecy," he said, feeling pompous. "I'll tell you later."

He didn't want to say what was really bothering him. Yildiz had said it was impossible for anyone to know that he was meeting his prime minister at the Hilton. Yet somehow RAA not only knew but was able to prepare and implement a complex and deadly plan on short notice. Zammit knew that if an adult male had tried to approach Amurkhan for an autograph, he would have been instantly buried under a pile of secret service agents. The use of the boy was ingenious. He tried not to think of the word, but it slithered into his brain anyway: *elaborate.*

"How's the analysis going?" he asked Richards.

"I have some bad news."

Zammit suddenly felt very tired. He remembered how short of sleep he was. "The only kind of news around these days. What?"

"The cyanobacteria is genetically engineered. It's a hybrid, so it's difficult to predict its life cycle. It appears to have three stages. First, massive blooming. Second, generation of toxin. Soon it will enter the third stage."

"What's that?"

"Reproduction."

"But it *has* been reproducing. That's why there's so much of it."

Frankie Richards shook her head. "It's been *altered*. I've analyzed the stromatolites and those fleshy bulbs that are growing on the surface. I'm not yet sure what they are or what they contain. But they appear to be reproductive organs."

"Bacteria don't have reproductive organs," Zammit protested. "They're asexual."

"I'm the microbiologist, Mike. Don't forget what a peculiar creature this is. A few species of cyanobacteria reproduce through cell division, fragmentation of colonies, then formation of sexual reproductive organs called fruiting bodies. But in natural cyanobacteria the fruiting bodies are microscopically small. The basketball-sized bulbs in the reservoir are colossal by comparison."

Wearily Zammit rubbed his face. "How much work did Biopreparat do on this stuff, anyway?"

"A lot. What bothers me is the fact that it's a weapon. Who knows what capabilities they built into it? There's another thing—"

"Piece of cake!" cried Kang gleefully. He typed furiously. "A five-year-old could hack this thing."

Richards took Zammit's arm. "Mike, there's something else. The samples we're getting back in Seattle. Analysis is taking forever because they're contaminated. All of them."

Despite the earnest look on her face, Zammit smiled. "How can you contaminate contamination?"

She punched him in the arm. "Sometimes your sense of humor really bugs me. It isn't funny. It's like they've been heated or something. Junk, weird stuff. We found nicotine, of all things. Like somebody swished a cigarette butt through the sample. We're trying to detect parts per trillion of particular substances and this garbage swamps everything."

Zammit thought hard. "The samples are coming from the dam. The Turks smoke. Maybe there's someone at the dam besides Ruslan Glinka who's in on the plot."

The door opened. It was Costopoulos and Yildiz. The Turk was pale as he was introduced to Richards. "Pleased to meet you, colonel. Mike has told me good things."

As Yildiz fished for his cigarettes, Zammit asked, "How goes the interrogation?"

Yildiz flicked his lighter and inhaled as if he wanted smoke to come out his toes, then shot two blue columns from his nostrils.

"Let's say it's in its terminal stages. I'm glad you told me about the possibility of suicide weapons. We removed them in time."

"Any information?"

"They babble about the Koran. I hate fanatics. They're not reasonable."

"Where's Graves?" asked Zammit.

"On the phone to Washington. They are very upset, so he had to tell them."

Zammit's eyes were hard. "The White House leaks like a sieve. The information has to be completely restricted to the president and his immediate staff."

Yildiz coughed. "Graves knows that as well as you do." He pointed at Kang. "Does he know what he's doing?"

"Yes, I do," replied Kang, not taking his eyes from the screen. "And I'm in."

As the others gathered around the table, Zammit whispered in the Turk's ear, telling him what Frankie Richards had said.

"Contaminated?" Yildiz's eyes searched his. "Could this be a natural phenomenon?" Zammit shook his head. "No way."

The Turk's jaw muscles bunched. "I'll call the dam immediately and have it checked."

As Yildiz left the room, Zammit walked over to where the others were staring intently at the screen.

"Where did this machine come from?" asked Kang.

Zammit replied, "The Turkish police had a file on the leader of the RAA assassination team, knew his address. They raided his apartment and found the computer there. It was hidden under the floorboards. He forgot that he'd set the clock alarm. It was beeping."

"I thought Islamic fundamentalists hated the West and Western technology," said Kang.

"They've always been selective about what parts of Western culture they hate," replied Costopoulos. "Iranian mullahs who rant against America use television to tell their people how awful it is. When the Ayatollah Khomeni was dying, he was hooked up to every modern medical device you can name, and damn the expense."

Kang grinned. "I see what you mean. If they hate the West so much, why don't they give up the Sidewinder missiles and go back to using bows and arrows?"

"Let's concentrate on the task at hand," said Zammit. "What's in there?"

"It's in a foreign language. But there aren't a lot of files. And look here." He hit a few keys. "This guy never cleans out his e-mail. He's saved 388 messages. Here's the first one."

Costopoulos peered. "It's in Turkish."

"I thought Turkish writing was all that swirly stuff, like Arab calligraphy," said Kang.

As he read the first message, Costopoulos said, "Racially, Turks and Arabs are completely different. Kemal Ataturk wanted a new written Turkish language, one based on the Latin alphabet. He called in a team of scholars and asked how long it would take. They said six years. He said, 'You have six months.' And they did it."

He touched Kang on the shoulder. "Next."

He turned to Zammit. "They did a nice job. It's a logical language, easy to learn. Incidentally, if you want to make a Turk angry, call him an Arab. They think of themselves as Europeans who just happen to be Muslim." He read another message. "Next."

After three more messages Costopoulos said, without taking his eyes from the screen, "I need a pad of paper and a pen."

Zammit opened a desk drawer and found both. Stavros scribbled furiously as he read. Ten minutes later he was done with the e-mail. Kang opened the other files, and the Greek found nothing important. As he sat on the edge of the desk reading his notes, Colonel Yildiz came in. "Nothing," he said to Zammit. "No indication that other personnel would have the remotest connection with causing contamination in the samples."

Zammit shrugged. He didn't believe it, but he knew the Turk had had a rough day. He wondered if the RAA terrorists were dead. "OK. Let's see what Stav has."

The Greek flicked through the pages. "Of the 388 messages, 264 are old or of no interest to us. But there are 124 messages that are either to or from someone named *ghazi*. Requests for weapons. Requests for dates, times. Requests for drugs."

The Greek stared at the white ceiling, frowning. "And some interesting ones inquiring about the role of RAA in the structure of government in the new fundamentalist Turkey, once the 'unclean one' is dead."

"What does *ghazi* mean?" asked Richards.

" 'Warrior,' " said Yildiz. "The nickname for Ataturk, the great leader. In today's Turkey, to call yourself *ghazi* would be like an American politician saying his name was George Washington."

Costopoulos looked thoughtful. "It seems to me we are dealing with someone who has a substantial ego. Not to mention delusions of grandeur."

"Wait a second," interrupted Kang. "There's a hidden file."

Costopoulos looked. "*Ghazi* is a code name for someone called Abdul Jamal."

"Anyone heard of this guy?" asked Zammit.

A brief silence. "Wait a moment," said Stavros. "There's a reference to the rivers of Babylon and a knight. Pitiful attempts at being cryptic."

Zammit pulled the tattered e-mail message from his pocket. "My mysterious correspondent. Mr. Jamal. Obviously the man who incited the RAA terrorists to assassinate Amurkhan. Who is he? What is he supposed to get out of this plot?"

"The reference to the overthrow of the government is obviously connected with what the PKK told you about when RAA tried to recruit them," Yildiz said to Zammit. "And to a fundamentalist, the 'unclean one' is obviously Amurkhan."

"I beg your pardon?" came a cool singsong voice.

They turned and stared.

Standing in the doorway, in her trademark white skirt and jacket with her sunglasses tucked in the pocket, was Thamar Amurkhan.

34

A small smile played over Amurkhan's mouth as she saw the looks of astonishment on every face but Yildiz's and Zammit's.

As she walked into the room, she said, "Thank you again, Dr. Zammit, for suggesting at the Dolmabahçe Palace that I use a body double."

"I'm so sorry she's dead. Who was she?"

"A member of our Secret Service. The resemblance was astonishing. She died instantly, praise Allah. She knew the risks when she was recruited, but you always hope it never comes to something this ugly. I'll make sure her husband and family get a handsome pension."

Frankie Richards spoke. "Why don't the news reports mention that you're still alive?"

Amurkhan's almond-shaped eyes appraised her. "If what Dr. Zammit has told me is true, the conspirators will take my death as a signal. If they know I'm alive, they might alter their plans. I'll stay dead until two or three days before the election, hiding with the help of Colonel Yildiz. Then I will reveal myself to the people, along with details of the assassination attempt. The sensational publicity should ensure victory. I'm sure even Muslims can appreciate a resurrection from the dead."

"I agree with that strategy," said Zammit. "We'll keep these guys in the dark, keep them guessing. They must have a tight schedule. Let's see if we can ruin it."

"What about the riots?" asked Kang.

"We can keep them under control," replied Yildiz. "We have a tremendous advantage because we know the prime minister is alive and in control of events, and her opponents and the conspirators don't."

Zammit turned to Costopoulos. "Stav, find Graves and ask him to get some information on Jamal." The Greek nodded and left. Zammit expanded on the two-front war scenario and the contamination in the reservoir giving the Iraqis an excuse to invade.

Eyes like green ice, Amurkhan said, "It all sounds plausible, Dr. Zammit, but we can certainly handle Anwar Hussein. I don't care how many men or how much armor this General Bled throws at us, he will find it impossible to win. Also, Ankara and Istanbul have a combined population of 9 million. Even if by some miracle he wins, he will find it impossible to govern the populace. And we will still have armed forces in the rest of the country. We will counterattack."

As Zammit was reminding her that General Bled controlled several hundred nuclear weapons, an army officer stuck his head in the door and spoke to Yildiz and Amurkhan. Zammit felt a sense of foreboding at the looks on their faces. "What is it?"

Amurkhan was furious. "The Iraqi army rolled across the border about ten minutes ago. Along with the Syrians. We'll be fighting a war on three fronts."

Colonel Graves strode into the room with a sheaf of papers in his hand, followed by Costopoulos. "Our satellite surveillance has just shown—"

"We already know," said Yildiz.

"What exactly are you facing?" asked Zammit.

They all listened intently, including Thamar Amurkhan, as Colonel Yildiz spoke. He had asked for a large map of the Middle East, now fastened to the concrete wall with tape. Zammit was amused to see him adopt a fussy schoolteacher manner. "This is a brief overview—I cannot go into details in front of foreigners, for reasons of national security. I'm sure you understand. Army command assures me they have things under control, for the moment."

He glanced at a sheaf of paper in his hand, then tapped on Iraq with a pointer. "Notice the border between Iraq and Turkey. It is only about 150 miles wide. That is a narrow space in which to jam large numbers of men and armor for a full-scale invasion, given the very poor roads in the area. You could end up with a bottleneck. It is almost 300 miles from the Iraqi border to Urfa and the Ataturk Dam—how do you say it in American slang?"

"As the crow flies," replied Zammit.

"Thank you. It also looks as if they may try for Ahlat, in the north, on Lake Van. Same problems. All of this is very rough terrain, and we will contest every inch of it. But that is not my main point."

"What about the air force?" asked Colonel Graves.

"Thanks to the United States and our membership in NATO, we have modern aircraft. Iraq does not. We estimate they may have as few as 500 aircraft, many of which are not serviceable. Air power for the Iraqis will be a neglible factor. And most of their tanks are still old Soviet-era T-72s. Ground forces are the mainstay of their army. But they do have very strong capabilities in antitank warfare, as well as sophisticated tube artillery. May I continue?"

Graves nodded.

"Iraq has a population of some 25 million and a land area of about 168,000 square miles. . . . Yes?" Yildiz asked irritably.

Kitson Kang had muttered something under his breath. "Sorry," he said. "But calculations like this are one of my hobbies. Iraq is about twice the size of Idaho."

Zammit grinned.

"To continue. Iraq is"—Yildiz gave a slight bow to Kang—"twice the size of Idaho. Active armed forces 350,000, reserves 650,000, 3000 battle tanks, and aircraft I have mentioned before."

He tapped the pointer on Syria, after glancing again at his papers. "Their border with us is a little over 300 miles. Population 20 million. About 72,000 square miles . . ." He looked at Kang expectantly.

"Slightly larger than North Dakota."

"Thank you. Army 350,000, reserves 400,000." He flipped a page, and then another. "I . . . I seem to have misplaced the information about their air force and navy."

Amurkhan did not look amused but she said, "Never mind. Continue."

Yildiz cleared his throat. "The problem is that with Iraq and Syria as allies, the front is 450 miles long. Also, Syria is less than 70 miles from the Ataturk. But their armed forces are pitiful, and we are concentrating our efforts at the moment on destroying them. Then we will concentrate on the Iraqis."

"And then there's us." He tapped on Turkey. "Population over 70 million. Our enemies' population, in total, is only 45 million. Turkey's area, 302,000 square miles—"

Kang said, "Bigger than Texas."

"Army 525,000, reserves 400,000—"

There was a knock at the door. Yildiz opened it. He listened for a moment to a visibly tense army officer, then turned and said, "Madam Prime Minister?" Amurkhan strode over and listened as well. Zammit saw her lips tighten.

She turned to them. "Things are not going well. The Syrians are proving unexpectedly difficult. We must transfer units from the north, despite Dr. Zammit's advice not to fall into the conspirators' trap. The lecture is over. I must attend to business, and try to save my country."

"Once you move enough troops to the southeast, General Bled will launch his invasion in the north," warned Zammit. "You'll find yourselves in a three-front bloodbath."

Amurkhan turned to Graves. "We can count on American assistance?"

"Of course," said Graves. "But our resources in the area are small. If you can't hold them off until we assemble a strike force with our NATO allies, and if Bled gets into the conflict with nuclear weapons, I can't guarantee anything."

Amurkhan turned to Yildiz. "In case the conspirators have other surprises in store, I want to stay here at your headquarters so I am absolutely safe. I want an immediate briefing on the present situation. And, Colonel Yildiz, I would also like to know why your intelligence people failed to pick up any hint about Syrian involvement in this invasion."

With a curt nod to the others Yildiz accompanied Amurkhan out of the room. Zammit did not envy him the next several hours.

"Christ, what a mess," said Graves.

"Before Yildiz started his lecture, you came into the room with some documents. What are they?" asked Richards.

"CIA information on Abdul Jamal."

Zammit said to Kitson Kang, "Keep hacking that laptop in case there's more information hidden somewhere. The rest of you come with me. There's a boardroom upstairs with some AV equipment. I want to show you something. Then I want to hear what Colonel Graves has to say."

They took the elevator up to the third floor and walked down a carpeted hallway into the boardroom. The navy blue drapes were closed. Zammit twitched them aside to reveal an immense sunset over the Bosphorus. The cloth-of-gold sky was bleeding red, as if pierced by the minarets on the horizon.

Zammit closed the curtains as the others chose their seats, then walked down the hall to speak to a staff officer. Returning to the boardroom, he said, "I asked for coffee and tea, and they fell all over themselves saying that isn't enough. I assume Thamar told them to give us the red carpet treatment. I hope everyone likes Turkish food."

"There are four great cuisines in the world," said Costopoulos. "Chinese, Italian, French, and Turkish."

Zammit took his seat. "Some bells have rung in the past few hours. First, there's Lazar Smegyev's cult and its involvement with the bioweapon in the Ataturk reservoir."

He picked up a remote control and aimed it at the screen. The image appeared to be a starburst on a field of grass. He pressed a button and the picture was enhanced. The forms making up the starburst were bodies in white robes. All were charred, as if they had been set on fire and incompletely burned.

"What the hell is this?" demanded Graves.

"An aerial photo of the murder-suicide of sixteen members of a French doomsday cult called the Order of the Solar Temple," replied Zammit. "Cult members included professional people, politicians, and wealthy socialites. Among other things, they believed that suicide instantly transported them to a new world on the planet Sirius. To make it even more pathetic, Sirius is not a planet, it's a star."

"Like the Heaven's Gate cult and their belief that suicide would transport them to the spacecraft following 1997's Hale-Bopp comet," observed Graves.

"Exactly," replied Zammit. "But at least the Heaven's Gate and Solar Temple members were intent just on killing themselves." Once again he pressed the remote control. The image of an ugly, heavyset blind man with long black hair and oriental features appeared on the screen. "Shoko Asahara, leader of the Japanese cult called Aum Shinrikyo, or Supreme Truth. Asahara ordered his followers to release a chemical weapon called sarin, a nerve gas invented by the Nazis, into a Tokyo subway train. More than 5,000 people were injured."

"I remember this one," said Costopoulos.

Zammit continued. "Asahara recruited scientists, government officials, and other prominent citizens. He also had ties with the military and organized crime. He conducted experiments on his acolytes and was amassing a huge arsenal of weapons—conventional, biochemical, and nuclear."

"Yes," said Stavros. "As I recall, their beliefs were quite bizarre, based on a series of science fiction novels."

"Isaac Asimov's *Foundation* series," interrupted Frankie Richards. "About the destruction of civilization and its reconstruction through a small band of survivors."

Costopoulos nodded. "Asahara intended to wipe out the human race and start over. It was all quite insane."

"The terrifying thing," added Graves, "is that it was the first time in history any independent group, without protection or sponsorship by a government, had access to weapons of mass destruction. God knows what could have happened if they hadn't been caught."

"True," said Zammit. "And now the same thing is happening again. Only it's not based on fiction but on historical fact mingled with myth and legend. But although these Japanese cultists were insane, they still weren't crazy enough to use a bioweapon, certainly not a genetically modified one whose effects on the environment would be inherently unpredictable. They had the sense, if you can call it that, to use something whose effects would be restricted to the immediate area."

"Interesting observation," mused Costopoulos.

Zammit turned off the AV. "That's it for my dog and pony show. My point is, we have a peculiar mix here. We've got cultists who believe some odd things. That's par for the course, cultwise. But we've also got Abdul Jamal, who likes sending taunting e-mail, invents drugs, and is obviously involved in planting the bioweapon. I'm baffled. Everything else about this conspiracy is meticulously planned. I can't believe they'd use a GMO, with its element of uncertainty and risk. There must be something we haven't thought of."

There was a knock on the door. Costopoulos opened it. Four people entered with steaming pots of coffee and tea.

"Haven't had coffee in what seems like ages," said Zammit. "Smells great."

The four returned with a trolley loaded with trays of sliced tomatoes, cucumbers, hard-boiled eggs, cold sliced lamb, feta cheese, four different kinds of olives, thick yogurt the color of butter, and pita bread. There was also a bottle of *raki*, a stack of plates, and a huge dish of what looked like doughnuts floating in thick syrup. "Aha!" exclaimed Stavros. "My favorite Turkish dessert. *Kadin gobegi*. The Turks are very fond of intensely sweet desserts."

"What does *kadin gobegi* mean?" asked Graves.

Stavros winked at Frankie. "It means 'lady's navel.' "

Richards threw back her head and laughed. "I'll leave that delectation to you gentlemen."

"I can smell the *raki* from here," remarked Zammit, pouring himself a tiny porcelain cup of thick Turkish coffee and dumping in a teaspoon of sugar. He downed it, careful to avoid the grounds at the bottom, and poured himself another, as well as a glass of *raki*. He sniffed it appreciatively. "I love that licorice smell."

As they filled their plates and started to eat, Graves shuffled through his papers. "Abdul Jamal. Not much information, but enough to indicate he's despicable."

Zammit opened up a pita and stuffed it with lamb, cheese, tomatoes, and cucumber topped with a thick dollop of yogurt. "Continue. Why would he send me an e-mail message, apart from the fact that he seems to be a cocky bastard?"

"With a substantial ego, not to mention delusions of grandeur," added Costopoulos, spooning syrup over his pastry.

Graves shrugged at the Greek. "You're the expert on that kind of thing. All I know is what's in the file. Jamal's from an old trading family in Oman, a feudal sultanate in the southeastern Saudi Arabian peninsula, right on the Persian Gulf. Lots of money, but although the family has a reputation as sharp traders, they're apparently decent people. Jamal was the family's pride and joy. They sent him to the Sorbonne in Paris, where he was academically brilliant. In fact, he's rumored to be a genius. Offered several academic positions, which he turned down in favor of business. Then he went as bad as maggoty meat. Actually, it's obvious he was bad from birth."

"How?" asked Frankie Richards.

"Criminal activity of various sorts. He's the kind of guy who, if he was given the choice of doing something legally or illegally, and the profit was going to be the same, would take the illegal route just for kicks. Got involved in a variety of shady deals in sunny places, mainly in the Middle East and Southeast Asia. Arms deals, drug trafficking, the occasional financial swindle. Even slavery, which is an old Omani standby. Apparently he can really turn on the charm if he wants to, and his manners are impeccable, but he's rumored to have a vicious temper and to have committed several murders though never charged. He has a reputation as a gourmet, also as a sexual predator and sadist."

"A man of appetite, you might say," observed Costopoulos.

Graves nodded. "There've been a variety of rape and assault charges over the years but no convictions. Victims and witnesses recanted their testimony before trial or disappeared."

"Charming," said Richards. "What does this psychopath look like?"

Graves sipped thick Turkish coffee as he slipped a couple of photographs out of the file and pushed them over to her. "Made a pile of money, lived in a ritzy neighborhood in Paris until a financial scam backfired. Operated a complex Ponzi scheme in several Eastern European countries a few years ago. Took advantage of the fact that most former Iron Curtain citizens wouldn't know a legitimate investment deal if they found it swimming in their soup. Bankrupted millions of people with pyramid investments that collapsed. Made the mistake of running the same scam in the former East Germany. It's always a mistake to piss off the Germans. Law enforcement agencies got involved, he killed a couple of his partners, been on the lam ever since. Cuba, before it got too hot for him. North Korea, same thing. Myanmar, formerly Burma, one of the most corrupt dictatorships in the world. Now he's in Tuvanistan, which is the bottom of the barrel."

"I've heard of it," said Frankie. "The dictators are Ivan and Anastasia Popov. Supposed to be a dreadful couple."

"Official name is Republic of Tuvanistan, but if it's a republic, I'm a Hindu dancer," snorted Graves. "It's sandwiched between Armenia, Georgia, Chechnya, Ingushetia, North Ossetia, Dagestan, Tatarstan, and those other alphabet-soup countries close to Turkey's eastern border."

"Well, it's a perfect location for Jamal as far as this plot is concerned. He couldn't get any closer to the action unless he was in

Turkey itself. So this creep is Muslim?" asked Zammit. "He can't be a fundamentalist."

Graves spoke around a mouthful of stuffed pita. "Nominally a Muslim. 'How're you going to keep him down on the farm, now that he's seen Paree?' That kind of thing. Finds it useful to pretend, so he can use fanatical Islamic groups, just like he manipulated RAA."

Costopoulos interrupted. "Islam is a noble and profound religion, professed by roughly a billion ordinary decent people who are not extremists. Judging Islam by Abdul Jamal or Anwar Hussein is like judging Roman Catholicism based on the behavior of the head of the Sicilian mafia. It's not a question of religion, it's a question of gangsters."

Frankie Richards was examining the two photos of Abdul Jamal.

"What is it?" asked Zammit.

"He's handsome, but there's something desperately wrong with this man. He's forty-five years old but has no lines on his face." Frankie's instincts were kicking in. "And there's a weird sort of glare at the back of his eyes."

"A youthful appearance is often typical of psychopaths," said Costopoulos. "Because they have no conscience, they never worry about anything, so they never have trouble sleeping at night. No wrinkles."

"Speaking of gangsters," said Graves, "Jamal should feel right at home in Tuvanistan. He's staying in the presidential palace with the Popovs." Briefly he filled them in on the couple and their reign. "It's like Germany under the Nazis," he concluded. "The natural order of things is reversed. The decent people are dead or in prison, and criminals run the place."

The door opened. Costopoulos listened, then turned to Zammit. "Call for you. From Sevastopol."

Zammit walked down the hall toward one of the duty stations. A soldier handed him the receiver and he heard a familiar croaky, smoky voice. "Irina?"

"I have news. Two pieces. First, you are dealing with a biological weapon that was stolen. Correct?"

"Yes."

"Another has been stolen. Just had a call from one of my sources in Novosibirsk, in Siberia. Last night someone broke into the virology institute called Vector and took several vials of smallpox."

"Jesus Christ," said Zammit. "How could they do that? Isn't it guarded?"

"There are two night watchmen. Or rather were—they were murdered. But no money for any protection more sophisticated. The building is not secure, and the intruders somehow knew how to get into the refrigeration units."

Zammit was stunned. "This is incredible. You guard something like that in a sealed vault with an army division."

He heard the click of a cigarette lighter and the rasp of Markova's lungs as she inhaled. "You don't know how bad it really is. During the last coup attempt, when the smallpox was still stored at the Research Institute for Viral Preparations in Moscow, the institute's director was so worried about rebels stealing the stuff that he opened the fridges, removed all the smallpox, stuffed it in his coat and briefcase, and took it home with him on the subway. He stored it for several days in his own refrigerator. His wife almost had a stroke when he told her. That's when they moved all the smallpox samples to Siberia, very far away, to be safe. Obviously, not safe."

Zammit rubbed his face with his free hand. "What's the other piece of news?"

"One of my sources at the Sevastopol naval base tells me that General Bled has taken sudden leave of the maneuvers and gone out of the country."

"Where?"

"Some hole of shit called Tuvanistan. It is located—"

"I know where it is," interrupted Zammit. "Irina, are you sure about this?"

"Of course. Bled can't go to the toilet without letting his senior staff know where he is. According to my source, he signed out for forty-eight hours to go to the capital of Tuvanistan, Blavatsk. The contact number he gave is one assigned to the communications center of the presidential palace. There aren't many people who know where Vector is, or how to get into it and the refrigeration units. Bled may have stolen the smallpox and is taking it to Tuvanistan."

Zammit's mind raced as the information sank in. He heard Markova say something. "What?"

"Tuvanistan is like something out of Kafka. You know, that story of his, *In the Penal Colony*. Why would Bled go there with smallpox?"

"I think I know," said Zammit.

"What?" demanded the journalist. "You know the routine: I feed you stuff, you feed me stuff. Why is Bled in Tuvanistan?"

"I can't tell you now," Zammit replied. "But if things work out, I'll feed you the biggest scoop of the last thirty years and personally nominate you for the Pulitzer Prize."

"The what?"

"Never mind. In America it's a big deal. I'll be in touch."

He hung up and headed back down the hall. As he entered the boardroom he briefed the others, then said, "Hey, Stav. You speak any Tuvanian?"

The Greek's eyes narrowed. "A little." He rattled off a series of throaty eating noises interspersed with tongue clicks and retching sounds.

"Crikey," said Colonel Graves. "That's the ugliest language I've ever heard."

Costopoulos shrugged. "Non-Indo-European. Possibly Finno-Ugric in origin. Or Old Caucasian. I know enough to order a meal in a restaurant. Why do you ask?"

Zammit explained what Markova had said.

"Both in Tuvanistan and both at the palace!" exclaimed Richards.

"Exactly," said Zammit. "Two bad apples in the same rotten barrel. And to mix in an Islamic metaphor, if the mountain won't come to Mohammed, then Mohammed goes to the mountain. According to Irina, Bled may have the stolen smallpox, and we have to stop him. Colonel, what are the chances of sneaking into this country?"

"You could sneak in," Graves replied. "But you'd never get out. They hate foreigners, every third person is a spy, and they shoot first and ask questions never. As far as getting through the electrified fence and into the palace, forget it."

"There must be a way," said Zammit. "Stav, could you function if we somehow managed to sneak into this nightmare country? I could pretend to be a mute or something."

Costopoulos shook his head. "As I said, I speak restaurant Tuvanian. We get a hundred feet into the country, a secret police thug says something to me, I reply, 'Eggs over easy,' and we're dead. Won't work."

Frankie Richards reached over, took Costopoulos's spoon, and ladled some syrup into her mouth. "I can get you in," she said loftily.

They stared at her. Finally Zammit overcame his astonishment. "*You* can get us into this concentration camp of a country?"

"Yes, I can."

"Let me guess. You're going to bat those big green eyes, and those two psychopaths are going to issue a gold-plated invitation?"

Frankie Richards batted her big green eyes and smiled. "Precisely. And not just a gold-plated invitation. We're going to walk in through the front door and be greeted with smiles and champagne."

Zammit gazed at the fine bubbles streaming up through the golden liquid. He sipped from his fluted glass and enjoyed both the taste and the sensation—champagne always felt as if it was giggling in his mouth. He held up the bottle and looked again at the black and orange label. "Stav, what does *Veuve Clicquot* mean?"

Costopoulos looked up distractedly from the files Graves and Morgan had given him on General Bled, the Popovs, and Abdul Jamal. He had chewed his pencil almost in half. Zammit had never seen him look so worried.

"*Veuve* is French for 'widow,' " he replied. "Upon the death of Monsieur Clicquot, the founder of the firm, his spouse took over and made it one of the world's great champagnes."

Zammit spooned a mound of black caviar onto the delicate square of a blini and popped it in his mouth. He looked around the luxurious cabin of the Gulfstream V jet that was part of the personal fleet of aircraft belonging to Ivan and Anastasia Popov.

"So this is how dictators live. No wonder so many people want to be one." Despite his jocularity, he was worried too but couldn't think of any other way to do things. He looked out the window at the whipped-cream clouds far below. They looked solid enough to land the aircraft on. The robin's-egg-blue sky stretched away in all directions. Kang was at the dam with Connie Palaeov, still doing analyses, and Cairo Jackson was in Istanbul with Graves and Yildiz.

It was less than thirty-six hours since the assassination of Amurkhan's double, and so far no one suspected that the Turkish leader wasn't dead. As anticipated, her supposed assassination had set off riots and violence. But Colonel Yildiz was managing to keep them under control because Thamar Amurkhan was secretly working with the National Security Council. Zammit couldn't even imagine how bad the situation would now be if the RAA assassination team had killed the right person. He assumed the Turkish government's ability to keep everything under control was something Jamal and his co-conspirators had not anticipated. And he hoped that not knowing the reason—that a crucial aspect of their plot had failed—they were starting to feel uncertain themselves.

Zammit wondered grimly what other surprises might be in store. Jamal was obviously a meticulous planner who arranged things so that he was always one step ahead of his enemies. He thought again about the elaborateness of the reservoir poisoning and the murder of Boris Kazov. But if you did something in a complex way, you increased the possibility of accidents and failure.

The scientist shrugged. You could drive yourself crazy with this kind of speculation. They would find out soon enough. It was obvious that General Bled couldn't launch his invasion of Turkey until he returned from Tuvanistan. Irina Markova said he had signed out for forty-eight hours, which meant he would be in the Blavatsk palace for only another eight hours. Not a lot of time.

Zammit glanced at his watch. They were just an hour away from landing in Blavatsk. He had no idea what to expect except the possibility of danger. Given what he'd learned about Abdul Jamal, he didn't want to involve Frankie Richards in this mess, but she was the only way they could get safely into the country and, most importantly, into the palace.

He walked down the aisle. Richards was examining the contents of her painting case, the size of a fishing tackle box. The cargo hold contained several rolls of canvas, an easel, stretchers, and other materials too big to go into the main cabin of the sleek corporate jet. She was muttering to herself. "Viridian, cadmium red medium, primary magenta, primary cyan, cerulean blue, raw sienna . . ."

From the next seat she picked up a couple of color photos the Popovs had sent her over the Web, scrutinizing them so that she could make the proper selection of colors for their portrait. Zammit leaned over her shoulder. "I still can't believe how easy this was. I thought we'd have to don blackface and camouflage gear and parachute into the country at midnight, armed to the teeth."

Frankie put down the photos and made a couple of notes. "As I said, the Popovs contacted me several months ago when they heard about my work. After discovering what sort of people they are, I politely declined the commission. When I contacted them to say that I was in the Crimea and able to accept the commission after all, they snapped it up." The Popovs had insisted on sending one of their own personal aircraft to pick up Richards and her traveling companions. Her easels and paints had been air-expressed from Seattle.

Jack Morgan strolled up and caught the last part of the conversation. "Explain to me how you got the paranoid Popovs to admit the rest of us into the country as well."

"It was easy," said Richards. "You have to know what sort of people you're dealing with. As a sought-after portrait painter for the rich and famous, I'm a celebrity. Everyone knows celebrities travel with entourages—bodyguards, personal trainers, hairdressers, and the like. If you don't act like a prima donna, nouveau riches like the Popovs think you're nothing special."

"What if they had refused?"

"That's easy too. If they'd balked at admitting all of you, I would've thrown a tantrum prima donna-ish enough to make the eruption of Krakatoa look trivial. They would've caved in." She grinned at Zammit. "I'm not a bad actress, you know."

Costopoulos came down the aisle and leaned over to pick up the photographs. "A rabid dog would have enough sense to stay away from these two. The more I ponder the files, the less I think this is a good idea."

"Speaking of acting," Richards continued, "you all have to remember your roles. It won't be hard, because they won't expect you to say anything. Mike, you'll be a bodyguard." She turned to Jack Morgan. "You're young and slim, so you're the hairdresser. Try to act swishy—they'll expect it. Stavros, you're my official translator or assistant or personal art historian or something. Look learned. And you'll all have to be very attentive and deferential to me."

"Costopoulos has a point," said Morgan. "What are we supposed to do when we get to Tuvanistan? Maybe the Popovs are in on this plot too, although it seems a little large scale for them. They're basically smash-and-grab types. How do we even know we'll see Abdul Jamal? Or General Bled? That palace is huge. And even if they do meet us, maybe neither of them likes surprises."

"I've explained it before. We're doing this because we don't have enough time to play a waiting game," said Zammit. "Also, the Popovs don't know who we are, and there's no reason for them to tell Jamal or Bled that we're coming. That way we can take them by surprise. Also, we have to find the smallpox."

Zammit said to Frankie, "Do the Popovs know you work for INERT?"

"I doubt it. As you know, I keep my work with the agency very quiet. Anyway, people aren't interested. They think botany and microbiology are boring."

"See what I mean?" said Zammit to the others. "And even if the Popovs do find out who we are, what's it to them? They just want their portrait painted. If they do smell a rat, the worst they can do is toss us out of the country. Graves, the CIA, and the White House know we're there, and they'll raise a stink if anything happens to us. Frankie's a celebrity, and the last thing a couple of social climbers like the Popovs want is to get a reputation as bad hosts. And remember that Abdul Jamal is a guest in their country too—it isn't as if he runs the place. We might be able to pump him for information over cocktails or something."

"Abdul Jamal will talk to us, and it isn't a question of cocktails," said Costopoulos grimly. "That's what I'm afraid of. He won't be able to resist. This thing with the e-mail message to Mike was a flashy thing to do, very theatrical. He'll be dying to talk to Mike, for sure. I doubt if Bled will be anywhere in sight."

"Good point," said Zammit. "Just as Frankie's kept her involvement with INERT out of sight, very few people know of my work with the Knights of Malta. How could Abdul Jamal have found out? And why did he send me the message before Amurkhan even made the request that I get involved? Is he psychic or something? How did he know I'd have anything to do with it?"

As Richards examined a new sable brush, Stavros took Zammit's arm and whispered, "A few words?"

"Sure." They walked farther down the aisle and sat across from each other. "What?"

"I want to make some suggestions about how to handle someone like Jamal."

"Shoot," said Zammit.

Costopoulos poured himself some more champagne and drained it at a swallow. "You are dealing with a charming, intelligent, and manipulative man whose personality can suddenly switch to the most violent kind of behavior. That is because he is a psychopath."

Zammit interrupted. "You wrote a famous paper on this, as I recall. And a best-seller based on the paper."

Costopoulos nodded. "I needed money, and a popular textbook was the way to do it. I will refresh your memory. People believe all psychopaths are killers, but most are not. The characteristics that make up a psychopathic personality are found in many people who never kill anyone—we call them subcriminal psychopaths. As with everything else in life, it's not black and white—you're one and I'm not. There are degrees, little tendencies, personality quirks that don't necessarily have to turn into anything monstrous but can do so when exacerbated by circumstance or environment."

Zammit nodded. "Go on."

"In fact, many successful, driven people have psychopathic elements in their personalities. The ruthless back-stabbing executive, the wheeler-dealer with the flashy lifestyle who turns out to have been looting pension funds and defrauding widows and orphans. People renowned for their risk taking and lack of regard for others."

"I get the general idea."

Costopoulos continued. "They are often successful at what they do because they have an uncanny ability to fool other people, to take them in. But this is accompanied by a very low frustration threshold. Let's say a psychopath is stealing from a business, which is common—after all, they are not constrained by the conscience that would prevent you or me from stealing. Their employer finds out and confronts them. To escape from the situation, the psychopath invents a dying grandmother who doesn't exist or a cancerous tumor they don't have. They will tell these lies with convincing sincerity, because whenever a psychopath tells a lie, he truly means it at the time he's telling it. It's merely a way of getting what he wants, of taking you in."

Zammit poured them both more champagne.

"But if lies and charm don't work, what can they do? Argue, of course, but arguing is stressful, frustrating. The last thing you want to do is frustrate a particular type of psychopath, because without warning they will lash out violently. The interesting thing—and it's one of the key points about such people—is that after they have lashed out, perhaps hit, maimed, raped, or killed someone, they will regard themselves as blameless. They will think, it was the victim's fault for not believing me—if only they'd believed me, they'd still be alive."

Zammit nodded. "Makes sense, in a bent sort of way."

"They often seem perfectly normal until their desires are thwarted. Then they attack. They have no empathy for others, treating them as things, as if human beings were cardboard cutouts the psychopath could move around as he pleased. But if a cutout refuses to be moved around, the psychopath will become violent. It must do as he wishes, and after all it's only a cardboard cutout, so where's the harm in hacking it to pieces and burying it in the woods somewhere?"

Zammit looked at his watch. "We're going to be landing soon."

"The e-mail message really bothers me. He seems to know obscure things about your life. It's a form of provocation. It means he thinks he's in complete control. Why is he so confident? This ties in with the sexual stuff—he's obsessed with bondage, restraints. Once again, very controlling."

Zammit said thoughtfully, "The drugs Jamal manufactures are the ultimate in control. It's one thing to control a person's body, another to control his mind."

Costopoulos blinked. "I hadn't thought of that. Damn."

Zammit grinned. "Stav, you think too much. You're going to give yourself a brain cramp. Relax. We'll do what we can and move on. Fear is information without the cure. We'll find the cure somehow."

The Greek shook his head. "I can't let it go. Why does he think he's going to win? How can he be so confident?"

Zammit yawned. "Stav, we're building this guy up based on CIA files. Maybe he'll turn out to be someone we can throw around like a ping-pong ball."

Costopoulos sighed. "Perhaps. But psychos have weaknesses, and it's the nature of the psychopathic personality not to recognize their own flaws."

"Such as?"

"In Jamal's case, he knows he's intelligent because he's been told that by other people all his life. That means he probably thinks he's more intelligent than he actually is, because psychopaths tend to be narcissists. Any man who believes that about himself is going to make mistakes. You could exploit Jamal's inflated assessment of his own cunning."

Zammit nodded as he filed this information away.

"He is controlling. Make him feel not in control—it will upset him very much. Tell him something he doesn't think you could know—it'll rattle him. The obsessive collecting of women, of art, of recipes—he's a greedy, covetous man. Greed is one of the seven deadly sins. If necessary, you could turn Jamal's greed against him and make it truly deadly."

Costopoulos pointed down the aisle toward Frankie Richards

gazing out the window lost in thought. "Her instincts are even better than mine. Compared to her, when it comes to figuring out life, I have to read the manual, line by line. She's worried."

There was a sudden whine as the engines changed pitch. They were descending into the unknown.

 "I've come to one conclusion for sure," said Mike Zammit as they lounged in the gray leather interior of the white stretch limousine. It smelled of fine leather, polished wood, and something else he couldn't put his finger on. The limo was pulling away from the Blavatsk airport and taking them to the presidential palace.

"What's that?" asked a glum Stavros Costopoulos.

"Nothing on earth inspires less confidence than the sight of a Tuvanian policeman."

The airport was a ramshackle structure of peeling paint, cracked concrete, and grimy smeared windows, despite being heavily fortified. A high stone wall surrounded it, topped with barbed wire and wicked scythelike shards of broken glass. As guests of the president they had been greeted by a contingent of unhappy-looking officials in cheap Soviet-era suits. When one of these officials thought he was being looked at, he would flash a white, sharkish smile so patently false it was worse than no smile at all. Generally swarthy, with black hair and eyes, there was a hint of Arab in some of the faces, although most had the rounded skulls with flat backs typical of the ancient Ilyrians. But it was the eyes that told everything. Deep black pools, bright and wary, they glowed with hungry resentment.

They were the eyes of a people who had found themselves caught between two tectonic plates of history—Christianity and Islam—that through an accident of geography and religion just happened to collide in the Caucasus and the Balkans. They had endured and thrown off invasions by the armies of Rome, Attila, Byzantium, and Genghis Khan before finally being smothered for half a millennium by the dead weight of corrupt Ottoman rule.

They were the eyes of sheep stealers and bandits, of sharp traders with sharper knives, of snipers who always aimed at the genitals, of people who engaged in mindless vendettas that lasted hundreds of years and left mutilated bodies to rot in lonely country lanes. Hard, cruel, untrusting eyes, the eyes of people it would be unwise to turn your back on.

As guests of the president, they did not have to go through customs, and immigration was a perfunctory affair. It was never hard to spot a state under siege—the presence of hundreds of soldiers and police was a giveaway.

Once they left the fortified airport compound and hit the potholed highway leading to the capital, Zammit remembered that there were two airports in Tuvanistan, one about five miles west of the city and another some twenty miles to the east. Having flown from Istanbul, they had landed at the western one. When he questioned why such a small country would need two airports, Colonel Hakim Yildiz had said, "Two fast exits are better than one," obviously referring to the unstable political situation. With a spike of unease, Zammit remembered the Turk's response when Zammit briefed him on their decision to go to Tuvanistan. Yildiz had listened in morose silence, shaken his head, then used his middle finger to pull down the lower lid of his right eye. Zammit knew what this universal Mediterranean gesture meant: Keep your eyes open—beware. Yildiz escorted them to the airport and saw them off with the words "*Gechmis olsen.*" Zammit asked Costopoulos what it meant. Stav looked unhappy. "Roughly translated, it means, 'May it be behind you.' "

As he contemplated the landscape, it occurred to Zammit that the shiny American armored car was like a swan traveling down a river of sewage. He had seen poverty in a lot of places, from Rio de Janeiro to Calcutta, but rarely had he seen a landscape as blasted as this one. Huge piles of rubble were heaped by the roadside between dead gray trees and rusted vehicles. They passed the occasional sway-backed mule hauling a wooden cart filled with giant bundles of rushes or twigs. The drivers were gaunt and looked haunted. Farmland lay between the airport and the city, but the crops looked sickly, as if they had been poisoned or lay under a curse. Off in the distance Zammit could see a pall of black smoke, no doubt from the oil fields. Under a leaden sky he watched as peasants prodded staggering farm animals pulling plows that would have been familiar to a medieval farmer.

As they approached the capital in its setting of trash, he could see minarets and domes on the horizon, along with several towering milk carton shapes that indicated Stalinist-era buildings, examples of Soviet Brutalism. All were partially obscured by a brown fog of oil-field smog that clung greasily to the trees and left oily streaks on the windshield. There was a pervasive smell of burning

hydrocarbons, wood smoke, and ashes. He was reminded of Dzerzhinsk.

Suddenly he was hit in the face with a blast of strong scent. He
flinched. Everyone else did too.

"What the hell was that?"

"Lilac," said Morgan. "I really hate lilac."

"I rather like it," said Stav, "but this is awfully strong."

Richards was examining the side panels of the limo's interior.
"Little nozzles. Looks like they're programmed to spray scent into
the car periodically, so the Popovs don't have to smell their own
country."

As they entered the city, people stopped and stared, often darting into doorways. Curtains twitched aside as invisible watchers
observed their passage. Feral dogs snarled over piles of trash, and
emaciated children with the reddish hair of the chronically mal-
nourished crouched on the cracked and buckling sidewalks.

The limousine swerved left as they passed a column of men
shuffling down the middle of the road in leg irons. Their collective
gait was peculiar—none of them were moving their left arms. It
gave the creeping column the look of a centipede that had had a
stroke which rendered its left side immobile.

The men in the column were guarded by soldiers with rifles and
clubs and slavering German shepherd dogs on chains with choke
collars. Some of the men looked sideways as the limousine passed
the column, with the haunted eyes of those who wished themselves dead.

"Oh my God," whispered Frankie Richards. Zammit stared. In
addition to the shackles around their ankles, the prisoners were
fastened together, one to another. The red streaks of blood on their
ragged prisoner's uniforms told the tale. They were strung together
with yards of metal wire that had been inserted through the flesh
of their triceps.

Zammit's eyes grew cold and thoughtful. He remembered Irina
Markova's comment about Tuvanistan being like something out of
Kafka's *In the Penal Colony* and tried to recall the story. Slowly it
came back—it was about an island prison where the commandant
had devised a machine to which prisoners were strapped and then
had the crime for which they were being punished incised into
their flesh by a slowly lowered device of needles and razors called
The Harrow. He'd first read it when he was about fourteen, and
it was still lodged in his brain like a splinter.

In contrast to the gray and begrimed streets, they could see in the distance a giant gilded dome rising into the sky. The white limo swung around a corner, and suddenly they were on a broad boulevard. At the end squatted the vast bulk of the presidential palace, secure behind the pylons of its giant electrified fence. Armored vehicles and squads of soldiers were everywhere. At the front gate of the palace the limo stopped, surrounded by soldiers. Swarthy faces peered at the driver, then at the passengers. The gates swung silently open, and they were waved through.

The limo swung around the sweep of the grand driveway and halted in front of the broad flight of marble steps that led up to the front portico. Red carpeting covered the steps, and a group of people waited at the top. Some wore suits, others balloon pants, fezzes, and embroidered shirts, and they held a variety of odd-looking instruments. It took Zammit a moment to realize they were musicians. Uniformed flunkies opened the doors of the limo as others started removing their luggage and humping it up the side of the staircase.

As they trudged up the marble steps, the musicians began playing, a squealing cacophony of oriental half-tones. As they neared the top, the expressions on the musicians' faces reminded Zammit of beaten white poodles at the circus, in red velvet hats, unhappily jumping through hoops. As at the airport, there was a delegation of officials in dark suits and big smiles topped with unsmiling eyes. One of them spoke into a cell phone and waited expectantly by the grand entrance, his eyes sweeping the surrounding area.

Men with machine guns looked alert, and even though the streets were virtually deserted, squads of uniformed men patrolled the perimeter outside the fence. Zammit realized that they were there in case of snipers. He remembered to stand behind Frankie Richards and look alert himself, as a bodyguard should.

They faced the delegation. A well-fed man with a black moustache and hot black, wary eyes stepped forward and bowed to Richards. "Welcome to the presidential palace," he said in heavily accented English. She smiled graciously and inclined her head. This was the sign for a general round of bows and smiles where mouths smiled but eyes didn't.

They were escorted into the palace, through doors that appeared to be solid bronze. Despite the size of the palace entry, they found themselves in a narrow hallway with metal walls, like cattle in a chute, shuffling toward a security checkpoint and an airport-style metal detector. It was obvious the Popovs had no intention of allowing anyone into the building without a thorough check.

Zammit couldn't shake the feeling that a black presence was waiting for them somewhere inside this palace. As he went through the metal detector it squealed sharply. A man with a machine gun faced him and held out his hand. Zammit reached into his jacket and pulled out the 9 mm automatic from the shoulder holster underneath his left armpit. He handed it to the man.

Their guide smiled a nonsmile. "It is secure here. Dr. Richards will be safe. Your gun will be returned when you leave."

Zammit looked at Morgan. Without a word the agent reached into his own jacket, handed over his weapon, and strode through the metal detector.

As they set off down the corridor away from the security checkpoint, Zammit pondered what Costopoulos had said on the plane. As he reviewed what they had seen on the drive into the city, he realized that this visit might have been a mistake. One word kept reverberating in his mind.

Defenseless.

 Zammit sat on the edge of his bed and bounced experimentally up and down. He had expected they would be taken directly to meet the Popovs, but their guide had said, "I am sure you would like to be shown to your suites. The president wished to be here to greet you personally on your arrival, but pressing affairs of state require his immediate attention."

"I wonder who's being executed," Morgan muttered to Zammit as they took the elevator up to their rooms. They each had their own suite. The suites were grouped around the artist's, which was the largest and most ornate, with a pink satin canopy bed. Zammit's luggage was next to his bed, which was round and the size of a patio. After a few moments' puzzled contemplation, it finally evoked a memory—old 1970s photos of Hugh Hefner in the Playboy mansion, on the same kind of bed, with a velour robe, a pipe, a smirk, and lots of bosoms. Zammit sniffed—the musty smell of disuse mingled with the delicate Middle Eastern odor of attar of roses. At least it wasn't lilac.

There was a big TV in the room. He walked over and switched it on. It appeared to be the beginning of a local program. It struck him as familiar, yet bizarre. A baritone in a blue suit, loud tie, and improbable hairdo was saying something in a foreign language. From the sound-and-fury-signifying-nothing soundtrack, he figured it was the local news.

He picked up the remote and surfed the channels. Static and snow. Obviously Tuvanians were expected to make do with just one station. He returned to the single source of news, just in time to see a tracking shot of a man he recognized as President Popov descending to earth on a cloud to stand on a mountaintop in a crude video special effect. Once earthbound, Popov stood, arms akimbo, looking stern and godlike as a computer-generated breeze ruffled his clothing. The camera cut back to the improbable-hairstyle man, who began reading what Zammit assumed was the news in Tuvanian. The news anchor had the chiseled features, resonant voice, and general air of false sincerity of news anchors the world over.

Just like the anchorman, the film clips were like TV the world over. Most stories were trivial yet heightened with false drama because there was air time that had to be filled and not enough real drama to fill it with. Clips showed Popov touring an oil refinery, the president and his wife at some official function, ruddy-cheeked peasants driving state-of-the-art tractors, tending fertile fields bursting with produce.

Zammit's eyes narrowed. He didn't know what the news anchor was saying, but the modern machinery and baskets of vegetables didn't jibe with what he had seen on the drive from the airport. Obviously propaganda. Badly done propaganda at that.

Finally he figured out how this was different from American news programs. U.S. programs showed this kind of thing at the end, when they were desperate to fill the last five minutes—stats on the Iowa corn harvest, the welfare recipient who'd won the lottery. American programs always started with a disaster, because every news producer knows that channel-surfing viewers like to watch disasters. That's why ninety percent of the interesting events in the world aren't reported on the evening news. Unlike a train wreck or a plane crash, a complex financial scandal doesn't come with an eye-catching film clip. Besides being difficult to report, it's boring for viewers to watch.

Zammit also realized that in a perfect peoples' paradise like Tuvanistan, there could never, ever be disasters to report.

He turned off the TV and opened the minibar. More Veuve Clicquot. He tossed some ice into a crystal goblet, selected a small bottle of Glenfiddich, and poured. He swirled the whiskey-covered cubes around, thinking hard. Based on what he had seen so far, it seemed unlikely the Popovs would be part of the complex plot they had uncovered—they wouldn't be clever enough to think of something so elaborate, much less execute it. And based on what he had learned about Abdul Jamal, it seemed equally unlikely that such a controlling and suspicious person would discuss the weather with the Popovs, much less anything more complicated. Knowing they were in the palace somewhere, he wondered how to discover the precise whereabouts of General Bled and Abdul Jamal and the smallpox. He also wondered what he would say to them if they did meet. He drained the goblet and shrugged. He'd worry about it when the time came.

He stripped off his clothes and went to take a shower. The bathroom was huge, tiled in blue- and ivory-colored marble.

Zammit noticed a pile of magazines with garish covers beside the toilet. He picked up the top one and flipped through it. It was a display of brutal pornography. Obviously the Popovs made certain assumptions about the sort of hospitality that should be extended to a guest's bodyguard. It was also obvious that they made those assumptions based on their own tastes, or the tastes of their own bodyguards. He felt a sickening lurch in the pit of his stomach as he realized the sort of people he was dealing with.

He threw the magazine back onto the pile, then picked up the stack and tossed it into a nearby closet, slamming the door. Now he really needed a shower. As he unwrapped a bar of expensive soap, he felt a faint reflex surge of adrenaline, remembering the pictures. Even though they were pathetic and loathsome at the same time, at some deep primitive level he responded to photos of other people having sex. As he turned on the water, he reflected that God sure screwed people up during the process of wiring their brains. No wonder the human race was outbreeding everything but the insects, and could think up plots like the contamination at the Ataturk Dam. He remembered his conversations with Grand Master Angelo Fortucci and felt a black tide of cynicism rising in his soul. God had to be a spider.

As he toweled himself under the ceiling's infrared lights, the heat made him drowsy. On a gold hook near the marble sink hung an ankle-length bathrobe in thick burgundy velour. He put it on and walked back into the bedroom. As he lay down on the bed he wondered if there was a surveillance camera in the suite. He assumed there was. He scanned the room but couldn't spot anything. To hell with it. You want to watch me snore, be my guest. He lay back, dozed, and dreamed.

He started awake at the sound of a knock on the door. It took him several moments to remember where he was. As he heaved himself off the bed, he realized how tired he was. And he was still sore from his ordeal underground. I must be getting old, he thought. Don't bounce back the way I used to.

He opened the door. It was Costopoulos. "I've been informed that dinner is at eight." He looked into Zammit's eyes, concerned. "You look ill."

"Bad dream," said Zammit shortly. "Black tie and tails? Like they told Frankie when she called?"

Stav grimaced. "Tuxedos at dinner. A gangster's idea of class."

Zammit pointed at the pen in the Greek's pocket. "Is that on?"

"Yes."

"Good. The masking device will prevent anyone from over-hearing our conversation, in case they're listening."

Zammit smiled. "It's not often I see you in a monkey suit. Remember to put the cummerbund on right side up."

Jack Morgan appeared, pointing at his masking device. "I hear we get to play Fred Astaire and Ginger Rogers."

Zammit nodded. "I have to keep reminding myself that I'm a bodyguard, and bodyguards don't speak unless they're spoken to." He thought again of the magazines and the unspoken truths they uttered about the mindset of the Popovs and the nature of the country they ran.

Frankie Richards appeared in the doorway. She surveyed Zammit's burgundy velour bathrobe. "How are things at the Playboy mansion these days?"

"Groovy," deadpanned Zammit.

She gave him a searching look, sensing the same disquiet Costopoulos had noticed. "What is this cabal of my employees up to?"

"Discussing the upcoming ordeal," replied Stav glumly. "I find it hard to smile at these people."

"They have trouble smiling at you," said Zammit. "Frankie, when do we meet the monstrous couple?"

She glanced at her watch. "Soon. We get a guided tour of the palace first, in about twenty minutes. Then a formal introduction to the Popovs, just before dinner. They want to meet all of us. Remember your roles, for God's sake."

"I hate fake identities," said Zammit. "I tend to forget who I'm supposed to be, halfway through the job."

"Me too," said Jack Morgan. "I failed that test once at Langley. As part of our CIA training we had to do role-playing—how to survive interrogation, that kind of thing. Once I had to pretend to be completely deaf while the other guys in class played my captors and tried to intimidate me. Shouted at me and so on. I was doing really well until they left me alone for a few moments, then one guy looked over at me in horror and said, 'Christ, there's a cockroach on his head.' I reached up to brush it off and . . ." The young agent gave a grin that made him look even younger than he actually was.

As the others returned to their suites, Zammit closed the door. He made himself do fifty push-ups to get the blood pumping and clear his head. As he forced himself through the last five, he remembered that Abdul Jamal was a notorious sexual predator. He put on his tuxedo, struggling as he always did with the studs in the cuffs. On his third attempt to get the tie on properly, he glanced over at Catula, motionless and blank-eyed in the suitcase on the floor. He wished he'd left the insectoid with Aunt Julia back on Malta. Too late now.

He gave his cummerbund a final tug, opened the door, and stepped into the hallway.

 The interior of the Blavatsk palace resembled a gigantic gold jewelry box stuffed with furniture, antiques, and paintings, all jumbled together. Purple embossed wallpaper, pink velvet upholstery on faux Louis XIV chairs, a fake Venus di Milo and a small-scale imitation of Michelangelo's David, only in bronze, massive marble tables topped with all sorts of third-rate antique knick-knacks, with the occasional priceless piece. Zammit got the impression the Popovs would place the same value on a Picasso as they would on a black velvet painting of Elvis. He remembered what Costopoulos had said—a gangster's idea of class.

He stayed close to Frankie. She had her hair up somehow—the style had a name, but he couldn't remember it—and wore an ankle-length, high-necked black silk dinner dress with lace sleeves that stopped at mid-forearm, with a string of pearls around her neck, a delicate gold bracelet that looked as if it had been woven, and black shoes that added about three inches to her height. She looked positively regal and smelled great, and if she was wearing any makeup apart from a little mascara, he couldn't tell. She was all charm when talking with the guide, but when his back was turned she gazed about with a look of horrified fascination.

The ballroom was at least thirty yards across, with white and black marble flooring, pink satin wallpaper, and chandeliers in multicolored Venetian Murano glass. The domed ceiling was a riot of white plaster moldings, cherubs blowing trumpets, and pastoral scenes with voluptuous half-naked maidens dabbling their toes in babbling brooks. Zammit had had enough conversations with Frankie about the history of art to recognize the rococo style when he saw it, with its cotton candy pinks and baby blues, and these ceiling paintings were the worst imitations of Tiepolo and Fragonard he had ever seen.

Jack Morgan sidled up to him and muttered, "Are they blind?"

There was a Las Vegas–style casino, with some thirty tables set up for blackjack, as well as roulette, slots, and keno. It was empty of players and lacked the usual casino stink of sweat, stale perfume, cigarette smoke, and boredom. Dealers stood at attention behind each table, decks of cards fanned out on the green baize in front of their chip trays. They weren't the usual plastic tokens but real coins—gold and silver, apparently, and mostly antique. Zammit wanted to examine them, but it wasn't the sort of thing a bodyguard would do. It was obvious the dealers were expected to stand at attention during their shift, in an empty casino, in case the Popovs or their guests had a sudden desire to play a few hands at three in the morning.

He'd seen similar places in the United Arab Emirates, where just a generation before the 1970s oil boom the local sheik would have considered himself fortunate to have a sand dune to pitch his tent on. Now there were palaces and desalinization plants and lush lawns where the sheik could take his shoes off and walk on fresh green grass, an experience entirely unknown to his ancestors. Desalinization plants. It struck him that unless they could find a solution to the cyanobacteria, there wouldn't be any more functional desalinization plants in the Persian Gulf states, and no more green grass either.

The communications center was a jarring contrast to the rest of the palace, with its banks of monitors and machine gun–toting guards behind bullet-proof Plexiglas. They were not granted a tour. He made a mental note of the center's location.

There was no sign of Abdul Jamal or General Vladimir Bled. Zammit wasn't surprised—the palace was so big you could hide half the crowd from a Super Bowl game in the building and never see them. Their guide talked the whole time using the monotone of professional tour guides the world over.

"This is the House of the Large Fountain," he announced as they walked into a huge room. "It is a replica of the original house found in Pompeii." Frankie Richards made appreciative noises, and Zammit noticed that it was indeed a precise duplicate of the residence excavated from the volcanic depths of the buried city. In addition, it was stuffed with replicas of ancient statuary made to look the way they would have looked when they rolled out of some craftsman's workshop in the 1st century A.D. It was odd to see ancient statues as they had originally been—not the pale clean stone of museum antiques, but heavily painted, with flesh and hair tones, gilded clothing, and gemstones for eyes.

Zammit walked around the room, intrigued, and relieved not to see any more pink, but trying to look bored because a real bodyguard wouldn't be interested in this kind of thing. He found himself standing in front of a Roman-era pornographic drawing scratched into the plaster wall of the replica building. There was a graffito in Latin underneath the drawing. He stepped back a couple of paces to get a better look so he could decipher the inscription. He'd gotten as far as "Livia's a slut, Falco's a whore, if wishes had mouths they'd . . ." when his heels hit something.

He turned and looked behind him. A block of fused coins, about a cubic yard in size. It was similar to those he had seen in the underground temple. He stared at it. How had such a treasure gotten here? Something this valuable would never have been put up to auction when it was unearthed. It would have been whisked off to a Turkish museum under heavy guard. Theft of antiquities in Turkey was a serious offense.

Once again he felt the pieces of some complex puzzle whirling in his brain, but they still didn't fit together. What was it Sultana had said? Iraq had been moving troops and armor to the border before the cyanobacteria in the reservoir had been discovered. He now knew the reason for that. The Resistance Army of Allah had approached Sultana and the PKK, asking for their cooperation. He now knew why. Suddenly he remembered what else she'd said: "Other people have been observed in the area. They are heavily armed, stealing antiquities."

He stared at the block of coins. How had the Popovs acquired something like this? Was it their employees who were the well-equipped and heavily armed people stealing antiquities from ancient sites around the Ataturk Dam? If so, were they in on the plot too? Mentally he filed the block's existence away for future reference.

They headed down yet another ornate hallway to yet another huge room. "The presidential collection of modern art," announced their guide, surreptitiously looking at his watch. Richards made appreciative noises again, less enthusiastically this time. Zammit wandered to the end of the room and stood before a locked glass case. It contained a bronze plinth on which was mounted what appeared to be a piece of driftwood with five rusty beer bottle caps nailed to it. He peered at the discreet brass nameplate, which read MONA LISA 23.

Costopoulos joined him. They stared at the piece in silence. Finally Zammit said, "I think we ought to start a new school of art."

"Yeah?" said the Greek.

"We'd call it the Shit School of Art."

"Why?"

"Then people could stand in front of something like this and with perfect accuracy say, 'Look at that shit.' "

They moved down another hallway. Zammit now only half-listened to the guide because the spiel was always a variation on the same theme—the genius and sophistication of the Popovs, the marvels they had performed for their country, the undying gratitude of the masses. Frankie Richards was still smiling, but it was starting to look a little forced.

". . . and so the glory of the Fatherland is reflected in the achievements of our brilliant leader and his consort," concluded the tour guide. Consort? thought Zammit. What is this, the 18th century? He looked at the guide and held his eyes. He raised an eyebrow in a deliberately provocative way, as a test. Did he believe this crap? The man's eyes flicked away. Nope.

The guide made a flourish, like a conjurer about to perform a particularly difficult trick. "And now, you will have the honor of meeting Their Excellencies Ivan and Anastasia Popov."

 A footman in yellow livery escorted them to the door of what appeared to be an enormous library. Zammit looked at the shelves of books that teetered into the air. All were leather bound with gilt lettering on the spines and looked as if they had never been opened.

Another footman in livery marched through the library door carrying a silver tray filled with champagne flutes and a couple of bottles. "More Veuve Clicquot," muttered Costopoulos. "Must have a franchise."

As they waited, tense and lost in their own thoughts, Zammit walked to the window and gazed out over the courtyard and the buzzing fence toward the dilapidated town beyond. He sipped the fizzy golden liquid without appetite. The window was a solid sheet of thick glass and, from the look of it, could stop an artillery shell. A few moments later he heard a noise and turned. Standing in the doorway were President Ivan Popov and his wife, Anastasia.

Often people seen only in photographs are either smaller or larger than expected when finally met. It was the same with the Tuvanian dictator and his wife. From the photos he'd seen, Zammit had assumed Ivan would be a beefy man of maybe six foot two and 280 pounds. Instead he found himself staring at a round-shouldered man of perhaps five foot six with a head too large for his body. He noted the low forehead, ferrety eyes, weak chin, and wet lips. He could smell a bucket load of some sort of male cologne, even from where he stood ten feet away, and noted also the two garish rings, a diamond pinkie and a cabochon ruby.

Anastasia was even more startling. A 44D, if Zammit wasn't mistaken, her breasts like half-empty sacks of grain, with orange hennaed hair. She had startling turquoise eyes, heavy makeup, and had obviously made at least one plastic surgeon very rich.

The two of them smiled at Frankie Richards, which was a little like seeing a couple of sharks wearing bonnets—it didn't come naturally to them. "Dr. Richards," said Ivan in surprisingly good English, an oily smile greasing his face. "How delightful to meet you. I am glad you could accept our commission."

"So am I," said Frankie, with apparent sincerity. The woman

really is a good actress, thought Zammit. "As I mentioned, I am here just briefly to discuss what poses you want, clothing, and so on. I will then do the preliminary sketches and certainly the faces, which are impossible to paint from photos. For the clothing and background, I can paint from photos when I work on the portrait back in America."

As Zammit listened to this exchange, he remembered that the term "peasant cunning" had come up more than once in Graves's briefing on the Popovs. They had isolated Tuvanistan from virtually all contact with the outside world except for vicious right-wing elements in Russia. The country was a strange amalgam of medieval and modern—a style of government that would not have seemed strange to a 12th-century serf, conducted with incessant surveillance, torture, and the latest weaponry. He thought of the train of shackled prisoners with the steel wire threaded through their flesh and realized he was reflexively clenching and unclenching his right fist.

Ivan Popov's smile vanished as an aide entered the room and whispered urgently in his ear. A look of alarm crossed his face, and he appeared paralyzed with indecision. He muttered to Anastasia, who barked something in Tuvanian at the aide, who promptly fled.

"Will you excuse us for a few moments?" said Anastasia, seizing her husband's arm and dragging him through a side door.

They stood and waited for the return of their hosts. After a few moments Zammit walked over to Stavros and said quietly, "I get the feeling President Popov is not exactly the sharpest quill on the porcupine. No doubt who's the power behind that throne."

Costopoulos nodded. "Poor bastard. That woman makes Lucrezia Borgia look like Mary Poppins."

"He's probably being shorn of the last remnants of his manhood even as we speak."

"I don't give this autocracy much longer."

Zammit drained his glass. "Why not?"

"This country is a slave state, but Tuvanians are natural-born rebels and have been for at least 2,000 years. Eventually it'll blow."

"I agree," said Jack Morgan. "And apropos of nothing in particular, I don't like the way El Presidente looks at me."

Costopoulos smiled. "You're a hairdresser, remember? He got his start pimping for the Communists. He has leapt to a conclusion about your sexual orientation. Don't turn your back on him, and for God's sake don't bend over."

"Bedfellows make strange politics," observed Frankie Richards.

Suddenly the door opened and the autocrat reappeared, his head still nodding on automatic pilot as he received final instructions from his wife. Before the door closed on a final burst of emphatic syllables, Zammit caught a brief glimpse of flaming red hennaed hair and two reptilian turquoise eyes. Anastasia was about to take care of business, and Ivan was being left with the task of playing host.

As he sidled back into the room, the dictator made hand-washing movements and wet his lips with his tongue. He looked sheepish, as befits a man who has just been shorn.

Morgan muttered in Zammit's ear, "To paraphrase Jerry Lee Lewis, whole lotta grovelin' goin' on."

"You know, hands and eyes are the hardest things to render in paint," said Richards smoothly. "Sir Joshua Reynolds, one of the greatest portrait painters, was so bad at it that his subjects are usually portrayed with drapery hiding their arms and hands."

Ivan Popov was obviously grateful for her effort to ignore what had just happened. Zammit stared out the window. They had just learned something important about the autocrat—he was dumber than his wife and subservient to her.

Another footman appeared and spoke to Popov. Apparently the banquet was ready. The walk down the corridors to the dining room seemed to take forever. Zammit wondered what would be served for dinner. He noticed shadowy figures everywhere, muttering into cell phones. Secret police. He reminded himself why they were there. Talk to Bled, if possible. Jamal as well. Were the Popovs involved? Mentally he braced himself to expect anything.

 The banquet hall would not have been out of place in the palace of Versailles. Mirrors, chandeliers, white moldings, gilt. The gleaming mahogany table was twenty feet long, laden with crystal, china, and gold. Footmen in yellow livery stood along the walls, like actors in some Ruritanian farce.

Costopoulos and Richards sat, with much fussing and pulling out of chairs by footmen. Stavros was getting star treatment in his role as Frankie's personal art historian. As a mere hairdresser, Morgan was at the far end of the table. As a bodyguard, Zammit was next to Frankie.

There were two empty chairs across from Zammit, each with place settings. Other palace guests must be on their way. It occurred to him that the dinner table atmosphere was much as it would have been on the *Titanic* if passengers had known beforehand it was going to sink and there wouldn't be a band.

Dinner was a succession of heavy foods in cream sauces. A cream of mushroom soup. A salad of greens he couldn't identify, smothered in a blue cheese dressing that appeared to be made with overripe gorgonzola. Cabbage dumplings in sour cream. The main dish seemed to be lamb in a white sauce sprinkled with capers, but the sauce had curdled, and the lamb had a fatty, off smell. He noticed that Frankie was just picking at it. Grimly he ate, trying to avoid the gristle. The china was Limoges, the crystal Baccarat. From the heft, the knives and forks were solid gold.

Frankie and the Popovs chatted back and forth. The Popovs appeared intent on impressing her with the number of American celebrities they knew. The names Zammit recognized were third-rate movie stars whose careers had faded long ago. Frankie was handling it well, gracious and polite.

Anastasia had a white Persian cat. It groomed itself, sprawled on a stool beside her on a pale blue velvet cushion. Zammit's eyes flicked to the giant picture facing him above a priceless 15th-century gilt Venetian mirror. Painted on aquamarine velvet, the same cat stared at him with eyes made of genuine sapphires.

His attention was caught by something Ivan Popov was saying. "Perhaps we could have a séance later this evening. We have our own personal medium who puts us in touch with the spirit world. Just last week I had a conversation with Genghis Khan." I'll bet, thought Zammit.

As Popov expressed his high opinion of Madonna's vocal talents, a door opened at the far end of the room. A heavy-set but muscular man of about six foot three, in a double-breasted tuxedo, approached the table. Swarthy face, ebony hair silvering at the temples. He spread his big hands and smiled dazzlingly. "My apologies. Business. No rest for the wicked."

He glanced at the contents of the plates. "Mutton again? Excellent! I see we have other guests. May I have the pleasure?"

Ivan Popov wiped his greasy mouth and stood. "Abdul Jamal, this is the world-famous artist Frances Richards. She has agreed to paint our portrait."

"Miss Richards." Jamal took her hand. "Or should I say, Dr. Richards?" Zammit felt an icy finger trail down his spine. The Omani held her fingers to his lips, his eyes never leaving hers. From Frankie's rigid posture, she was finding this unpleasant. He remembered her reaction to the photos of Jamal.

Another smile. His charm was in overdrive. "Of course I am familiar with your work. I know the human body can be rather difficult." Zammit's stomach lurched.

"I mean, to portray. Tell me, is it true the two most difficult parts of the human body to render convincingly in paint are the eyes and the hands?"

"Yes," replied Richards. She was looking directly at Jamal, but Zammit knew her well enough to know she was making an effort. He remembered what she had said about the glare at the back of his eyes.

Jamal was introduced to Costopoulos, in his role as Frankie's personal art historian. The two men shook hands. Zammit saw the look on the Greek's face. You'd have to know him to read the look. He's just realized Jamal knows who we are. As the Omani pulled out his chair, he cast a glance in Zammit's direction. A faint smirk appeared on his face, then he leaned forward to talk to Frankie. But Jamal, no matter how dangerous, was just a guest. The Popovs ran the place, and their eagerness to be courteous to Frankie was palpable.

"I like Kandinsky and Klee," Jamal said. "I suppose it's my Muslim upbringing, the fact that they are abstract artists. As you know, Islam prohibits representational art. The Impressionists are so boring, don't you think?" His voice deepened and darkened. "Renoir's women, with their enormous breasts and vapid faces. And his colors—his choice of palette made them look like fruit. Juicy, edible, human fruit."

Even Ivan and Anastasia Popov picked up on Jamal's tone of voice. He remembered what Costopoulos had said on the plane: "Jamal thinks he's in control. Why is he so confident?"

Suddenly the Omani turned to Zammit. The switch from tormenting Frankie was disconcerting. "I'm always interested in meeting new people, learning new things. Your bodyguard looks more intelligent than most. I am interested in his opinion."

Zammit kept his face impassive. "I don't know anything about art." No gun. He gazed down at his place setting, noting what was there.

Jamal said, "Not art. Politics. The death of the Soviet Union makes the world a much more interesting place than it was before." He gestured toward the Popovs. "Crisis is opportunity for those willing to exploit it. Today the four largest nuclear powers are the United States, Russia, the Ukraine, and Kazahkstan. In a world where a nation of camel-riding pastoralists can be the fourth-largest nuclear power, anything can happen. Including permitting our hosts to have their own country. It will also permit me to have my own country."

Zammit remained silent, even though he was surprised—he had assumed all along that the new country would belong to Bled and Smegyev. What was going on? He remembered what the Greek had told him—rattle Jamal.

Jamal turned to Frankie. "Did you choose an idiot as a bodyguard?"

Zammit spoke. "With freedom comes responsibility. Power must be tempered with judgment and respect for others."

The financier smiled. "An unusual opinion for a bodyguard. Did you enjoy your magazines?" Zammit realized that Jamal, not the Popovs, had placed them in his suite.

"You did, didn't you?" asked Jamal softly. "At some primitive level, you responded to them." It was true. Again the deep, dark voice. "So, you see, we are alike, you and I."

What was going on? Zammit stared down at his plate. He's intelligent, and he must know he's not normal, that other people aren't sexual predators and killers. It must bother him somehow.

Suddenly he had it. I'm a contestant in some sort of competition. For whatever reason, he wants me to admit the two of us are alike. That because I responded to the pornography, even in a minimal way, I'm the same sort of person he is. If I admit that, he'll think he's won a victory over me. But I am not like him. I may be an animal in my physiology, but I am more than a beast.

"No, we are not alike," said Zammit. Waiting for whatever was coming next, he flexed his leg muscles underneath the table, surprised at how rubbery they felt.

Jamal smiled. "It was Shakespeare who said, 'There is nothing either good or bad, but thinking makes it so.' That's why he could create a character like Richard III, a villain who reveled in villainy. I love Shakespeare, his instinctive knowledge that life is meaningless. 'We are such things as dreams are made on, and our little lives are rounded with a sleep.' "

Jamal leaned forward. "Tell me, bodyguard, do you know what existentialism is?"

"Yes," said Zammit. "The philosophical doctrine that man forms his essence in the course of the life he chooses to lead. How you choose is who you are. Do you cheat on your taxes? Fool around on your spouse? Watch a child being beaten and do nothing about it? Hear someone tell a cruel joke, and laugh even though you don't feel like it? Have sex with a woman even though she says no, stop? You do these things, and I can tell you who you are. You are a cheat, a coward, a hypocrite, and a rapist, and it doesn't take a lot of hand-wringing to figure that out."

"Very, very good," said Jamal. "A philosophical bodyguard. But you've left out the rest of it."

"I'm listening."

"A person chooses the life they lead, but you are assuming some sort of moral grounding. But a person's choices take place in a universe that is purposeless and irrational. In a universe without meaning, all acts are morally equivalent. Man only knows he exists by doing. And in the overall scheme of things, what he does, the choices he makes, doesn't matter."

Zammit recalled his conversation with Grand Master Fortucci on the nature of evil. This man is morally insane. Of his own free will, he chooses to do evil. "I disagree."

Open-mouthed, the Popovs were trying to follow this exchange.

"I know you," said Jamal. "You are a Knight of Malta, but you have no faith in anything but your machines. I have faith in power. Mao Zedong said power grows out of the barrel of a gun. What is a gun? A machine. How are we different?"

Zammit thought, Why is he trying to get me to admit that we are similar? He tried to explain, to himself as much as to Jamal. "Imagine the captain of a ship embarking on a voyage. The ship is your life, the captain is your soul. As you embark on the voyage, someone gives you a book. It contains instructions for the voyage. But you cannot open the book until you are out of sight of land. You are on the infinite ocean with no means of navigation. Lost, you open the book. But it is almost impossible to read. You can decipher certain words, certain instructions. They give you some vague idea of which way to go. You are frustrated because you can't understand the rest. But because you have no choice, you follow the instructions, as best you can, on your voyage through life."

Jamal smiled. "I have such a book, and it is not as mysterious as yours. It's very detailed. It is my bible. Perhaps you know it. 'I believe the worst about everyone, including myself, and I am seldom mistaken.' "

"Machiavelli. *The Prince*. Not the choice I would make on my journey through life."

"It works for me," said Jamal.

"In his own life he was a political failure. Why choose as a guide someone whose ideas didn't work even for him?" Zammit gestured around the room. "If you're so smart, how come you're here and not in Paris?"

Jamal's smirking smile was suddenly fixed. There was a red flare from his eyes.

"You will never find refuge, not even if you have your own country. You will always be a fugitive because you are always fleeing from yourself."

Jamal's face was suddenly congested. Too late Zammit remembered what Costopoulos had said—the last thing you want to do is frustrate a psychopath, point out his flaws, his lies, make him angry. It wouldn't take much to push him over the edge. With cold detachment he evaluated Jamal's size and probable strength. Heavy hands. Bigger than I am by thirty pounds.

Zammit raised his glass. "A toast. Here's to those who wish us well. And those who don't can go to hell."

Jamal's voice was thick with rage. "Despite what you say, we are alike, Dr. Zammit. A final quote. 'Whoever fights monsters should see to it that in the process he does not become a monster. When you look long into an abyss, the abyss also looks into you.' Nietzsche. Look into your own abyss, Dr. Zammit, and see what is there."

"What is going on here?" demanded Ivan Popov. "I don't understand any of this. I thought this man's name was Davis, and he is Frances Richards's bodyguard."

The door opened and Wurban Ice plodded in. He whispered to Jamal. The Omani's face changed, as if a mask had been ripped off. Zammit was suddenly afraid.

The financier regained his composure and muttered something back. Ice left the room. "I have just been informed that millions of dollars worth of education have been wasted. It appears that many of my star pupils from the Imam Hatip have been arrested by a certain Colonel Yildiz. In particular, seventy members of the Turkish military."

He looked at Zammit. "I suppose I have you to thank for this?"
"Yes."

"Well," said Jamal, "the waste of money and effort is irritating, but it doesn't matter. I always make sure I have a fallback position."

The room was filling with the Popovs' personal bodyguards. Ivan Popov stood. "I didn't order you to come in here. Get out!"

Jamal spoke. "Shut up, you clod-hopping authoritarian. They won't leave without my orders."

Zammit realized that the financier had subverted the palace guard. That's why he was so confident. Jamal turned to Zammit. "I am in control here." He looked at Frankie Richards. "Dr. Richards is a beautiful woman. She will come to realize it is not an asset."

Zammit thought, There are at least ten men in this room apart from Jamal. I can't fight them all. He gazed at his place setting. You are a scientist. Scientists use instruments.

Suddenly he heard a familiar sound. He stared at the floor.
Catula.

It had gotten out of his suitcase. As he had conjectured, Dikka must have installed a battery to jump-start it after a certain length of time. Its movements were hesitant. The robot didn't like open spaces. Then Catula saw Anastasia's white Persian cat. The insectoid's red camera eyes swiveled on their mounts as it stopped, perfectly motionless.

Come on, thought Zammit. You really hate cats.

The white Persian had seen Catula too. It stood on its cushion, with a hunting look. As it leapt off the stool, Jamal saw Catula as well. "Get that cat out of here!"

Zammit had forgotten how fast the robot could move. The Popov's bodyguards took one look at Catula and fell all over each other trying to get away. Suddenly all was chaos.

Chaos was opportunity.

He seized a dinner plate from the table. He'd noted the shape before. He threw it like a frisbee at the bodyguard closest to him. The plate hit him in the forehead with a *thunk*. Costopoulos and Morgan were following his lead, throwing glasses and plates. Zammit seized a couple of dinner knives and hurled, saw them hit home. The bodyguards weren't shooting, so they must have orders not to kill them. He saw Catula battling the cat. The robot was winning.

He was a good fighter, but there were too many. He threw every combination he could think of. Right, left, overhand right, make the brain slosh around in the skull. Hit them hard, hit them often. They were hitting him back, but he realized he could take it. At forty, he could still do it.

But there were too many of them, and he was getting tired. He dropped a couple of guards and found himself facing Wurban Ice, just as he saw Morgan and Costopulos flee the hall. He couldn't see Frankie. The Hungarian was holding his hands in a strange way. Karate expert. He slammed Ice's face hard, two overhand rights in a row. But Ice didn't go down.

He threw a left just as the Hungarian lowered his head and punched. Zammit's hand slammed into the top of his skull. Stabbing pain as a metacarpal snapped. And then he was falling.

 When Zammit came to, he couldn't move. He was imprisoned in some sort of portable bondage harness, like the ones he'd seen in Jamal's pornographic magazines, arms behind his back, wrists bound. He twisted his aching head. There was a chain attached to the wrist cuffs. The chain ran through a pulley at the top of the harness's black metal frame. His feet were flat on the ground, but if the chain was racheted up, he'd find himself dangling in the air, as his shoulders slowly dislocated.

Blearily he looked around. The decor was the same as in the rest of the palace. It was a private suite, with high ceilings, furnished with gilt French antiques, pink velvet upholstery, and purple watered-silk wallpaper. It looked like an expensive bordello except for a large mahogany desk in French Third Empire style against one wall.

Wurban Ice stood in a corner, red marks on his face where Zammit's blows had found their mark. The Hungarian stared with flat hostility. Zammit peered at something on the floor beside the bodyguard. A fused block of ancient coins, like the ones he'd seen in the underground temple and the Popovs' museum. It must have been Jamal's men Sultana and the PKK had spotted looting the buried cities near the Ataturk Dam.

There was someone else, sitting on a chair. A young girl with sherry-colored hair and crocus-blue eyes. Hands on her knees, she was completely motionless, staring straight ahead, like an ancient Egyptian sculpture. Her feet were bare, and she was naked from the waist up. On her lower body she was wearing what appeared to be a tight bikini bottom made of black latex. He couldn't see very well, but her eyes were wide open. They appeared vacant but alert at the same time, as if she were drugged.

He forced his aching head around. Another woman in a chair, only she was bound and fully dressed. He recognized the clothing.

Frankie. Her cheek was bruised.

He shifted his weight, ignoring the thudding in his head. He twisted his wrists. His bonds felt like leather cuffs. Leather stretches. You are stronger than most people. He twisted harder.

His left hand felt as if it had been pounded with a sledgehammer. "Frankie?" he croaked.

"Mike?"

"What the hell is this?"

"Jamal's suite in the palace. We were brought here after being knocked out. Morgan and Costopoulos escaped from the dining hall. I don't know where the Popovs are."

Zammit raised his chin at the motionless girl. "Who's she?"

"I don't know."

"She's Circassian," came a voice from the doorway. It was Jamal, in his tuxedo. "Acquired her a few days ago. She's being trained."

He stood in front of Zammit. "Stupid thing to do, coming here. Had to ride to the rescue, didn't you? I knew you would, if you figured it out this far."

"I didn't know you'd subverted the palace guard. That you control this place."

"I'm always one step ahead of my enemies."

"Where are the Popovs?" asked Richards.

"Dead. Stupid people with bad taste in everything, even governance. Good riddance." He walked to a marble table covered with bottles, selected one, and poured himself a drink.

Zammit tried to think. Bled and Smegyev were partners, along with Anwar Hussein and the Syrians. Bled supplied the big stuff—military expertise, nuclear weapons, troops. Bled's men were fanatical members of Smegyev's cult, which supplied morale. Smegyev and Bled together were trying to fulfill the monk Nestor's prophesies about the enthroning of the Holy Chosen One as tsar in Istanbul.

But Jamal was the mastermind of this plot. Why? All he supplied were drugs. Narcotic and hypnotic, plus powerful amphetamines. What were the amphetamines for? What was he getting out of this? Zammit remembered what Costopoulos had said: Jamal needs to talk, to explain himself and his cleverness.

"This is very clever," said Zammit. "But what do you get out of it?"

"I'm tired of running. I want my own country."

"But Bled has troops, nukes, Smegyev and the cult. It will be *their* country. You're just a dope dealer."

Jamal drained his glass. "Why are the Iraqis and Syrians part of this plot? Do you think Bled or Smegyev could broker a deal with them? Of course not. It was my idea, and without me, it has no chance of success. They all know that, which is why I'm in charge."

Frankie Richards spoke. "If you want your own country, why not Tuvanistan?"

"My partners don't want Tuvanistan. For religious reasons, they want Istanbul and a chunk of land between it and Ankara. They have nuclear capability, and I don't. Besides, who wants this pigsty of a country? Nothing but oil and misery. An economy based on a single commodity is always vulnerable. I hate being vulnerable."

Zammit knew what Frankie was doing. Keep him talking. "I don't understand how it's possible to have your own nation. I can see mounting a coup if you're part of the country's administration, a politician or a soldier, but not if you're a foreigner."

"You're less intelligent than I thought," sneered Jamal. "The Grimaldis of Monaco are Europe's oldest royal family. They have their own country because in the 13th century the original Grimaldi, a pirate, scaled the palace walls one night and simply took it. That's the trouble with people today. No initiative."

"That was 700 years ago," replied Richards.

Jamal poured another drink. "World War I. Four huge empires disappeared in four years, shattered into new countries. 1991. The Soviet Union blows apart into seventy nations and other autonomous regions. If that could happen a decade ago, it can happen today."

He paced the room. "The key thing is nuclear weapons. That's where Saddam erred when he invaded Kuwait. I needed a partner with nukes and military experience. Bled was the only logical choice." He shrugged. "Us having our own country is no more unusual than the Popovs having theirs. But to create a viable state, you must have weapons, agriculture, industry, legitimate leadership. You must also avoid the Bolshevik mistake, where you expect people to worship a theory. You must have more, which is why religion is such a godsend, no pun intended. A wonderful tool of control. A fundamentalist religion is even better, since it's simpleminded."

"Wait a minute," said Zammit. "You enlisted the Resistance Army of Allah to assassinate Amurkhan by pretending to be a devout Muslim. Most Turks are Muslim. Smegyev's cult is based on Russian Orthodoxy, so Bled's army of occupation will be Christian. How is that going to work?"

The Omani grinned. "I thought of that already. Our little state will have freedom of religion."

Zammit twisted his wrists. "Aren't you worried about the reaction from other countries?"

Jamal laughed. "The Americans and NATO will make outraged speeches, strictly for home consumption. Then they will make deals with us. They have to because we'll control Istanbul, one of the world's great ports. America did business with the Chinese after the Tiannemen Square massacre because they needed the trade. They launched the Gulf War to save Kuwait because they needed the oil. Same with us."

"Even with freedom of religion, you aren't going to hold Turkey," said Richards. "The population will rebel."

"I have a solution," said Jamal. "Got the idea from a book I read as a boy. A drug administered to the population to keep them docile. Soma." It sounded familiar but Zammit couldn't recall why.

Frankie's voice was heavy with irony. " 'O brave new world, that has such people in it.' "

"Precisely," Jamal smiled. "The idea of controlling people with a combination of biological engineering, drugs, and religion was brilliant. Huxley's *Brave New World* fused with my reading of Machiavelli, and so here we are. The drug is called POCS."

"P-O-X?" asked Zammit.

"No. P-O-C-S. I like the acronym because it's so ugly when you say it. Population Control Sedative. I've been testing it for years."

A thought struck Zammit. "You sent me an e-mail message before anyone else knew about the cyanobacteria. Why? How did you know I'd have anything to do with this crisis?"

"Don't be so modest. They always call you in on the big ones. Besides, I was keeping tabs on you. Do-gooders are so trusting."

What was he talking about? Zammit pointed his chin at Frankie, bound in the chair. "Why all of this?"

The financier walked over and stood before Zammit. "I am a vindictive man, and sooner or later I fix the wheels of every wagon that ever ran over me."

"I don't understand."

Jamal made a temple with his fingers and tucked it under his chin. "Several years ago. Pakistan. People getting sick from river water. You were called in. You found that the pollution came from a carpet factory discharging toxic effluent."

"I remember. A huge release of chemicals. It contaminated a

hundred miles of river." He recalled the worst of it. "The carpets were made by child slave labor. Hundreds of kids in a firetrap warehouse, chained to their looms, their only food a bowl of rice a day sprinkled with rotting fish. The windows were sealed and the doors locked."

Jamal shrugged. "That is not important. You found the factory. You persuaded the American government to mount sanctions to halt child labor. You almost ruined a profitable business."

Zammit stared into the man's eyes. "So it was you. But there's something you're omitting. Before I could investigate the factory itself, you torched the building. And everyone in it. All those kids, burned alive."

"You were moving too fast, and I had to destroy the evidence."

"What evidence?"

"The carpet business itself was not important. But to make carpets, you must use chemicals. In a place like Pakistan, no one is going to check whether the drums entering the factory actually contain what is on the label."

Suddenly it was clear. "The factory was a cover for your drug research."

"Yes. You forced me to relocate to another part of Pakistan, at great expense and inconvenience. That is why you are here. I want my pound of flesh." Jamal turned and smiled a slow, rotten smile at Richards. Zammit's face turned to ice.

"You can't harm us," said Zammit. "Colonel Graves, the White House, and the CIA know we are here in Tuvanistan. Frankie is a celebrity."

Jamal walked over to Frankie. "I'll have fun with Dr. Richards. You, I will kill."

Desperately Zammit thought, He really means it. "There will be an international uproar. You'll be hunted down like an animal."

The financier looked at his watch. "What's keeping them?" He threw himself onto a sofa. "If the Princess of Wales can die in a spectacular car crash in the middle of Paris because of a drunken limousine driver, the same thing can certainly happen here. The Popovs are dead. Soon this nation will be in chaos, which will increase its already phenomenal rate of traffic accidents. I've arranged such crashes many times. If you do it correctly, not even an expert forensics team can tell it wasn't an accident. It's an underappreciated art form. Great crime has the aesthetic quality of great art."

"Who are you waiting for?" asked Richards.

"My idiot partners. Bled has to get back to Sevastopol."

Zammit thought furiously. Jamal was controlling. Having partners meant giving up control. "What are you going to do with them, once you don't need them anymore?"

Jamal yawned. "Bled will be found dead after a bender or die in a drunken fall. Smegyev will have a heart attack or something." He smiled at Frankie, then blew her a kiss.

Zammit felt very cold. It was worth a try. "I'll make a deal with you."

Jamal looked surprised. "What's that?"

"I notice you have a block of fused ancient coins. I also saw one in the House of the Large Fountain, in the Pompeii room. I know where there are many more. If you leave her alone, I'll tell you where they are and how to find them."

The Omani's eyes gleamed. "I gave that block to the Popovs as a gift, even though it pained me greatly to do so. Where?"

"Promise to leave her alone."

Jamal gazed up at the ceiling, musing aloud. "Such treasures are extremely rare. Rarer than women. I can always get more women."

"There are statues too. Greek originals. Also very rare."

"You'll tell me precisely where to find them?"

"Yes. If you promise to leave her alone."

"Deal," said Jamal. "Where and how?"

"When I arrived at the Ataturk Dam, I took samples from the reservoir. I was abducted by the PKK and taken to an underground temple they were using as a hideout."

Jamal grinned. "We wondered where you were. But you were unconscious when you arrived, and it was dark when you escaped. How do I find this place?"

"I escaped using a metal detector. When I reached the surface, I left the device turned on and jammed it into a crevice by the temple entrance. You'd be able to home in on the signal."

"Ingenious. Thank you. But you are obviously not a good businessman."

Zammit felt a sickening lurch in the pit of his stomach. Richards's face was white.

"Never, ever negotiate from a position of weakness." Jamal blew another kiss at Frankie.

There was a knock on the door.

 Wurban Ice plodded over and opened the door. General Vladimir Bled strode in, carrying a large black box and an attaché case. A faint sneer appeared on his lips as he glanced around the suite. Without a word he walked up to Jamal and handed him the box. Jamal gave it to Ice, who left the room.

Then Lazar Smegyev glided in, fingering his greasy black beard. There were stains on the front of his coarse brown monk's habit. The *starets*'s huge eyes stared at the motionless Circassian girl with reptilian avidity. Just like Rasputin, thought Zammit—a holy man who likes the ladies.

As Zammit twisted in his harness, three other men came through the door. He stared in astonishment. One wore a fringed jacket and a gray hairpiece chosen to match his Old Testament prophet–style beard. The two others were carrying machine pistols. One was lean and blond, the other short and ruddy with curly black hair.

Edward G. Pompo and his Irish bodyguards, Roy Dool and Fergus Cronin. Pompo gave him the same faint smirk as on the Molly Katz show. He remembered Irina Markova asking about cults forming alliances, about Smegyev being in touch with Pompo. So they were partners too.

"Gentlemen, please sit down," said Abdul Jamal. "Anything to drink?"

"Why are we meeting here?" asked Pompo as he sat. "This place is awful."

Jamal was oozing charm. Zammit realized he was trying hard to hold his peculiar coalition together. "Because we have reached a crucial stage in our plan. Because telephone calls or e-mail can be intercepted. And—"

Bled shouted, "And because everything is going wrong!"

Jamal gazed at him. Softly he said, "Had a few drinks already, I see."

The general's shaved, bullet-shaped skull gleamed with sweat. He thrust a forefinger at Jamal. "The political situation in Turkey is still stable, despite your assurances. Your Imam Hatip pupils have been arrested. My men still don't have Aggressor. Dr. Cabrinovic is behind schedule. I told him if it isn't ready by the time I get back, I will have him shot!"

Jamal was soothing. "Everything is under control. With a complex plan, things sometimes must be rearranged."

Bled twisted around to look at Zammit, jaw muscles bunched, piggy eyes bloodshot. "He's figured it out so far. You told me that wouldn't happen."

"So he's figured it out so far," shrugged Jamal. "Look at him. Completely helpless. This is as far as he gets. He will die here."

"What is Aggressor?" asked Zammit.

Bled blinked. "Methamphetamine cocktail. My men will be invincible."

"General, please shut up."

Bled twisted back toward Jamal and almost fell off the sofa. How drunk was he? "What for? You said this is as far as he gets."

He rose unsteadily and walked over to Zammit. "How do you overcome a normal young man's reluctance to kill a stranger who has done him no personal harm?"

"I don't know."

"Boot camp. Shave his head, exercise him to exhaustion, stand screaming two inches from his face, make him clean a hundred latrines with a toothbrush, make him cry like a baby. And he can't fight back."

Bled leaned forward. The smell of alcohol was overpowering. "You destroy his personality. Then rebuild it the way you want so he will kill on command. But even this isn't enough. Soldiers must be willing to die as well as kill. They must believe in something enough to die for it. Communism wasn't good enough to die for. In World War II soldiers didn't die for Stalin or Bolshevism. They died to defend Holy Mother Russia."

He gestured toward the monk. "Now Communism is dead. Everything is falling apart, and we weren't even defeated in battle. People just gave up. We have our own national personality, and democracy will not work. Thanks to the *starets*, I realize the greatness of Russia must be rediscovered in its glorious history. Many others realize it as well. Aggressor will ensure success."

"Smegyev is protected by powerful elements in the government. Like national security advisor Vyacheslav Radchuk?"

A look of loathing crossed Bled's face. That told Zammit everything he needed to know. If they managed to get out of here, Radchuk was the man to get to.

Jamal spoke. "General, I think you've said enough."

Bled didn't appear to hear. "We must have a strong leader, a religious leader. We will have a tsar."

"You mean the Holy Chosen One," said Zammit.

Bled blinked. "How do you know about that?"

Zammit persisted. "So who is this guy? Another partner?"

Jamal's voice was rising. "General!" He struggled to keep his face under control as he walked over. He crossed his arms and contemplated Zammit.

"You must have found Kazov's notes. The ones we tried to find when we ransacked his office. They contained information about *The Secret Chronicle* by the monk Nestor. Did Kazov enjoy his cobalt-60?"

"That was stupid," growled Bled. "If I'd known, I would've stopped it."

Zammit realized there was dissension between the partners. How to exploit it? Unsettle Jamal even more. He doesn't know we found the RAA terrorists' laptop and read all the messages. "So you had to assassinate the unclean one, did you? Clever, using the boy, wasn't it, *ghazi*?"

Jamal's mask started to slip. "How do you know that is my code name?"

"I know a lot more than you think I do."

More slippage. It was as if he were trying to approximate human features and not getting it quite right. "Excuse me for a moment," he said thickly. He left. Zammit could hear water running in the bathroom. Bled walked to the far end of the suite, opened his attaché case, and began reading a file.

Frankie Richards said to Pompo, "Why are you in on this?"

Pompo ignored her. He smirked and walked over to Zammit. "A bad thing is happening to you, Dr. Zammit." He adjusted his hairpiece. "I was the original partner on the religious end. American evangelists were working in Russia, with great success. Show biz—we know how to do it. Then the Duma passed a law favoring Russian Orthodoxy and forbidding proselytizing by foreigners."

He leaned forward and whispered in Zammit's ear so Bled and Smegyev couldn't hear. "The Russkies are paranoid about that sort of thing—you know, foreign influences. Drives them nuts." He raised his voice again. "That's when Smegyev was made part of the deal—besides, he knows a lot of stuff you can't even dream of, even though you're pretty good at faking what you don't know. I told Jamal I still wanted in. He thought it might be useful to have an American partner as well as a Russian one. Knowing the media angle, that sort of thing. Plus, with the Brotherhood of the She-Manitou being tax-exempt because it's a legally recognized church in America, it's a great way to launder money."

Zammit tried to insinuate himself into the fanatic mind. "How does laundering money, environmentalism, postindustrial society, and the She-Manitou fit in with an invasion of Turkey?"

"The spiritual environment must be cleansed. Western materialism and consumerism are corrupt and spiritually unfulfilling. Not so in Russia." He gestured at Smegyev. "Russian religious sects have always prized the 'holy fool' as the ultimate attainment of sanctity. With Jamal's drugs, we will have an entire nation of holy fools to educate in the proper way to live. Political systems are nothing, freedom of religion everything."

"So Jamal mentioned," said Zammit grimly.

"Besides, I should be able to make money selling my seminars. Those who God blesses, he makes prosperous."

Zammit raised his chin at the monk, who was mumbling a prayer, eyes closed. "What about the mad monk?"

Smegyev roused himself and glided over. Even though his hair and beard were greasy and his monk's habit stained, he didn't smell of anything except cologne and hair oil. Zammit realized that the peasant monk appearance was largely an act, to appeal to a culture-specific expectation of what a holy man was like. The wandering, filthy, God-blessed *starets* was a mythic part of Russian culture, just as an American evangelist had to have a swept-back, blow-dried pompadour, drive a Cadillac, and use his hands as if he were chopping the air into blocks.

"I am not mad. Russian civilization is the greatest ever known. It was Tsar Peter the Great who made the fatal error of embracing European ideas 350 years ago, creating a gulf between the wealthy aristocrats in their villas and the peasants who worked the land. Tolstoy and Solzhenitsyn both knew this—Mother Russia is rural and deeply religious, used to obedience. Everything foreign is corruption."

He pointed to his bulging eyes. "These are big for a reason. So they can see into the future. And the future is a tsar, enthroned in Constantinople, in the rose-red church of Holy Wisdom."

"Bullshit," said Zammit. "Your eyes look like golf balls because your thyroid gland is out of whack. A little medication, you might look halfway normal." The *starets*'s eyes bulged in anger, but he turned away, sat on the sofa, and began mumbling a prayer.

Zammit said to Pompo, "So how does Smegyev raise the dead?"

"It's amazing what can be concealed under a monk's habit. Whenever he does the resurrection stuff, he has a defibrillator unit strapped to his chest. An electrode runs from the unit to a prod attached to his wrist. He also has a syringe with a retractable needle concealed in his sleeve. The electrode jolts the heart back to life while the syringe delivers a shot of adrenaline."

"We had problems during the testing and training phase," said Abdul Jamal, toweling his face as he reentered the room. He now looked normal. He glanced at the monk with evident distaste. "Smegyev liked the show-biz part so much he would delay the resurrection. Brain death begins within three to six minutes, and he would wait too long, chanting and praying."

Jamal didn't like Smegyev. He had referred to Bled as an idiot. The partners were all pursuing their own agendas. Zammit realized they were each prepared to betray the others if the opportunity arose. He had a good idea who the winner would be.

Jamal appraised the Circassian girl and Richards, then turned to Zammit. "I suppose you believe in things like love, romance, the innocence of children, and the sanctity of motherhood?"

"Yes, I do."

"Then you're a fool."

Dool and Cronin were staring at the floor, listening intently.

General Bled closed his attaché case and walked over. He looked at the Circassian girl and Frankie. His lip curled. "I must go back to Sevastopol. *Starets*, let's get the troops ready, with a blessing from Our Lord in Heaven. Pompo, a brief word. Accompany us to the limousine."

Pompo turned to Cronin and Dool. "Stay here. I'll be back shortly."

"General," called Jamal. Bled stopped. "Don't forget who hatched this plot. Do as I advise, and everything will be fine."

Bled grunted, and the three men strode from the room.

Jamal stood in front of Zammit. "I don't like you." He saw the punch coming, tried to roll with it. Darkness, filled with pain beyond imagining.

When he awoke, he was still in the harness, arms numb.

"Frankie?" he croaked.

Jamal had taken off his tuxedo jacket and tossed it over a chair. Seeing that Zammit was conscious, he strolled over to Richards. From behind the chair, he plucked idly at her outfit. "Good taste in clothes."

He buried his face in the nape of her neck as she twisted away. "Italian. Aqua di Palma. Lovely scent. Although I'm sure not as nice as your own."

He caressed her face as she snapped her head away. He turned to Zammit. "Yours?"

"Nobody's!" spat Frankie.

Jamal leaned over and looked her right in the eye. "Mine," he whispered.

He walked over to Zammit. "The world exists, in its meaningless way, so I can do what I want in it. Everyone must do what I want." The Omani threw a hard left hook to Zammit's rib cage. Zammit felt something snap. Dimly he heard Jamal say, "So, Knight of Malta, Catholic defender against evil, where is your God now?"

Zammit struggled to breathe. At least one of his ribs was broken. He raised his head and looked around. Wurban Ice, smirking. The two Irishmen, Cronin and Dool. They were both staring at him. He realized that this was the first time they'd heard he was a Catholic knight.

Desperately he twisted his wrists against the bonds, skin tearing. Blood trickled down his hands. He could feel the leather cuffs start to slide. He pulled his bound arms outward as his shoulder joints popped. It was working, but not fast enough.

Jamal contemplated Frankie. "You must belong to someone. A waste for you not to be an engine of delight for a man." A rank goatlike smell came from him, filling the air with a fetid stench, as if the rottenness of his soul were finding physical manifestation. Richards stared at him, defiant.

The Omani leaned over the Circassian girl, still with her hands on her knees, staring straight ahead, motionless. "Haven't you wondered about her?" He walked over to the desk and opened a drawer, removing a syringe and a clear rubber-sealed bottle. He thrust the needle through the seal, filled the syringe, and walked over to Zammit. He waved it in front of his face.

"Population Control Sedative. There are several types. This one is particularly powerful. Hypnotic as well as narcotic." He tapped the syringe to get rid of any bubbles. "You've seen professional hypnotists? Members of the audience crawling around on stage, barking like dogs? This has the same effect."

He gestured at the Circassian girl. "I told her to remain in that position until told otherwise. She will do so until the drug wears off. She'll need another shot very soon. The interesting thing is that anyone under the influence of this drug will do exactly what they're told. *Anything.* And they are fully alert while they're doing it. Fully aware." He smiled at Frankie. "I can't wait to see how Dr. Richards performs."

Jamal walked over to the TV and VCR and inserted a cassette. "You did belong to someone once." Rough footage, clumsily shot. A waterfall. A jungle. A man, emaciated and ill, cuts and bruises on his face, as from a beating. Balding, his short beard peppered with gray.

"Adam!" whispered Richards.

Jamal paused the tape. "Sumatra. My men were searching for medicinal plants needed to make drugs. Searching a nature preserve, where collecting rare plants is illegal. Your husband discovered what they were doing and had the audacity to demand that they stop." He gestured at the screen. "You can see the results."

"Where is he? What happened to him?" Frankie screamed as she struggled against her bonds.

He held up the syringe. "Perhaps I'll tell you one day. When we've gotten to know each other much, much better."

He smiled at Zammit. "Anyone can rape a body. It's an art to rape someone's mind."

The cruelty of this was beyond imagining. When Zammit found his voice, it was clotted with rage. "You're evil."

Jamal laughed in genuine amusement. He walked over to Frankie, the gleaming needle held aloft.

God, thought Zammit, if you exist, help me now. His eyes searched the room. Find a weapon. What would Costopoulos do? Desperately he thought, Think like the Greek.

He had it.

Fergus Cronin and Roy Dool. Cronin's ruddy face was pale, staring at the carpet, his Skorpion machine pistol sagging. Dool stared at the floor too, looking ill. Realizing Zammit was watching him, his eyes flicked up.

A weapon doesn't have to be a piece of equipment. Choose your weapon. Choose it now.

"Hey Roy," croaked Zammit. "Roy Dool." The Irishman looked at him, eyes burning.

"When the idealistic young man you once were first joined the IRA to free your country, did you ever think you'd be part of something like this?"

"Shut him up," Jamal said to Wurban Ice.

The squat Hungarian plodded toward him, rolling his shoulders, ready to throw a barrage of punches. Zammit wasn't sure he would survive the assault.

"Did you, Roy?"

Dool stepped forward and loosed a burst from his pistol. "Step away from her, you piece of filth."

"What're you doing, Dool?" said Cronin.

Without taking his eyes from Jamal and Ice, Dool said, "C'mon, Fergus. He's right. When did we turn into a couple of monsters ourselves?"

Cronin stared at Dool. He hefted his weapon, then swung his gun around. At Jamal. "You and me, Roy Dool. As always."

Jamal's eyes glowed red from under his brows, like those of an insane animal in a cave. He stopped in front of Frankie. "You can't even imagine what I am going to do with the two of you."

Frankie's long right leg pistoned as she kicked Jamal in the groin. He doubled over, gagging. Her leg shot out again and cracked him on the side of the head, the spike of her shoe hitting him in the temple. He dropped to the floor.

Everything was happening too fast. Zammit was almost free. Wurban Ice fired at Dool as Dool fired at him. The Irishman fell. Cronin was shouting.

Zammit twisted free and hit the floor. His legs wouldn't hold him. He lifted his head and saw Ice grab Jamal and start hauling him from the room, firing over his shoulder to keep Cronin at bay. Cronin crouched behind a sofa. Zammit couldn't see Dool, but Frankie was still bound. Cronin couldn't get a good shot at the fleeing men because she was in the way. Then they were gone.

Zammit tried to rise and fell, forehead pressed to the floor. Voices shouted in his ear, people tugged at his arms. He was upright. It was Morgan and Costopoulos, both armed.

"Tried to get here sooner," panted Morgan. "What is this chamber of horrors? Why does it smell like a farmyard?"

Zammit's head ached. Someone in the doorway, firing. One of the Irishmen. Ahead of him Frankie, still bound.

Step by step. Scientific method. "Help the Irishmen," he croaked.

He staggered across the room toward Frankie and gazed blearily around. Scientists use instruments. Desk. Scissors. An instrument. He fumbled for them and started cutting. Soon she was free. She took him by the shoulders as he began to fall. She couldn't hold her head steady, and her eyes were too bright. "Mike, are you all right?"

"Yeah," he lied. "You?"

She nodded. It was a lie. He could see it in her soundlessly screaming eyes.

Black rage rose in his heart, choking him. Jamal was going to pay for this. Gunfire. Fergus Cronin, crouched in the doorway, firing down the hall. Where was Dool?

Tears began streaming down Frankie's face. He was about to put his arms around her when Cronin shouted, "Where's Roy?"

Dool was slumped against a wall. One bullet had creased his eyeball and others had stitched gaping holes across his torso. Blood poured from the wounds. There was nothing to be done.

Zammit took the dying terrorist in his arms. "Thanks, Roy."

The man's lips moved but he couldn't hear. Zammit leaned forward. "What?"

"Redemption," whispered Roy Dool. "Did I get them all?"

"Who?"

"Jamal, Ice. Does that make up for the rest of my life?"

Dool was dying in some faraway place, beyond even pain. Comforting the dying was more precious than telling the truth. He looked in the Irishman's remaining eye and lied. "Yes, you did."

"Good." Dool was fading away. "Bless me, Father, for I have sinned."

He thinks I'm a priest. Desperately he tried to remember the prayer, the giving of absolution. He hadn't been to Mass or a funeral in years. I absolve you of your sins. What was the Latin? Remembering, he made the sign of the cross on his own, then the Irishman's chest. "*Ego te absolvo a peccatis tuis, in nomine Patris, et Filii, et Spiritus Sancte. Amen.*"

The terrorist whispered something sibilant. Zammit leaned forward, weariness filling his soul, not wanting to be false. No choice. "Say again, my son."

"Desperate," whispered Dool. "Life is a desperate business." His head fell to one side, and Zammit knew he was dead. His remaining eye stared from his face like a searchlight someone had forgotten to turn off.

"Thanks, Roy."

He realized there were people standing over him. Richards, Cronin, Morgan, and Costopoulos.

"Ah, Jesus," said Cronin as he looked at Dool's body. Frankie Richards held the videocassette in her hand.

"Where are Jamal and Ice?" asked Zammit.

"Probably escaped by now. I heard he always had a jet fueled and ready at the airport in case he had to flee. It looks as if staff and soldiers are looting the palace now that Jamal has escaped, the Popovs are dead, and no one is in control. They'll stay away from this area for a while because they know we're armed."

Zammit couldn't move. Cronin bent down and grabbed him by the arm. "Come on, Knight of Malta. It's not over yet."

 Frankie Richards helped Zammit to the bathroom, where he splashed cold water on his face, then rinsed the blood from his mouth. A loose tooth moved back and forth as he swished. He cleaned the blood off his arms and hands with a towel. As far as he could tell, he had at least one cracked rib and a broken left hand, which was swelling like a balloon. His clothing stuck to him, wet and clammy with Dool's blood.

"Frankie. Adam. That videotape. He may still be alive."

Her eyes were desolate. "I can't go down that road right now, OK? I'll start screaming and not be able to stop."

He was wobbly. Frankie helped him back to the main room. The Circassian girl was sobbing, huddled on the floor. Costopoulos knelt, several feet away, talking to her quietly in her own language. The sound was hypnotic, as Zammit knew Stavros intended it to be.

"Hey, Stav." He looked up.

Zammit knew it was a stupid question, but he had to say something. "She OK?"

The Greek's eyes swept over him, then Frankie. "Physically, yes, as far as I can tell without touching her. Having a male touch her right now would be a bad idea. But she's only been prisoner for a few days, so I think she'll be all right. Circassians are very tough people. Her name is Yasmin." At the sound of her name the girl looked up. Behind the tears her eyes were now clear.

"Mike, can you stand on your own?" Frankie's eyes were flicking in and out, in and out, like a light switch someone was toying with. Jamal's cruelty. "I want to help Yasmin get into something other than that bikini thing." Zammit nodded, and she walked over to one of the closets.

Cronin was in the doorway, his eyes searching the corridor.

"Anything?" asked Zammit.

"All quiet," replied the Irishman. "But not for long."

Zammit looked around the suite, the empty harness, the chairs, the bullet holes in the walls. "Jack, search this place. He lived here. People store valuables where they live." Jamal's tuxedo jacket, draped over a chair. "Clothes first. Wallet, phone numbers, anything."

Morgan searched the jacket. "Bingo." He held up a black square. "Computer disk." He searched another pocket. "Booklet with numbers in it. Looks like code."

"Take them," said Zammit. "See if there are more disks or papers. Search everything." A wave of weariness engulfed him. "I have to lie down."

Lying on the silk Bokhara carpet, trying to both think and quell the pain in his body, he could do neither. He passed out.

He was roused by a voice.

"Hey," said Morgan. "What's this box? Found it in one of the other rooms. It's got some sort of symbol on the side." He placed it on the floor.

Zammit tried to focus his eyes. The container was yellow with the symbol of a black circle with three interlocking horned crescents. "It's a biohazard box," he croaked.

"Well, the lid was popped when I found it," said Morgan. "Open a couple of inches. I haven't opened it any more."

Swell, thought Zammit. An open biohazard box. "Open the lid all the way. Don't put your face directly over the interior, and try not to breathe."

Leaning away, Morgan flipped the lid open, then waved his hand over the top of the box. "The interior is cold. Some sort of refrigeration unit." Cautiously he peered inside. He started violently and scrabbled away from the box. "Jesus Christ, that spider thing is in there!"

Zammit crawled over and looked inside. Catula was curled up, its plug inserted into a socket inside the box. "A portable refrigeration unit has an internal power source. Probably batteries."

"Who put it in the box?"

"No one. The spider has three programming commands. The first two are to eat and hide. By getting into the box, it's doing both. When attacked by the cat, it was following the third command—defend yourself."

Something was wrong about this. It struck him. Spargo's insectoids were programmed to hide but not if finding a refuge meant something as complex as opening a container.

If his face hadn't hurt so much, he would have smiled. Catula was evolving. Evolving fast. Most people think you're a nasty bit of business, thought Zammit. But you're a smart little insectoid, and even if you're ugly, I think you're sweet.

He said to Morgan, "Let's see if I can find the off switch before Catula figures out what I'm doing." He reached inside as fast as he could. The robot sprang to life, its tentacles scrabbling. His fumbling fingers found and flipped the tiny toggle switch. Catula's little red eyes slowly turned black. It was now asleep. As a precaution he pulled the robot's plug out of the socket.

A wave of nausea rolled him onto his back. Dimly he thought, Biohazard box.

"There's other stuff in here besides the spider," said Morgan.

Eyes closed, Zammit said, "Remove the robot and find out what's underneath. It sounded like the tentacles were scraping on glass."

"Is it going to attack me? I've got a thing about spiders."

"It's not going to attack you. Take it out."

Moments later he heard, "Lab stuff. Tubes. A dozen of them."

Zammit opened his eyes. Morgan was holding up a glass tube the size of the cardboard inner tube of a paper towel roll.

"Jack, I can't see very well. Describe it to me."

"There's another smaller tube inside and a bunch of seals and valves on top. Label's in Russian."

"What does it say?"

"Doesn't make sense to me." Laboriously he spelled out the word. "V-A-R-I-O-L-A. Variola. What the hell's variola?"

Zammit felt his face turn to ice. He rolled over and propped himself up on one elbow. "Jack, I don't want to alarm you, but please don't drop that tube. Variola is the scientific name for it. You are holding in your hand one of the world's last remaining vials of smallpox."

Morgan paled.

"This must be what was stolen a few days ago from Vector, the Russian virology institute in Novosibirsk, in Siberia. Bled must have brought it in that big black box. Why, I don't know. But given the chaos in this palace, we can't leave it here. Put the tube carefully back inside. Make sure it's firmly in its padded rack. Then put Catula on top, close the lid, and lock it."

Then he remembered how Catula had been able to get out of his suitcase in the first place and battle Anastasia's white Persian. Dikka's battery pack, to jump-start the robot so it could drag itself to a power source. The last thing he wanted was for Catula to be jump-started in the biohazard box and start thrashing around to the sound of breaking glass. Then he remembered—he'd flipped the toggle switch. The insectoid was asleep until manually turned on again.

"Find anything else in these rooms?"

"More disks. There's a laptop too, but it caught a bullet so I have no way of finding out what's on them."

With an effort, Zammit sat up. "Take the disks."

Cronin came over. He was carrying Roy Dool's weapon as well as his own, and his pockets were stuffed with spare clips of ammunition. "Seems reasonably quiet. We should get out of here. Do we have a plan?"

"Yes," said Zammit. "We get to the communications center. Make some quick calls. On our tour of the palace I noticed they have PCs there as well as phones. We can check those disks." With an effort, he got to his feet.

They staggered down endless hallways trying to find the communications center. Zammit had to be half-carried. Yasmin was still barefoot but dressed in one of Jamal's shirts. Cronin was point, Morgan guarded the rear. The palace was in chaos, being looted by palace staff and soldiers. They were stripping paintings off the walls and lugging ornaments. The sight of Cronin with his machine pistol and Morgan with Dool's weapon was enough to send them scurrying. "Where are we going?" panted Morgan.

"We're getting close," said Zammit. "Next corner, take a right at the Ming vase." The vase was gone, but he recognized the massive porphyry marble table it had sat on.

Finally they reached the communications center. Soldiers milled around. Cronin fired a burst and they fled.

Zammit said to the Irishman, "Guard the corridor and fend off anybody who tries to get in here." Cronin moved to the door.

Morgan surveyed the banks of glowing PC monitors. "Quite a setup." He pointed at the video cameras near the ceiling. "Never did want to be a TV star." He picked up a chair and swung, smashing them to pieces. "Spies do not permit others to watch them, unless of course it's a trick. CIA 101. What now?"

"We have to let people know what we've learned and ask for a pickup," said Zammit. "Let's start with Colonel Yildiz and Colonel Graves."

Gunfire from the corridor. As Costopoulos grabbed a phone, Fergus Cronin pulled out an empty clip and rammed a full one home. "If you're going to reach out and touch someone, do it now, some unpleasant people want this room."

Costopoulos called Yildiz and told him to send an escort of fighter planes to the Tuvanian airport five miles west of the capital. He then briefed Graves and told him what Zammit had observed—that although the cult reached into the Kremlin, national security advisor Vyacheslav Radchuk was not part of it.

Zammit interrupted. "Arrange a meeting with Radchuk. Tell Graves I want to be there. Once we get out of here."

"You're quite an optimist," said Morgan.

Costopoulos spoke into the phone, then listened intently. "Graves says Radchuk is paranoid. Doesn't want to meet with Western intelligence people because it'll give ammunition to his enemies in the Kremlin. Also, he'll want to know where Graves got his information."

Zammit's brain raced. "Tell Graves to call Yury Bogov. Bogov and Radchuk were both senior officers in the KGB. See if Yury will vouch for us. Contact Irina Markova as well. She can confirm what Boris Kazov found out about Smegyev's cult."

Costopoulos transmitted this to Graves. "Colonel says good idea. But they are careful about verification of sources. Bogov doesn't know Graves. How can he confirm the request comes from you?"

It seemed so long ago. "Neanderthal man," he said.

"What?" asked Stavros.

"Yury will remember. Tell Graves to quote to Bogov what I told him about the mafia thugs at Dzerzhinsk. He'll remember."

Costopoulos told Graves what to say to Bogov and hung up. "Why do you want to meet with Radchuk?"

"I'll explain later," said Zammit, feeling for the wall. He leaned his forehead against it and closed his eyes.

"Apparently the Turkish army is standing fast, and it's still a secret that Amurkhan is alive. Yildiz thinks they've arrested all the fundamentalist sympathizers in the army and government who were Jamal's pupils. The Iraqis and Syrians are being ground to pieces, but it's slow going. The Turks have had to transfer military units from the north. If Bled invades, he'll have an easy time of it."

Face pressed against the wall, Zammit was aware that Frankie Richards was on the phone. It sounded as if she was speaking with someone in Seattle. Her voice was quavering. He tried to hear what she was saying. Irrationally he thought, *It's just the friction of my face against the wall that's holding me upright.*

"Doc, are you all right?" It was Morgan.

He didn't answer or open his eyes, concentrating on keeping his legs from buckling.

Morgan again. "He seems to be out of it."

Costopoulos. "Nothing is ever as it seems, young man. Michael, speak to me."

Zammit's voice was a whisper. "When I was in high school, I was on the track team."

"See?" said Morgan. "He's out of it."

"A sprinter. Fastest guy in school. We had a weak 400-by-400-meter relay team. The coach always had me run anchor, the last leg. By the time I got the baton we were almost always behind. At the championships, by the time I got the baton I was last in a field of eight. The leader was thirty yards ahead of me. I ran in an outside lane and still passed everyone. I don't know how I did it. I pulled every muscle in my body and threw up for an hour afterward, but we won. After, I asked the coach why he always made me anchor."

Zammit pushed himself away from the wall and swayed. A great weariness filled him. "He said it was because he knew I was the kind of guy who never gives up. And I'm not going to give up now. What does Frankie have to say?"

"She's still on the phone," said Morgan. "I'm not a scientist, but it sounds as if the team in Seattle has discovered something horrible about the cyanobacteria. They've analyzed the underwater pictures taken by the *Alliant*. Something about the stuff growing downward. There's also news about those fleshy bulbs growing on the surface. Dr. Richards got this strange look on her face, then she started talking technical and I couldn't follow."

"Just hung up," said Costopoulos.

"Let me talk to her."

Richards appeared. He could tell from her gaze that he must

look dreadful, that his face was swelling even more. She moved to put her arms around him. Zammit held up his hand. "Don't!" She stepped back a pace, a look of uncomprehending hurt on her face.

Zammit knew he was on the verge of losing it altogether. Frankie's touch might be the little thing that could shove him over the edge into total collapse. He couldn't afford to think about anything except the problem at hand.

Her look told him he had cut her to the quick. She's trying to comfort me, but she's badly hurt too. That videotape. Her ordinarily pale skin was paper white, and he could see a vein throbbing in her neck. The pupils of her eyes were huge. It's just sinking in, the horror of what might have happened to her husband, the horror of what Jamal would have made her do under the influence of the drug.

He was about to say something when there was more gunfire from the hallway. Cronin was crouched against the door frame. Yasmin was crouched there too. She had Dool's gun.

"We can't make any more bullets!" shouted the Irishman.

Painfully Zammit touched his face. "That guy could punch the wet out of water," he said to Frankie, wanting her to understand why he had just done what he'd done, that he couldn't allow her to touch him.

As if in a trance, she ignored the remark. "The situation at the reservoir is critical. The cyanobacteria is changing."

"Changing how?"

"It has three life stages. Growth, generation of toxin, then reproduction. Unfortunately, the terminal phase is going to be a little different from what I expected."

Grimly Stavros said, "I don't like the way you emphasize the word *terminal.*"

"I'm listening" said Zammit.

"The underwater shots taken by the *Alliant* show that the cells you identified have now developed into filamentous hollow tubes."

"Go on."

"The tubes consist primarily of cytoplasm, interspersed with fluid-filled spaces. Imagine grabbing a handful of cooked spaghetti and immersing it in water. The spaghetti hangs down in the water. Only it isn't spaghetti, and it's growing."

"I understand," said Zammit.

"Downward, toward the reservoir floor. There are billions of filaments. They are growing downward for a purpose."

"Why?" asked Morgan.

"Survival."

Talking about this allowed Richards to detach herself emotionally from the horrors she had witnessed and barely escaped. "Keep going," Zammit encouraged.

"Bacteria are among the oldest and most abundant organisms on earth. But they are structurally simple. Just rigid vessels filled with DNA and cytoplasm. They lack the elaborate features of most other organisms' cells. But this structural simplicity belies an extraordinary sophistication in manipulating their environment. This involves communicating with each other."

Morgan was incredulous. "Bacteria talk to each other?"

"Yes. These biochemical discussions can result in amazing behavioral and even structural changes. They talk to survive. And it works. Why do you think cyanobacteria are almost 4 billion years old? They are one of evolution's great winners."

"I'm listening," said Zammit.

"They live in colonies. We used to think these colonies were groups of rugged individuals that had little to do with each other or with cells in another colony. Not true."

She now looked almost calm. "As I said, these chemical discussions can result in astonishing changes. In this case, when nutrients are in short supply, millions of cells assemble into complex multicellular structures called fruiting bodies."

"I never did understand this part. Why would they do that?" asked Costopoulos.

"We've stopped feeding the cyanobacteria, right?"

"Right."

"So it's begun to starve."

"Right."

"Allowing yourself to be starved to death is not sound evolutionary strategy. An organism must find some way of continuing to exist. So now it is entering the terminal stage of its life cycle, one that will allow it to survive even though it is starving and trapped in the reservoir."

Jack Morgan suddenly looked ill. "You mean it has a way of escaping?"

"Yes. Starvation provokes a survival response—maturation of

the fruiting bodies, leading to reproduction. Not through cell division this time. Through sporing."

"I am getting a bad feeling about this," said Stavros.

"What exactly are spores?" asked Morgan.

"Thick-coated cells, resistant to heat, dessication, and long-term starvation. Ordinarily, fruiting bodies are just big enough to be seen by the naked eye, but with the GMO, it's different. And those thousands of basketballs contain trillions of tiny spores."

Zammit saw Yasmin place Dool's empty gun on the floor and start firing a pistol instead. It wouldn't be long before they were both out of ammunition.

"Approximately four hours after starvation sets in, the cyanobacterial cells send an SOS to other cells, using a chemical signal called Factor A—a homoserine lactone."

"Dr. Richards, what's it mean in English?" asked Morgan.

"Factor A is a distress signal telling other cells they are in danger of starving. Once the other cells say, hey, you're right, they all release Factor C, a small protein that starts the process of spore maturation."

"How long does that take?" asked Zammit.

"Even with the distance the chemical signals have to travel, I'd say anywhere from forty-eight to seventy-two hours."

"Christ," said Morgan.

Richards continued. "From what I can tell, the spore maturation and release process is not complete until the filaments touch bottom and anchor themselves. At present, they are quite delicate. As far as we can tell, all that changes once they touch bottom. Then a further chemical reaction takes place, and the filaments suddenly turn into stalks of fibrous material, like bamboo. Imagine an impenetrable underwater jungle of tough stalks."

"So once it's anchored, it spores?"

"No, the spores are forming, but they're still immature. Once anchored, the chemical signal is given to induce spore maturity, followed by another signal for release. The fruiting bodies burst open, and the spores are released into the wind."

"Trillions of spores," said Costopoulos tonelessly.

"I wish I'd taken biology in college," said Morgan. "What are we looking at here, and what can we do about it?"

"The green stuff is starving, which is the signal to breed by maturing spores in the basketballs. Once the spores mature, the balls burst. The spores, which have giant wings for such tiny bodies—did I mention that?—get lifted into the air by the slightest breath of wind. This carries them into the atmosphere. Far away, to another body of water, which may or may not contain the nutrients they need to resume a new life cycle."

"How far?" asked Zammit.

"Hundreds, perhaps thousands of miles."

"More cyanobacteria in another location?" asked Morgan.

"Yes."

"Another body of water fills with green slime and poison?"

"Correct."

"And we have no antibiotic that will kill the cyanobacteria," stated Costopoulos.

"No."

"Or the spores."

"No."

"And no antidote to the endotoxin itself."

"No."

Morgan spoke. "So we're up shit creek without a paddle."

"You are one smart fella," said Frankie Richards.

"Wait a minute," said Costopoulos. "Once it's in a new location, it has to eat. And not just anything, it has to eat organophosphates. Without someone like Ruslan Glinka to supply nutrients, it'll die."

"You're forgetting something," interrupted Zammit. "They had to be fed in the reservoir because the Euphrates is nutrient-poor and there's no agriculture in the area. No use of organophosphate pesticides on fields, no runoff from the soil into nearby water bodies. But that changes within a few hundred miles of the Ataturk Dam. Some of the most intensively farmed lands in the world, with the highest use of pesticides. The Ukraine, Russia, Hungary, Italy, Egypt. Ponds, lakes, rivers, and reservoirs with high levels of organophosphates."

"The bacterial equivalent of Christmas dinner, all year round," said Frankie.

"This stuff will spread its spores all over the world?" asked Morgan.

"Within weeks."

"But not the oceans? Please say not the oceans."

Richards frowned. "Good point. This is a GMO. Perhaps, like AIDS, it can mutate very fast to adapt to different environments. Many of the world's oceans are badly polluted. Unless we can think of something, it is probable the entire planet will revert to what it was 4 billion years ago—water and poisonous green slime."

"Well, I think something should be done about this," said Morgan.

"I am open to suggestions," said Richards.

Zammit waggled his loose tooth. Think. The meeting at the Dolmabahçe Palace. The Turkish general saying that war was about strategy and tactics, minimizing your own losses while maximizing the enemy's. What had he said? "This way, everyone loses."

Once again, he felt the pieces of a complex puzzle whirling around in his brain. Some pieces of that puzzle were now in place. Where did the other pieces fit? As he stared at one of the computer monitors, a jigsaw piece suddenly slipped into place.

"Jamal's disks," said Zammit. They stared at him, surprised at the sudden energy in his voice. "The one he had in his tuxedo pocket. If he carried it on his person, it must be important."

Morgan sat in front of a PC, inserted the disk, and started typing. After a few moments he said, "Encryption codes. Complicated ones." He pulled Jamal's booklet from his jacket and flipped the pages. "Same stuff."

"He was concerned about computer crashes and not being able to access the disk, so he put the information on paper as well," said Zammit.

Morgan flipped more pages. "Each code has a date and a time beside it. Most of them are crossed off." He smiled. "He changes his encryption codes at least once a day. The old ones, he crosses off the list." He peered at a page. "Here are the only codes that aren't crossed off. They have today's date."

"That means they're still usable," said Zammit.

"Hang on," said Morgan. "One of them contains letters from the Cyrillic alphabet."

Zammit leaned over and stared. "Is it the only one with Russian letters in it?"

"Yes."

"That must be the code he uses to communicate with General Bled. What about the other disks?"

Morgan pulled them from his pockets and quickly checked them, one by one. "Messages he's sent. All of them are signed *ghazi*."

"I'm starting to get the picture," said Frankie.

Zammit nodded. "We're going to send a message to General

Bled, using Jamal's current encryption code. This communications center must have its own automatic ID signature, so Bled will know it came from here. The message will be waiting for him when he gets back to Sevastopol. The message will appear to be from Jamal. Stav, read some of these messages. Can you imitate Jamal's style?"

"Yes. I'll keep it simple to minimize the possibility of errors that will make Bled suspicious."

"What's the point of sending a message in the first place?" objected Morgan.

"Bled is on his way back to Sevastopol," explained Zammit. "He has no idea what just happened here. As far as he knows, everything is fine. It was obvious to me that he has a healthy respect for Jamal's intelligence. If he knows a message came from the palace communications center, and if he believes it's from Jamal, he'll follow whatever advice it contains. And don't forget, when he was here, he was drunk. He's obviously a highly functional drunk, but he'll do whatever Jamal advises."

"What advice are you going to give?" asked Morgan.

"Hold off on launching his invasion of Turkey for precisely forty-eight hours. Keep it terse, say some new development has come up. A minor problem, but it has to be dealt with. Just delay the invasion."

"How is that going to work?" demanded Morgan. "He won't fall for it. What if he calls back to the palace to get an explanation? Everyone's fled or dead."

Zammit's mind was racing. "We'll also tell him there's been a revolt and the Popovs are dead. He knows damn well what the political situation is in this country, so a revolt won't surprise him. Because of the revolt, Jamal's had to flee. But everything is under control. Just delay the launch."

Richards interrupted. "What if Jamal, wherever he is, contacts Bled on his own and Bled finds out our message is fake?"

Zammit pointed at the encryption codes on the glowing screen. "Those codes are complex. He carried them on his person because he couldn't memorize them. Now he doesn't have the disk anymore, or his notes. Any message he sends to Bled that isn't properly encoded and doesn't come from here, Bled isn't going to believe. Jamal and Bled are now incommunicado."

Quickly they composed a terse message telling Bled to delay

launching the invasion for forty-eight hours, signed it *ghazi*, and fired it off into cyberspace.

"I still don't understand," said Jack Morgan. "A delay isn't going to do anything. The war is still raging, and the Iraqis and Syrians are losing. The political situation in Turkey is stable. Maybe Bled will get this fake message and call the whole thing off."

"He can't," said Zammit. "By disobeying explicit orders from both the Kremlin and Kiev to stop maneuvers, he's gone too far. Once Radchuk finds out about this plot, Bled is a dead man. He *has* to invade. The cult members are cranked up, Smegyev is urging him on, and he has all those nukes. He still has reason to feel confident of success, delay or not."

"But we still don't know what to do about the crap in the dam," protested Morgan. "Dr. Richards said the planet is going to revert to water and green slime, invasion or not. The whole world is going to die, and there's nothing we can do about it."

Zammit fiddled with the loose tooth, wincing. "Jack, remember in our initial briefing about Biopreparat, you said something about how their bioweapons are designed to be immune?"

"Yes," said Morgan. "They're designed to be immune to antibiotics."

"That's not what you said. You said they were designed to be immune to *Western* antibiotics."

He turned to the rest of them. "We agreed it would be insane to use a naturally occurring bioweapon, much less a genetically altered one. Jamal is morally insane, but he's brilliant and leaves nothing to chance. He would never rely on something as inherently unpredictable as a GMO. And Bled isn't an idiot either."

The others were perfectly still.

"There is a single condition under which it would not be insane to use this bioweapon."

They stared at him. The tooth came loose. He pulled it from his mouth, gazed at it wearily, and tossed it across the room.

"It wouldn't be insane if you had the antidote."

 Mike Zammit looked at the walls and wondered if somehow they contained echoes of the anguished screams of every tortured soul who had died in this place.

He was in the notorious Lubyanka Prison, headquarters of the secret police ever since the building was taken over by the Bolsheviks in 1918. It had been used for decades as an administrative headquarters, prison, and interrogation and execution center. Formerly occupied by the KGB, the Lubyanka was now home to its successor, the Russian Federal Security Service. He glanced at Graves, Morgan, and Costopoulos, all staring at the floor. Yury Bogov was bumming a cigarette from Irina Markova. She was chain-smoking. It was only thanks to Bogov that they'd been able to get in on such short notice.

They had escaped from the communications center in the Blavatsk palace and found the palace garage. It was being looted by the Popovs' mechanics and drivers, but gun to his head, one of the limousine drivers sped them to the airport. At the hangar they learned that Jamal and Ice had escaped in a jet, destination unknown. Four F-15s arrived and escorted them back to Istanbul without incident. Their various wounds were treated. Then they flew to Moscow. Frankie Richards was now back at the Ataturk Dam with Cairo Jackson, making preparations in case national security advisor Vyacheslav Radchuk agreed to cooperate.

In case.

Zammit glanced at the white plastic cast on his left hand. Still the tornado whirled in his brain. How did it all fit together? There was one thing he had realized on their escape from Tuvanistan, and it worried him almost as much as the contamination in the reservoir.

Abdul Jamal had known they were coming. How? There's something I'm missing, thought Zammit. Something vital.

The door opened and Vyacheslav Radchuk marched in. He was of Ukrainian descent, stocky, about five foot eight, with salt-and-pepper hair and bandy legs. In the puffy, sallow face, his small eyes looked like raisins in pools of buckwheat dough. He wore an expensive Italian suit that didn't fit properly and held a cigarette. His index finger was bright yellow all the way to the knuckle.

Bogov stood as Radchuk stopped in front of him. The national security advisor had the look of a man who expected at any moment to find a shiv in his back. Bogov introduced them all. Eyes bright and wary, the two former KGB spies contemplated each other.

"Hello, Yury," said Radchuk, in good English. "Long time no see."

"Hello, Vaya," replied Bogov. "Still on the old career treadmill, huh?"

"Yeah. You're freelance now. You like it?"

"I like it."

"I envy you. This place is hell."

"It always was," said Bogov. "Are we through with the pleasantries?"

"Yes." Radchuk crushed out his cigarette. "When you told me your information I almost had a heart attack." He gestured at Zammit. "Apart from looking like he's been run over by a truck, is he OK? You trust him?"

"Yes," said Bogov. "He's worked for our government before. He's smart, tough, and honest."

"Good," said Radchuk, contemplating Zammit. "Haven't met anyone like that in . . . well, never, actually."

Radchuk appraised Colonel Graves. "I am sure word has already gotten out that I am having an unexpected meeting with an assistant to the president of the United States and that I have not invited any politician or civil servant to attend. That's bad enough. I am also meeting, in private, with a CIA agent. This will get me into a great deal of trouble." He looked at Irina Markova. "And meeting with a journalist like her, in private, is a death sentence. This better be good."

"I assure you—," began Graves.

Radchuk held up a yellow index finger. "One moment." He walked over to a filing cabinet by his desk. He opened the bottom drawer and removed four small antennas. He carefully placed one in each of the four corners of the room. Then he sat in his desk chair, opened one of the drawers, and fiddled with something.

"Mr. Radchuk, what are you doing?"

Radchuk gestured at the antennas. "If there were any more bugs in these walls I'd have to hire an exterminator. Ninety years' worth of listening devices. I suppose we could tear the walls down, which would take forever. Once they were back up again, they'd start filling with more bugs. I have no idea how many of the bugs now in the walls are operational or who might be using them."

He reached into the drawer and flipped a switch. "Good. Now we can talk. I have reason to believe my secretary is a spy. For General Bled, in fact."

He pointed again at the antennas. "Broad spectrum noise generator. An electronic cone of silence. The device that generates the field is in this drawer. Any electronic equipment other than a watch won't work in this room as long as it's on. That includes telephones and listening devices in the walls. Markova, try your cell phone."

She did. "Dead."

"Got the idea on a tour of FBI headquarters in Washington. The entire building is a huge cone of silence. Good thing there are no windows in this room. Then I'd have to worry about long-distance laser listeners who could overhear my conversations by picking up voice vibrations from the glass." He lit another cigarette. "Now, what is this about, and why should I care?"

They filled him in as Radchuk's ashtray quickly filled with cigarette butts. By the time they were finished, the national security advisor had his head in his hands.

"So," concluded Graves. "If you help us, you will accomplish a number of things. First, you may help save the world from death by poison. Second, you will help stop the war that is currently raging. Third, you will prevent the formation of a hostile new nuclear power right next door to you. Fourth, you will help destroy an international fugitive and criminal. Finally, you will annihilate General Vladimir Bled."

"*Razborka*," said Bogov.

"What?" asked Zammit.

"Settling of scores. Getting even." The former KGB man was watching Radchuk carefully. "Vaya? What do you think?"

Radchuk stood and walked over to a filing cabinet. He opened it and removed a glass and a bottle of vodka. He poured himself a stiff shot, tossed it back, wiped his mouth, and sat down again.

He turned to Irina. "I want copies of your files on Smegyev and Bled."

"OK."

Radchuk lit another cigarette. "Four times I have started files on those two. Four times the files disappeared. Everyone thinks I'm powerful. In some ways I am. But I can't even trust my own staff."

He stared moodily at the walls. "OK. Here's how it is. I don't care about Abdul Jamal. He's not my problem. I don't care about this American evangelist either. Once I have proof from Markova's files about Smegyev, I will take action. The day I can't at least handle some crazy monk is the day I blow my brains out."

He scratched his cheek. "A rod of plutonium and cobalt-60 used to kill Boris Kazov. Well, at least we found one of them. I wonder where the other twenty-six are. A problem for another day."

He turned to Graves. "The problem for now is Bled, the army, and those nuclear weapons. His mafia allies might pose a difficulty too." His puffy face lifted in a humorless smile. "You heard the joke? In Russia, the law is like a lamp post—you can always get around it." The smile disappeared. "The Russian mafia has more money than God, and they are just as powerful."

"I don't believe the mafia will be a problem here," said Graves.

"Maybe not," said Radchuk, rubbing his face. "Maybe yes. It is tiring, always trying to think of every possibility."

Morgan spoke. "Why can't you just order other army units to take Bled out? They have nukes too."

Radchuk smiled again. "Ah, to be so young and naive. First, I am sure you understand why we don't want a nuclear war on our own soil. There's also the fact that, despite our propaganda during the Cold War, our missiles never were accurate, and now they're old. We've always suspected that if one day we had to launch them against Washington, we'd end up raining death on a town in Kansas. Second, I know Bled, and he would start such a war here in Russia if he felt trapped. He is also a brilliant strategist and a stubborn fighter. Third, there are many other military men and politicians who are members of Smegyev's cult. Even in the Kremlin."

He gestured around the room. "Why do you think I have this setup? At least I can have a confidential conversation in my office. But because of the cone of silence, the phones don't work, so I can't make any calls. Once I walk out that door and start giving orders to do something about Bled, someone in this building will quietly pick up a phone. Informed of our plans, he may decide to launch his invasion ahead of your forty-eight-hour deadline, regardless of any message he thinks he received from Jamal."

Zammit interrupted. "Bled must have a headquarters. Where is it? It must be a place where he has complete control, including secure storage for his arsenal and the bioweapon. Wherever the cyanobacteria came from, the antidote must be there too. What do you call the bioweapon?"

"Cyanostrom."

"Have you ever tried it before? Experimentally, on a large scale?"

The Ukrainian's eyes flickered. "Unfortunately, no."

"So there was no one in Biopreparat with any idea how its life cycle might play out, whether it might be unpredictable."

"No."

Costopoulos spoke. "Do you know the name of the antidote?"

"Anticyanostrom."

"Well," said Zammit, "that's simple enough. How do you spell them in Russian?" Radchuk spelled them as Morgan wrote down the names.

"Do you know what the antidote is?" asked Zammit. "Its chemical composition, optimum delivery system, anything?"

"No."

He tried again, as discouragement rose in his heart. "Do you know how much of it there is?"

"No. However, there are stocks in storage in other secret cities."

Zammit thought hard. "If I had designed this GMO, I'd use the same engineering on the antidote. Superconcentrated, dessicated with sugar, instantly dissolvable in water. But I won't know that until I can test it. I must take some of it back to the Ataturk Dam where my microlab is. Once again, where is this material stored?"

Radchuk looked hunted. As a professional spy, he was used to collecting and hoarding information, not giving it away.

"Come on," said Zammit. "We're running out of time."

He could tell the Ukrainian had reached some momentous decision. Radchuk took a deep breath and stared him straight in the eye. "Secret city Talitsa-4. It's in the Crimea. It's a small one and the only one located in a populous area, apart from a facility near St. Petersburg."

"St. Petersburg?" asked Bogov incredulously.

Radchuk looked hunted. "You didn't hear it from me. Bled controls Talitsa completely. His warehouse and research facilities are there. My information is sketchy, but that's where he stores everything."

Costopoulos interrupted. "Can't you at least give the order to attack the warehouse with paratroopers or something? Capture it and hold it at all costs?"

Radchuk's voice was cold. "For the reasons I have just explained, no, I cannot. I am helpless."

"Bullshit," said Yury Bogov. "I know you, Vaya. You would never find yourself in a situation where you were completely helpless. You're too smart for that. You have something, even if it's little stuff. Give."

The two old spies stared at each other. Zammit expected an explosion of anger from Radchuk, but there was none. "Vaya," whispered Bogov. "You might get to save the world. It's not often an old spy like you is a hero. At least you may be able to destroy Bled. *Razborka.*"

"I can't do it myself," said Radchuk. "I can't give an order to restock toilet paper without everyone knowing about it. But nobody knows about the conversation in this room except us."

He turned to Zammit, eyes appraising. "I've heard stories about you. If you want the antidote, you're going to have to get it yourself."

Zammit almost laughed, until he realized Radchuk was serious. "And how do you suggest I do that?"

The national security advisor rose and walked over to a giant wall safe. "Since the files on Bled and Smegyev vanished, I've kept all my good stuff in here. It has four combinations, as well as six encryption codes I change four times a day. Getting it open is going to take a few minutes. By the way, it is also wired with enough plastic explosive to level this building. When I installed it, I made sure every employee here knew about it. So far, no one has touched it."

Five minutes later Radchuk laid a box on his desk and shut the safe. He beckoned them all over as he removed the contents. There was a large roll of paper, an odd-looking pen, several blank forms about the size of credit cards, a stencil, and a set of contact lenses in a plastic case.

"I'm supposed to break into secret city Talitsa-4 and steal the antidote using this junk?" said Zammit. "I'm not McGyver."

Radchuk smiled. "I love that show. And yes, that's the plan."

He picked up the roll of paper and spread it out. "Here are detailed blueprints and a layout map of the warehouse at Talitsa-4. Bled may have moved things around a bit, I don't know. But here are the research labs, loading docks, and transportation bay, and he can't move those. Forklifts, cranes, the usual. There is a small airport at the back."

"I don't even know where this place is," protested Zammit. "These plans won't do me any good unless I can actually get there and get inside. And I can't fly a plane."

"I can," said Jack Morgan. "All types. A hobby of mine." He sighed and colored. "OK, I learned to fly most of them through flight simulators and computer games. But doing the real thing won't be much different. Doc, you can't do this yourself, especially not with a broken hand. I'll fly the plane."

Zammit stared at the young agent for a moment. Morgan's eyes were very bright. "OK."

He turned to Radchuk. "What else is in this pitiful collection?"

Radchuk held up the forms, the stencil, and the pen. "These blank forms are security passes. Standard issue, for entry into all the secret cities." He pointed to an iridescent strip. "The latest magnetic code. Also, I have all the necessary stamps and seals." He pointed to an old typewriter in the corner. "I'll fill them out properly. The passes will get you through the first set of security gates. But not without Bled's signature on the bottom."

He held up the pen. "Bled uses a special pen, with ink that is luminescent under ultraviolet light. His signature is verified by running it under a fluoroscope. Obtaining the pen was hard enough. For the ink, we had to scrape some off an old signature, do a spectroscopy, and recreate the formula from scratch. The stencil is for forging Bled's signature. I have been practicing."

Zammit pointed at the contact lenses. "What use are those?"

"The security passes are for the first checkpoint. The second one, leading to the research labs and loading docks, is more difficult. You must press one of your eyes against a scanner, which reads the pattern in your iris. Anyone whose iris pattern is not in the data bank doesn't get in. It's more accurate than fingerprints."

Radchuk held up the box. "And fingerprints can be faked— stick-on pads and such. Iris patterns can't be faked. At least not until now. I'm proud of this—I don't believe it's been done before."

He opened the box and gingerly removed a lens. "Because he drinks so much, Bled's eyes are going. He needed surgery and had contact lenses made. The surgeon photographed his eyes. I arranged for an office break-in by an agent with a camera, so that's how we know the patterns of both his irises. I was also able to get a duplicate pair of lenses, only nonprescription. I had his iris patterns and color imprinted on them. Believe me, neither of these tasks were easy. When you and Morgan approach the door, you will each wear one lens. Keep in mind that when the lens is in your eye, you can't see through it. You'll be completely blind in one eye for as long as the lens is in."

Zammit grinned. "This is clever. Why didn't I think of it?"

Radchuk put the lens back in the case. "Because you're not a spy. Count your blessings."

Zammit thought for a moment. "But we have three problems. First, how do we get to Talitsa-4 in the first place? Second, I don't speak or read Russian. Somebody asks me a question, I'm dead. Third, we'll need uniforms."

"Uniforms are not a problem. As far as getting there, I will tell you how. In downtown Sevastopol, there is what appears to be a vegetable warehouse. But in the basement, through the secret entrance on which these security passes will work, there is an underground train, a subway. It will take you to the secret city in about an hour."

"Don't worry about language. I'm fluent," said Morgan.

"Besides," said Markova, turning to Zammit, "based on what we've learned from the files, Bled and his research staff do ugly experiments on soldiers. You look awful. You're just the victim of an experiment that didn't work, and as a result you cannot talk. Jack can explain that to anyone who gets suspicious."

"I hardly think the two of you will be able to do it alone," said Costopoulos. "I too am fluent in the language. And I've always harbored an illicit desire to be an actor."

"Two more things," said Zammit. "If this does work, and we do somehow manage to get the antidote onto a plane and take off, we will be pursued. Can you give us cover?"

"I'll work on it."

"Also, I doubt if the amount of antidote we can load onto a single plane will be enough. We'll need more, from other secret cities. Air freight it to the Ataturk Dam. Call Colonel Yildiz and tell him you will be violating his airspace but that you are not Bled's invasion force. Work out some sort of signal."

Radchuk's face was a mask of furious concentration. "I don't know if that is possible."

"You're a smart guy, Vaya," said Bogov. "Figure it out."

It was a challenge. Zammit could tell from the anger in Radchuk's eyes. "All right, I will. Let's get working on the documents and uniforms. And Dr. Zammit?"

"Yes?"

"If you fail, I cannot help you. I will deny that we ever discussed this."

"Understood."

Radchuk reached for Zammit's hand and shook it firmly. "Good luck."

Zammit stared at the gray concrete wall flashing by. There was a whooshing sound from the constant rush of air and a *whackity-whack* from the wheels. The rocking motion was soothing.

As he leaned against the side of the car, he glanced down at his uniform, that of a Russian army private. He looked at the two people seated across from him—Morgan in a sergeant's uniform and Costopoulos in a white lab coat with a pocket protector, some pens, and a clipboard.

They were on the subway that led from the vegetable warehouse to Talitsa-4. With Radchuk's assistance, they had no trouble accessing the secret entrance that led to the underground platform. The security passes had been verified, and so far their journey had been uneventful. The car was filled with people who looked just like them—technicians, scientists, and soldiers. Most of the soldiers had the emaciated faces and shaved heads of abused recruits, but there were some who looked like Morgan. Most of the soldiers looked alert and normal, but some did not. Zammit knew these were the ones who had been used as guinea pigs by Smegyev, Bled, and Bled's Director of Clinical Research and Development, Dr. Bratko Cabrinovic. Their eyes were vacant, they had difficulty sitting upright, and some were drooling. Without being obvious, Zammit studied them so he could imitate their behavior to some extent. He gazed at his reflection in the glass. With the battering he had taken, he certainly looked like an experiment gone wrong.

Having Costopoulos play a scientist instead of a soldier had been a last-minute change in plan. They realized they would have easier access to the lab area if one of them looked as if he had unquestioned authority to be there. Stavros hadn't liked this change: "So we get into the lab area. A technician asks me a question. I speak Russian, but I don't speak science. What am I supposed to say so I don't arouse suspicion?"

"I'll feed you the answer somehow," Zammit had replied.

"What, in English? You're supposed to be a brain-damaged mute."

On the one-hour journey, Zammit ran through everything he had endured in the past several days. Pieces of the jigsaw puzzle still whirled in his brain and refused to fit into place. Step by step, he thought. First, get the antidote.

The train clattered to a stop and the passengers departed. There were wheelchairs for those too damaged to walk. The security checkpoint was manned by soldiers in combat gear with machine guns. Costopoulos took Zammit's card out of his uniform pocket as Zammit stared vacantly into space, hoping he looked convincingly brain damaged. First the guard verified the iridescent magnetic strip on their three passes. Zammit was aware that the man was appraising him and wondered why. I can't be that bad an actor, he thought. Finally, as the guard ran the cards under a fluoroscope to verify Bled's signature, he said something to Costopoulos. The Greek gave a brusque reply that seemed to be satisfactory. But the guard did not return their security passes. Costopoulos asked a question, the guard replied, and they were waved through.

Without their passes.

The three had memorized the layout of the secret city's warehouse by studying the plans Radchuk gave them. If they ran into problems, Costopoulos carried the blueprints and layout diagram concealed under scientific papers on his clipboard. Zammit wanted to ask what was going on, but there were too many people around them as they proceeded down the long concrete hallway that led into the bowels of the warehouse. The hallway ended in a cavernous space that was one of the main sections of the building—all steel girders and concrete, typical warehouse construction, although the girders seemed unusually sturdy.

In the open area, the crowd dispersed and Zammit could finally talk. He tried to speak without moving his lips. "Talk to me."

"The guard asked, 'Since when did they start beating people up?' I replied it was necessary to establish a certain drug's effects on the ability to endure pain."

"What about our security cards?"

Morgan replied. "He said they expired in an hour anyway and wouldn't be of any use. He said we'd have to go to the main permitting office, submit proof of identity, then get new cards issued. Standard procedure. In short, if we want to leave this place by the main door, as it were, and take the train again, we're out of luck. We're trapped in here."

They kept walking. Other hallways fanned out from the main room like spokes. "This way," said Costopoulos. From the bustle of activity, it was obvious that preparations were being made for the invasion.

As they walked through the cavernous room, warehouse shelving units rose forty feet high until they were lost in the dim vastness near the ceiling. The shelves were stacked with crates and drums, some clear white plastic, others black metal. Every one had on its side a sign or symbol indicating its contents. Some held weapons, from antitank guns and machine pistols to surface-to-air missiles. Others had the international symbol for radiation or the yellow emblem of a black circle intersected by three horned crescents that indicated a biohazard.

Morgan gestured at the shelving and its lethal contents. "War in a box."

Their footsteps echoed hollowly on the concrete floor. In the distance, knots of people in white lab coats. There was a distant rumbling sound, as if large pieces of machinery were working overtime. They could see the gleaming rectangle of the foot-thick stainless steel door that led to the most secret part of the warehouse.

"We are approaching the research labs, chemical manufacturing area, and transport bays," said Costopoulos, checking the diagram. "Where are those lenses?"

Morgan pulled the plastic case from his pocket. "Tell me again how we do this?"

Zammit replied. "We have two lenses and three eyes. I will create some kind of diversion so I can get the lens out of my eye and palm it to you so you can fit it into your eye and get through the scanner too. You're not going to have any saline solution to lubricate the insertion, so you'll have to get it right the first time."

Morgan handed the plastic case to Costopoulos. The two lenses floated in a saline solution. They paused momentarily as the Greek took a lens on his fingertip, popped it into his left eye and blinked. "Work OK?" asked Zammit.

"Yes," said Stavros. "Odd feeling, to be suddenly blind in one eye. Loss of stereoscopic vision."

"Remember," said Zammit. "Bled's irises are a peculiar color. Do not look at anyone directly while wearing the lens. You'll have one eye that's your own color and another that isn't. It wouldn't take an Einstein to notice the difference."

He took a lens on his fingertip, popped it into his right eye, and blinked furiously. "Stav, I see what you mean. Once we're through that security checkpoint, I suggest we get these out fast." They continued walking.

"Start drooling, Doc," said Morgan to Zammit.

Zammit put his hand on the young agent's shoulder and leaned. "Should've gone to drool school. Excess saliva is hard to produce in situations like this."

A technician looked up. His eyes narrowed at the approach of three strangers. He started to say something, then Costopoulos let loose with a burst of nasty-sounding Russian. The man flinched and stepped aside. Costopoulos marched up to the iris scanner and pressed his left eye against it. There were three loud beeps, and a green light glowed above the big steel door. Morgan seized Zammit's head and assisted him in pressing his right eye against the scanner. Beeps and a green light.

Zammit's legs suddenly buckled and he sagged to the floor, clutching his face. He was aware of the technician moving in to assist. Once again, some barks of Russian from Costopoulos made the man back off. Jack Morgan leaned down to stare him in the face and ask if he was all right. Zammit popped off the lens and held it, shining, on one fingertip. As he pretended to struggle to his feet, Morgan took the fragile disk and put it into his eye, wincing and blinking. Zammit wondered if the scanner would sound an alarm upon seeing the same iris pattern twice in a row within less than a minute. Morgan pressed his eye to the scanner. Three beeps and a green light. No.

They were in.

 Once through the huge steel door, the rumbling sound was louder.

"Out," said Zammit. Costopoulos removed the contact lens from his eye. So did Morgan. The CIA agent took both lenses, placed them carefully back into the plastic case, and handed it to Zammit, who slipped it into his pocket.

Stavros lifted the papers on his clipboard and studied the layout plans for Talitsa-4. "This way." They walked down a wide hallway. At the end were three branches. One branch, to the left, led to a series of glass-walled lab facilities. Zammit recognized the usual paraphernalia of a research laboratory. But there was something else as well—several large clear plastic isolation tanks. They contained the limp and motionless forms of naked young men, obviously the subjects of experiments. Zammit's eyes narrowed. He'd like to have five minutes alone with Dr. Cabrinovic.

The hallway straight ahead led to a series of conveyor belts. They rumbled loudly at full speed. There was daylight at the end of the hallway to the right. Through an open bay, Zammit could see loading docks, forklifts, and cranes, as well as the tail of an enormous aircraft.

And ranks of pallets filled with 200-gallon black drums. All had different colored labels.

Zammit moved toward the conveyor belts.

"Hey, Doc," said Morgan. "You're looking way too alert for someone whose brain has been fried."

"We have to move fast. You see anyone around?"

"Technicians and soldiers in the distance. Otherwise, no."

Zammit approached the conveyor belts and stared. There were four systems. Only two were operating. On both, thousands of tiny white pills bounced along the line, but each system was heading toward a different packing destination. He moved around to study the destinations of the two conveyor belts and quickly returned. "System is completely automated. That's why no one's here." He plucked a white pill from one line and examined it closely. Another white pill from the second line. He turned them over, looking at both sides of each pill, thinking furiously.

"What is it, Doc?" asked Morgan.

Zammit held up the tablets. "The one in my left hand goes into drums with a blue label. The one in my right goes into drums with a red label. Obviously two different drugs." He smiled. "Remember General Bled saying that Cabrinovic was behind in his refining? That if the material wasn't ready by the time he got back, he'd have him shot?"

"That's what you told us," said Costopoulos.

"Well," said Zammit, "in his desperate rush to manufacture this stuff, Dr. Cabrinovic has made a terrible mistake." He slipped the pills into the right- and left-hand pockets of his uniform and darted toward the drums.

"Jack, what do these labels say?"

Morgan stared at the ranks of drums. There were hundreds of them. "Blue labels say POCS. There are two types of POCS. Pills and a liquid—an aerosol."

"The aerosol is probably a variant of the stuff Jamal was going to use on Frankie," said Zammit. "Spraying from aircraft, I expect. You can't force millions of people to take pills. An aerosol version of the sedative will be used initially to stupefy the populations of Istanbul and Ankara. Show me where the label for the aerosol version is different from the label for the pills." Morgan pointed, then moved to another set of drums.

"Green labels say Cyanostrom. The bioweapon."

"We've had enough of that already. Keep going."

"Red labels say Aggressor."

"The amphetamine and hormone cocktail Bled will use on his troops."

"Yellow labels say Anticyanostrom."

"Good." Zammit's eyes searched the area. He walked over to a workbench and stared at its scatter of equipment. He turned and gazed at the loading dock and an array of forklifts, thinking hard.

"What is it?" asked Costopoulos.

"I have an idea," replied Zammit. "Jack, approach that group of soldiers and techs in the distance and tell them they have to load as much of the Anticyanostrom as they can onto the biggest plane out there."

"What about the rest of these drums?" asked Morgan.

"We can't take them," said Zammit. "Too many, and we don't have time."

"Then let's torch the place as we leave, destroy this stuff."

"Thought of that already. Look at those girders, all this concrete. Even if we had something to torch this building with, the fire wouldn't spread. And we don't have explosives."

Morgan's eyes flickered as he gazed over Zammit's shoulder. "Houston, we have a problem."

Zammit turned. The group of soldiers and technicians was gathered in a knot, staring at them and whispering among themselves.

"Get moving," said Zammit. "Yell, threaten to have them shot. Say the order to load comes directly from Bled and you'll report them if they don't obey. They already know the stuff has to leave, so the order won't be a surprise. Stav, you go too, add an air of authority. Keep shouting at them so they don't have time to think. Jack, order them to prep the plane first. Fuel, maintenance, whatever. Get the forklifts lined up and ready too. But tell them they can't actually start loading the drums until thirty minutes from now." He turned to the Greek. "Stav, you give a direct order that no one is to approach this area for the same length of time."

"What the hell?" said Morgan.

Zammit saw a soldier and a technician leave the group and start walking down the corridor toward them. "Go." The two marched off. Moments later he heard both men shouting and the sound of running as the soldiers and techs rushed to obey their orders.

He strode over to the workbench, picked up the piece of equipment he had noticed before, and started to work.

His broken hand and aching ribs made it harder and slower than it should have been. Sweat was running down his face by the time he was almost done. He panted with exertion, the dull ache in his ribs now a stabbing pain. Hold yourself together for just a little longer. He tried to breathe shallowly. Finally, it was finished. He laid the device back on the table, swaying. Don't faint now. He sat down on the workbench, head between his knees, and fought the black clouds that threatened to engulf him.

He looked up at the sound of approaching footsteps. Costopoulos said, "My God, Michael. You look like death."

"Never mind," said Zammit. "Plane ready?"

"Yes."

"Give the order to start loading."

"OK. They want to know why they have to stay away from here. I can't stall them any longer."

"Doesn't matter now." Zammit rubbed his face. "They can enter the area. I'm going to sit in that corner. Give them some reason why I'm here and why they have to leave me alone. Tell me when we're ready to leave."

"OK."

Wisps of black cloud writhed across his vision. "Help me get over there." Stavros hauled him to his feet and into the corner. He sat down on the floor, leaned against the wall, and closed his eyes. He heard bustling movement, pounding footsteps, barked orders, the rumble and thump of forklifts. He wasn't sure how long he was there, but gradually his breathing slowed and he didn't feel as nauseated. He remembered what Aunt Julia had said: You're a knight of the Order. That toughness is in your blood. You'll need it someday. You're right, Julia, he thought. I'm going to need every ounce of it.

"We're ready." It was Costopoulos, looking worried. As he helped Zammit to his feet, he said, "We have to get out of here fast. One of the techs asked me a question about the behavior of granules in a centrifuge, and of course I didn't know what he was talking about. Got a funny look on his face and now he's disappeared. I've also been asked why an army sergeant will be flying the plane." He reached into his lab coat pocket and handed Zammit a pistol. "Jack says, just in case." The scientist stuffed it in his jacket. "From the looks on the faces of the soldiers and techs, I've given the last order that will be obeyed."

"Where's Jack?"

"On the plane, studying the controls. We must go now."

Footsteps echoed in the corridor. A tall spindly man in a white lab coat bounded down the hall toward them from the direction of the lab facilities. Zammit thought he looked like an ostrich. A soldier was with him. Zammit leaned against the Greek and stared vacantly at the soldier. The man stopped in front of Costopoulos and said something sharply. Even without knowing Russian, Zammit understood and recognized the name. Dr. Bratko Cabrinovic was identifying himself and demanding to know who they were. Costopoulos said something sharp in response. Zammit recognized the name Vladimir Bled. Cabrinovic flinched. Stav was reminding the research director what Bled had said about shooting him if the drugs weren't ready. Cabrinovic's emulike eyes darted about as uncertainty and fear battled suspicion. Suspicion was winning.

Zammit started to slide to the floor. The soldier moved toward him. He straightened suddenly and moved behind the man.

Caught by surprise, the soldier was slow to react. Zammit slipped his arm around the man's neck and placed him in a choke hold.

As the man fought against him, Zammit saw Cabrinovic attack Stavros. Neither man was a trained fighter, but Costopoulos was winning. Finally the soldier was unconscious. Zammit dropped him just as the Greek missed with a haymaker and lost his balance. Cabrinovic seized his arm and started whirling Costopoulos around. When the tall man let go, Costopoulos slammed heavily into the engine casing of a forklift and fell to the ground, clutching his chest. Cabrinovic pounced, fingers extended like talons. He was going for the eyes. As he clawed at Costopoulos's face, Zammit lunged, fist raised, and hit him with a vicious rabbit punch to the back of the head. Bled's research director fell without a sound.

Zammit knelt over the Greek. "Stav?"

He had long fingernail slashes on one cheek, but his eyes were undamaged. Costopoulos struggled to catch his breath. "Hurts," he gasped. "Get out of here."

Zammit looked around. The soldier and Cabrinovic were still out. Going for the eyes. Dirty fighter. He rolled Cabrinovic onto his back. Taking the contact lenses from his pocket, he forced open the man's eyelids and dropped one lens in each eye. Then he seized the rifle and helped Costopoulos to his feet. Dragging the injured Greek, he headed through the deserted loading area for the plane, Jack Morgan, and freedom.

 **48**

Morgan was standing in the cockpit, a pistol pointed at the head of a terrified mechanic. "Where the fuck have you been?"

"Had to fight our way out," gasped Zammit, panting from the exertion of hauling the Greek up the metal ramp into the cabin. "Stav's hurt."

He laid Costopoulos and the rifle on the floor and looked around. The cargo hold was packed with black drums with yellow labels. The stink of Jet A1 turbine fuel, stale motor oil, and hot metal was overpowering. "Cargo bay closed?"

"Yes."

"This thing is huge. What kind of aircraft?"

"Military cargo plane. Ilyushin 76. More precisely, an IL-76MD. They call them Mike Deltas. One hundred and sixty-five-foot wingspan, a hundred and fifty feet long."

"Name *Ilyushin* mean anything?"

"I think it's Russian for 'crate.' Must be one of the original ones, built in 1974. A sort of sky truck. They've sealed the emergency exits with duct tape, for Christ's sake."

"Can you fly it?"

"Guess I'll have to."

"Will it get to the Ataturk Dam?"

"I remember the specs from the flight simulators. Has a maximum takeoff weight of about 171,000 kilos. It was already half-loaded with crates of weapons and Semtex plastic explosive. We didn't have time to take them off. This guy says that with the drums it's close to being overloaded but it should get airborne."

"Answer the question, Jack."

"With maximum payload, it'll go over 1800 miles at 480 miles an hour. I've already checked the maps. It's about 500 miles from here to the dam. Piece of cake, if I can get it off the ground."

"So we can be there in an hour?"

"Yes."

Costopoulos moaned. Zammit went to him and bent over. His chest was heaving, lips turning blue. "Stav. You OK?"

"No."

He tore open the Greek's lab coat and shirt. There was a deep purple abrasion on the left side of his chest.

"What is it?" asked Morgan.

"Broken rib, collapsed lung. Ask if this plane is pressurized."

Morgan asked the question. The mechanic's eyes flickered uneasily as he answered.

"He says sometimes. The airframe has cracks in it, and they haven't finished with maintenance yet."

Zammit thought furiously. "If we have to fly high, and if this isn't pressurized, Stav will die of hypoxia."

"With this huge payload and a cracked airframe, we might also shake to pieces in midair," said Morgan grimly.

The scientist hooked a thumb at the mechanic. "Do we need him anymore?"

"Probably. Crew is supposed to be two pilots, a flight engineer, a navigator, a radio operator, and two loadmasters. But I can't fly this thing and hold a gun to his head at the same time."

"I have to look after Stav. After I've fixed him up, I can be navigator if necessary." Zammit appraised the mechanic. He was stocky, with a round face, slanted Tartar eyes, and hands like shovels. His overalls were greasy, and his face shone with sweat and fear, eyes pleading.

"He can be our flight engineer. Ask his name and if he's a member of Smegyev's cult." Morgan barked the questions. A look of confusion crossed the man's face. He talked until the agent interrupted him.

"Fedor Slavutych. Unless this guy's a great actor, he doesn't know anything about Smegyev. Says he's never been here before. Was ordered to come two days ago, been working nonstop on the planes. Mechanic for twenty years in the Soviet air force. Says he can take apart and put together one of these things blindfolded. Says he's a working stiff from Kazan, has a wife and kids, please don't kill me."

"Tell him we are agents of the Moscow government. If he helps us, he won't get killed, he'll get a medal and lots of money." Morgan talked. The man's eyes blinked. He smiled an honest peasant smile and replied.

Morgan looked relieved. "He says OK. Says he'll show me what I need to know and that he's test-flown these things unofficially."

"Let's go," said Zammit.

Morgan stuffed the gun in the belt of his uniform. He sat in the pilot's seat and contemplated the controls as Slavutych took the copilot's seat. "Damn, those video game people are good," he said. "Just like the real thing." The four Soloviev D-30KP turbofans screamed to life. He taxied away from the loading docks and started to swing the huge plane around.

Slavutych pointed through the windshield and spoke. Morgan said, "Fedor says this plane is close to overload. We're going to need every inch of runway to get aloft."

"We can't do anything about it," said Zammit. "Just get out of here." He ran back and looked through the still-open cabin door. At one of the loading docks he saw a tall man in a white lab coat leaning against the metal door frame, sobbing convulsively. He straightened and held his arms out in front of him as he lurched forward, like Boris Karloff in *The Mummy*. He took a few steps and pitched off the end of the loading dock, falling six feet onto the pavement. It looked as if he had broken at least one leg and an arm. "Well, Dr. Cabrinovic," said Zammit softly. "How do you like being the victim of an experiment?"

As the man rolled on the cement in agony, several soldiers appeared on the metal platform. Zammit seized the rifle and fired. They ducked back into the opening. "Come on, Jack!" he shouted over the rising shriek of the engines. "It's Chuck Yeager time!"

He saw Morgan ease the throttle. The big cargo jet started to roll down the runway. As it gathered speed, the old plane shuddered and clanked. "Shake, rattle, and roll!" yelled Morgan. Zammit and Slavutych seized the cabin door and heaved it shut. The scientist darted back into the cockpit and peered through the windshield at the runway flashing underneath.

"This is going to be mighty close," said Morgan grimly.

Shuddering and straining, engines screaming like banshees, the Ilyushin slowly lifted into the air just as the last bit of runway disappeared under the wheels.

Airborne.

 **49**

Zammit bent over Costopoulos. "Stav, I'm going to have to do something. It isn't going to be pleasant." Eyes half-closed, the Greek nodded.

Zammit headed for the cockpit. The plane was shuddering so badly he could hardly keep his feet. Fedor Slavutych's eyes searched the control panels. He pointed at dials and talked rapidly as Morgan used both hands to struggle with the throttle, fighting for lift.

"It's like flying the Queen Mary!" he shouted above the shrieking engines. "Christ, this thing is heavy." He gritted his teeth as he strained at the throttle. "I feel like I'm physically lifting it myself!"

Zammit shouted in his ear. "Remember, this isn't a video game. It's a real plane, carrying too much weight. It's old, has a cracked airframe, and a maintenance history I suspect has not been impeccable. Be prepared for anything."

"How's Costopoulos?"

"Not good. Ask Fedor if there's an emergency medical kit on this crate."

The mechanic listened to Morgan and nodded. He disappeared into the back of the plane and returned with a white box with a red cross on the side. Zammit opened it. "Syringes, sutures, needles, tubes, bandages, local anesthetic, foil packets of disinfectant swabs, rubber gloves, the works."

He tore open one of the foil packets. Completely dried out. "How old is this stuff anyway?" He handed the box of anesthetic to Slavutych. "Jack, ask him the expiration date."

Morgan asked. "September 15, 1998. Been expired almost five years."

"Damn," said Zammit. "I have no choice. Fedor, is there anything in this plane that has tubing, medical disinfectant, anything?" Morgan spoke. The mechanic again disappeared into the bowels of the aircraft. Zammit headed down into the glass cage at the bottom of the nose cone, where the navigator would be stationed. He established their bearing and bounded back into the cockpit to give the information to Morgan. "Keep heading due southeast, in a straight line." He stared through the cockpit windshield. They were now over water. The Black Sea.

"Jack, our ETA is about an hour?"

"If we don't get shot down by the Russian, Ukrainian, or Turkish air force? Yeah."

"Send the signal. You remember the frequency?"

"Seared into my brain. But is there anyone to respond to it at the other end?"

"I hope so." Hearing a rattling sound, Zammit turned. Slavutych was pushing a cart. Zammit grinned. "What the hell is a beverage cart from a commercial airline doing on a military cargo plane?"

Morgan listened for a moment. "Fedor says the pilot of this craft got it from an Aeroflot flight attendant in exchange for a couple of machine guns."

Zammit knelt and examined the cart. It was filthy. Metal canisters of soft drinks, connected with stiff plastic tubing. He tore off a length of tubing. A coil of thin wire was attached to one of the cart's legs, presumably to fasten it to something so it wouldn't roll in turbulence. He unspooled a couple of feet of wire, straightened it, and bent it back and forth until it snapped. He examined the bottles and selected the one with the highest alcohol content. Overproof Armenian brandy. He rummaged around in a drawer, found knives, forks, and spoons. No scalpel. He searched his pockets, found what he wanted. An OLFA Touch-Knife.

Morgan and Slavutych were talking in the cockpit. They were gaining altitude. If they got high enough, the Greek was going to die.

He bent over Costopoulos. Eyes closed, lips bluer than before. He returned to the cockpit. "How's it going?"

"Good," said Morgan. He glanced at the material Zammit held in his hands. "What now?"

"I have to operate, get that lung fixed. I just hope the anesthetic is still good."

The agent hooked a thumb at the kitchen utensils. "You going to operate on him or eat him?"

"I may need these," replied Zammit. "I realize it's not the Mayo Clinic way, but I have no choice."

"What's the wire and tubing for?"

"I'll insert the wire into the tubing to stiffen it. Tell Fedor he's entering the surgical profession." The mechanic paled.

Zammit and Slavutych returned to Costopoulos. The scientist

fetched an empty basin from the beverage cart, tore open a sealed plastic container of napkins, and laid several on the metal floor of the aircraft. With the brandy, he sterilized the tubing, both inside and out. He rubbed alcohol along the length of the wire, then selected one of the rubber gloves. Using more wire, he secured the glove around the end of the tube with an air-tight seal, then cut two fingers off the glove.

He rolled Costopoulos onto his side, having decided to make the incision on the side, the part of the chest that moves least.

He laid everything carefully on the napkins and mimed what to do next. The mechanic held his hands over the basin as Zammit poured brandy over them. Zammit did the same to his own hands, scrubbing vigorously, making sure to clean the cast too. He mimed making the incision and inserting the tube. Fedor nodded.

Zammit opened the box of anesthetic. The clear bottle had a blue rubber seal on top. He tore the plastic off a syringe, thrust the needle through the rubber, and withdrew four cc's of liquid. He tapped the syringe to get rid of any bubbles, then leaned over Costopoulos. "Hey, Stav." The eyes slowly opened. "I have local anesthetic, and I'm not sure if it's going to work. I'm injecting the area where I'm going to make the incision and insert the tube. Let me know if and when it feels numb. I'm not going to lie to you. This might hurt like hell." He injected the incision site.

Costopoulos's voice was faint. "I laugh at danger, I flirt with death. What's with the glove?"

"I've improvised a flap-valve. When you exhale through the chest tube, positive pressure is generated within the thoracic cavity, pushing air through the tube and the cutoff fingers of the glove. When you inhale, the walls of the glove fingers are sucked together by the negative pressure, preventing air from accumulating in the cavity. If air and pressure are allowed to accumulate in the cavity, they kink the large veins around your heart. You go into shock and die."

"Sorry I asked. I'm numb."

"Jack!" shouted Zammit.

"What?"

"Any sign of pursuit?"

"Not yet."

"Let me know if there is. We might have to do evasive maneuvers. Give me ten minutes steady flying, and Stav lives."

"Roger."

With the OLFA Touch-Knife he made a small, deep nick in the skin, then punched in the tube with the flap valve on the end. Minutes later Zammit sewed up the wound with brandy-sterilized sutures as Slavutych tossed the instruments into the basin. Zammit poured more brandy over the mechanic's hands, then did the same with his own.

"At least he's not going to have one hell of a scar." He took a swig from the bottle. Not a lot left. He handed it to Slavutych. Fedor drained the rest. The mechanic's eyes were darting. He looked down at Costopoulos, held up a forefinger, and headed to the cockpit.

Wearily Zammit rose and followed. The two were talking. "Fedor looks like he's had an idea. What's up?"

Morgan grinned. "He says if we fly real low and slow, forty or fifty feet off the sea, their radar won't be able to track us. And in case the operation didn't work, Costopoulos won't die of hypoxia, because we're not flying high."

"OK," said Zammit. "An aerial version of the low-speed O. J. Simpson chase. Just make sure this crate doesn't stall. He headed down into the glass navigator's cage, then returned. "Entering Turkish airspace in about ten minutes."

"Yeah," said Morgan grimly. "In an Ilyushin. If the Turks send F-15s after us, we're finished."

"We'll have to wait and see if the signal got through. As for whether Radchuk worked something out with Yildiz ..." He shrugged.

Zammit returned to Costopoulos. The Greek whispered, "I heard heaven is filled with angels. I always visualized them as female. Because I'm looking at your ugly mug, I assume I'm not dead."

"That's right," said Zammit. "Lie back and relax."

"Two o'clock!" shouted Morgan. "Fighters. Can't tell who they are."

Slavutych handed Zammit a pair of binoculars. He watched for a few moments. Three fighter planes, moving in fast. "I'm not an expert on aircraft," he said. "I presume they're MiGs."

"Can't be," said Morgan. "MiG-29s are small short-range fighters. They're not capable of flying a distance like this without being refueled in midair. Let me see."

He peered through the binoculars. "Shit. Sukhoi-30 Flankers. Fighter-interceptor, range of 2500 miles. Can go over Mach 2.3.

Incredible engines. Only mass-manufactured plane in history capable of breaking the sound barrier while climbing vertically. Only fighter capable of the Cobra maneuver. Scary as hell. Like an F-15 on steroids. They must be within range. Why aren't they shooting us down? We're a sitting duck."

"Because," said Zammit, "we're carrying the antidote. They shoot us down, the antidote drowns in the sea. They're going to try and herd us, force us back to Talitsa-4."

"More planes," said Morgan. "Ten o'clock. We're screwed."

Zammit stared through the binoculars. "More Sukhoi-30s. Five of them."

"Shit creek, no paddle," said Morgan. "At least we tried."

The fighters were closing fast. There were two spurts of flame and white propellant from one of the jets approaching at ten o'clock. Missiles. Zammit looked at the planes in the two o'clock position. A direct hit. The sky filled with flame. The remaining Su-30s soared through the sky, in a swirling dogfight. Five against two. He watched as the two Sukhois were destroyed.

Slavutych said something to Morgan. "What?" asked Zammit.

"Wants to know what's going on. Wouldn't mind knowing myself."

"Radchuk found a way to meet Yury Bogov's challenge. He responded to the prearranged signal we sent on a special frequency, the signal telling him we were on our way and needed help. The original plan was for Radchuk to arrange with Yildiz to have Turkish jets show up and fight Bled's pursuit force, so Radchuk could preserve deniability. But that would've meant Turks fighting Russians. An act of war. It would have given Bled and his people in the Kremlin the perfect justification for their invasion of Turkey. This way it's Russian fighters against Russian fighters. No possibility of an international incident, no excuse for Bled."

Zammit pointed. "It appears we now have an escort to the Ataturk Dam."

Morgan glanced at his instruments and grinned. "We are now in Turkish airspace. Not an F-15 in sight. Radchuk and Yildiz obviously worked something out. Hot diggity dog." He waved at the Su-30s flying on either side of them. The pilots waved back. "Vaya, next time we meet, the first bottle of vodka is on me." He explained to Slavutych.

The radio crackled to life, and Morgan started talking. Zammit examined Costopoulos. His lips were no longer blue, and although he was in pain, he was out of danger. "Hey, Doc!" yelled Morgan. "The Su-30 pilots want us to fly higher. Can we do that without killing Costopoulos?"

Zammit returned to the cockpit. "Yes. Just don't try setting any altitude records."

Shuddering and groaning, the big cargo plane ascended. They were now over land. In the glass nose cage Zammit examined a map and checked their coordinates, then scrambled to the cockpit. He pointed to a cluster of buildings in the distance. "That must be the town of Niksar."

Slavutych was staring intently at the control panel. He looked worried. He pointed and said something to Morgan. Zammit leaned over to take a look. Needles were quivering at the far end of their dials, creeping toward red lines. "What is it?"

Jack looked grim. "These engines are hotter than a two-dollar pistol."

"Will we have to land before we get to the dam?"

"Maybe."

Zammit eyes searched the horizon. "That must be the town of Hekimhan. It's not far now."

Minutes later they spotted something shining like a mirror on the horizon. Water. "We're approaching the reservoir," said Zammit. "This northern end is the only part that the cyanobacteria hasn't contaminated yet."

Soon they were flying over a green mat. "Jack," said Zammit, "radio our Sukhoi escort and tell them you want to move west so you're flying over land. If we have to ditch, I don't want to do it in this crap."

"Christ, no," said Morgan, reaching for the receiver.

Minutes later they were circling the Ataturk Dam. Morgan spoke urgently into the receiver with staff on the ground. "They want to know how heavy we are. I told them my best estimate and they freaked out. The runway isn't made to take a weight like this. They think we're going to break through the pavement at 200 miles an hour and tear off the undercarriage. The plane will be ripped to pieces and explode. We still have almost a full tank of Jet A1 fuel."

"The stuff is not particularly volatile," said Zammit. "But you mentioned earlier that some of the crates in the back contain Semtex. If we crash, that fuel, mixed with the plastic explosive, will create a bang so big it'll wake up Hong Kong."

He pointed at the gauges. "And we can't fly around forever, or make it to another destination. Those dials just red-lined. The engines are about to burn out." He looked at the mechanic. "He knows this plane. Ask him."

Morgan talked. Slavutych shrugged, grinned, and replied. Morgan grinned back.

"I'm waiting," said Zammit.

"Fedor says this plane is beautifully designed. Has over a dozen huge wheels under the nose cone and fusilage. Great weight distribution, so it can operate on very poor runways. The runway and tarmac only have to be able to withstand a pressure of six kilograms per square centimeter." Morgan spoke into the receiver, listened, and smiled. "No problemo."

He flipped a series of switches. Fedor pointed at a lever, and Jack pulled it. They heard the whine and thump of landing gear being lowered. Their escort of five Su-30s peeled away and headed for home. Morgan headed in for a landing. With the slightest thump and bounce, they were taxiing to the maintenance warehouse and loading docks.

Morgan smiled blissfully. "Man, those video game people are good." He slapped Fedor's back affectionately.

 Once off the plane, Zammit asked for the infirmary's physician and a stretcher. When they arrived, he told the man how he had reinflated the lung and ordered him to complete the procedure with an underwater seal. The doctor did a quick examination of Costopoulos and said he was going to be all right.

Then he looked at Zammit. "You have been badly beaten and are very pale. Come with me."

"Can't," he said.

"Then I will get you a painkiller."

"No thanks. I'm so tired it'll make me stupid. I can't get stupid."

"I insist on examining you."

Zammit rubbed his face and winced as he felt his broken rib scrape. "OK. Give me a few minutes and I'll be in your office. Look after Costopoulos."

As they took the Greek to the infirmary, Zammit ordered maintenance staff to unload the antidote and bring the first drum into the warehouse. He fetched the microlab and laptop from storage, opened the drum, and started to work. Morgan and Slavutych stood by anxiously.

Zammit examined a slide under the microscope. "Where is everyone?"

Morgan replied, "I'm told Dr. Richards is here, along with Dikka Spargo, Kitson Kang, and Cairo Jackson. Never met them, but I must say your colleagues have weird names. Colonel Yildiz is in Istanbul, making sure Prime Minister Amurkhan is protected. The election is four days from now. Your colleague Connie Palaeov is in Istanbul too."

Zammit started keying information into his laptop, wincing as he used only the index finger of his broken left hand. Without taking his eyes from the screen, he said, "I have to talk to Frankie."

When Richards arrived, she gestured at Slavutych. "Who's he?"

"A helpful fellow and a damn fine mechanic," said Zammit. "I won't be much longer." As he matched his new information with the computer's database, Morgan filled Frankie in on what had happened.

"Are you sure Stav is going to be OK?" she asked.

"Pretty sure," replied Zammit. "It's hard to operate with a broken hand. I'm glad I took that training in emergency medivac surgical techniques a couple of years ago." He stared at the screen, then turned to Richards. Her face was impassive. He remembered how hurt she had looked when he hadn't let her touch him.

"The video. Was there . . . ?"

"Nothing more about Adam's fate. I'm sure he's dead." She was all business, but he could tell she didn't want to believe what she was saying. No time to get into it now, and it was obvious she didn't want to talk about it. "As soon as you landed, I talked to Connie in Istanbul," she said. "Colonel Yildiz wasn't available—he's in conference with Amurkhan and the National Security Council. I filled Connie in and told him to explain to Yildiz what's happening with the arrival of the treatment. Then Yury Bogov phoned, wanting to know if you'd arrived safely. Apparently Radchuk pulled in every favor he was ever owed and twisted arms. He's in big trouble with the Kremlin for doing this solo. Barely holding things together. Approximately forty tons of the antidote are being air freighted from a couple of other secret cities, Sverdlovsk-17 in the far north and Vozrozhdeniya-2 on an island in the middle of the Aral Sea. There's more antidote in other secret cities, but they're controlled by allies of Bled's, and Radchuk can't get into them. The cargo planes will have military escorts in case Bled tries to intercept them. It'll be hours before they get here."

"Tell me more."

"No one knows Amurkhan is still alive. The water situation is desperate—crops are dying, and soon people will be too. The Turkish army is grinding the Syrians and Iraqis to pieces, but they're fighting hard. It looks as if Bled fell for the fake message we sent. Even with the theft of the antidote, it seems he's still going to launch the invasion."

"He has to. He's reached the point of no return," said Zammit. "There's more of the antidote elsewhere, and besides, Bled must have the formula. Can't be that hard to manufacture more, if his allies control some of the secret cities. Anything else?"

"According to Bogov, given what Bled will throw at them, the remaining Turkish forces in the north will be overrun."

Zammit was silent.

"Mike, I know that look. There's something you're not telling me."

Wearily he rubbed his face. "God, I feel awful. A Russian private's uniform is itchy in this heat." He gestured at the computer screen. "I've done some analysis on the antidote. I figured out part of it but not all. You're the expert in microbiology, and I'm not. I don't understand some of it. Have a look. I'm going to get this rib checked."

As Zammit headed for the infirmary with Morgan and Slavutych, Frankie sat down in front of the laptop.

The physician's examination showed that Zammit indeed had a broken rib and that the cast on his hand didn't need replacing. He taped Zammit's chest to stabilize the rib and gave him a handful of vitamins.

When Zammit returned, Frankie said, "Good news."

"What?"

"Every member of the anonymous Biopreparat research team who invented this should win the Nobel Prize for Chemistry."

"Talk to me."

Richards gazed up into the hot blue sky. "These drums contain at least one superconcentrated antidote. It binds with chlorophyll."

Zammit frowned. "The substance that makes all green plants green. Photosynthesis. Chlorophyll absorbs energy from sunlight and transforms light energy into chemical energy."

"Correct. In all plants, chlorophyll is located in chloroplasts. Except for cyanobacteria, the only organism on earth where the chlorophyll is located in photosynthetic membranes at the cell periphery."

Light dawned in Zammit's eyes. "So that's it. Located on the outside of the cell, it's vulnerable."

"You've got it. The antidote binds to the chlorophyll on the cell periphery. Once the two are bound together, sunlight is suddenly not a source of life but a source of death."

Zammit grinned. "The antidote makes sunlight poisonous to cyanobacteria?"

"Yes."

"Wow," he said. "Take an organism's basic survival mechanism and turn it into its worst enemy. That is fiendishly clever."

"What did you find?" asked Richards.

"There is a second treatment as well. As I suspected, they used the same technique as they did to engineer the bioweapon. Miniscule sugar beads that dissolve instantly in water. The toxin molecules produced by the cyanobacteria become bound to the synthetic sugar, an oligosaccharide. It, in turn, is attached to particles of diatomaceous earth."

"Chalk," interrupted Richards. "A harmless natural substance that cannot be absorbed by the human body."

"Precisely. The combination of sugar and chalk is a sort of toxin sponge that binds up the poisonous molecules. The human intestine will not absorb chalk. The endotoxin is bound to the chalk, so the body won't absorb it, either. If it doesn't get into the bloodstream, you can't die. It simply gets expelled."

"You mean, I could take a glass of poisonous water from the reservoir, mix it with the antidote, drink it, and nothing would happen?"

"That's right."

Richards threw back her head and laughed. "In other words, once this is in the reservoir, water can be released?"

"Theoretically, yes." Zammit glanced at the computer. "One moment." He keyed an equation. The hard-drive light blinked furiously as the machine flashed through its calculations. "The question is, how much do we need? We'll know in a couple of minutes. And how fast does the organic material dissolve once it's exposed? We can't release water if the dam's intakes and machinery are incapable of filtering out organics."

"How do we deliver the treatments?"

"Spray them over the reservoir. We'll need planes. As far as I can tell, biplane crop dusters could do it. Also, put it into smaller canisters and drop them through the muck into the water underneath."

"That leaves us with one insurmountable problem. Sporing."

Zammit closed his eyes. His hand hurt, and so did his chest. He had never felt so tired. "Because it's never been field-tested, the bioweapon's behavior is unpredictable. The Biopreparat team probably didn't know it could reproduce through sporing as well as cell division, so they never came up with a way of dealing with the spores."

"We can't allow it to spore. Once it gets into the oceans, all the pharmaceutical factories on earth working full time couldn't make enough antidote to get rid of it. The world will die."

"I know," said Zammit wearily. "We'll have to think of something."

The hard drive stopped clicking. Zammit checked the screen. "We don't have enough. We'll have to wait for Radchuk's cargo planes."

Richards interrupted. "The filaments are close to reaching the reservoir floor. I am a botanist and microbiologist. I cannot even imagine how we can stop the sporing."

"There has to be a way," said Zammit. "I refuse to be beaten by green slime."

He heard pounding footsteps and turned. It was Cairo Jackson. "Mike, Colonel Yildiz just phoned. He sounds totally creeped out. He wouldn't explain anything, just said you have to fly to Istanbul immediately. Some sort of crisis. He's sending a helicopter."

Zammit turned to Frankie Richards. "All the info is in the laptop. Wait for the arrival of Radchuk's cargo planes. I'll meet with Yildiz and get back here as fast as I can."

Jackson and Zammit walked through the warehouse toward the elevators. Zammit concentrated on putting one foot in front of the other.

"Frankie filled me in," said Jackson. "Given what happened in Tuvanistan, I'm amazed you're here at all. You look terrible. Are you sure you're all right?"

"Yes," he lied.

They took the elevator up to the locker area. "Cairo, go talk to the helicopter pilot when he gets here. Find out what Yildiz is so worried about."

"OK."

Zammit walked toward the lockers. Dikka Spargo was seated at a table. The metal in her face gleamed under the lights. She had inserted a small flashlight through one of her eyebrow hoops, and she read a book and fiddled with something at the same time. "Hey, boss. You're looking kind of *inert*."

Zammit couldn't summon a smile. "What are you doing?"

"Waiting for some results about that crap in the reservoir. Reading Clive Cussler's *Inca Gold*. This guy is really good. How come we never do something as exciting as hunting for treasure? Meanwhile, I'm following your orders."

"What orders?"

Dikka snapped a couple of pieces together and held up an object. "You said you wanted the robots to make noises so people don't get startled. I made a couple of dozen little prototypes. They make different sounds. When we're done here, you tell me which sounds you like."

Zammit stared at the insectoid in her hand. "Dikka, do they have to be so ugly?"

She looked hurt. "I think they're cute." She rose and walked over to a set of duffel bags in the corner. "I borrowed one of your travel bags. Hope you don't mind. I didn't have one large enough to carry my tools plus the robots." Zammit shook his head. The teen flipped aside the tag with the scientist's name on it, opened the bag, placed the insectoid into the bag and zipped it shut. "They're all in here."

The scientist remembered what had happened with Catula. "Did you install a battery pack to jump-start them awake after a while?"

"No. They're too little. I'll have to invent a battery pack small enough to fit them. Won't be easy. I've installed a little broadcast generator in the bag. Fits on the bottom, on the inside, small and snug. To activate the insectoids, just flip the outside switch near the base. Wakes them all up instantly—it's a pain to do it manually, one at a time. They run around like crazy. As you requested, when they get within a few feet of someone, they make noises. I had fun with the noises. I took—"

Zammit knew what Spargo was like when she got started on the subject. "Dikka, I understand. Do me a favor. I'm going to get cleaned up. Tell Frankie I want a printout of the information about the two antidotes to take to Yildiz."

"OK." She darted out of the room.

He washed up and shaved, then dressed in the clothes he'd brought from Malta, so long ago—chinos, a dark green cotton shirt, and a black bomber jacket. What was Yildiz so panicked about? He transferred everything from the Russian private's uniform into his pockets and after a moment's reflection tucked the pistol into his jacket. He sat down on a bench, his head between his knees.

Spargo returned with a sheaf of paper. "Stick them in my bag," said Zammit wearily. "I'm going to lie down until the chopper gets here."

Dikka's eyes were appraising. "I'm worried about you, boss."

"I'm OK." Zammit lay down and was out in an instant.

He heard a voice and struggled from the deep black well of sleep. It was Kitson Kang. "Chopper's here."

Painfully he rolled off the bench, grabbed his duffel bag, and took the elevator down to ground level. As he boarded the Huey helicopter, he turned to Jackson. "Cairo, does this pilot know anything about why Yildiz wants to see me so urgently?"

"Guy doesn't know bugger-all," replied the big man.

Zammit nodded. "I'll be back as soon as I can." The big Huey shot into the air and zoomed away.

During the flight, Zammit fought the urge to sleep and tried to make sense of the tornado whirling in his brain. They had two treatments but no way of stopping the sporing process. As he meditated on the events of the past few days, he was again filled with a sense of foreboding. Abdul Jamal had known they were coming to Tuvanistan. How had he known? Where was he now?

A car and driver waited for Zammit at Yeltsikoy airport. He gazed at the glittering waters of the Sea of Marmara as they drove east along Kennedy Cadessi. Huge tankers, merchant ships and ferries plied the waters in the fading sunlight of early evening. He looked at the modern office buildings, the red tiled roofs of the older houses, the forest of slender minarets stabbing toward the sky. This time they were driving through Askaray district instead of around Sultanahmet. As usual, the streets were jammed with vehicles, the sidewalks swarming with pedestrians, as people headed home from work. Six million people.

It was now just hours before General Bled would launch his invasion. Grimly Zammit wondered which of these buildings would be rubble, how many bodies would lie on the pavement, the number of vacant-eyed zombies that would be wandering aimlessly, if he couldn't stop it.

The car pulled into the underground garage of the Istanbul headquarters of Turkish Intelligence. It seemed so long ago that he had been in this building. As they took the elevator up from the garage, he wondered what new crisis had occurred, one so urgent Colonel Yildiz had to see him personally.

The elevator stopped. Zammit stepped out. There was an unusually large number of men in the hallway, including soldiers. They turned to look at him, gazes openly hostile. Suddenly Colonel Yildiz burst through the crowd. His face was furious. He pointed a pistol at the scientist's head. "Dr. Michael Zammit, you are under arrest."

 The room was small and windowless. Zammit sat in a chair in the middle of the floor. Four soldiers stood along the walls.

"Colonel, what the hell are you talking about?"

Yildiz stopped pacing. "I can't believe I have been so stupid." He pointed his cigarette accusingly. "The assassination attempt on Thamar Amurkhan. Only three people on earth knew she was going to be at the Hilton—her, myself, and you. It was you who tipped off the RAA fundamentalists about where she would be and when."

"This is insane," said Zammit. "Why would I—?"

"And why did you go to Tuvanistan? I now know. To confer with your fellow conspirators. You are of Maltese descent. Historically, Turks and Maltese have hated each other. Tell me, Dr. Zammit, what do you get out of this plot?"

Zammit's head spun. What was going on? Suddenly another piece of the jigsaw puzzle removed itself from the whirling tornado in his brain and slipped into perfect place. He contemplated it for a moment, surprised at how cold and detached he felt.

"Well?" demanded Yildiz.

Zammit glanced at the duffel bag at his feet. He still had the Russian pistol in his jacket, and they hadn't frisked him. But there were too many of them. He'd be shot down in an instant if he drew the gun. His eyes narrowed as he looked at the bag. It had a tag on it, with his name. But there was a small switch near the base. Suddenly it came to him.

In his confused exhaustion, he'd taken the wrong bag.

"Colonel, I can explain everything. The information about the treatments is in this bag. May I?"

The Turk nodded curtly. Zammit leaned over and picked it up. He flipped the switch, felt the bag suddenly seethe with movement. He pulled it open, turned it upside down, and emptied its contents on the floor.

Tiny multicolored robots instantly scattered across the room, scuttling everywhere. The Turks stared in horror. The stunned silence was broken when an insectoid got too close to an astonished Yildiz. "Meep meep!" it said in a surprisingly loud voice. Another stopped in front of a soldier. His eyes bulged from his head. "AAAOOOOGGGAAAHHHH!" There was an eruption of sound— whistles, sirens, meep-meeps, and "Dive! Dive!" from one of the larger robots as the insectoids spun across the floor. The noise was deafening.

Pandemonium. Soldiers leapt onto chairs and scrambled onto tables. One opened the door and fled. Another tried stamping on a particularly nasty-looking robot. The third programming com-mand—defend yourself. Little hooks popped from the ends of the tentacles, and the insectoid swarmed up the soldier's leg. He screamed and tried to bat it away.

Zammit grabbed the pistol from his jacket and hit Yildiz as hard as he could across the back of the head, then seized him by the collar and dragged him down the hall to the elevators. One was open. Soldiers rounded the corner. Zammit snapped off two shots and punched the button for the underground garage. The doors swished shut. He searched the colonel's uniform. Car keys, fas-tened to a plastic tag with a stall number. He fished in the left pocket of his chinos and found what he wanted. He held up the little white tablet.

Population Control Sedative. POCS.

What would be the optimal delivery system for such a drug in pill form? Ingested drugs had to be absorbed through the intestinal wall. Too long. You'd want it to work instantly. Also, pills could be spat out. Not the stomach and intestine. The thin membranes of the mouth. As Yildiz moaned, he decided. He forced open the Turk's jaws and tucked the pill between his cheek and gum. It started dissolving instantly. The doors swished open. Zammit heaved the man to his feet and dragged him to the car. He threw him into the passenger seat and got behind the wheel. The engine roared to life. Tires squealing, he shot toward the exit ramp. People were running after the car and converging near the exit. There was a burst of gunfire behind him. He flinched as bullets stitched holes in the trunk. The car smashed through the barricade and onto the street.

It was evening, and rush-hour traffic was over. Zammit thought about what he had to do. He glanced at Yildiz. The Turk was upright but motionless. He had an odd look on his face, eyes va-cant and alert at the same time. Zammit remembered Yasmin, and what Jamal had said. Were the pills as strong as the liquid?

"Colonel. Lift your right arm and place your index finger on the windshield." Slowly, Yildiz obeyed.

"Nod twice if you think you are capable of following a complex explanation." Two slow nods.

"Say yes if you can speak."

"Yes." The Turk's voice was toneless. Zammit's lips tightened. This demonstration of POCS's power provided a sickening illustration of what could have happened to Frankie. He drove through the Beyoglu district, heading out of Asia toward the European part of Istanbul. Traffic was light. He crossed the Ataturk Bridge and turned onto Ordu Cadessi. To his left he could see the Beyazit Tower. Straight ahead were the Topkapi Palace, the Blue Mosque, and the rose-red church called Hagia Sophia, the Church of Holy Wisdom, now a museum. As he drove, he talked nonstop to Yildiz, eyes searching. Finally he saw it and pulled over. "Stay here."

It was a bus station with a big yellow sign and the black letters PTT, which meant a bank of public telephones. For a few Turkish lira he bought a plastic and metal telephone debit card known as a *telekart*. Walking to one of the yellow phones, he inserted the card and dialed the only member of the INERT team still in Istanbul.

"Connie? Zammit. We got trouble. You're going to have to help me." He explained how he had escaped from Turkish Intelligence headquarters.

"No, I can't tell you where I am and you can't come and get me. Every police officer and soldier in this city is after me. I have a better idea. You know Hagia Sophia? About 400 yards from the Blue Mosque. It's rose-red and has four minarets around it, like spacecraft about to launch? Good. There's a park with flower gardens and a big pool with a fountain. Meet me at the fountain in half an hour." He hung up.

Wearily he climbed back into the car. Yildiz was still motionless. He wondered how long the effects of the drug lasted. Zammit leaned back, fighting a fatigue so deep he thought it might stop his heart. He rubbed his face. With clinical detachment he noticed that his right hand was trembling, as if with palsy. He tried to remember the last time he had eaten anything and couldn't. He looked at his face in the mirror, the bruises and cuts, the deep lines, the utter exhaustion. If he could just hold himself together for a little longer. Miles to go before I sleep. He turned the key in the ignition. "Showtime," he whispered.

 **52**

Zammit parked the car along the avenue of small shops in front of Hagia Sophia. He talked rapidly to Colonel Yildiz, hoping he understood everything he'd been told.

As he got out of the car, his right leg buckled and he fell to the pavement. With an effort he stood. He leaned into the vehicle before shutting the door. "Stay here."

He walked down the street, concentrating on putting one foot in front of the other. He crossed Alemdar Cadessi, the broad boulevard in front of Hagia Sophia, and headed for the park. At this time of night there weren't many people around. A slight breeze rustled the trees. The sweet smell of roses was overpowering. Dew sparkled on the grass, a fairy spill of tiny silver sequins. A fall moon hung in the sky like a giant pearl snuggled on blue velvet. Shadows and moonlight played with each other. Chiaroscuro. The contest of darkness and light. Where one ruled, the other could not. He had a sickening flashback to what might have happened to Frankie, the video of Adam, the horror that was Abdul Jamal. He found the big pool with the fountain and stepped into the vegetation nearby. Hidden, he leaned against a tree trunk, waiting for Connie Palaeov. He knew he was standing on some of the most blood-stained ground in history. Blood pounded in his ears. In his exhaustion, he thought he could hear 2,000 years' worth of spectral screams. So many deaths, so much senseless ugliness in the world.

He remembered what Grand Master Fortucci had said—evil exists, and we have always fought it. Aunt Julia had said, You're a knight of the Order. That toughness is in your blood, and you will need it someday. He needed it now. He checked himself out, piece by piece. His legs were rubbery, his right hand still shaking. He felt faint. Methodically he visited his physical and spiritual wells and noted, for the first time in his life, that they were dry. He had nothing left.

He closed his eyes. You're a scientist. Figure it out. Slowly his eyes opened as he remembered. The only option. He reached into the right-hand pocket of his chinos and took out the little white tablet.

Aggressor.

He used his broken left hand to steady his right as he opened his mouth and slipped the pill between gum and cheek. He closed his eyes. Nothing. Noth . . .

A neutron star exploded in his body. A burst of energy filled him, and a strange neon-lit curtain rose in his brain. He opened his eyes. Everything was sharper, clearer, more definite than it had ever been. He could see in the dark. He could hear sounds he'd never heard before. He flexed his right hand. No more trembling. He flexed his broken left hand, inside the cast. No pain.

His sea-blue eyes glowed, and his head shot up like a panther's at the rustling sound of approaching footsteps.

Zammit stepped from the shadows. Startled, Constantine Palaeov whirled around.

"Hello, Connie. Betrayed anyone lately?"

The young Russian faced him warily. "What are you talking about?"

"Cut the crap. I know it was you."

Palaeov looked him up and down. "So you figured it out. Jamal said you were smart." The light in Palaeov's eyes was not quite sane.

"It took me far too long to realize I was harboring the viper in my bosom."

"I was careful. What gave it away?"

"Little things. Jamal always being several steps ahead of me, knowing my every move. When technicians went to fetch Ruslan Glinka at the dam, he was on the phone. The instant he saw them he tried to run. He was on the phone with you, wasn't he? You were warning him that we'd figured out his involvement and to get the hell out of there."

"Yes."

"All the samples coming from the reservoir being contaminated. You were supervising the collection of samples. You also destroyed the original samples at Urfa."

"Yes."

"It wasn't just you. Jamal made mistakes. In Tuvanistan. People freak out the first time they see Catula. Jamal didn't. When he saw the robot and Anastasia's white Persian going after each other, he shouted, 'Get that cat out of here!' How did he know the robots even existed, and how did he know Catula hates cats? Somebody told him."

"That wasn't very smart of Abdul," said Palaeov.

"Other things. When I told him about the blocks of coins in the underground temple, he knew I was unconscious when I was brought there and that I escaped at night. How did he know that? Him saying, 'We wondered where you went.' Who's 'we'?"

"My opinion of the man is dropping like a stone," said Palaeov, surveying the area. He flexed an arm and his biceps bulged.

Connie was bored with talking. Zammit waited, arms loose at his sides, trying to quiet the raging tide of adrenaline in his system. "Where's Jamal?"

"He wanted to be here, but he's not feeling well. Dr. Richards popped one of his testicles."

"Couldn't have happened to a nicer guy," said Zammit. "The final piece fell into place when Yildiz arrested me. Frankie told you to brief him about the antidote. I can only imagine what concoction of lies you told him. He asked how the RAA assassination team knew Amurkhan was going to be meeting him at the Hilton. She knew, he knew, and I knew. You knew because I told you. I've had a feeling for a long time that pieces of a puzzle weren't fitting together, but now most of them are. The only reason we were able to break into Talitsa-4 and steal the antidote is because it all happened so fast and in such secrecy that you didn't know. What was the purpose of having Edward G. Pompo and me together on the Molly Katz show?"

Connie grinned. "That was an accident. Earl Stone booked you on at the last minute, when he learned you were coming back from Dzerzhinsk. Synchronicity is a strange thing. Man, Pompo was angry at the way you humiliated him."

"Why did you do this, Connie?"

"It was Jamal's idea. He even wrote the letter I sent you, begging to be hired. He said you'd hire me because you're a do-gooder, and do-gooders are trusting and easy to manipulate. He knew they'd bring you in to solve the cyanobacteria. We needed some way of keeping an eye on you."

"I'll repeat the question. Why did you do this?"

"For the reasons I just mentioned. Besides, according to the prophecy, I must prove myself against a worthy opponent."

"What are you talking about?"

"I am the Holy Chosen One. The direct descendant of the last Byzantine Emperor, Constantine XI Palaeologus Dragases. He supposedly died on May 29, 1453, but his body was never found. That's because he escaped. First to the Despotate of Morea, badly wounded and raving. When Mehmet II captured Morea, he was taken to the monastery of St. Sava, near Kemerovo, way on the other side of the Urals. He was off his head for a long time, couldn't speak. Eventually had a son with a local girl named Natalka, so the dynastic line was continued."

"That is the biggest load of crap I have ever heard in my life," said Zammit.

"It's true." Palaeov's gaze was appraising. He flexed his other arm. "The monastery's had the last emperor's personal possessions stored there ever since. It's all in *The Secret Chronicle*, by Nestor. See this?" The heavy gold signet ring gleamed in the moonlight. "The last emperor's personal seal."

"You shouldn't read fiction, Connie, if you're going to mistake it for real life."

"It's not fiction. It is destiny. It is foretold."

"Why now? Why you? It's been over 500 years since the fall of Constantinople."

"The timing was never right." Palaeov was moving, toward an open area. "Monks aren't much good at organization, and they don't have armies. It's happening now because of the chaos in Russia. It allowed Lazar Smegyev to get established. His ability to raise the dead appeals to people. It was Bled who bribed members of the Duma to ban proselytizing by foreign missionaries, which is how Smegyev was able to flourish. Lazar is from the St. Sava monastery, so he knows about all this history. When Bled joined the cult, Smegyev let him in on the secret. Bled was doing business with Jamal, which is how Jamal found out. As I said, monks aren't much good at large-scale organization. Jamal brokered the whole deal."

"So what happens now?" asked Zammit.

Palaeov glanced at his watch. "Midnight attack. Bled invades in less than two hours. He will win. I will be crowned emperor of the new Byzantium." He pointed at the vast bulk of rose-red Hagia Sophia, looming in the darkness. "In there. Nothing can stop us."

"I wouldn't be too sure," said Zammit.

The big Russian stopped his slow circling. "The prophecy says I must prove myself against a worthy opponent. Jamal said you are worthy, and I agree with him. But the only way to truly prove myself is in battle."

Zammit waited. The muscles in his legs were twitching spastically. He was clenching and unclenching his right hand.

The Russian grinned. "They told me to wait for Wurban Ice, just in case. But I'm bigger, stronger, and younger than you. You're tired, you're hurt, and you're old. I'm going to beat you to death."

"Connie, I wouldn't bet the farm on that."

Palaeov lunged. Zammit stepped to his right and threw his first punch.

They fought for a long time. Zammit found he could move faster than he had ever moved in his life. Palaeov wasn't a trained fighter, but even though he was muscle-bound and slow, the Russian outweighed him by at least fifty pounds and had a chin like concrete. And the Aggressor in Zammit's system couldn't restore the structural integrity of his left hand. He could feel broken bones grinding against each other. The hand was now not just broken but shattered. Throwing lefts was as effective as throwing porridge. Palaeov tried grappling, wrestling, using his size to get Zammit on the ground. The scientist refused to go down. He seized the Russian's right arm, braced the elbow against his knee, and pulled backward. Palaeov screamed as his elbow broke. Zammit got behind him. Choke hold. The huge muscles of the Russian's left arm strained as he tugged in vain at Zammit's arm. He rammed his elbow into Zammit's ribcage. No pain. He started clawing frantically. Zammit could feel the writhing body against him, smell the Russian's sweat. He squeezed harder. Just as Palaeov was about to go limp, Zammit heard a sound.

He turned. A squat figure was plodding toward him. White-blond hair, a man built like a 350-pound fireplug. Wurban Ice. Zammit let go of Palaeov. A spike of incandescent rage shot through him. He threw an overhand right at Ice, so hard it stopped him in his tracks. Zammit lifted the Hungarian off the ground and hurled him. He landed near a stone bench. The moaning Russian was getting to his feet. Suddenly Zammit saw a figure lurching toward them. Yildiz. His motions were jerky, his balance uncertain. But he was moving toward Palaeov, and he had a pistol in his hand. As the Turk threw himself at the Russian, Zammit lunged at Ice. Jamal's bodyguard slipped on the grass and fell. Zammit tipped over the heavy stone bench as easily as if it were plywood, pinning the Hungarian's legs. He straddled Ice and started hitting him with his right fist. The karate expert was hammering him with his hands, but Zammit didn't feel any pain. It was as though his entire system were screaming with rage. He rode the Hungarian like a cowboy on a bull. Was it possible to punch your way to China? It seemed like a good idea. He closed his eyes and tried.

He wasn't sure how long he was at it, but slowly he became aware that someone was calling his name. He stopped and looked over. It was Yildiz. He was leaning against a tree, his pistol pointed at Palaeov. The Russian was whimpering on the ground and clutching his elbow. "Dr. Zammit, I believe he has been dead for some time."

He looked down. Where Ice's head should have been, there was a pile of raw meat with some splinters of white bone poking through. He wiped his bloody hands on the Hungarian's clothes and stood. He wasn't even breathing hard. He walked over to Yildiz. The Turk's eyes were still strange. Zammit realized the colossal effort of will it must have taken him to fight through the effects of the drug and come to his aid.

"Thanks, Yildiz."

"The name's Hakim. Call my people. We'll take him to headquarters and—"

"No, we won't," said Zammit. He seized the pistol from the Turk's hand and faced Palaeov. "My friends were hurt. Frankie almost spent the rest of her life as a sex slave. Twenty thousand people are dead and thousands more sick. The world may die. Somebody has to pay for all that. *Razborka*." He raised the gun. "Show muscles, Connie. I told you they were no good." He shot the Holy Chosen One between the eyes.

Zammit gazed at the carpet of cyanobacteria. It glistened under the hot sun as if coated with oil. In the heat, the stink was overpowering. Cairo Jackson was standing beside him, holding a padded laptop bag. Superaware because of the Aggressor still in his system, Zammit could tell the big man was spending more time casting sideways glances at him than looking at the fetid contamination in the reservoir. Getting cleaned up before leaving Istanbul, Zammit had looked in a mirror. It had taken him a few moments to realize he was looking at himself.

"So that's the situation," said Jackson. "The cargo planes arrived from the secret cities with another forty tons of antidote. Radchuk's people found every member of Bled's invasion force sitting at the controls of their weapons, staring vacantly into space. Bled's committed suicide, Smegyev and Pompo have been arrested, and the Syrians and Iraqis have given up. Tell me again how you did it."

"The warehouse in Talitsa-4. The drums of bioweapon, antidote, POCS, and Aggressor. I examined the pills bouncing down the conveyor belts. In his rush to manufacture the stuff, Cabrinovic failed to add any coloring to the pills or stamp marks on them so they could be distinguished from each other. To the naked eye, the sedative and amphetamine tablets were identical. I noticed a heat gun on a workbench. As Morgan and Costopoulos kept everyone away from the loading area, I melted the labels off the drums and switched them around. Bled's troops took the sedative. How's Yildiz?"

"Looks stunned, says he has a crashing headache. How do you feel?"

"I could sip hot lead and spit out rivets."

"Obviously they made Aggressor more potent than the sedative."

"Obviously."

Jackson gestured at the oily green mat that stretched to the horizon. "With the defeat of the Iraqis and Syrians, the Turkish air force is able to supply planes that can spray the two antidotes and drop canisters under the water. But we can't stop the sporing. Frankie has been running scenario after scenario. The stuff is going to anchor itself in about four hours. Then it spores. Nothing can stop it. The world will die."

"I refuse to be beaten by green slime," said Zammit.

Jackson held up the laptop. "Mike, you want this? Run some scenarios yourself?"

He gazed at the huge white cast on his left hand. The physician in Istanbul had looked at it and shaken his head, slopped iodine all over it, muttered something about gangrene, given him a bottle of penicillin, and offered morphine. Zammit had refused the morphine. "If Frankie can't figure it out using a computer, neither can I. It's going to tell me we've lost."

His mind raced. A muscle convulsed in his cheek. Jackson was watching it. Zammit tried to stop the spastic twitch and couldn't. "Planes fly. Birds fly."

Jackson's eyes searched his battered face. "Mike, you are scaring the hell out of me. What are you talking about?"

"You know how much Stav hates computers. He once said, 'Planes and birds fly, but the way they fly couldn't be more different. A plane is a machine. It flies through the power of its engines and clever engineering of the wings. Birds fly because they're born that way. A bird can go places aircraft never could. A computer is just a machine that operates through sheer calculating power.' My brain is like a bird. It can do things that laptop can't. For example, lateral thinking. I'm going to let my imagination fly."

Jackson's eyes searched his. "What do you want?"

"A pad of paper, some pencils, and thirty minutes of solitude."

They took the elevator up to Yildiz's office. Zammit told Jackson to gather everyone in the boardroom down the hall and wait. He sat and stared at the walls, then started drawing aimlessly on the paper. After a few moments, he realized he'd broken the nib and was tearing through several sheets at once, so he stopped. He closed his eyes. His mind strobed, images flashing crazily.

His parents, dead at sea in a winter storm, drowned in their yacht. Drowned in water. Birds. Planes. Flying. Wings. Spores developing wings. The spores were the result of fruiting bodies. Bodies. Palaeov and Ice. Cutting bodies. Cutting open Costopoulos to reinflate the lung, on the IL-76. How did planes fail in the air? Cracks in the airframe. Weak. Metal fatigue, leading to shearing. The cyanobacteria floated on the water like a carpet. Carpets. Some were made by shearing the wool. He gazed at the cast on his hand. Weak. Shearing. Pulverized.

He had it.

Zammit burst through the boardroom door with such force he threw it off its hinges. He was aware of it leaning crazily. Everyone in the room was looking at him as if he were crazy. Aggressor. He knew he was talking too loudly.

"How do you deal with a carpet of contamination? Carpet bombing!"

He seized a piece of chalk and started hacking at the blackboard. "Frankie said that until the filaments anchor themselves, they're delicate. Weak. If they can't anchor themselves, the cyanobacteria can't spore. The war is over. Colonel, how close are the nearest bomber forces?"

Yildiz was pale but seemed alert. "Twenty minutes' flight time away, near the Syrian border."

"Give the order for every bomber within 500 miles to arrive here, with depth charges, bombs of any sort."

The chalk kept breaking. He hurled it across the room. "The cyanobacteria is already dying because we've stopped feeding it. The explosions from the bombing will shear the filaments, pulverize them, turn them into slurry. They won't be able to anchor, so it can't spore. We have the antidotes. All we have to do is spray them."

Jackson protested. "Bombing will destroy the filaments, but it will also break open the fruiting bodies. That will release the spores anyway."

Zammit turned to Frankie Richards. "You said the wings are the last things to develop on the spores."

She looked at him warily. "Yes."

"Have the wings developed yet?"

"No. It'll be another three hours, as far as I can tell."

"Good. We carpet bomb the reservoir. The fruiting bodies may break open, but the spores don't yet have wings, so they can't fly. They fall into the water and drown. The antidotes destroy them, neutralize any remaining cyanobacteria and toxin, and make the water drinkable."

Dead silence.

"Move!" roared Zammit.

Everyone scrambled. "Yildiz. A word."

As the others left the room, the Turk said, "It's Hakim. You look like a madman. What do you want?"

"Patrols. Within a thirty-minute flight radius of here, due west and southwest. Any unusual movement, any unusual presence, you report it to me. I also want a chopper on standby for my personal use."

"What for?"

"Just do it."

 **54**

From the dam's crest, Zammit watched the motley collection of heavy bombers, crop dusters, and fighter planes make endless passes over the reservoir. He held his hands over his ears. Aggressor made everything brighter and louder than it would ordinarily be, and the sound of screaming engines and explosions was painfully loud. The cyanobacterial carpet floating on the water seethed like green scum in a boiling pot.

He had supervised the loading of the antidote onto the planes. Depth charges, missiles, spray canisters, all had their guts modified to carry a load of miniscule sugar beads. It was a patchwork job, as each weapon was fitted with timed explosive charges. Dangerous, improvised work, but nothing had blown up in anyone's face, run after screaming run, bomb after bomb, as the green carpet heaved and geysers of oily green muck shot twenty feet into the air, then collapsed with a wet splat. In his superaware state, he thought he could actually see the color shift as the cyanobacteria was destroyed.

Cairo Jackson bounded up.

"How's it working?" asked Zammit.

"Couldn't be better. Yildiz sends a message."

"I'm listening."

"Couple of cargo planes and helicopters spotted by a patrol about thirty minutes from here, due west. Desolate area. Nonmilitary aircraft. He said you'd want to know."

Zammit nodded. "Everything here is under control. Only one more thing to do."

"Am I reading this right?"

"About why those planes and helicopters are at the underground temple? Yes. In his insane greediness, he couldn't resist."

"You've taken that amphetamine. God knows how long the effect will last, but it can't be much longer. It's taken you way up, and when it wears off, you're going to crash and burn. Way down. Someone has to be there to catch you when you fall."

"I know," said Zammit. "I don't care. Vengeance is mine, sayeth the Lord."

"We're going to find him sooner or later. Doesn't matter if we get him now. You're on the verge of complete collapse. I refuse to let you kill yourself."

"I don't care. Vengeance is mine, sayeth the Lord."

The big man looked deep in his eyes. "Ask yourself the question General Custer should have asked himself before the Battle of the Little Bighorn. Is this the hill you want to die on?"

Zammit's face was a carved mask of aggression, exhaustion, and misery. "Yes."

Cairo shrugged. "OK. Let's go."

"I'm not asking you to die with me."

"You're not asking. I'm volunteering. We've known each other since we were kids. This is personal for me too."

Five minutes later they were in a Huey, thundering west. Zammit had paid a visit to the storage area as Jackson collected weapons and flashlights. Yildiz wanted to send soldiers with them, but Zammit explained that the underground temple was a labyrinth designed to kill intruders: "The last thing we need is a stomping herd of soldiers falling through holes in the floor. Stealth is the best way to deal with this."

"It isn't working!" shouted Jackson. "There's no signal from the metal detector you jammed into the crevice by the entrance!"

"Jamal's probably removed it or turned it off. Doesn't matter. Grab those binoculars."

"What am I looking for?"

"I paid close attention to our flight path when you rescued me after I escaped. The landscape is all brown. Look for a formation of stones and boulders about ten feet high and a depression in the ground 200 yards to the east of it. In the depression, there will be two white plastic distilled water containers."

Twenty minutes later, Jackson shouted, "I see them!"

The Huey landed, dust swirling in choking clouds. Zammit's sea-blue eyes glowed through the murk as he leapt to the ground. They headed for the entrance to the underground temple.

**55**

"How did you get out of here without a flashlight?" panted Jackson.

They darted down the corridor, beams of light swinging crazily. They tried to move fast while avoiding the holes in the floor. Rough yellow stone, shadows, dust, and stifling air seemed to squeeze against them like a physical presence.

"We're heading to the temple's central shrine," gasped Zammit. "That's where the treasures are stored. Jamal will have people with him. It's going to be hard for him to move all that stuff in this trap. He's a meticulous planner, so be prepared for anything."

"Where are his choppers and cargo planes? There were no aircraft by the temple entrance."

"Probably did a quick mapping tour of the temple complex and found an entry more suitable for moving the loot."

"Why do you keep looking up at the roof?" asked Jackson.

Zammit pointed to his left. "Near the ceiling. The red fluorescent arrows. I used a felt-tipped marker when I escaped the first time." He grasped Cairo's arm. "We're getting close."

They extinguished their flashlights and pressed against the wall. Lights and movement. Dim figures, half-hidden by swirls of dust, wrestled with dollies and carts laden with statues and blocks of fused coins. The sound of voices, as they crept down the corridor. There were portable lights in the central shrine. Zammit waited until a group of men left with a burden of treasure and silence fell. He stepped into the stone room. A yawning space of rough-hewn yellow stone, a vault rising into the gloom like a primeval cathedral. Crude oblong niches hacked in the rock. The statues they had contained were gone. Only two blocks of coins were left among the debris littering the floor.

Dressed in a black aviator's suit, Abdul Jamal had his back to them, a gun in one hand, a cane in the other. He was contemplating the bronze statue of a Greek goddess, her weight resting gracefully on her left hip as she gazed sightlessly at him. The whites of her eyes were alabaster, the irises made of emerald or jade.

"Hello, Abdul," said Zammit. "Having a little trouble getting it up lately? At least you can't hurt a woman made of bronze."

The Omani slowly turned. His face was gaunt and had a greenish tinge in the flaring lights. With a visible effort he composed himself. His voice was thin. "Why am I surprised? How did you find this place again, once I removed the metal detector?"

"White plastic and distilled water. You figure it out. I'm not in an explaining mood."

"I understand you managed to kill both Ice and Palaeov. I am impressed. How?"

"Aggressor."

"I see. Well, you must at least allow me credit for inventing good drugs." He peered more closely. "I notice you are twitching a little, Dr. Zammit. I've never tried it myself, but I understand the aftereffects of Aggressor are singularly unpleasant. Including flashbacks that can last for years. That didn't bother us at the testing stage, since the drug was to be administered to soldiers in continuous doses until their hearts burst or their brains failed. They're just soldiers—it's their job to die."

Zammit gestured at the remaining treasure in the room. "Where?"

"I have another refuge. It's not Paris, or even Blavatsk, but it will do for the time being. I always have a fallback position."

"So I've noticed," said Zammit. "It's taken me a while to figure that out. When dealing with someone like you, I need one too."

He heard the sound of stealthy footsteps creeping down the corridor. He glanced at Cairo Jackson, staring at Jamal with loathing. But without the superawareness of Aggressor, the big man couldn't hear the approaching enemy. Zammit fanned through his options as if they were cards in a poker hand, and made a decision. He waited, trying to quell the convulsing muscle in his cheek. Suddenly five of Jamal's men darted into the room, machine guns at the ready. Too many. Jamal said, "Unless you feel like the Earp brothers at the OK Corral, I suggest you surrender your weapons." Wordlessly he and Cairo handed over their guns.

Jamal's eyes narrowed. "You have a fallback position in a situation like this?" He raised his pistol and aimed. "I can't even imagine what it is. I should have killed you immediately. Should I ever run across anyone like you again, I will not make the same mistake."

What Costopoulos had said. Use the man's ego against him. "You're like Napoleon," said Zammit.

The Omani gave a wary smile and lowered the gun. "Goodness, a compliment."

"It isn't intended as one. Napoleon's career rested on the bodies of two million Frenchmen, whom he murdered in his insane quest for personal glory. Even when exiled to Elba, he managed to escape and return to France. I forget how many soldiers died at Waterloo. As long as he was alive, he was a danger. Same with you."

Jamal shrugged. "History doesn't care whether you're a nice guy. We make our own destiny. The purpose of life is existence, and the price is violence. Nature, red in tooth and claw. To act is to exist."

Zammit looked around the room. Five heavily armed men, plus Jamal. Jackson and himself, defenseless. *You're a scientist. Figure it out.*

He gestured. "May I? As one connoisseur to another?"

The Omani's eyes were wary. "Yes. But very, very slowly."

He watched Zammit examine the glittering block of fused coins near the oracle niche. "Beautiful, isn't it?"

"Yes." Zammit stepped into the oracle niche, as if examining the walls. Slowly he lowered himself onto the stone throne where the priest would have sat. The niche was virtually identical to the one in the Hypogeum on Malta, the one excavated by his great grandfather Sir Themistocles. He looked above his head and saw a hole. The male oracle would have sat on this throne and spoken during religious ceremonies, in a normal tone of voice. The bizarre acoustical properties of the place would have served to echo his words throughout the vast circular temple. He thought of Radchuk and his cone of silence. This was the reverse. He'd always wondered if the acoustical effect was as spectacular as rumored.

He was about to find out.

"So, you won't tell me where you are taking all the treasure you're stealing from the central shrine of this temple? Where your next refuge is?" In his superaware state, he thought he heard a faraway resonance, like the ringing of a deep, sonorous bell.

"No. But it doesn't matter. As with everyplace else, my refuge will be filled with useful idiots. Such people make up most of the human race. I'll come up with another plan. It's like Bled, the drunken fool. He was worried he would be seen as a traitor to his country. Can you believe anything so stupid? What's that saying?"

Zammit remembered. " 'Treason doth never prosper, for if it does, none dare call it treason.' "

"I've always enjoyed associating with well-read people. We are alike, you and I, despite your resistance to the idea. Perhaps we could have been friends. Talked about books, had some laughs, planned how to conquer the world."

"Not a chance," said Zammit. "We are not alike. 'What does it profit a man to gain the whole world, if he loses his own soul?' "

Jamal sighed. "Sir Thomas More. To be beheaded because you disapprove of Henry VIII's divorce. Religion—it's not good to take it so seriously. You're a Knight of Malta. You believe things I do not. People are animals. The concept of the soul was an invention of the ancient Greeks, an intellectual artifact, an attempt to give meaning to an existence that is meaningless."

"We've been down this road before. I'm tired of this conversation."

"You cannot refute me, so you avoid the issue. You're a scientist, yet you live like a monk. Celibate and alone. You've never had sex with Dr. Richards?"

"No. I prefer to make love."

Jamal shook his head. "Making love. Never grasped the concept."

"That video of Adam Richards. What happened to him? Is he alive?"

"My little secret. Tell Frances I said so. I like the idea of her waking and screaming at four in the morning."

From his seat on the stone throne, Zammit saw a lithe figure slip into the room.

It had worked.

He rose and stepped from the oracle niche. He could hear other approaching steps, footsteps the others couldn't hear. There was a sudden spasm in his abdomen. The spastic twitch in his face was getting worse. His right hand was starting to shake. Aggressor was wearing off. Just a little longer. Miles to go before I sleep.

He spoke to the shadowy figure. "I hope I didn't hurt you when I escaped."

Sultana stepped into the light, muscles tense. "No." Her pale gray eyes appraised Zammit. "I was half a mile from here, and I heard your voice as clearly as if you were standing next to me."

"Fallback position," said Jamal. "Oh, this is rich."

Sultana's eyes flicked to Cairo Jackson, then to the guards, then to Jamal. As she got a good look at the Omani, her face settled into a mask of rage and hatred. *"You!"*

"Hello, sweetheart," said Jamal. "Long time. I always wondered what happened to you. Bulked up a bit, I see."

He turned to Zammit. "She was a favorite of mine. When she tried to kill herself, I made the mistake of sending her to a hospital, where she escaped. The only one ever to do so. The perils of fondness. I should never let my good nature get in the way."

Men lunged into the room. Flowing trousers, tight bomber jackets, wide sashes, and coiled turbans. Wild, romantic countenances, with hooked noses, great shocks of long black hair, and dark, intense eyes. Sultana shouted something in Kurdish, and the PKK members aimed their AK-47s at Jamal's men. The burst of gunfire was deafening.

Zammit grabbed Sultana's hand and ducked as he ran from the room. Cairo Jackson followed. They headed down a stone corridor, their flashlights throwing crazy beams of light. Zammit could hear footsteps in pursuit.

Their footfalls thudded as they dashed down the corridor, leaping over and around floor holes as if in some lethal obstacle course. As they passed an intersection, Sultana panted, "How do you know where you're going?"

Zammit pointed at the fluorescent red arrows near the ceiling. He looked over his shoulder at the lone flashlight beam and pursuing figure thirty yards behind.

"Jamal can't follow fast. Doesn't know about the arrows, and he's hurt. He . . ." Zammit stumbled, his legs rubbery. Aggressor was wearing off. His exhausted body was burning out. Cairo and Sultana hauled him to his feet and they lurched forward. There was no sound except the scraping of their feet, labored breathing, the footfalls behind. Zammit's balance was going. He almost plunged through holes in the floor, saved only by Cairo and Sultana as they held on to his arms. Cones of light shot through the darkness as they staggered down the hallway like some crippled tripartite beast.

Suddenly they inhaled sweet fresh air. The corridor started to slant steeply upward. Zammit was being half-dragged. Ahead, a dim light illuminated a set of carved stone stairs. They divided at the top, with a broad set of steps angling around to the right and out of sight. The other set was narrow, crudely carved, and twisted away to the left, appearing to vanish into nothingness.

Sultana and Cairo started up the right-hand set of stairs.

"No," whispered Zammit. "Other one."

"Mike, that can't be right," said Cairo. "You can see that—"

With his remaining strength, Zammit forced them to stop their ascent. "Other one." He looked behind him. Jamal was close behind. "Now." He seized their hands and forced them. He dragged them up the narrow, uneven steps that angled sharply to the left and disappeared into darkness. They turned the corner and pressed their bodies to the rough stone wall.

Thudding footsteps, the sound of panting. The footfalls stopped. They saw a beam of light flashing from one staircase to the other, heard labored breathing. Then the scrape of boots on stone.

Jamal had chosen the right-hand staircase.

Silence. Then a grunt, and a crashing sound, as if something heavy had fallen into something deep.

Zammit staggered to the bottom of the steps. Both hands against the wall, he slowly mounted the right-hand stairwell. "Careful," he whispered over his shoulder.

They peered around the corner. There, on the final step, were Jamal's cane, his gun, and his flashlight. Cairo's beam searched the emptiness, found the sheer drop into the narrow, smooth-walled rock chamber. He leaned over and peered. "It's like the opening of a very deep coffin."

"That's what it is," said Zammit. He leaned over and gazed into the opening of the crypt. His hand was trembling so much he had trouble holding the flashlight. Twenty feet below, Jamal was lying on a carpet of rags and bones. His legs were twisted beneath him, his face contorted in pain and rage.

"Not even a professional rock climber could get out of that," said Zammit. He dropped the flashlight into the crypt and called down. "So you can see what's about to happen to you. Vengeance is mine, sayeth the Lord."

Back against the wall, legs buckling, he reached into his jacket and removed the container.

"Jesus, Mike," said Jackson.

Zammit's eyes were desperate. "Vengeance is mine, sayeth the Lord." His hand was shaking so badly he was afraid he would drop it. He looked at Sultana, the muscular body, the pale gray eyes, the broken nose, the scars.

He handed it to her. "*Razborka*. Care to do the honors?"

"What is it?" she asked.

"A vial of smallpox. You have to pop the seals on top. You'll hear a hissing sound as the vacuum of the outer container dissipates. Remove the inner container, the one with the virus. It's glass. Make sure you throw it hard enough that it shatters on the stone."

He turned to Jackson. "Cairo, grab that stone lid." The big man struggled with the heavy rectangle as Sultana popped the seals. A sound like the hissing of a deadly snake, then she held up the gleaming glass vial.

Zammit leaned once more over the crypt. "Abdul. Company's coming. And it hasn't eaten in a long, long time."

He nodded at Sultana. She leaned and threw. The sound of

breaking glass. A rising scream from the crypt, suddenly muffled as Jackson wrestled the stone lid on top of Jamal's coffin.

They both turned to him. They were saying words, but Zammit couldn't hear. He tried to speak. His mouth moved but nothing came out. His body sagged like a marionette whose strings were being cut, one by one.

He pitched forward and slammed face first into the dust.

Epilogue

The party was in full swing.

Under a starlit sky, on the roof of the Lascaris fort, people sipped Maltese wine, devoured Aunt Julia's hors d'oeuvres, and chatted. From the beach below came shrieks as adventurous guests leapt into the cool water. It was the annual INERT New Year's Eve party, the one Zammit always held. Every year he flew his staff and friends to Malta, from wherever they were in the world, for a big bash.

Frankie Richards stood by the satellite dish and watched the crowd. Fergus Cronin was by the parapet talking with his girlfriend, Yasmin the Circassian. The Irishman was attentive and gentle with her. She had a fiery temper, but she always seemed relaxed when he was around.

Frankie saw Sultana talking with Colonel Graves. Apart from occasionally running a hand over her ebony hair, she was motionless, her pale gray eyes never leaving his face. Her muscular body leaned toward his. Graves was unusually animated, his face flushed. She couldn't hear what they were saying, but their body language said it all. Sexual attraction was an odd thing.

Sitting in the middle of the stone paving, like a group of kids, Jack Morgan, Rocco Pullicino, Colonel Yildiz, Lloyd Lavender, Earl Stone, and Grand Master Angelo Fortucci played with Catula. The robot had developed an inexplicable fondness for chasing and retrieving Ping-Pong balls. Perhaps that's why you hate cats so much, Frankie thought; your mentality is essentially canine.

Kitson Kang arm-wrestled with Cairo Jackson, using both hands and all his weight against the big man's right arm. Biceps bulging, Cairo was winning.

Dikka Spargo, her facial hoops and studs glinting in the moonlight, was dissecting a small robot, trying to explain things with her hands, watched by Fedor Slavutych. The mechanic was fascinated by the creatures. Tiny insectoids, eyes shining, plastic bodies glowing, roamed everywhere on the stone floor, softly going "meep meep" whenever they got too close to anyone. Dikka had been told to get rid of the loud sound effects.

Yury Bogov, Vyacheslav Radchuk, and Irina Markova were leaning against the parapet, chain-smoking cigarettes, sharing a bottle of vodka, and rapidly getting drunk. Radchuk was laughing so hard he was bent double. Finally he straightened and wiped his eyes, wheezing. "Oh, that was a good one."

Frankie saw Markova grin at the two old spies, heard her speak in her croaky, smoky voice as she fired up another cigarette. "Ever hear about Brezhnev and his mother?"

The two men shook their heads, listening intently.

"Brezhnev lived the good life—big villa in Crimea, a dozen cars, Cadillacs and Rolls Royces. Caviar and champagne all the time, expensive suits from London. One day Brezhnev brought his little old mother to the villa. She was a peasant. He showed her everything. 'Well, mama,' he said proudly. 'What do you think?' She said, 'Leonid, this is all very nice. But what happens if the Bolsheviks come to power?' "

The two men roared. Radchuk bent double again, clutching his side, wiping his eyes. "Oh, that was a good one," he wheezed. "Remember about Krushchev, the crate of Georgia peaches, and Mao's raincoat?" The three collapsed in laughter, snorting and giggling.

Frankie smiled sardonically. KGB humor. They staggered off, the men with their arms around Markova, to fetch another bottle.

Two days before the election, Thamar Amurkhan had revealed she was still alive. She won in a landslide. The Iraqis and Syrians were back within their own borders, imprisoned by a blockade of UN sanctions and watched by a huge NATO force in the area. Pure water and hydroelectric power now flowed from the Ataturk Dam. Russian authorities had raided the St. Sava monastery at Kemerovo where the Emperor Constantine's treasures had been hidden for so long. There was an argument going on between the Turkish and Russian governments over whom the treasure belonged to. They had asked Mike Zammit to mediate. He had refused.

Disinfected and sealed, the underground temple was now being explored by archaeologists.

Abdul Jamal turned out to be unusually susceptible to variola. He died in an isolation ward, his only monument the fact that he was history's last victim of smallpox. Unable to help him, physicians closely monitored his condition. Frankie had inadvertently seen a photograph on Zammit's desk and wished she could erase the memory. The pustules covered his entire body, so close to-gether that each suppurating crater was touching the next. His face looked as if someone had thrown a shovel full of putrefaction on it. The virus had eaten into his mouth, creating a crazed grin. One of his eyes had disappeared in a pool of pus, and the other shone with the black light of utter madness. It was as if the rottenness of his soul had somehow ascended to his face and found physical manifestation. The doctors gave him morphine to deaden the pain, but it hadn't worked well. At the end they decided to administer heroin. Zammit was informed of the decision. After a few mo-ment's silence, he agreed. Later, Frankie asked him why. He had replied, "Because I am *not* like him," and turned away.

Mike Zammit spent three weeks in intensive care, after being airlifted from the temple. The doctors had said he was in a state of physical and emotional collapse, and they couldn't understand how he had been able to function. Since getting out of the hospital, he hadn't eaten much and had lost twenty pounds. He spent a lot of time in his office, the door closed. Not knowing he was there, she had walked in once without knocking. He was staring out the window, tears running down his face. The aftereffects of Aggressor included mood swings, angry outbursts, and emotional coldness. The doctors couldn't predict how long the aftereffects would last. She was afraid the drug had changed Zammit forever.

When he wasn't in his office, he was in the machine shop work-ing on an improved version of the microlab. Since the Ataturk crisis, the world had been unusually quiet, and they hadn't had to deal with any large disasters. Zammit's left hand had been recon-structed, the pulverized metacarpals replaced with titanium rods held in place with pins. He had started boxing again, now the hand was healed, and the cold fury with which he attacked the heavy bag resounded through the gym at INERT headquarters for hours on end, unnerving everyone.

Costopoulos sauntered over. There had been no complications from his collapsed lung. He raised his glass to Frankie, looking deep into her eyes. "Not like you to be a wallflower."

His gaze flicked toward the gaunt figure leaning against the far parapet, almost hidden in shadow. "Maybe you could be wallflow-ers together."

She didn't reply. Since Zammit had gotten out of the hospital, she had tried many times to talk with him the way they used to, to no avail.

Costopoulos raised his glass. "Here's to the new year. Hope it's better than the last."

"Stav, what happens when the spirit dies?"

The Greek fell into a prolonged and brooding examination of his wineglass. Finally he said, "We are the same as our ancestors 100,000 years ago. The emotions are the same. Hate. Fear. The need for respect. Love. Certainly we've seen enough of hate and fear this past year."

She waited.

"The first man or woman to use their fingers to paint an animal with red ochre deep in the Lascaux caves was expressing the eternal human desire for meaning. But all of it comes down to one thing in the end. One thing only."

"What's that?" She knew the answer.

Costopoulos gazed out over the sea glittering under the moon as the winter waves crashed against the towering cliffs. She could tell he was trying hard to help her. "You know Sophocles? The Theban plays?"

"Yes."

"*Oedipus at Colonus.* Written in the 5th century B.C. 'One word frees us of all the weight and pain of life: that word is love.' " His cynical brown eyes looked into her soul. He knew. She didn't say a word.

"Not that I have to tell you about it." He lifted his chin at the shadowy figure. "Go to him. Explain. He must understand, or he will destroy himself. I've tried, and so has Fortucci. He won't listen. The evil prosper, the good die young. It's the way it is. He cannot wipe all the tears off all the faces of all the people who are hurting in this world."

He waited for her response. She gave none. The Greek drained his glass. "See you around." He walked away.

She watched the figure leaning on the parapet. The hard lines around the eyes and mouth were deeper than before. She remembered what the dying Roy Dool had said: "Life is a desperate business." And so it was.

She watched him as he watched the storming sea. She wanted to put her arms around him, but she thought of her husband, his fate still unknown, of Zammit speaking so sharply when she had tried to comfort him. Everything between us has changed. He is changed, perhaps forever. She watched him for a few moments, and decided.

Frankie Richards quietly turned and walked away.

Zammit's eyes searched the horizon, trying to understand the surging rage of the fathomless ocean, as if it were sending him a message he might somehow be able to interpret, if he could just listen for eternity.

Afterword

How much of this is true?

The biological warfare agency Biopreparat exists. At its peak, it employed some 60,000 scientists. It is part of a vast network of secret cities across the former Soviet Union. The network was first established in 1942 by Stalin's security chief Lavrenti Beria as part of the USSR's fight against Hitler. Today, sixteen of the secret cities specialize in nuclear or biological warfare research and production. When all the Russian defense ministry's weapon-design facilities are included, the total number of secret cities rises to eighty-seven.

Huge quantities of nuclear and biological warfare material have vanished from these places since the demise of the Soviet Union. No one in the West knows exactly what goes on in these secret cities, what stockpiles of weapons exist, or who controls them.

Biopreparat's mandate is to take known biological warfare pathogens and make them resistant to Western drugs. In 1994 work began on developing a superplague, a genetically engineered hybrid of smallpox and Ebola, called blackpox. It is not known where this lethal organism is now stored or who controls it.

There was an explosion at the Biopreparat facility in secret city Sverdlovsk-17 in 1979 (Sverdlovsk is now called Ekaterinburg). This resulted in a deadly release of weapons-grade anthrax. This is just one of many accidents that have occurred in various of the secret cities over the past half-century. As a result, Boris Yeltsin issued an executive decree ordering the closure of Biopreparat and the cessation of all biowar research. According to intelligence sources, this order has been ignored. Not even the Russian president knows all that goes on in the dark, corrupt world of his own country's increasingly out-of-control military establishment.

All the technology described in this story exists now or is in development.

After the fall of Constantinople in 1453, the body of the last Byzantine Emperor was never identified with certainty. The last direct male heir of the Palaeologus dynasty was Theodore, descended from the Emperor Constantine's brother Thomas. Impoverished and obscure, Theodore died in 1636 in Cornwall, England. A cadet branch of the imperial line can still be found today, living in southern Italy.

Russian ambitions to conquer Constantinople/Istanbul can be found in any history book. Even today, right-wing politicians make rabid speeches about it. As a condition of his empire's participation in World War I, Nicholas II, the last tsar, demanded the city as a prize once the war was won. The other Allied powers reluctantly agreed. Only the Bolshevik Revolution prevented the achievement of this historic quest.

Russian religious cults are very strange. Russian organized crime—armed with weapons stolen from huge military stockpiles— is the most vicious in the world. The Russia I describe is the chaotic Russia of today.

Malta and its history are as described. The modern Knights of Malta exist. The Hypogeum, with its bizarre acoustic properties and sinister traps, can be visited by any tourist, as can other megalithic temples (in Turkey as well). The learned and much-beloved Sir Themistocles Zammit (1864–1935) was a medical doctor as well as an archaeologist and historian. He is credited with discovering the source of the deadly bacteriological infection known as Malta Fever (the microbe *Brucella melitensis*, which causes brucellosis).

The Ataturk Dam and reservoir exist, as does the rest of the vast Southeastern Anatolia Development Project. I would like to see the 200 unexcavated ancient cities in the area examined by archaeologists before the reservoir fills and they are drowned forever, but this is unlikely to happen. Turkey has so much history that the government feels it can afford to lose some if it means striving toward a better future. In Istanbul, extremist members of the fundamentalist party want to turn Hagia Sophia, the Church of Holy Wisdom, back into a mosque.

The Kurdish problem is an ongoing saga of violence and brutality, with no end in sight. And no matter how much we might want to ignore the fact, there are far more people in the world like Abdul Jamal, Vladimir Bled, and the Popovs than it is comfortable to think about.

It is ironic that a planet consisting of two-thirds water is called "Earth." Seen from space, our planet seems rich in water, but only 2.5 percent is freshwater, and much of that is inaccessible, locked away in glaciers and ice caps. Less than one-hundredth of 1 percent of the world's water is both drinkable and renewed annually through rain or snow. As Earth's population grows over the next fifty years to 9 or 10 billion people from the present 6 billion, water may become more precious than gold.

And, as this story describes, the world's worst water problems are in the Middle East.

There will be a war over water in the Middle East within our lifetime. It is inevitable. As the Turkish visionary Ishak Alaton says, "I firmly believe that just as the 20th century was the century of oil, the 21st century will be the century of water."

Just as inevitable as water wars is the use of biological warfare. I can only quote Dr. Leonid Rvachev of the Russian Laboratory of Epidemiological Cybernetics: "Terrorist use of biological weapons is not a matter of if, but when."